A TEXT BOOK OF

DATA STRUCTURE

For

Semester - I

SECOND YEAR DEGREE COURSE IN ELECTRONICS / ELECTRONICS AND TELECOMMUNICATION ENGINEERING / INDUSTRIAL ELECTRONICS

Strictly As Per the New Revised Syllabus of

Dr. Babasaheb Ambedkar Marathwada University, Aurangabad

(2013-2014)

G. R. PATIL

M.E. (Electronics),
Associate Professor in E & TC Department,
Army Institute of Technology,
Dighi, PUNE.

NIRALI PRAKASHAN

Advancement of knowledge

DATA STRUCTURE (SE EC / E & TC / IE BAMU)   **ISBN 978-93-83525-50-8**

First Edition   :   September 2013

© : Author

Published By :

NIRALI PRAKASHAN

Abhyudaya Pragati, 1312, Shivaji Nagar,
Off J.M. Road, PUNE – 411005
Tel - (020) 25512336/37/39, Fax - (020) 25511379
Email : niralipune@pragationline.com

DISTRIBUTION CENTRES

PUNE

Nirali Prakashan
119, Budhwar Peth, Jogeshwari Mandir Lane
Pune 411002, Maharashtra
Tel : (020) 2445 2044, 66022708, Fax : (020) 2445 1538
Email : bookorder@pragationline.com

Nirali Prakashan
S. No. 28/25, Dhyari,
Near Pari Company, Pune 411041
Tel : (022) 24690204 Fax : (020) 24690316
Email : dhyari@pragationline.com
          bookorder@pragationline.com

MUMBAI

Nirali Prakashan
385, S.V.P. Road, Rasdhara Co-op. Hsg. Society Ltd.,
Girgaum, Mumbai 400004, Maharashtra
Tel : (022) 2385 6339 / 2386 9976, Fax : (022) 2386 9976
Email : niralimumbai@pragationline.com

DISTRIBUTION BRANCHES

NAGPUR
Pratibha Book Distributors
Above Maratha Mandir, Shop No. 3, First Floor,
Rani Jhanshi Square, Sitabuldi, Nagpur 440012,
Maharashtra, Tel : (0712) 254 7129

BENGALURU
Pragati Book House
House No. 1, Sanjeevappa Lane, Avenue Road Cross,
Opp. Rice Church, Bengaluru – 560002.
Tel : (080) 64513344, 64513355,
Mob : 9880582331, 9845021552
Email:bharatsavla@yahoo.com

JALGAON
Nirali Prakashan
34, V. V. Golani Market, Navi Peth, Jalgaon 425001,
Maharashtra, Tel : (0257) 222 0395
Mob : 94234 91860

KOLHAPUR
Nirali Prakashan
New Mahadvar Road,
Kedar Plaza, 1st Floor Opp. IDBI Bank
Kolhapur 416 012, Maharashtra. Mob : 9855046155

CHENNAI

Pragati Books
9/1, Montieth Road, Behind Taas Mahal, Egmore,
Chennai 600008 Tamil Nadu, Tel : (044) 6518 3535,
Mob : 94440 01782 / 98450 21552 / 98805 82331, Email : bharatsavla@yahoo.com

RETAIL OUTLETS

PUNE

Pragati Book Centre
157, Budhwar Peth, Opp. Ratan Talkies,
Pune 411002, Maharashtra
Tel : (020) 2445 8887 / 6602 2707, Fax : (020) 2445 8887

Pragati Book Centre
Amber Chamber, 28/A, Budhwar Peth,
Appa Balwant Chowk, Pune : 411002, Maharashtra,
Tel : (020) 20240335 / 66281669
Email : pbcpune@pragationline.com

Pragati Book Centre
676/B, Budhwar Peth, Opp. Jogeshwari Mandir,
Pune 411002, Maharashtra
Tel : (020) 6601 7784 / 6602 0855

PBC Book Sellers & Stationers
152, Budhwar Peth, Pune 411002, Maharashtra
Tel : (020) 2445 2254 / 6609 2463

MUMBAI

Pragati Book Corner
Indira Niwas, 111 - A, Bhavani Shankar Road, Dadar (W), Mumbai 400028, Maharashtra
Tel : (022) 2422 3526 / 6662 5254, Email : pbcmumbai@pragationline.com

www.pragationline.com   info@pragationline.com

Preface ...

It gives me immense pleasure to present this book on **DATA STRUCTURE**. This book is strictly written as per the new revised syllabus of Dr. Babasaheb Ambedkar Marathwada University, Aurangabad.

Any good work undertaken requires blessings, support encouragement and guidance.

All praise and honour to Lord Ganesha, Shri. Babamaharaj Arvikar and Gurumauli Naik Aai. Their blessings helped me in completing this book.

I would like to thank management and Principal AIT, Pune for their encouragement to write this book. The support provided by our HOD Dr. B. P. Patil and Surekha K. S. is worth mentioning here. A big thanks to Dr. G. K. Kharate, Dr. D. S. Bormane, for their constant encouragement. I would like to thank my guide Prof. V. K. Kokate for his suggestions and guidance.

The faculty and staff of AIT, Pune deserves special thanks, for their support.

This book provides an introduction to the theory, practice and methods of data structures and algorithms. The concepts of data structures and algorithms are presented with ample numbers of examples and programs.

My sincere hope is that the material presented in the book will be useful to readers.

Nirali Prakashan put the book, what we thought of into reality. My sincere thanks to Shri. Dineshbhai Furia, Shri. Jignesh Furia and Shri. M. P. Munde. The books could be completed in time, due to sincere and hard work of Nirali Prakashan's staff namely Mr. Malik Shaikh and Mrs. Prajakta. We thank them all.

Finally, I would like to thank Dr. Mrs. Sangeeta Patil for her moral support during long and aduous task of writing this book.

At the last but not the least, we are also thankful to the reader. Any suggestion for the improvement of this book will be acknowledged and well appreciated.

3ʳᵈ September, 2013
Pune.

G. R. Patil

Syllabus ...

Unit I: Introduction to Data Structure and Advance Concepts in 'C'   (06)

Introduction to Theory of Data Structure and its Data Types, Primitive and Non-Primitive Data Structures, Abstract Data Structure, Arrays: One Dimensional and Two Dimensional Arrays, Arrays as an ADT Insertion, Deletion and Traversals of Arrays, Pointers: Basic Concept, Concept of Functions and its Types, Structures: Array of Structures, Passing Structure to Function, Storage Classes.

Unit II: Stacks and Queues   (06)

Stack, Stack as an ADT, Representation using Arrays and Linked List, Applications of Stack, Concept of Infix, Postfix and Prefix Expressions. The Queue and its Representation, Queue as an ADT, Circular Queue, Priority Queue, Applications of Queue.

Unit III: Linked List   (08)

Definition, Concept, Operation on Singly Linked List, Circular Linked Lists, Doubly Linked Lists, Operations like Insertion, Deletion, Searching, Updating, Applications of Linked List such as Polynomial Manipulation, Comparison of Singly Linked, Circularly Linked and Doubly Linked List.

Unit IV: Graphs   (06)

Definitions, Basic Terminology, Representation and Implementation of Graphs, Graph Traversals, DFS, BFS, Shortest Path, Spanning Tree, Minimum Cost Spanning Trees.

Unit V: Trees   (08)

Definition, Basic Terminology, Operation on Binary Trees, Linked Storage Representation for Binary Search Trees, Basic Operation on Binary Search Tree such as Creating a Binary Search Tree, Searching, Tree Traversals, In-order, Pre-order, Post-order, Tree Application for Expression Evaluation and for Solving Sparse Matrices.

Unit VI: Sorting and Searching   (06)

Different Sorting Tech, Selection Sort, Bubble Sort, Merge Sort, Quick Sort, Heap Sort, Shell Sort, Radix Sort, Comparisons between Different Sorting Techniques, Sequential Searching, Binary Searching, B-trees, B+trees.

***

Contents ...

Unit IV: Graphs — 4.1 - 4.52

***

Unit I

INTRODUCTION TO DATA STRUCTURE AND ADVANCE CONCEPTS IN 'C'

1.1 Introduction

In this chapter, basic concepts of data structures and algorithms will be introduced. We will see how data can be organised and how various operations can be performed. Algorithms and their time complexity will also be discussed alongwith space complexity.

1.1.1 Basic Terminology: Elementary Data Organisation

First let us look at the various terminologies that will be used throughout this text.

(i) Data: It is a collection of values or information.

For example, A set of integers.

(ii) Data item: It is a single value in the set of data.

For example, A number 10 in set of integers.

(iii) Group items: It is a data item that can be divided into subitems.

For example, A record of student containing his Roll No, name, date of birth, marks etc.

(iv) Entity: It is something that has certain properties (attributes) which may be assigned values.

For example, In students list, each student is an entity.

(v) Entity set: Entities with similar attributes is called entity set.

For example, All students in a list of entity set.

(vi) Range of values: A set of all possible values that could be assigned to a particular attribute.

For example, Roll Nos of students may range from 1 to 70.

(vii) Information: It is meaningful or processed data.

For example, Sorted list of students.

(viii) Field: It is a single elementary unit of information representing an attribute of an entity.

For example, rollno, name, date of birth are fields because they represent attribute of student.

(ix) Record: It is a collection of field values of a given entity.

For example, Record of a student.

101 Amit 05 April 1994.

(x) File: Collection of records of the entities in a given entity set.

(xi) Primary key: The field which uniquely identifies the record.

For example, Roll no of student is primary key.

(x) Fixed-length record: All records in the file having same amount of space requirement i.e. they have same number of fields.

(xi) Variable length record: Records in the file may have different lengths.

The way in which data is organised is called data structures. Collection of records as discussed above is also a data structure. But data may be organised in a more complex types of structures as well. So that we can maintain and process the data more effectively.

1.1.2 Data Structures

The logical or mathematical model of a particular organisation of data is called data structure. There are two criteria on which the choice of data model depends:

    (i)   It should reflect the relationship of data in real world.

    (ii) It should be simple so that the processing of data can be done effectively.

Thus, a data structure can be defined as a set of domain D, designated domain $d \in D$, a set of functions F and set of Axioms A. Thus, the triple (D, F, A) denotes data structure d, where,

    D is domain means range of values.

    F is functions means operations.

    A is Axioms means semantics of operations i.e. rules of operations.

Data object is a set of values. In a data structure, we describe a set of data objects and how they are related.

Data structure may be divided into two types:

(i) Primitive: The data structures related to atomic data types i.e. they cannot be further divided are called primitive data structures or simple data structures or primary data structures. For example, int, float, char.

(ii) Non-primitive: The data structures which are composite in nature or derived from basic data types are called non-primitive data structures. For example, array, structures, file, lists etc. They are also called as secondary data structures.

Non-primitive data structures can be further classified as:

(i) Linear data structures: In this the elements form a sequence or arranged in hierarchical manner. For example, arrays, linked list, queues, stacks.

(ii) Non-linear data structure: In this data is not arranged in sequence, i.e. each element may have multiple successors or predecessors For example, trees, graphs.

Now, let us briefly discuss the various data structures.

Arrays:

A linear or one-dimensional array is a list of finite number of similar data elements referenced by a set of consecutive numbers called indices.

For example, $a_0, a_1, a_2, ..., a_n$ are elements of an array. In C language they are denoted using brackets as a[0], a[1], a[2], ..., a[n].

We can have array of integers, array of real numbers, array of names, array of records etc.

Linked lists:

It is a list elements in which each data element is stored alongwith address of its successor as shown below in Fig. 1.1.

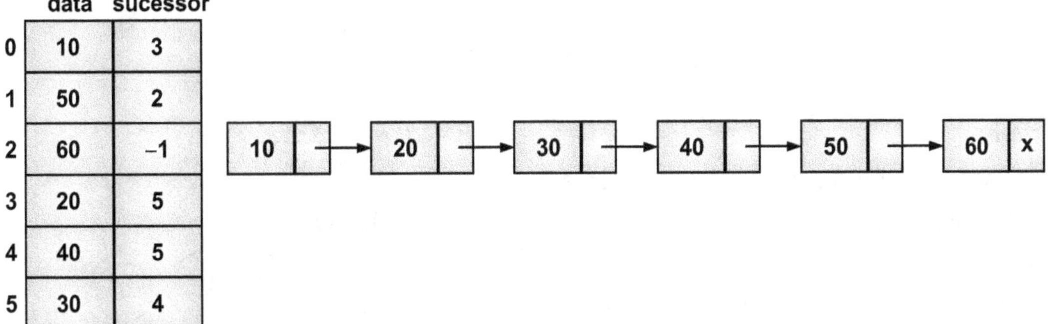

Fig. 1.1: Linked organisation of data

Stacks:

It is a Last In First Out (LIFO) type of data structure in which insertion or deletion can be made only at one place called top as shown in Fig. 1.2.

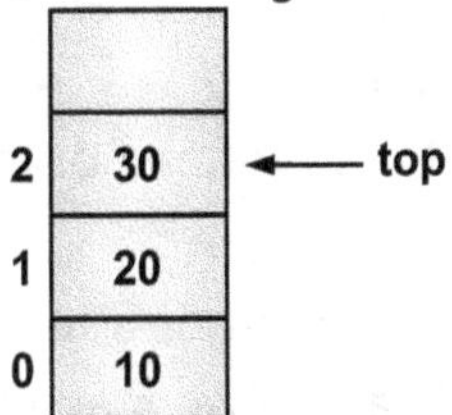

Fig. 1.2: Stack

Queue:

It is a First In First Out (FIFO) type of data structure in which deletion can take place at one called front and insertion can take place at the other end called rear as shown below.

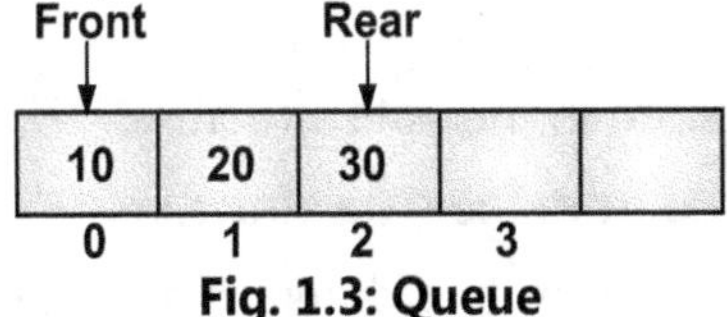

Fig. 1.3: Queue

Trees:

Data may contain hierarchical relationship between elements. This data can be stored using a tree type structure whose starting element will be at the root of the tree as shown below in Fig. 1.4.

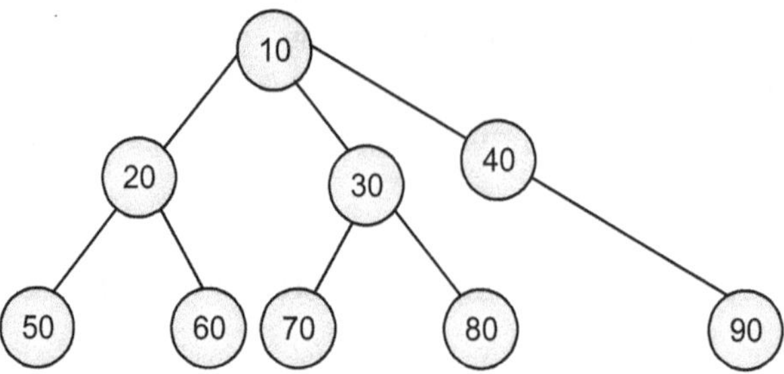

Fig. 1.4: Tree

Graph:

Information to be stored some times contain a complex relationship which may be represented in the form of graph. For example, In a computer network the packets are transmitted from one node to another. The cost of transmission of these packets can be represented as below in Fig. 1.5.

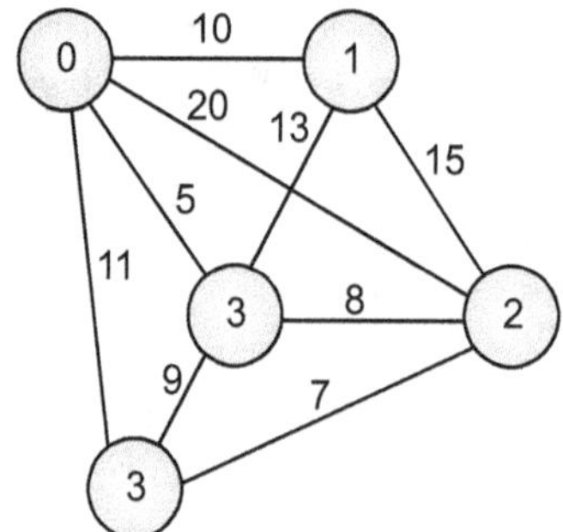

Fig. 1.5: Graph

1.1.3 Data Structure Operations

The various operations that need to be performed on the data stored in the data structure are:

(i) **Searching:** It is finding between location of a record or records based on a particular key. For example, in a student database we may need to find student or students with more than 50% marks.

(ii) **Sorting:** Arranging the records in some logical order. For example, we may need to arrange the student records in descending order of percentage.

(iii) **Traversing:** Accessing each record exactly once so that we can process the records one by one.

(iv) **Inserting:** Adding a new record in the data structure.

(v) **Deleting:** Removing a record from the data structure.

(vi) **Merging:** Combining records from two different structures. For example, we may want to combine two linked lists.

(vii) Copy: Making one or more copies of the record or records in the data structure.

(viii) Reverse: Reversing the order of the data stored in the data structure. For example, We may want to reverse the list of numbers stored in an array.

1.1.4 Abstract Data Type (ADT)

Abstract Data Type (ADT) is a tool for specifying the logical properties of a data type. Data type as you know is set of values and the operations on these values.

ADT is a mathematical concept that defines data type. In ADT, we do not specify how the set of operations is implemented. So when we define an ADT, we are not concerned with implementation details.
The ADT is a useful guideline for the implementers and a useful tool for programmers so that they can use data type correctly.

If we have an ADT, there will be some operations specified in it as functions. If a program wants to perform these operations it can do so by calling the appropriate function. Now, suppose the implementation of these functions in ADT is changed, that will not affect the program in which these functions are used. Then if you have some addition to ADT, that will also not affect the program.

With an ADT, we are not concerned with how the task is done. We know that it can be done. ADT consists of set of definitions that allow programmers to use the functions while hiding the implementation. This generalisation of operations with unspecified implementation is known as abstraction.

ADT is defined as data declaration packaged together with the operations that are meaningful for the data type.

There are many ways in which ADT is specified. An ADT consists of two parts:
1.   Value definition
2.   Operation definition.

1.   **Value definition:** It has collection of values for the ADT. It consists of two parts:
   (i)   **Definition clause:** It consists of actual data.
   (ii)   **Condition clause:** It consists of restriction on data.
2.   **Operation definition:** It defines operations in ADT in 3 parts:
   (i)   **Header:** Similar to function header.
   (ii)   **Precondition (Optional):** It specifies restrictions that must be met before operation is done.
   (iii)   **Post condition:** Specifies what operation does.

Example: Array as ADT

```
        value
/* Definition
Array_type a [size];
```

/* Operation Definition

/* To store n elements in array */

    void store (Array_type a, int n);

/* To display n elements of array */

    void disp (Array_type a, int n);

/* To find length of array */

    int length (Array_type a);

/* To append an element in array */

    void append (Array_type a, int x);

/* To modify an element in array */

    void modify (Array_type a, int p, int x);

/* To remove an element */

    void remove (Array_type a, int p);

/* To search an element */

    int search (Array_type a, int x);

/* To sort the array */

    void sort (Array_type a);

/* To insert an element */

    void insert (Array_type a, int p, int x);

1.2 Arrays (One Dimensional and Two Dimensional)

When we declare variables as:

    int a, b, c;

Compiler reserves 3 memory locations to store 3 integer numbers.

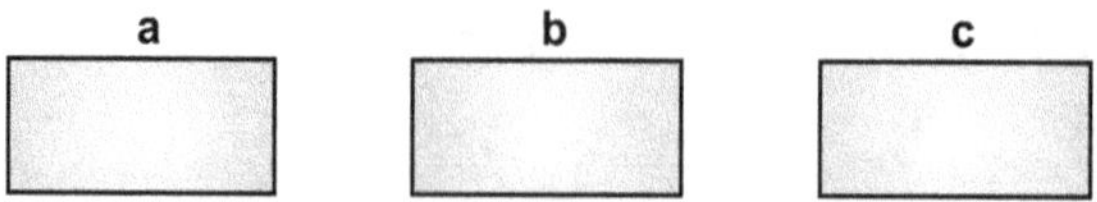

Fig. 1.6: Memory allocation for variables

In case, we want to store more numbers, say 1000 we have to have those many variables declared. But this is going to be inconvenient for the programmer.

C provides a convenient way to declare as many variables as you want using arrays. Arrays are defined in number of ways:

1. An array is a group of related data items that share a common name.

2. An array is a collection of elements of same type which are stored in continuous locations in memory. For example, suppose we want to store marks of 50 students or salaries of 25 employees, we can use arrays. In short, a list of data items of same type can be stored in an array. Arrays can be single or multidimensional. Let us first look into single dimensional arrays.

1.2.1 Defining an Array

We can declare any array variable to store them. Array is declared as

    data_type array_name [size];
    For example, int a[100];

It means we declared 100 variables of integer type. These variables have the same name a. The size can be any integer constant. The above declaration reserves 100 locations in the memory to store integer numbers.

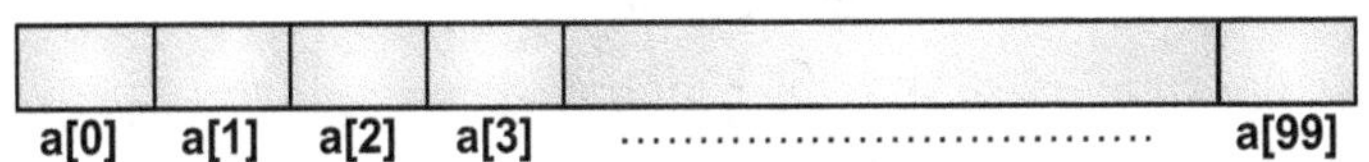

Fig. 1.7: Memory allocation for single dimensional array

These locations are a[0], a[1], ..., a[99] are called elements of array. They are just like any other variable names.

1.2.2 Reading into an Array

To read elements into an array we can use for loop as,

    for(i=0;i<n;i++)
    scanf("%d", &a[i]);

where n is the number of elements in the array, n can be any number less than size of the array. When i=0, first element entered from keyboard gets stored in the location a[0], when i=1 second number entered is stored in location a[1] and so on.

Similarly, if array elements are real (say float x[100]) then we can write,

```
for(i=0;i<n;i++)
    scanf("%f", &x[i]);
```

1.2.3 Printing an Array

The elements in the array can be displayed using for loop as

```
for (i=0;i<n;i++)
printf("%d \n", a[i]);
```

Thus, when i = 0 the element stored in the location a[0] gets displayed. When i = 1, the second element in the array gets displayed and so on.

1.2.4 Processing an Array

Array elements can be processed the same way we process other variables i.e. just like we write c = a + b; we can write,

```
a[2] = a[0] + a[1];
```

Numbers stored at location a[0] and a[1] in the array are added and the sum is stored in the location a[2]. Similarly we can have,

	sum = a[0] + a[1];
or	avg = (a[0] + a[1]) / 2;
or	a[10] = 20;
or	a[5] = 4;
or	a[9] = a[8]; etc.

It means we can take any element in an array randomly and process it.

1.2.5 Examples on Array

Now let us write some programs to understand how single dimensional arrays are used.

Program 1.0: To store and display the elements in an array.

```
void main( )
{
    int a[10], i;
    clrscr( );
```

```
        for(i=0;i<10;i++)
            a[i]=i*10;
        for(i=0;i<10;i++)
            printf("%d \n", a[i]);
        getch( );
    }
```

Explanation:

1. The declaration int a[10]; will reserve 10 integer locations a[0], a[1], a[2], ... a[9].

2. The first for loop puts values 0, 10, 20, ..., 90 in the locations a[0], a[1], a[2], ...a[9].

3. The second for loop displays the values 0, 10, 20, ..., 90.

Program 1.1: To display first 10 Fibonacci numbers.

```
    void main ( )
    {
        int a[10], i;
        clrscr( );
        a[0]=0;
        a[1]=1;
        for(i=2;i<10;i++)
            a[i]=a[i-1]+a[i-2];
        for(i=0;i<10;i++)
            printf("%d \n", a[i]);
        getch( )
    }
```


Explanation:

1. The declaration int a[10]; will reserve 10 integer locations a[0], a[1], a[2], ... a[9].

2. Since first two Fibonacci numbers are 0 and 1 they are stored in a[0] and a[1].

3. The first for loop starts with i=2 and calculates the ith Fibonacci number.

4. The second for loop displays all the Fibonacci numbers.

5. The output will be 0 1 1 2 3 5 8 13 21 34.

Program 1.2: To accept numbers from users and display them in reverse order.

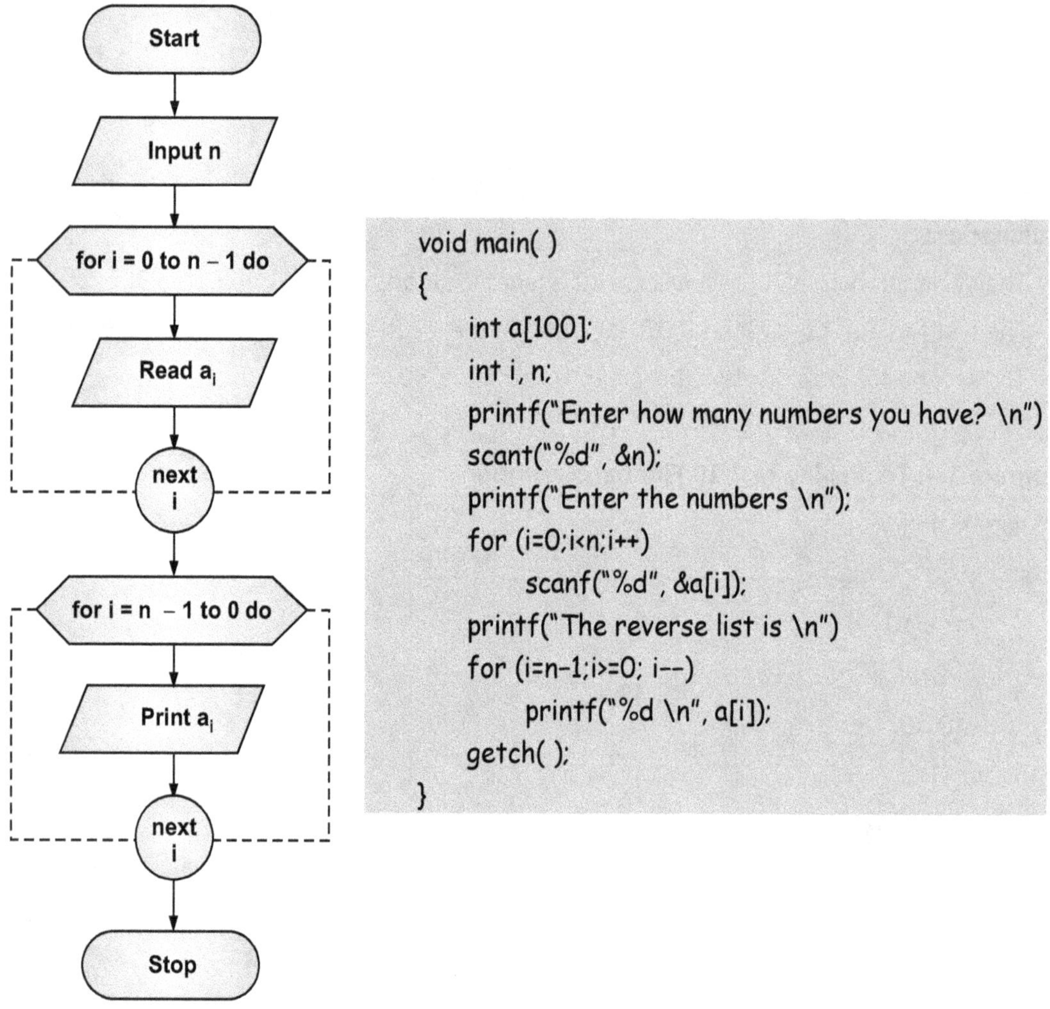

Fig. 1.8: Flow chart for program 1.2

Explanation:

1. First, for loop accepts numbers from users and stores them into an array.
2. Since, the last numbers will be in an $(n-1)^{th}$ location, the second for loop which displays the elements starts with $i = n - 1$ and goes upto 0.

Note: Most of the array related programs will have 3 parts, viz. reading the elements in an array, processing the array and printing results.

Program 1.3: To count number of odd and even numbers in a list.

```
void main( )
{
    int a[100];
    int i, n, oc = 0, ec = 0;
    printf("Enter how many numbers? \n");
    scanf("%d", &n);
    printf("Enter the numbers \n");
    for (i=0;i<n;i++)
        scanf("%d", &a[i]);
    for (i=0;i<n;i++)
    {
        if (a[i]%2==0)
            ec ++;
        else
            oc ++;
    }
    printf("Even numbers are %d \n", ec);
    printf("Odd numbers are %d \n", oc);
    getch( );
}
```

Program 1.4: To count number of positive numbers, negative numbers and zeros in a list.

```
void main( )
{
    int a[ 100];
    int i, n;pc=0;nc=0;zc=0;
    printf("Enter how many numbers? \n");
    scanf("%d", &n);
    printf("Enter the numbers \n");
    for (i=0;i<n;i++)
        scanf("%d", &a[i]);
    for (i=0;i<n;i ++)
    {
        if(a[i]>0)
```

```
                pc++;
            if(a[i]<0)
                nc++;
            if(a[i]==0)
                zc++;
        }
        printf("Number of positive numbers=%d \n", pc)
        printf("Number of negative numbers=%d \n", nc)
        printf("Number of zeros=%d \n", zc)
        getch( );
}
```

Program 1.5: To find sum, average, standard deviation of n numbers.

Explanation: We can write a program to find sum and average of numbers without using array. But to find standard deviation, we have to have an array because the numbers accepted from the user will be required second time to find standard deviation. It is given as

$$sd = \sqrt{\frac{\sum_i (a_i - \bar{a})^2}{n}}$$

where, $\bar{a}$ is Average of the umbers.

Hence to find standard deviation, we have to first find average and then find the $\sum_i (a_i - \bar{a})^2$

where, $i = 0$ to $n - 1$.

```
    #include <math.h>
    void main( )
    {
        float a[100];
        float s, avg, sd
        float i, n;
        printf("Enter how many numbers? \n");
        scanf("%d", &n);
        printf("Enter the numbers \n");
        for (i=0;i<n;i++)
            scanf("%f", &a[i];
        s=0;
        for (i=0;i<n;i++)
```

```c
            s=s + a[i];
        avg = s/n;
        printf("Sum is %f \n", s);
        printf("Avg is %f \n", avg);
        s=0;
        for (i=0;i<n;i++)
            s=s + pow(a[i] – avg, 2);
        sd=sqrt (s/n);
        printf("Standard deviation is %f sd);
        getch( );
    }
```

Program 1.6: To find maximum of given n numbers.

```c
    void main( )
    {
        int a[ 100];
        int i, n, max;
        printf("Enter how many numbers? \n");
        scanf("%d", &n);
        printf("Enter the numbers \n");
        for (i=0;i<n;i++)
            scanf("%d", &a[i]);
        max = a[0];
        for (i=1;i<n;i++)
        {
            if (a[i]>max)
                max = a[i];
        }
        printf("Maximum is %d \n", max);
        getch( )
    }
```

Program 1.7: To search a number from a given list of numbers.

```c
    void main( )
    {
        int a[100];
```

```c
    int i, n, s, flag;
    printf("Enter how many numbers? \n");
    scanf("% d ", &n);
    printf("Enter the numbers \n");
    for (i=0;i<n;i++)
        scanf("%d", &a[i]);
    printf("Enter number to be searched \n");
        scanf("%d", &s);
    flag = 1;
    for(i=0;i<n;i++)
    {
        if(a[i]==s)
        {
            flag = 0;
            break;
        }
    }
    if(flag==1)
        printf("Found");
    else
        printf("Not found");
    getch( );
}
```

Program 1.8: To convert decimal number into binary.

```c
    void main( )
    {
        int a[50];
        int i, x, q;
        printf("Enter the number \n");
            scanf("%d", &x);
        i=0; q=x;
        while (q>0)
        {
            a[i] = q%2;
            q = q/2;
```

```
            i++;
    }
    n=i;
    printf("The Binary number is .... \n");
    for(i=n-1;i>=0;i--)
            printf("%d", a[i]);
    getch( );
}
```

1.2.6 Initializing an Array

Just like we initialize memory variables at the time of declaration e.g., int x = 10; array elements can also be initialized as

int a[ ] = {10, 20, 30, 40};

It will initialize the elements of the array a as

a[0] = 10, a[1] = 20, a[2] = 30, a[3] = 40;

Here note that there is no need to declare size, since we are specifying the data to be stored in array. Let us consider following example.

```
void main
{
    int a[ ] = {10, 20, 30, 40};
    for (i=0;i<4;i++)
    {
        a[i] = a[i] + 10;
    }
    for (i=0;i<4;i++)
        printf("%d \n", a[i]);
}
```

Output of the above program will be

20

30

40

50

1.2.7 Two Dimensional Array

Sometimes, we have a group of numbers represented in terms of rows and columns. e.g., table of values.

Table 1.1

	Item 1	Item 2	Item 3
s1	10	40	10
s2	20	30	20
s3	30	50	50
s4	10	20	60

In mathematics, this table of values is represented in terms of matrix. It consists of rows and columns. The table given above can be represented in C using two dimensional array as

  int table[4][3];

Thus, two dimensional array can be declared as

  var_type   name [row_size] [col_size];

e.g. int a[10][10];

It will reserve 100 locations in the memory to store 100 integer numbers. The names of the locations will be

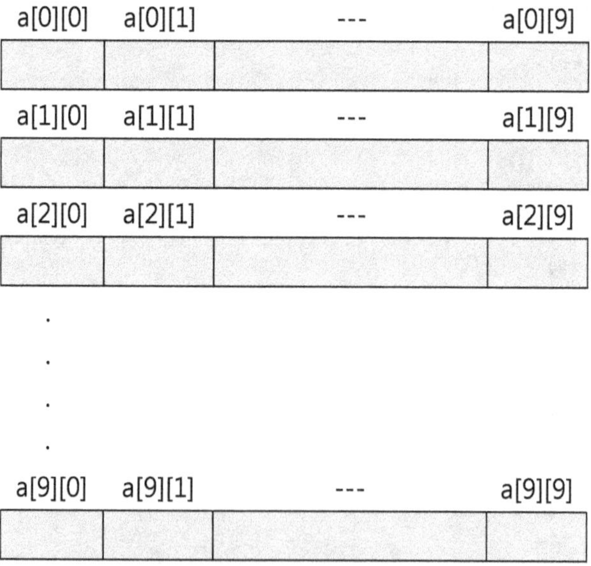

Fig. 1.9: Memory allocation for 2-D array

1.2.8 Reading into two Dimension Array

To read data in single dimensional array, we use single for loop. Here, we have to use nested for loop. Foe example if an array consists of m rows and n columns. We can write

```
for(i=0;i<m;i++)
for(j=0;j<n;i++)
    scanf("%d", &a[i][j]);
```

The outer for loop runs for m times and the inner n times. The elements will be accepted row wise. This is called as row major representation of the two dimensional array.

1.2.9 Displaying the Two Dimensional Array

To print the elements stored in two dimensional arrays, nested or loop will be required as follows:

```
for(i=0;i<m;i++)
{
    for(j=0;j<n;j++)
        printf("%d", a[i][j]);
    printf("\n");
}
```

Note: printf ("\n"); statement is used to transfer the cursor to next line after a row is over.

1.2.10 Processing Two Dimensional Arrays

Just like we access any element in a single dimensional array randomly, we can access any element in two dimensional array for storage of value or calculation purpose.

```
e.g. a[0][0]   =   10;
     sum       =   a[0][0] + a[1][1] + a[2][2];
     a[0][0]   =   a[0][0] + b[0][0];
     a[2][2]   =   a[0][0] + a[1][1];
```

1.2.11 Examples on Two Dimensional Arrays

Now let us write some programs based on two dimensional arrays.

Program 1.9: To find sum of two matrices.

There will be three matrices involved here. Three two dimensional arrays will be required to store the three matrices. The addition is carried out element by element.

```
i.e., c[i][j] = a[i][j] + b[i][j];
```

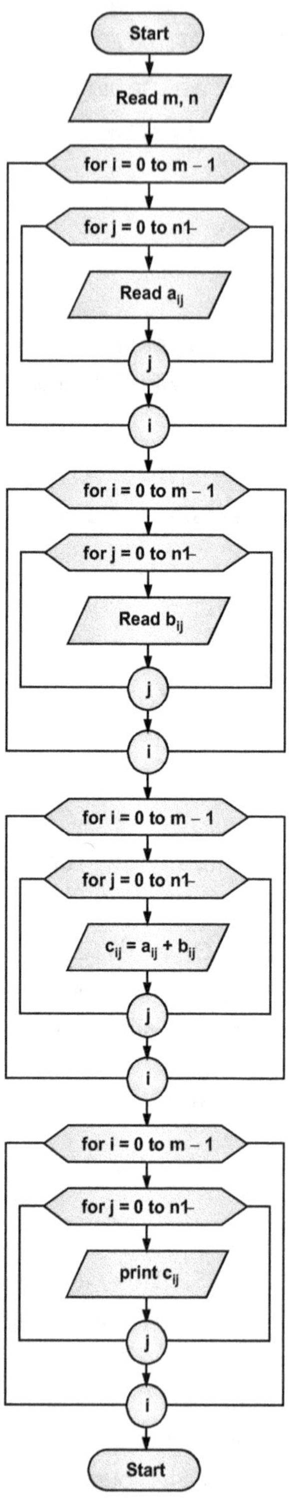

Fig. 1.10: Flow chart for matrix addition

```c
void main( )
{
    int a[10][10], b[10][10], c[10][10];
    int i, j, m, n;
    clrscr( );
    printf("Enter order or matrices \n");
    scanf("%d%d", &m, &n);

    printf("Enter first matrix \n");
    for(i=0;i<m;i++)
        for(j=0;j<n;j++)
            scanf("%d", &a[i][j]);
    printf("Enter second matrix \n");
    for(i=0;i<m;i++)
        for(j=0;j<n;j++)
            scanf("%d", &b[i][j]);
    for(i=0;i<m;i++)
        for(j=0;j<n;j++)
            c[i][j] = a[i][j] + b[i][j];
    printf("Resultant matrix is \n");
    for (i=0;i<m;i++)
    {
        for(j=0;j<n;j++)
            printf("%d", c[i][j]);
        printf("\n");
    }
    getch( );
}
```

Explanation:
1. Order means number of rows and columns of the two matrices to be added. It is same for both matrices hence same variables m and n are used.
2. The two matrices are accepted from user and stored in 2-D arrays a and b.
3. The third nested for loop adds the elements of a and b and stores the result in c.
4. The matrix c is displayed by the 4"h Nested for.

Program 1.10: To find sum of all major and minor diagonal elements in a given matrix.

```c
void main( )
{
    int a[10][10];
    int m, n, i, j, s, s1;
    printf("Enter order or matrix \n");
    scanf("%d%d", &m, &n);
```

```c
        printf("Enter the matrix \n");
        for(i=0;i<m;i++)
             for(j=0;j<n;j++)
                  scanf("%d", &a[i][j]);
        s = 0; s1 = 0;
        for(i=0;i<m;i++)
        {
             for(j=0;j<n;j++)
             {
                  if (i==j)
                       s = s + a[i][j];
                  if(i +j==m – 1)
                       s1=s1 + a[i][j];
             }
        }
        printf("Sum of major diagonal %d, minor diagonal %d", s, s1);
}
```

Explanation:

1. Diagonal elements will have row and column number same hence the condition i == j is tested for adding the elements.

Program 1.11: Write a program to find transpose of a matrix.

```c
void main
{
    int a[10][10], b[10][10];
    int i, j, m, n;
    printf("Enter order of matrix \n");
    scanf("%d%d", &m, &n);
    printf("Enter the matrix \n");
    for(i=0;i<m;i++)
         for(j=0;j<n;j++)
              scanf("%d", &a[i][j]);
    for(i=0;i<m;i++)
    {
         for(j=0;j<n;j++)
              b[j][i] = a[i][j];
    }
    printf("The transpose is \n");
```

```
    for(i=0;i<n;i++)
    {
        for(j=0;j<m;j++)
            printf("%d", b[i] [j]);
        printf("\n");
    }
}
```

Explanation:

1. Array a stores the matrix of the order m x n whose transpose is to be stored in matrix b.
2. After reading the elements in a, the elements of a are copied to b one by one. The element in the ith row and j^{th} column of a is copied to j^{th} row and i^{th} column of b.
3. Note that third loop which prints the elements of b has n first and m next because the transpose will have order n × m. i.e., it will haven rows and m columns. e.g. Transpose of 3 × 2 will be 2 × 3 matrix.
4. We cannot write the statement b[i][j] = a[j][i] instead of b[j][i] = a[i][j]. Find out the reason.

Program 1.12: To print product of two matrices.

```
void main
{
    int m, n, k, p, 1, i, l;
    int a[10][10], b[10][10], c[10][10];
    clrscr( );
    printf("Enter order of 1st matrix \n");
    scanf("%d%d", &m, &n);
    printf("Enter order of 2nd matrix \n");
    scanf("%d%d", &p, & l);
    if (n!=p)
    {
        printf("Invalid order");
        exit (0);
    }
    printf("Enter 1st matrix \n");
    for(i=0;i<m;i++)
        for(j=0;j<n;j++)
            scanf("%d"; &a[i][j]);
        printf("Enter 2nd matrix \n");
```

```c
        for(i=0;i<p;i++)
            for(i=0;j<l;j++)
                scanf("%d", &b[i][j]);
        for(i=0;i<m;i++)
        {
            for(j=0;j<l;j++)
            {
                c[i][j] = 0;
                for(k=0;k<n;k++)
                    c[i][j] = c[i][j] + a[i][k] * b[k][j];
            }
        }
        printf ("Product is \n");
        for(i=0;i<m;i++)
        {
            for(j=0;j<l;j++)
                printf("%d", c[i][j]);
            print("\n");
        }
        getch( );
    }
```

Explanation:

1. First matrix is stored in array a and has order m × n. second matrix is stored in array b and has order p × l.

2. Number of columns of first matrix should be equal to number of rows of second matrix. Hence, if n!=p the error message "Invalid matrices" is displayed and exit(0) statement terminates the program.

3. The process of multiplication will require Nested for loops. The outer for loop with variable 1st will keep on changing the row number of 2nd matrix. The second for loop with variable j will keep on changing column of 2nd matrix. The third for loop will do the sum of multiplication of ith row elements of first matrix and jth column element of second matrix and the result will be stored in 3rd matrix's ith row and jth column.

    e.g., when i = 0, j = 0, k runs from 0 to n − 1. The value

    a[0][0] * b[0][0] + a[0][1] * b[1][0] + ... + a[0][n − 1] * b[n − 1][0] will be stored in the location c[0][0] and so on.

4. The resultant matrix c is of the order m × l. Hence, the last nested for loops run for m × l times.

1.2.12 Initializing Two Dimensional Array

Just like we initialize one dimensional array, we can initialize two dimensional arrays as follows:

    int a [ ][3] = {10, 20, 30,40, 50, 60, 70, 80, 90};

It means we are storing the numbers in the array as follows:

    a[0][0] =10   a[1][0] =40
    a[0][1] = 20   a[2][1] =50
    a[0][2] =30   a[1][2] =60 etc.

Note that it is necessary to have column size mentioned as a[][3] otherwise it will become difficult for the compiler to allocate memory.

If number of columns is not specified, the array can be initialized as

    int a[ ] [ ] = {(10, 20, 30}, {40, 50, 60}, {70, 80, 90};

Program 1.13: To find sum of elements in a matrix

```
void main( )
{
    int i, j, s = 0;
    int a[ ][3] = {10, 20, 30, 40, 50, 60, 70, 80, 90};
    for(i=0;i<3;i++)
        for(j=0;j<3;j++)
            s = s + a[i][j];
        printf("Sum is % d", s);
        getch( );
}
```

Multidimensional Array:

We can have more than two dimensional arrays as well. For example, a three dimensional array can be declared as

    int a[2][2][3];

There will be total 12 elements in this array. These elements will be a[0][0][0], a[0][0][1], a[0][0][2], a[0][1][1], a[0][1][2], a[1][0][0], a[1][0][1], a[1][0][2], a[1][1][0], a[1][1][1], a[1][1][2].

While initialising the multidimensional array the leftmost dimensional can be omitted.

e.g. int a[ ][2][3] = {0, 1, 2, 3, 4, 5, 6, 7, 8, 9, 10, 11}

1.3 Pointers

Pointer is a very powerful tool which allows programmer lot of flexibility and help in improving efficiency of the program. This concept is important because almost all data structures are based on pointers.

1.3.1 Basic Concepts of Pointer

First thing that should be clear to you is, we are writing a program which is going to be executed by a machine which has memory and each location in memory has an address. When we declare a variable say int a; a location in the memory is reserved to store an integer number.

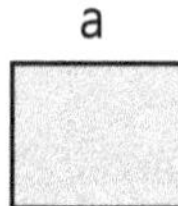

Fig. 1.11: Memory allocation for a

We have the location name as 'a'. The computer which is a digital device. gives number to the location which is called as address of that location. It is just like we give some nice name to our home and Municipal Corporation identifies it with House Number or Survey No. etc. Thus, the memory variable will have associated with it an unique address as shown in Fig. 1.12.

Fig. 1.12: Address of a

What if I want to know the address of that variable? It is possible to access the address of a variable using & operator. The operator & (ampersand) gives address of the corresponding variable. Thus, in above case, &a will be 10000. The address will be solely decided by the computer and not by the programmer. Let us write a program to understand this concept.

Program 1.14: Program to illustrate address of (&) operator.

```
void main( )
{
    int i = 4, j = 8;
    printf("value of i = %d\n", i);
    printf("Address of i = %u\n", &i);
    printf("Value of j = % d\n", j);
    printf("Address of j = %u\n", & j);
}
```

Explanation:

1. In program 6.6, we have two variables declared as i and j. The situation in the memory will be as shown in figure 1.13.

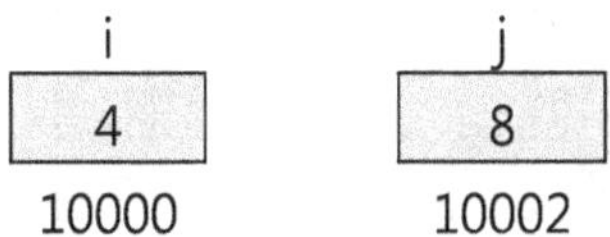

Fig. 1.13: Memory allocation and address of i and j

Here we are assuming that the address of i and j are 10000 and 10002 respectively. The output of the program will be as follows.

Value of i=4

Address of i = 10000

Value of j=8

Address of j = 10002

2. Note that while displaying address %u is used because the address will never be negative number. It is displayed as unsigned integer.

When C program is executed the RAM consists of operating system, the program and the data involved in the program in separate areas. The data area is nothing but the space reserved for the variables in the program. The space in RAM is measured in bytes. Each cell in RAM is of 1 byte. The address is given to each byte in RAM.

Generally, following is space allocation for each variable type

1   byte for char

2   bytes for int

4   bytes for float and long time

8   bytes for double

Hence, when we declare variables as below the memory allocation will be as shown in Fig. 1.14 (a) (Refer Appendix A for further details).

int a, b;

float x, y;

char ch;

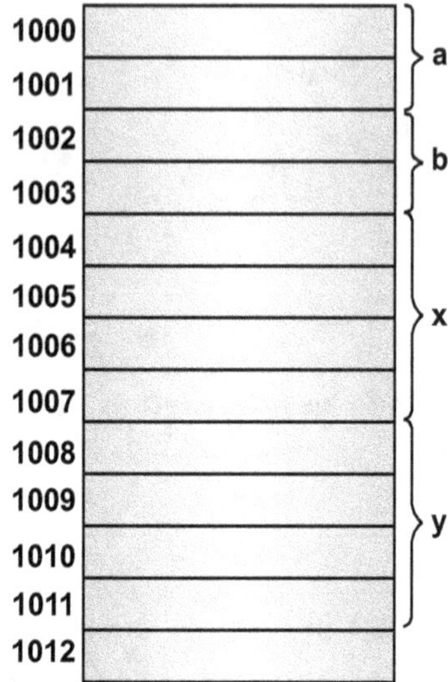

Fig. 1.14 (a): Memory allocation for variables

Just like we have & operator giving address of a variable, there is another operator called operator which gives value stored at a particular address. It is called indirection operator. e.g. *(&a) will give value stored at address of a, which is nothing but value stored at a only. Let us consider one more program to illustrate the concept.

Program 1.15: Use of & and * operator.

```
void main( )
    {
        int i = 3;
        printf ("Value of i = %d \n", i);
        printf ("Address of i = %u \n", &i);
        printf ("Value of i = %d \n", *(&i));

    }
```

1.3.2 Pointer Declaration and Initialisation

There are three basic types of variables in C viz. int, float, char. If a variable is of type int, it will store only integer type data. It is possible to store address of a variable in memory. C provides a pointer type variable which is capable of storing address of another variable but of same type.

A pointer variable is declared as,

int *p;

Thus, a pointer variable is declared like any other variable with * preceding the variable name. It means we are declaring a variable p which is a pointer type variable and it is capable of storing address of any integer variable. We can use this variable to access the value stored in another location. Suppose we have 2 variables declared as follows:

    int a = 10;

    int *p;

Two locations will be reserved in the memory as shown in Fig. 1.15.

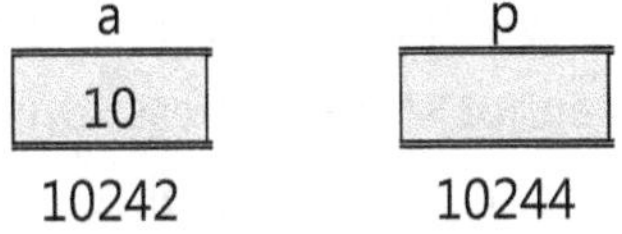

Fig. 1.15: Memory allocation for a and p

Now, if I write a statement as

    p = &a;

address of a (i.e., &a) will be assigned to p as shown in Fig. 1.16.

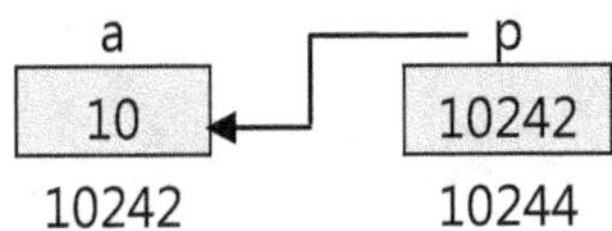

Fig. 1.16: Pointer p pointing to location a

It means p has the address of a i.e., p is pointing to a as shown and *p will give value stored at a. Thus, if we store address of a variable in a pointer type variable we can access the value stored in that variable through the pointer type variable.

Let us consider a program:

Program 1.16: To illustrate pointer variable & operator.

```
    void main( )
    {
        int *p;
        int a = 10;
        p = &a;
        printf ("Value of a = %d \n", a);
```

```
        printf ("Address of a = %u \n", &a);
        printf ("Value of p = %u \n", p);
        printf ("Value of a = %d \n", *p);
}
```

Output of the program will be

```
    Value of a = 10
    Address of a = 10242
    Value of p = 10242
    Value of a = 10
```

Note: We can have float and char type pointers also. The float type pointer can store only address of float type variable. It cannot store address of int or char variable. Similarly, char type pointer can store only address of char type variable. Following program has all the three pointers.

Program 1.17: To illustrate pointer variable & operator.

```
    void main( )
    {
        int *pi, a=10;
        float *pf, x=1.2345;
        char *pc, c = '*';
        pi= &a;
        pf= &x;
        PC= &c;
        printf ("%d \n", *pi);
        printf ("%f \n", *pf);
        printf ("%c \n", *pc);
    }
```

Output: 10

              1.2345

                 *

Now, consider some more programs.

Program 1.18: To illustrate operations with pointer variable.

```
void main( )
{
    int a = 10,b=20, *p, *q, c;
    p = &a;
    q = &b;
    c = *p + *q;
    printf ("Sum is %d \n", c);
}
```

Output: 30

Explanation:
1. Address of a is stored in p (a is pointed by p) and address of b is stored in q (b is pointed by q).
2. *p will be 10 and *q will be 20.
3. Variable c will store sum of value stored at a location pointed by p (i.e., a) and value stored in a location pointed by q (i.e., b).

Note: The indirection operator * has higher precedence than the arithmetic operators +, –, *, /.

Program 1.19: To illustrate operations with pointer variable.

```
void main( )
{
    int a = 10, *p;
    p = &a;
    *p = *p + 100;
    printf ("Sum is %d \n", a);
}
```

Output: 110.

Explanation:
1. p = &a will store address of a in p (a is pointed by p).
2. *p will be 10.
3. The statement *p = *p + 100 means the sum of value stored in a location pointed by p and 100 will be assigned to a location pointed by p.
4. Hence, *p = *p + 100 is equivalent to a = a + 100.

Program 1.20: To illustrate operations with pointer variable.

```
void main( )
{
    int a = 10, b = 20,.c, *p;
    p = &c;
    *p = a + b;
    printf("Sum is %d \n", c);
}
```

Output: 30

Explanation:

1. p = &c will store address of c in p (c is pointed by p).
2. *p will be garbage initially.
3. The statement *p = a + b means the sum of a and b will be assigned to a location pointed by p which is nothing but c. Hence, *p = a +.b is equivalent to c = a + b.

Program 1.21: To illustrate operations with pointer variable.

```
void main( )
{
    int *p;
    *p = 100;
    *p = *p *10;
    printf ("%d\n", *p);
}
```

Output: 1000

Explanation:

1. *p = 100 will store the constant number 100 in a temporary location and p will point to this location as shown in Fig. 1.17.

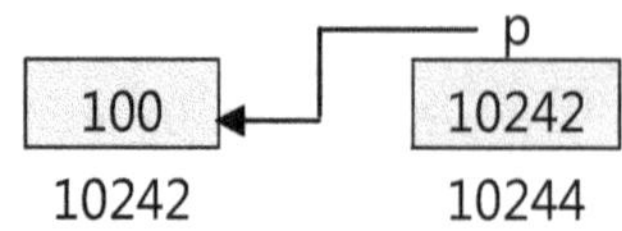

Fig. 1.17: Pointer to a constant

2. The statement *p = *p *10 will store product of location pointed by p and 10 into a location pointed by p itself.

1.3.3 Pointer to a Pointer

Let us consider a program to illustrate this concept.

Program 1.22: To illustrate double pointer.

```c
void main( )
{
    int a = 4,*b, **c;
    b = &a;
    c = &b;
    printf("%u \n", &a);
    printf("%u \n", b);
    printf("%u \n", c);
    printf("%u \n", &b);
    printf("%d \n", a);
    printf("%d \n", *b);
    printf("%d \n", **c);
}
```

Note that there are two pointers b and c. b is a single pointer and c is a double pointer. b stores address of integer variable. c can store address of another integer variable.

1. Let us assume following situation in memory when a, b and c as declared.

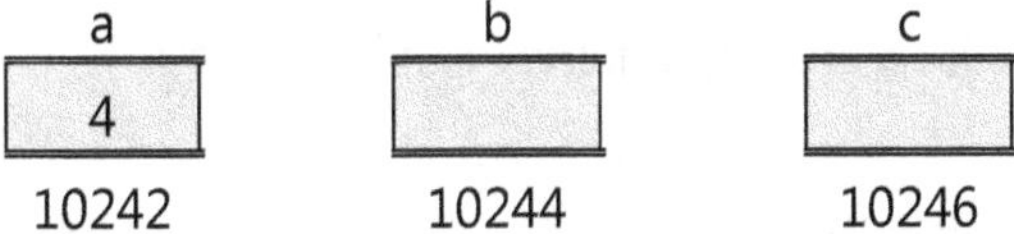

Fig. 1.18: Memory allocation for a, b and c

2. When the statements
    b = &a;
    c = &b; are executed, the memory contents will be as shown in Fig. 1.19.

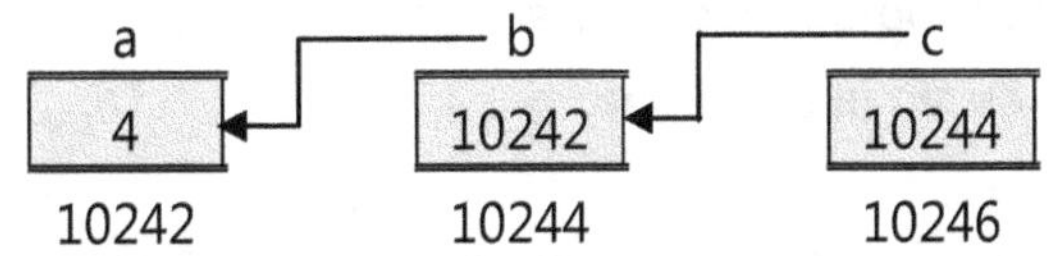

Fig. 1.19: Pointer to a pointer (double pointer)

*b will be value stored at 10242 i.e., a
**c = value stored at (value stored at 10244)
    = value stored at 10242
    = 4

3. Hence, output of program will be,

    10242

    10242

    10244

    10244

    4

    4

    4

1.4 Introduction of Function

Programs which we have seen till now were very simple. In practice, the programs we need to write are lengthy and more complex. In such cases, it becomes very difficult to write, debug and maintain the program. Let us see how it can be simplified through the use of functions.

Suppose we are given a complex task, what we do is, divide the task into small modules, so that each module can be worked out separately and then we combine those modules.

While writing lengthy and complicated programs, we can do the same thing. A program is divided into small subprograms. In C, these subprograms are called as functions. Thus, functions are programs, which do a specific task. These functions can be used in any of our programs. Thus once functions are written, they can be reused.

The advantages of using these functions are:
1. The program becomes compact.
2. The program becomes readable.
3. It is easy to debug the program.
4. Program development process becomes faster.
5. Future modification to program becomes easier.
6. The function can be reused in other programs.

We have already used some of the functions provided by C complier, which are called as inbuilt or library functions such as clrscr( ), getch( ), pow(x, n), sin(x) etc. The function clrscr( ), clears the screen. The pow function finds power of x raised to n etc. The programs for doing these things is already written by somebody else, we are just using these functions.

We can write such functions which are called as user defined functions.

1.4.1 How to Write a Function?

For writing a simple function, the format is,

```
Return_type function_name( )
{
    Declarations if any
    Body of function (code)
}
```

Return_type will be discussed later. Right now let us use it as void.

Suppose we want to write a function to display a message "Hello"

```
void print_hello( )
{
    printf("Hello \n");
}
```

This function can be called in any of your program. Just like we declare variables, we need to tell the compiler about the function before using it. It is called function prorotyping.

Program 1.23: Printing Hello

```
void print_hello( );
void main( )
{
    clrscr( );
    print_hello( );                 /* call to function */
    getch( );
}
void print_hello( )                 /* function header */
{
    printf("Hello \n");             /* body of function
}
```

Explanation:

1. The program execution starts first at main( ) function.
2. main( ) function first has call to clrscr( ) function which is an inbuilt/Library function. Because of this screen is cleared.

3. Then there is a call to print_hello( ) function. The control gets transferred to the function print_hello( ).
4. It will execute the statement in the function (printf) i.e. prints Hello
5. The control is transferred back to the main function.
6. Then there is a getch( ) function which waits till a key is pressed on the keyboard.

Thus, whenever there is a call to any function, the program control gets transferred to the called function. Unless and, until the function gets over, the control will not be transferred to the access point in the calling function. (In this case, main is a calling function). Consider another example:

Program 1.24: Multiple functions.

```
void fun1( );
void fun2( );
void fun3( );
void main( )
{
    clrscr( );
    fun1( );
    fun2( );
    fun3( );
    getch( );
}
void fun1( )
{
    printf("Function 1 is called \n");
}
void fun2( )
{
    printf("Function 2 is called \n");
}
void fun3( )
{
    printf("Function 3 is called \n");
}
```

Output of above program will be

    Function 1 is called
    Function 2 is called
    Function 3 is called.
    A function can be called into any other function as follows:

Program 1.25: Multiple functions

```c
void fun1( );
void fun2( );
void fun3( );
void main( )
{
    clrscr( );
    fun1( );
    printf("I am back in main \n");
    void fun1( )
    {
        printf("Function 1 is called \n");
        fun2( );
        printf("I am back in Function 1 \n");
    }
    void fun2( )
    {
        printf("Function 2 is called \n");
        fun3( );
        printf("I am back in Function 2 \n");
    }
    void fun3( )
    {
        printf("Function 3 is called \n");
    }
}
```

Output of above program will be

    Function 1 is called
    Function 2 is called
    Function 3 is called
    I am back in Function 2
    I am back in Function 1
    I am back in main.

1.4.2 Passing Parameters to Function

Now, let us write some more functions in which there will be local variable used for calculations. We know how to write a program for addition of two numbers. A separate function for this can be written and called in the main function as follows:

Program 1.26: Function to add two numbers.

```c
void add( );
void main( )
{
    clrscr( );
    add( );
    getch( );
}
void add( )
{
    int a, b, c;
    printf ("Enter any two numbers \n")
    scanf ("%d%d", &a, &b)
    c = a + b;
    printf ("Sum is %d \n", c);
}
```

The program will be executed as:

1. The starting point is main function where clrscr( ) will clear the screen.
2. The control is then transferred to the function add( ).
3. In the function add( ), two numbers are accepted, addition is performed and sum is displayed. The control is then transferred back to main.
4. The function add( ) has three variables a, b, c declared as int. We can have such declarations in the functions, just like we declare variables in main( ) function. Now suppose I write program 3.4 as program 3.5, will it be correct?

Program 1.27: Function to add two numbers.

```c
void add( );
void main( )
{
    clrscr( );
```

```
        print ("Enter any two numbers \n");
        scanf("%d%d", &a, &b);              // Error undefined identifiors
        add( );
        getch( );
}
void add( )
{
        int a, b, c;
        c = a + b;
        printf ("Sum is %d \n", c);
}
```

As far as the sequence of statement is concerned, program 3.4 and program 3.5 are same. But the program is not correct. The variables which are declared within the functions including main( ) function are called as Local variables. These are local in the sense that their scope is within that function only. When we go out of the function, these variables are not available outside the function, even if we have another set of variables declared in the called function with the same name. The memory space reserved for the local variables in the functions cannot be same, even if they have the same name. The way out for this is to pass the variables to the function. This is called Passing parameters. The function should accept these variables, for which there will be arguments of the functions. Number of parameters and number of arguments should be same.

The above program with parameter passing can be written as:

Program 1.28: Function to add two numbers.

```
    void add(int, int);
    void main( )
    {
        int a, b;
        printf("Enter any two numbers \n");
        scanf("%d%d", &a, &b);
        add (a, b);
        getch( );
    }
    void add (int x, int y)
```

```
{
    int z;
    z = x + y;
    printf("Sum is %d", z);
}
```

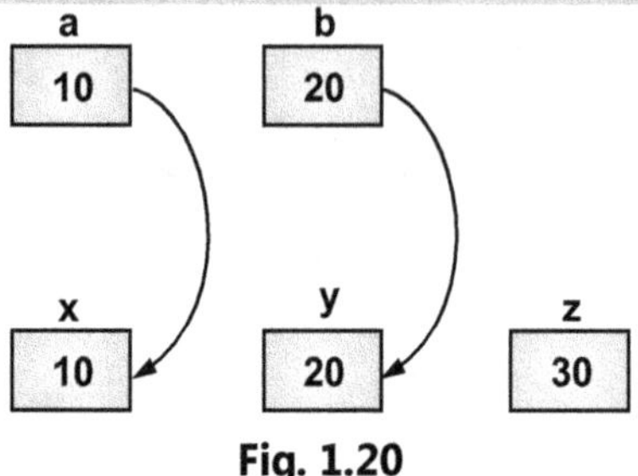

Fig. 1.20

Explanation:

1. main function is invoked first.
2. Two numbers are accepted and stored in a and b.
3. Function add (a, b) is called with value of a passed to x and value of b passed to y.
4. Sum of x and y is stored in z.
5. Sum is displayed.
6. Control is transferred back to main.
7. Main ends.

Program 1.29: Write a function to print square of a number.

```
void square(int);
void main( )
{
    int a;
    clrscr( );
    printf("Enter a number \n");
    scanf("%d", &a);
    square (a);
}
void square(int x)
{
    int y;
    y = x * x;
    printf("Square is %d", y);
}
```

Explanation:

1. main function is invoked first.
2. A number is accepted and stored in variable a.
3. Function square (a) is called with value of a gets passed to x.
4. Square of x is stored in y.
5. y is displayed.
6. Control is transferred back to main.
7. Main ends.

1.4.3 Returning a value from the function

In the two programs which we have seen above, if we want that the calculated value (sum or square) be available to calling function i.e. main function, then we can return a calculated value back to the calling function using return statement. When a function returns a value it will have return type. It is necessary that we should declare the prototype of the function which returns the value. It is similar to variable declaration. The prototype declaration format is

return_type function_name (arguments data_type)

return_type is the type of value returned by function. If a function returns an integer value return_type will be int. In the program above, we are returning value of z which is integer hence its return type is int. If a function does not return any value its return type is void. All the previous programs will have their return type as void. In the first program where we have print_hello function we could have declared prototype as:

void print_hello( )

The function add requires two integers to be passed to it and returns an integer hence its prototype will be int add (int, int). The complete program is given as follows:

Program 1.30: Function to add two numbers.

```
int add (int, int);                    // Prototype declaration
void main( )
{
    int a, b, c;
    clrscr( );
    printf("Enter any two numbers \n");
    scanf("%d%d", &a, &b);
```

```
        c = add (a, b);
        printf("Sum in %d", c);
        getch( );
}
int add (int x, int y)
{
        z = x + y;
        return (z);
}
```

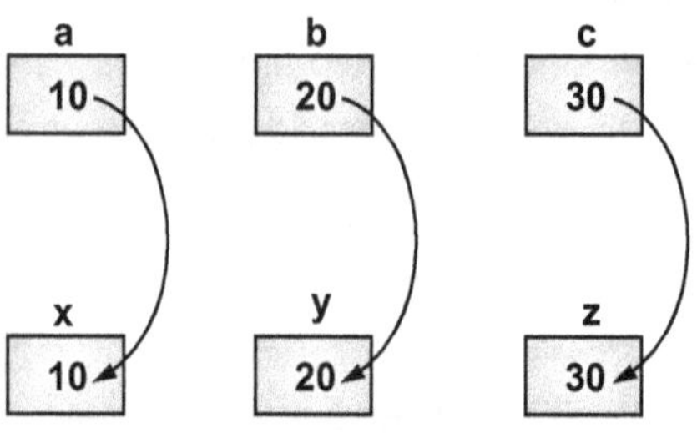

Fig. 1.21

Explanation:

Let us see how the above program works.

1. void main( ) function is invoked.
2. Two numbers are accepted and stored in a and b.
3. Function add (a, b) is called, it is an int type function. i.e., it is going to return an integer value which is going to be collected in the variable c.
4. Values of a and b get passed to x and y respectively.
5. Addition of x and y is stored in z.
6. Value of z is returned back to calling function (main function).
7. The value of z is collected in c.
8. Value of c is printed.
9. main( ) ends.

Program 1.31: Write a function to find square of a number.

```
float square (float);
main( )
{
        float x, y;
        printf("Enter number \n");
        scanf("% f ", &x);
        y = square (x);
        printf ("y=% f ", y);
        getch( );
}
float square (float x)
{
```

```
        int y;
        y = x * x;
        return (y);
    }
```

The above two functions can also be written as:

1. int add (int x, int y)
    {
        return (x + y);
    }

2. float square (float x)
    {
        return (x * x);
    }

1.4.4 Examples on Functions

Program 1.32: Write a function to find area of circle.

```
    float area (float);
    void main( )
    {
        float r, a;
        printf("Enter radius \n");
        scanf("%f ", &r);
        a = area (r);
        printf("Area =%f\n", a);
        getch( );
    }
    float area (float r)
    {
        float a;
        a = 3.142*r*r;
        return (a);
    }
```

Program 1.33: Write a function to find n!

```
float fact(int);
void main( )
{
    float f;                          //f will be large for large values of n hence float
    int n;
    printf("Enter a number \n");
    scanf("%d", &n);
    f = fact (n);
    printf(" Factorial = %.0.f", f);        // % 0.f will display 0 decimal places
    getch( );
}
float fact (int n)
{
    int i;
    float p = 1;
    for (i=l;i<=n;i++)
    p = p*i;
    return (p);
}
```

Program 1.34: Write a function to print sum of digits in a given number.

```
int sd (long int);
void main( )
{
    int s; long int n;
    printf("Enter a number \n");
    scanf("%ld", &n);
    s = sd (n);
    printf("Sum of digits %d", s);
}
int sd(long int)
{
    int s = 0, r;
    while (n>0)
```

```c
    {
        r = n%10;
        s = s + r;
        n = n/10;
    }
    return(s);
}
```

Program 1.35: Write a function to find x^n.

```c
float power (float, int);
void main( )
{
    float x, y;
    int i, n;
    printf("Enter x, n \n");
    scanf("%f%d", &x, &n);
    y = power (x, n);
    printf("Result = %f \n", y);
}
float power (float x, int n)
{
    int i;
    float p=1;
    for(i=1;i<=n;i++)
        p=p*x;
    return (p);
}
```

Program 1.36: Write a function to find maximum of two numbers.

```c
int max (int, int);
void main( )
{
    int a, b, c;
    printf("Enter any two numbers \n");
    scanf("%d%d ", &a, &b);
    c = max (a, b);
```

```
        printf("Maximum is %d", c);
        getch( );
    }
    int max (int x, int y)
    {
        if (x>y)
            return (x);
        else
            return (y);
    }
```

The above function can also be written as:

```
    int max (int x, int y)
    {
        return (x>y? x : y);
    }
```

Program 1.37: Using the function max written above, write a program to print maximum of 3 numbers.

We have 3 numbers say a, b, c. First find maximum of first two numbers a and b and store it in d. Then using the same again find maximum of d and c.

```
    int max (int, int);
    void main( )
    {
        int a, b, c, d, e;
        printf("Enter any 3 numbers \n");
        scanf("%d%d%d", &a, &b, &c);
        d = max (a, b);
        e = max (d, c);
        printf("Maximum is % d", e);
        getch( );
    }
    int max (int x, int y)
    {
        if (x>y)
            return (x);
```

```
        else
              return (y);
    }
```

The two statements,

```
        d = max (a, b);
        e = max (d, c);
```

can be replaced as d = max(max(a, b), c);

or the three statements,

```
        d = max (a, b);
        e = max (d, c);
        printf("Maximum is %d", e);
```

can be replaced as,

```
        printf("Maximum is %d", max (max (a, b), c));
```

Program 1.38: Write a function to find e^x.

We know that

$$e^x = 1 + x + \frac{x^2}{2!} + \frac{x^3}{3!} + \;.... \text{ upto n terms.}$$

Here, we need to write a function to find e^x. Let us give the name to the function as expo. This function will have two arguments viz. x and n. x is number whose exponentiation is required and n is number of terms. Within the function expo we can use the function fact which finds n!

```
    float fact (int);
    float expo (float, int);
    void main( )
    {
        float x, y;
        int n;
        printf("Enter x & n \n");
        scanf("%f%d", &x, &n);
        y = expo(x, n);
        printf("y=%f", y);
    }
    float expo(float x, int n)
```

```
{
    float s = 1;
    int i;
    for(i=1;i<=n-1;i++)
    {
        s=s+pow(x, i)/fact (i);
    }
    return(s);
}
float fact(int n)
{
    float p=1; int i;
    for(i=1;i<=n;i++)
        p = p*i;
    return (p);
}
```

Program 1.39: Write a function to print ^nC_r.

$$^nC_r = \frac{n!}{r! \, (n - r)!}$$

Explanation:

We can make use of function fact here as there are three factorial terms to be calculated.

```
    float fact (int);
    float ncr (int, int);
    void main( )
    {
        float y;
        int n, r;
        printf("Enter n & r \n");
        scanf("%d%d", &n, &r);
        y = ncr (n, r);
        printf ("ncr = %.0 f", y);
    }
    float ncr(int n, int r)
    {
```

```
        return (fact (n)/(fact (n – r)*fact (r));
}
float fact (int n)
{
        float p=1;
        int i;
        for (i=1;i<=n;i++)
                p = p*i;
        return (p);
}
```

Program 1.40: Write a function to evaluate

$$y = 4x^3 + 3x^2 + 2x - 1$$

Tabulate the values of y for x 0 to 1 with step of 0.1.

```
    float f(float);
    void main( )
    {
        float x, y;
        clrscr( );
        for (x=0; x<=1; x=x+0.1)
        {
            y = f(x);
            printf("%d \t %d \n", x, y);
        }
    }
    float f(float x)
    {
        return (4 * pow(x, 3) + 3 * pow(x, 2) + 2 * x – 1)
    }
```

Program 1.41: Write a function to convert decimal to binary.

```
    void dtob(int);
    void main( )
    {
        int n;
        printf("Enter number \n");
        scanf("%d", &n);
        dtob(n);
```

```
        getch( );
    }
    void dtob(int n)
    {
        int a[10], i;
        i=0;
        while (n>0)
        {
            a[i]=n%2;
            n=n/2;
            i++;
        }
        for(i=i-1;i>=0;i--)
            printf("%d", a[i]);
    }
```

1.4.5 Recursive Function

Till now we have discussed non-recursive way of writing the functions, now let us study recursive functions. A function can call another function. That function can call another function and so on. When this kind of chaining occurs, the function called in the end has to be completed first, then the second last, and so on. Similar nesting can occur, if a function calls itself. It is called as recursive function. The process of handling such calls is bit complex. Whenever a function is called, all the current variables are put aside in a memory location called as stack. When the function call gets over, those variables are retrieved back from the stack. We are going to study this in detail in Unit IV. Using recursive function, we can eliminate loops written in a function.

Let us consider a simple function hello which calls itself recursively.

Program 1.42: Recursive function to print hello.

```
    void hello( );
    void main( )
    {
        clrscr( );
        hello( );
        getch( );
    }
    void hello( )
    {
```

```
        printf("Hello \n");
        hello( );
}
```

Here, we are calling the function hello in main( ).

The function hello will print "Hello" and calls itself second time.

This will be repeated infinite number of times and the control will never be passed back to main. Thus, the program will keep on displaying Hello in infinite loop.

The program can be modified to print Hello finite number of times as follows:

Program 1.43: Recursive function to print hello n times.

```
void hello(int);
void main( )
{
    clrscr( );
    hello (3);
    getch( );
}
void hello (int n)
{
    if(n>0)
    {
            printf("Hello \n");
            hello(n-1);
    }
}
```

The function hello(int) now has a value passed to it. The function will be executed n times depending on the value passed to it in n. Here, n is 3.

1. First time the function is called with n=3, i.e., hello(3). Hello is displayed and the function hello(3−1) i.e., hello(2) is called. Note that hello(3) is not over.

2. Second time the function is called with n=2, i.e., hello(2). Hello is displayed and the function hello(2−1) i.e., hello(1) is called. Note that hello(2) is not over.

3. Third time the function is called with n=1, i.e., hello(1). Hello is displayed and the function hello(1 − 1) i.e., hello(0) is called. Note that hello(1) is not over.

4. Fourth time the function is called with n=0, i.e., hello(0). Now since the condition n>0 is false, hello(0) gets over. Where should the control return? It should go back to the point from where hello(0) was called i.e., hello(1). Since there are no statements left out to be executed in hello(1), it gets over and we go back to hello(2) and so on. Finally, the control will be transferred back to main. The process is depicted in Fig. 1.22.

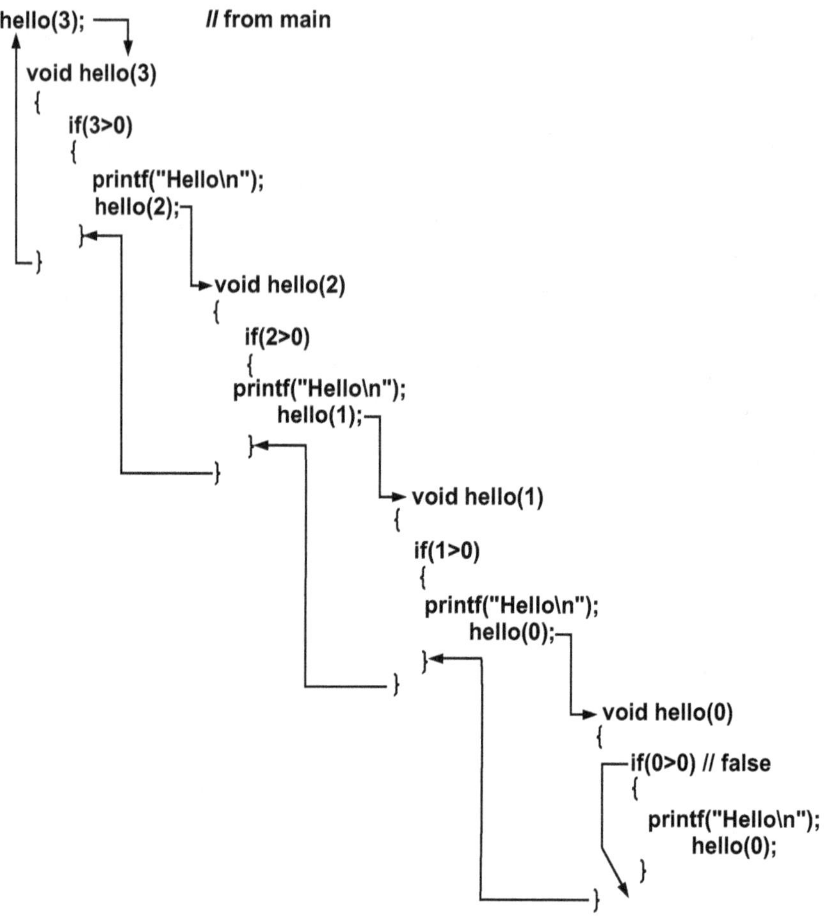

Fig. 1.22: Recursive function call hello(n)

Program 1.44: Recursive function to find factorial of number.

```c
float fact (int);
void main( )
{
    int n;
    float f;
    printf("Enter a number \n);
    scanf("%d", &n);
    f = fact(n);
    printf("Factorial is %f", f);
}
float fact (int n)
```

```
{
    if(n==0 || n==1)
            return (1);
    else
            return (n*fact (n-1));
}
```

Let us see how it works:
1. Main function is invoked first.
2. Value of n is read. Say 4.
3. A function fact (4) is called. We expect the function to return some value which is going to be assigned to f.
4. Value n = 4 gets passed to n in function fact.

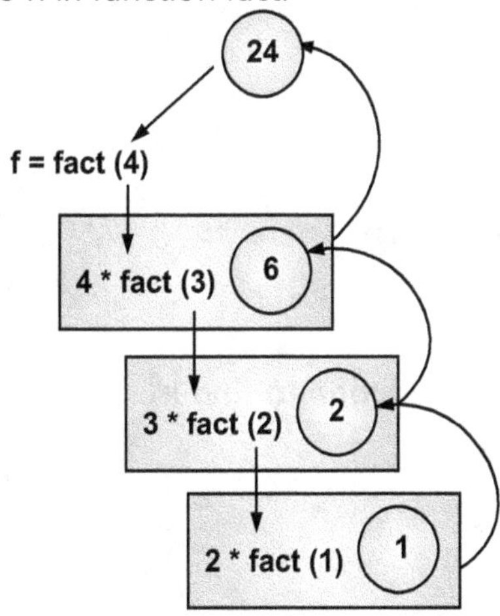

Fig. 1.23: Recursive function For n!

5. Since n==1 is false. return (4 * fact (3)) is executed. The value returned by this is going to be assigned to f. But in this statement fact (3) is a call to the same function. Hence, right now the value (Let us call it as c1) is not returned. Since fact (3) call is to be attended, 3 gets passed to n. Since again n==1 is false return (3 * fact (2)) is executed let it be c2. Again fact (2) is called with 2 passed to n. Here again n==1 is false and return (2 * fact (1)) is executed. Now there is call to fact with n = 1. Let it be c3. Hence n==1 is true hence 1 is returned. But to whom? To the calling function fact (1) whose execution gets over with its value becoming 1. Now c3 will be 2 * fact (1) = 2. It's value becomes 2. c2 becomes 6 and similarly c3 becomes 24. This value in turn is returned back to main function and assigned to f.
6. f is printed.
7. Main gets over.

Program 1.45: Write a recursive function to find sum of digits in a given number.

```c
int sd (long int);
void main( )
{
    int s;
    long int n;
    printf("Enter a number \n");
    scanf("%ld", &n);
    s = sd(n);
    printf("Sum of digits=%d \n, s);
}
int sd (long int n)
{
    if (n==0)
        return (0);
    else
        return(n%10 + sd (n/10));
}
```

Program 1.46: Write a recursive function to find x^n.

```c
float power (float, int);
void main( )
{
    float x, y;
    int i, n;
    printf("Enter x, n \n");
    scanf("%f%d"; &x, &n);
    y = power (x, n);
    printf("Result = %f \n", y);
}
float power (float x, int n)
{
    if(n==0)
        return (1);
    else
        return (x*power(x, n-1));
}
```

SOLVED PROBLEMS

1. **Write a recursive function to calculate nth term of Fibonacci number.**

Program 1.47: Recursive function to calculate nth term of Fibonacci number.

Solution:

```c
void main( )
{
    int n, x;
    printf("Enter n \n");
    scanf("%d", &n);
    x = fib(n);
    printf("The Fibonacci number is %d", x);
}
int fib(int n)
{
    if(n==0 || n==1)
        return (n);
    else
        return (fib(n-1)+fib(n-2));
}
```

2. **Write a menu driven program to implement Linear and Binary search and sorting of number.**

Solution: Earlier separate programs for linear and binary search, sorting were discussed. Now let us write functions for linear search, binary search, bubble sort, selection sort and insertion sort and use them in the main function which will have menu driven program. Since, we don't know right now how to pass an array to 4 functions, the array will be declared globally so that it can be accessed by all functions.

Program 1.48: Menu driven program for searching and sorting.

```c
#define MAX 100
int a [MAX];
int n;
void lsearch( );
void bsearch( );
void bubble_sort( );
void sel_sort( );
```

```c
void ins_sort( );
void read_list( );
void print_list( );
void main( )
{
    int ch;
    read list( );
    do
    {
        clrscr( );
        printf(" 1. Linear  search  \n 2.  Binary  Search  \n  3.  Bubble—sort  \n
        4. Sel_sort \n 5. ins_sort \n 6. Exit \n");
        printf("Enter your choice \n");
        scanf("%d", &ch);
        switch(ch)
        {
            case 1:  lsearch( );
                     break;
            case 2:  bsearch( );
                     break;
            case 3:  bubble_sort( );
                     disp_list( );
                     break;
            case 4:  sel_sort( );
                     disp_list( );
                     break;
            case 5:  ins_sort( );
                     disp_list( );
                     break;
        }
        getch( );
    )while (ch!=6);
}
void read_list( )
{
    int i;
```

```c
        printf("Enter number of elements in the list \n");
        scanf("%d", &n);
        printf("Enter the elements in the list \n");
        for (i=0;i<n;i++)
                scanf("%d", &a[i]);
}
void disp_list( )
{
    int i;
    printf ("sorted list is \n");
    for (i=0;i<n;i++)
            printf ("%d \n", a[i]);,
}
void lsearch( )
{
    int i, s, flag;
    printf ("Enter the number to be searched \n");
    scanf("%d", &s);
    flag=1;
    i=0;
    while (i<n)
    {
        if(a[i]==s)
        {
                printf("Found at location %d", i + 1);
                flag=0;
                break;
        }
    }
    if(flag==1)
        printf("Not found");
    }
    void bsearch( )
    {    int i, s, mid, l, u, flag;
        printf ("Enter number to be searched \n");
        scanf("%d", &s);
```

```c
            flag=1; l=0; u=n-1;
            while (l<=u)
            {
                    mid = (l + u) / 2;
                    if(a [mid]==s)
                    {
                        printf("Number found at location %d", mid + 1);
                        flag = 0;
                        break;
                    }
                    if (a[mid]>s)
                        u =mid-1;
                    if(a[mid]<s)
                        l=mid+1;
            }
            if(flag==0)
                    printf("Not found");
    }

void bubble_sort( )
{
    int i, j, index, max;
    for (i=0;i<n-1;i++)
    {
        for(j=0;j<n-1-i;j++)
        {
            if(a[j]>a[j+1]
            {
                temp = a[j]
                a[j] = a[j+1];
                a[j+1], temp;
            }
        }
    }
}
void sel_sort( )
```

```c
{
    int i, j, index, max;
    for (i=n-1;i>0;i--)
    {
        max = a[0];
        index=0;
        for(j=1;j<=i;j++)
        {
            if (a[j]>max)
            {
                max=a[j];
                index=j;
            }
        }
        a[index] = a[i];
        a[i] = max;
    }
}
void ins_sort( )
{
    int i, j, temp;
    for (i=1;i<n;i++)
    {
        temp=a[i];
        for(j=i-1;j>=0;j--)
        {
            if (a[j]>temp)
                a[j + 1] = a[j];
            else
                break;
        }
        a[j + 1] = temp;
    }
}
```

3. Write recursive function in 'C' to find GCD of given numbers.

Program 1.49: Recursive function in 'C' to find GCD of given numbers.

```c
int gcd(int x, int y)
{
    if(x<y)
    {
        t = x;
        x = y;
        y = t;
    }
        if((x%y)==0)
                return (y);
        return(gcd(y,x%y));
}
```

1.4.6 Functions and Pointers (Passing Parameters by Address)

A pointer is used to store the address. In chapter 3, we discussed parameter passing to functions. Any number of parameter can be passed to a function but function returns only one value. Let us consider a program as follows:

Program 1.50: Passing parameter by value.

```c
void modify (int, int);
void main( )
{
    int a = 4, b = 5;
    modify (a, b);
    printf ("a=%d \t b=%d n", a, b);
}
void modify (int a, int b)
{
    a = a* 10;
    b = b* 10;
    printf("a=%d \t b=%d \n", a, b);
}
```

Explanation:

The output will be

```
a = 40    b = 50
a = 4     b = 5
```

The reason is

1. In main function, a and b are initialized to 4 and 5

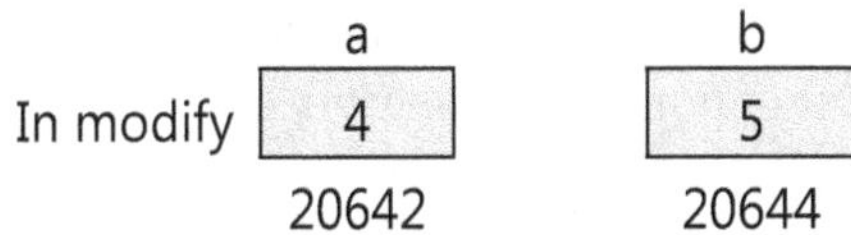

3. The next statements a = a * 10 and b = b * 10 modify a and b to 40 and 50. This modification is done in locations 20642 and 20644 and not in the locations 10242 and 10244.

2. We call the function modify with values of a and b passed to the function. Note that the values of a and b get transferred. The locations are not handed over to the function. These values get passed to a and b in the function which incidentally have same names. But their address is different.

4. Therefore when we go back to main function, the values in a and b remain 4 and 5 itself and hence we get output a = 4 and b = 5.

5. This is called as passing parameter by value. Thus, if we pass parameter by value, there is no effect on the passed variable after function call is over; even if function is modifying the passed values. Thus passing parameters by value, does not allow the modified values of the parameters in called function to be available in calling function.

What if we need to modify these values and get back?

We have to hand over the variables to the function. Therefore we have to pass the addresses of variables to the function. The passed addresses are to be stored in pointer type variable. This is called passing parameters by address or by reference. The function arguments will be pointers and the function prototype declaration will be

    void modify (int *, int *);

The program is as follows.

Program 1.51: Passing parameter by reference or by address.

```
void modify (int *, int *);
void main( )
{
    int a = 4, b = 5;
    modify (&a, &b);
```

```
        printf("a=%d \t b=%d \n", a, b);
    }
    void modify (int *x, int *y)
    {
        *x = *x*10;
        *y = *y *10;
    }
```

Output: a=40 b=50

Explanation:

Now let us see what happens when we execute the program.

1. Before function is called situation in the memory is,

a   b

| 4 | | 5 |

10242   10244

2. When function is called the address of variable a gets passed to x and address of b to y.

x   y

| 10242 | | 10244 |

Thus, x is a pointer to a and y is pointer to b.

3. In the function.

    $*x = *x* 10$ will modify value pointed by x to 40

    and $*y = *y *10$ will modify value pointed by y to 50

    i.e., the values of 'a' and 'b' are modified.

4. Hence after the function is over, the locations of a and b will be

a   b

| 40 | | 50 |

10242   10244

Thus, if we pass the parameters by address, the values will be accessible to the function and function can modify these values. This is also called as passing parameters by reference.

Now consider the following programs.

Program 1.52: Function to interchange values of two variables.

```
    void swap (int*, int*);
    void main( )
    {
        int a = 4, b = 5;
        swap(&a, &b);
        printf("a=%d \t b=%d \n", a, b);
    }
```

```c
    void swap(int*x, int*y)
    {
        int t;
        t = *x;
        *x = *y;
        *y = t;
    }
```

Output: a = 5   b = 4

Explanation:

1. Before function call in main( )

2. When function is called

3. When function is over

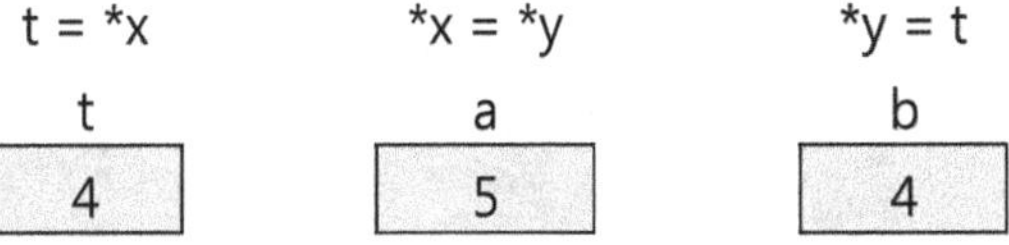

Program 1.53: Passing parameters by value and address.

```c
    void demo1 (int, int*);
    void main( )
    {
        int a = 10, b = 20;
        demo1 (a, &b);
        printf("a=%d \t b=%d \n", a, b);
    }
    void demo1 (int x, int*p)
    {
        x=x+10;
        *p=*p+x;
    }
```

Output: a = 10   b = 40

Explanation:

1. Before function call in main( )

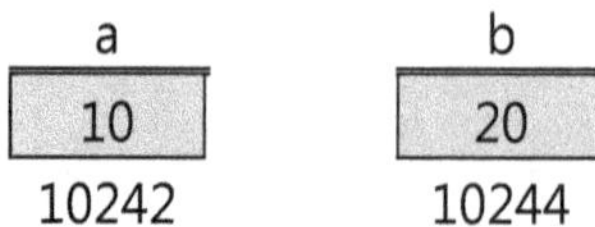

2. When function is called, x gets value of a and p gets address of b.

3. When function is over

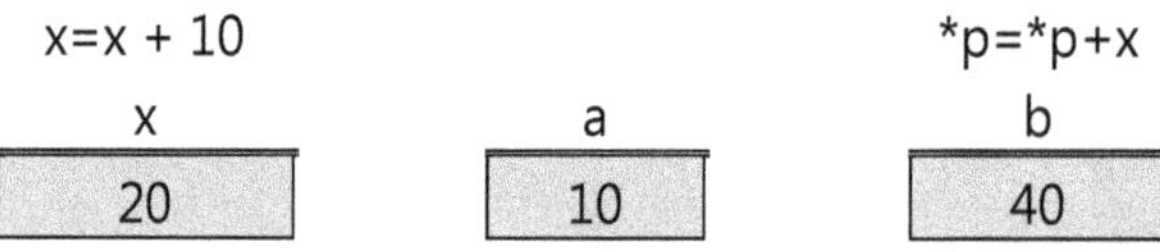

Note that a is passed by value hence it is not changed, whereas b which is passed by reference is changed.

Program 1.54: Passing parameters by value and address.

```c
void demo3(int, int*);
void main( )
{
    int a = 10, b;
    demo3(a, &b);
    printf("a=%d \t b=%d \n", a, b);
}
void demo3(int x, int*p)
{
    *p=x*x;
}
```

Output: a = 10   b = 100

Explanation:

1. Before function call in main( )

2. When function is called, x gets value of a and p gets address of b.

3. When function is over

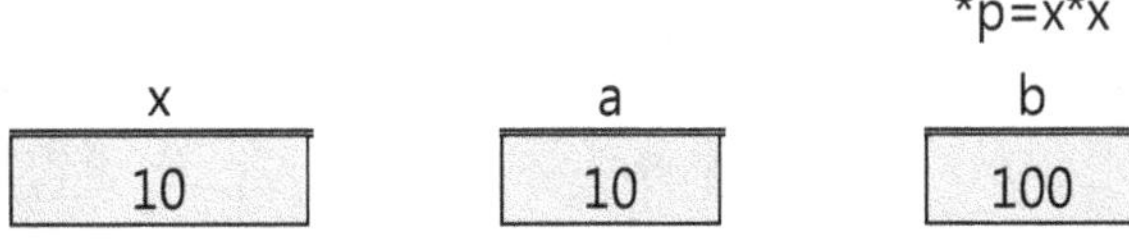

Note that a is passed by value hence it is not changed, whereas b which is passed by reference is changed.

Returning more than one values from function

We know that function can return only one value. By this time you must have realized that, using pointer we can make a function return more than one values. If we want the function to calculate more than one value and return them back, pass the variables in which you want to collect these values by address.

Consider the following program in which we have function to calculate sum and product of two numbers.

Program 1.55: Function to find sum and product of two numbers.

```c
void sp(int, int, int *, int*);
void main( )
{
    int a = 4, b=5, sum, prod;
    sp(a, b, &sum, &prod);
    printf("Sum=%d \t prod=%d", sum, prod);
}
void sp(int x, int y, int*s, int*p)
{
    *s = x + y;
    *p = x * y;
}
```

Output: sum=9   product=20.

Explanation:

The parameters a and b are passed by value whereas parameters sum and product are passed by address.

1. Before function call.

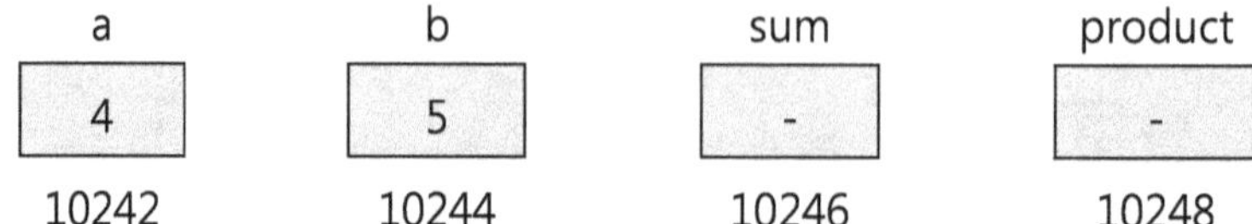

2. When function is called

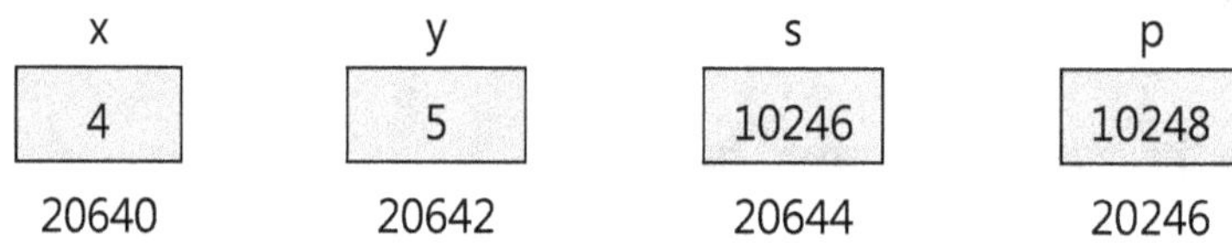

3. In the function,

$*s$ = sum = x + y = 9

$*p$ = prod = x * y = 20

Program 1.56: Function to find area and perimeter of a circle.

```c
void ap(float, float*, float*);
void main
{
    float r, area, peri;
    r = 10;
    ap(r, &area, &peri);
    printf("Area=%f \n", area);
    printf("Perimeter=%f \n", peri);
}
void ap(float r, float *a, float*p)
{
    *a= 3.142 * r * r;
    *p = 3.142 *2 * r;
}
```

Output: Area = 314.2   Perimeter 62.84

1.4.7 Arrays and Pointers

The most important use of pointers is that, we can use pointer variable to replace an array. Elements in an array are stored in contiguous memory locations.

e.g., int a[5] = {10, 20, 30, 40, 50};

will reserve 5 locations in memory as follows. With each element in the array will have its own address as shown

a[0]	a[1]	a[2]	a[3]	a[4]
10	20	30	40	50
1000	1002	1004	1006	1008

If we want to display the addresses of each element in the array, we can write

```
for(i=0;i<n;i++)
printf("%u \n", &a[i]);
```

Now, suppose we have an integer pointer p, we can store the address of first element in the array in it by writing,

$$p=\&a[0];$$

with the help of this pointer p, we can access any element in the array. Following program illustrates this.

Program 1.57: Accessing array elements through a pointer.

```
void main( )
{
    int a[] = {10, 20, 30, 40, 50};
    int *p;
    p=&a[0];
    for(i=0;i<n;i++)
        printf("%d \n", *(p+i));
}
```


When we declare array, its size needs to be specified at the time of writing the program unless we initialize the array as above. The problem in such case is:
1. If we have only few data items to be stored, much of the space in the array remains unutilized,

   e.g., if array is int a[100] and we are storing only 10 elements.
2. If we have more data to be stored than the size of the array, there will be overflow.

Using pointers, we can allocate memory to the data items as and when required, i.e., at the time of execution of program. Hence, we can also store as many data items as we want (of course not more than computers memory).

The allocation of memory at the time of compilation is called static allocation whereas the allocation of memory at the time of execution is called dynamic allocation.

malloc function

C provides malloc function to allocate memory to a pointer type variable.

Its usage is as follows ptr=malloc(no_of bytes). This will allocate a block of memory specified by no_of bytes, e.g., ptr=malloc(10) will allocate memory block of 10 bytes and address of first location will be stored in ptr.

1. Suppose we have a pointer variable int *p;
2. It will reserve a location in memory as shown in figure 1.24.

Fig. 1.24: Memory allocation for p

3. Now if we write p=malloc(10).
4. It will reserve 10 bytes of memory block and address of first location is stored in p as shown in figure 1.21. It is assumed that the address of first location is 1000. Each location will be 2 bytes since p is integer type pointer and it points to int type location which is of 2 bytes.

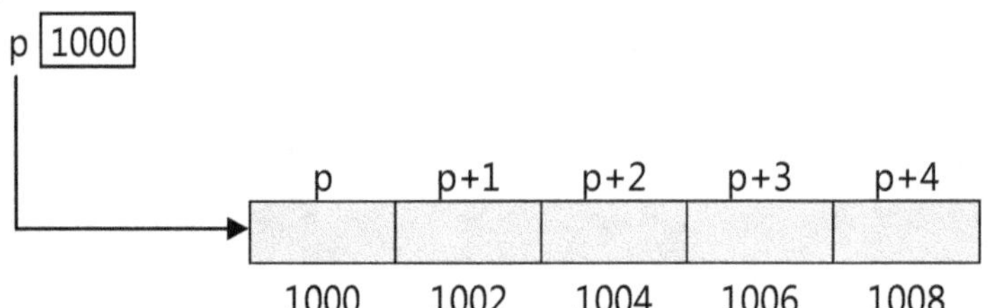

Fig. 1.25: Block allocation (malloc) to p

5. p has the address of first location. Address of next location is obtained by adding 1 to the pointer, i.e., p+1 will be address of second location, p+2 will be address of third location and so on.
6. *p will give value stored in a location pointed by p. *(p+1) will give value stored in second location. *(p+2) will give. value stored in third location and so on.
7. Thus if we have a single pointer variable, we can access all the successive locations pointed by it. In other words, a single pointer variable can be used in place of array. Array requires fixed size to be specified. It is Static allocation. Pointer variable allows dynamic allocation and we can specify the number of locations at the time of execution of the program.

Let us consider a program to illustrate this

Program 1.58: Program to illustrate dynamic allocation.

```
void main( )
{
    int *p;
    p=malloc(10);
    for(i=0;i<5;i++)
         *(p+i)=i*10;
    for(i=0;i<5;i++)
         printf("%d \n",*(p+i));
}
```

Explanation:

1. p is an integer type pointer.
2. 10 bytes of memory will be allocated to p as shown in Fig. 1.26.
3. The first for loop will store the values 0, 10, 20, 30, 40 in the 5 locations

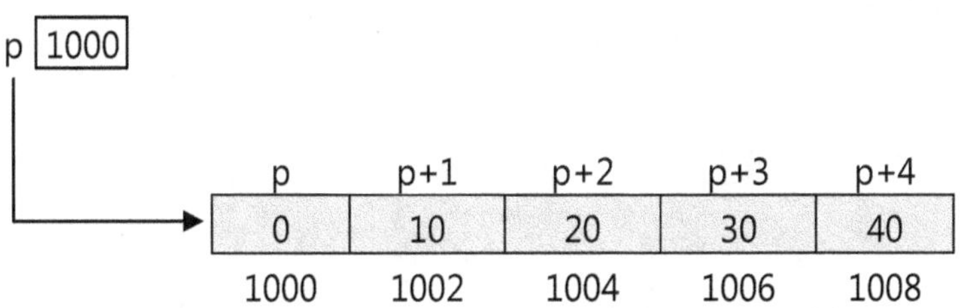

Fig. 1.26: Storage of data in the block

4. The second for loop will display these values

   There are some more issues related to pointers and malloc functions.

   (i) If we have a float type pointer, say float *fp, the malloc function will be:
$$fp = malloc(20);$$
   fp stores address of first location, then fp+1 will be address of second location and so on as shown in Fig. 1.27.

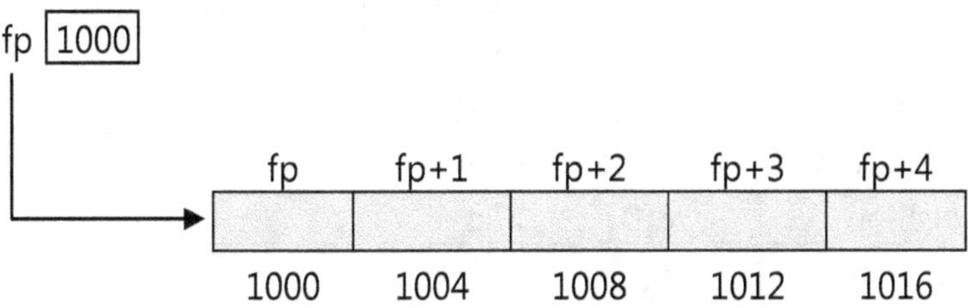

Fig. 1.27: Float type pointer

Note that the increment in fp by 1 is equivalent to increment of 4 bytes.
  (i) An operator called as sizeof is used to find number of bytes required by a variable or variable type, e.g., sizeof(int) gives 2, sizeof(float) gives 4 and sizeof(char) gives 1.
  (ii) The malloc function is used practically as:
       if p is int type pointer p = (int*) malloc (n*sizeof (int)) will allocate 2*n bytes of memory to the pointer variable p. (int*) is the return type of the malloc function. It is called type casting and is required, as malloc can return any type of address. If we are allocating memory for a float type pointer we should write (float*) before malloc.

Let us rewrite the above program to incorporate these.

Program 1.59: To illustrate use of malloc.

```
void main( )
{
    int *p, n;
    printf("How many numbers? \n");
    scanf("%d", &n);
    p=(int*)malloc(n*sizeof(int));
    for(i=0;i<n;i++)
         *(p+i)=i*10;
    for(i=0;i<n;i++)
         printf("%d \n",*(p+i));
}
```

In this program, we have only two variables p and n. Hence, only 4 bytes of memory is allocated at the time of compilation of program. When the user enters the value of n, that time memory is allocated to store exactly n integer numbers. It means only the required amount of memory is allocated not less, not more. Thus, pointer variable allows us to allocate memory as per the requirement.

Just to have analogy between array and pointer consider the illustration given in table 6.1.

Table 1.2

	Array	Pointer
Declaration	int a[10]	int *p; p=(int*)malloc(n*sizeof(int));
Address of 1st location	&a[0]	p
Address of 2nd location	&a[1]	p+1
Address of ith location	&a[i]	p+i
Value at 1st location	a[0]	*p
Value at 2nd location	a[1]	*(p+1)
Value at i^{th} location	a[i]	*(p+i)

Scale factor:

- The pointer variable is assigned address of another variable.
- We can also store address of a block of memory using malloc in it.
- It can also be assigned value of another pointer variable.
- The pointer variable can be added or subtracted with integer value. But this addition or subtraction is different from normal arithmetic.
- If we have a pointer p of some data type the increment or decrement will cause p to be incremented or decremented by the 'scale factor'. This scale factor will be dependent on data type of the pointer variable. For example, if we have a pointer variable int *p; and we write p = p + 1. The contents of the pointer p will be incremented by two bytes. If we have char *p; and we write p = p + 1. The contents will be incremented by one byte. Following are few more examples.

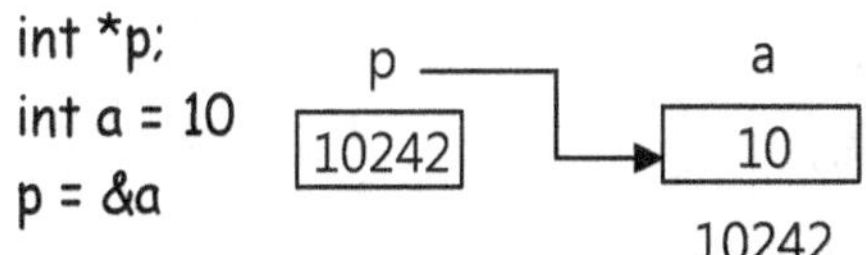

p = p + 1 will make p = 10244
p = p – 1 will make p = 10242
p = p + 10 will make p = 10262
p = p – 5 will make p= 10232

- The pointer variable cannot be multiplied.
- A constant value cannot be assigned to pointer variable.
- Two pointer variables of same data types can be compared. They can also be subtracted from each other.

Calloc:

Like malloc, calloc is another memory allocation function. The malloc function allocates only single block of memory space, whereas calloc allocates multiple blocks at a time. Its format is

$$ptr = (dats\_type *) calloc (n, size)$$

where, n is number of blocks of size will be allocated to the pointer variable ptr

For example,

$$ptr = (int *) calloc (10, sizeof(int));$$

will allocate to 10 blocks (20 bytes) for the 10 integers.
All the bytes in the blocks are initialized to zero in calloc.

Program 1.60: To find maximum of given n numbers.

```c
void main( )
{
    int *p;
    int i, n, max;
    printf("Enter how many numbers? \n");
    scanf("% d", &n);
    p=(int*)malloc(n*sizeof(int));
    printf("Enter the numbers \n");
    for(i=0;i<n;i++)
        scanf("%d", p+i);
    max = *p;
    for(i=0;i<n;i++)
    {
        if (*(p+i) > max)
            max = *(p+i);
    }
    printf("Maximum is %d \n", max);
    getch( );
}
```

Explanation:

1. Pointer p is allocated 2*n bytes of memory by malloc.

2. scanf accepts numbers and stores in locations whose addresses are p, p+1, p+2, ..., etc. Note that scanf requires addresses of locations where data is to be stored.

Program 1.61: To find sum, average, standard deviation of n numbers.

```c
void main( )
{
    float *p;
    float s, avg, sd;
    int i, n;
    printf("Enter how many number? n");
    scanf("%d", &n);
    p=(float *)malloc(n*sizeof(float));
    printf("Enter the numbers \n");
```

```
        for(i=0;i<n;i++)
              scanf("%f", p+i);
        s=0;
        for(i=0;i<n;i++)
              s=s + *(p+i);
        avg = s/n;
        printf("Sum is %f \n", s);
        printf("Average is %f \n", avg);
        s=0;
        for(i=0;i<n;i++)
              s=s + pow(*(p+i) – avg, 2);
        sd=sqrt (s/n);
        printf("Standard deviation is %f", sd);
        getch( );
}
```

1.4.8 Two Dimensional Array and Pointers (Array of Pointers)

Just like one dimensional address can be replaced by a pointer, two dimensional arrays can also be replaced by pointers. Each row of two dimensional arrays is a single Dimensional array. Hence for each row, we can use a pointer. Number of pointers required will be number of rows. An array of pointers can be used to represent or replace two dimensional array.

Let int *p[10]; be an array of pointers. It will reserve 10 locations viz. p[0], p[1], p[2], ..., p[9] to store addresses of each row.

Each row can be allocated memory using malloc.

p[0]=(int*) malloc(n*sizeof(int)) will allocate memory for storing n integers in first row.

p[0] will be address of 1st element.

p[0]+1 will be address of 2nd element.

p[0]+2 will be address of 3rd element etc.

p[1]=(int*) malloc(n*sizeof(int)) will allocate memory for storing n integers in second row.

p[1] will be address of 1st element.

p[1]+1 will be address of 2nd element.

p[1]+2 will be address of 3rd element etc.

In general, p[i]=(int*) malloc(n*sizeof(int)) will allocate memory for storing n integers in i^{th} row

p[i] will be address of 1st element.

p[i]+1 will be address of 2nd element.

p[i]+2 will be address of 3rd element etc.

p[i]+j will be address of jth element in i^{th} row.

The value stored in the ith row and j^{th} column will be *(p[i]+j).

Here is how you can replace two dimensional arrays with pointer.

Table 1.3

	Array	Pointer
Declaration	int a[10][10];	int *p[10]; p[i]=malloc(n*sizeof(int))
Address of ith row and j^{th} column element	&a[i][j]	p[i]+j
Value of ith row and j^{th} column element	a[i][j]	*(p[i]+j)

Look at the given program.

Program 1.62: To illustrate use of array of pointers

```c
void main( )
{
    int *p[3], i, j;
    for(i=0;i<3;i++)
    {
        p[i]=(int*) malloc(3*sizeof(int));
        for(j=0;j<3;j++)
            *(p[i]+j)=i+j;
    }
    for(i=0;i<3;i++)
    {
        for(j=0;j<3;j++)
            printf("%d", *(p[i]+j));
        printf("\n");
    }
}
```

Explanation:

1. Initially, an array of 3 pointer is created as shown in Fig. 1.28.

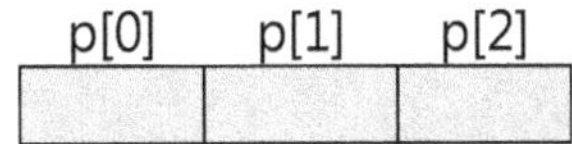

Fig. 1.28: Array of pointers

2. When i=0, p[0] is allocated 3 locations and 0, 1, 2 is put into these locations

p[0] → | 0 | 1 | 2 |

3. When i=1; p[1] is allocated 3 locations and 1, 2, 3 is put into these locations

p[1] → | 1 | 2 | 3 |

4. When i=2; p[2] is allocated 3 locations and 2, 3, 4 is put into these locations

p[2] → | 2 | 3 | 4 |

5. These values are displayed by second nested for.

Program 1.63: To find sum of two matrices using array of pointers.

```
void main( )
{
    int *a[10], *b[10], *c[10];
    int i, j, m, n;
    clrscr( );
    printf("Enter order of matrices \n");
    scanf("%d%d", &m, &n");
    printf("Enter first matrix \n");
    for(i=0;i<m;i++)
    {
        a[i]=(int*)malloc(n*sizeof(int));
        for(j=0;j<n;j++)
            scanf("%d", a[i]+j);.
    }
    printf("Enter second matrix \n");
    for(i=0;i<m;i++)
    {
        b[i]=(int*)malloc(n*sizeof(int));
        for(j=0;j<n;j++)
            scanf("%d", b[i]+j);
    }
    for(i=0;i<m;i++)
    {
        c[i]=(int*)malloc(n*sizeof(int));
```

```
        for(j=0;j<n;j++)
            *(c[i]+j) = *(a[i]+j) + *(b[i]+j);
    }
    printf("Resultant matrix is \n");
    for(i=0;i<m;i++)
    {
        for(j=0;j<n;j++)
            printf("%d", *(c[i]+j));
        printf("\n");
    }
    getch( );
}
```

Address Calculation of Elements in Matrix

Two dimensional array for matrix is defined by specifying number of rows and columns as,

    int a[10][10];

As already seen, 100 locations in the memory are reserved. Each location will have some address. There are two ways in which the elements in the matrix can be stored.

(a) Row major order,

(b) Column major order.

(a) Row major order:

In this representation, the elements are stored row wise. If there are m rows and n columns and base address i.e., address of first element is b then address of the element a[i][j] will be

$$b + (n \times i + j) \text{ size of element}$$

For example, size of element will be memory required to store one element. Suppose m = 3 and n = 3, i.e., we have array int a[3][3], then the address of the elements will be as follows:

Element	Address
a[0][0]	$b + (3 \times 0 + 0) \times 2 = b$
a[0][1]	$b + (3 \times 0 + 1) \times 2 = b + 2$
a[0][2]	$b + (3 \times 0 + 2) \times 2 = b + 4$
a[1][0]	$b + (3 \times 1 + 0) \times 2 = b + 6$
a[1][1]	$b + (3 \times 1 + 1) \times 2 = b + 8$
a[1][2]	$b + (3 \times 1 + 2) \times 2 = b + 10$
a[2][0]	$b + (3 \times 2 + 0) \times 2 = b + 12$
a[2][1]	$b + (3 \times 2 + 1) \times 2 = b + 14$
a[2][2]	$b + (3 \times 2 + 2) \times 2 = b + 16$

(a) Column major order:

In this representation, the elements are stored in memory column wise. If there are m rows and n columns and base address is b, then address of the element a[i][j] will be,

$$b + (m \times j + i) \text{ size of element}$$

For example, suppose m = 3 and n = 3, i.e., array is int a[3][3], then the address of the elements will be as follows:

Table 1.4

Element	Address
a[0][0]	$b + (3 \times 0 + 0) \times 2 = b$
a[1][0]	$b + (3 \times 0 + 1) \times 2 = b + 2$
a[2][0]	$b + (3 \times 0 + 2) \times 2 = b + 4$
a[0][1]	$b + (3 \times 1 + 0) \times 2 = b + 6$
a[1][1]	$b + (3 \times 1 + 1) \times 2 = b + 8$
a[2][1]	$b + (3 \times 1 + 2) \times 2 = b + 10$
a[0][2]	$b + (3 \times 2 + 0) \times 2 = b + 12$
a[1][2]	$b + (3 \times 2 + 1) \times 2 = b + 14$
a[2][2]	$b + (3 \times 2 + 2) \times 2 = b + 16$

1.4.9 Strings

String is an array of characters. Strings are used to manipulate text such as names, words, sentences, etc. A string is declared as:

```
char string_name[size];
e.g., char s[80];
```

The string declaration char s[80]; will reserve 80 locations to store 80 characters as shown in figure 1.29.

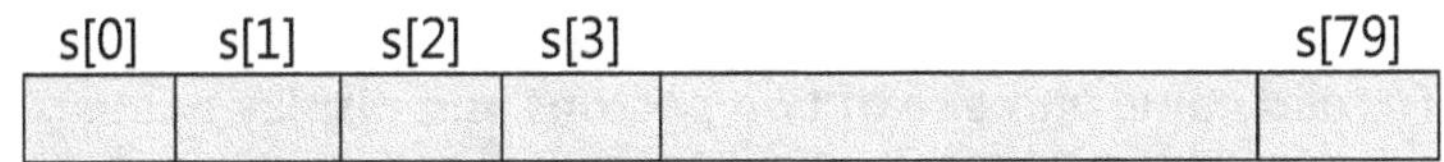

Fig. 1.29: String (array of characters)

But there is a difference between an array and string, as far as reading, printing and manipulation of string. The reason is when we read integer numbers; we have to give a space in between two numbers. But when we read a string, we cannot give a space between two characters. To read numbers in an integer array, we use a loop and scanf in the loop expects a delimiting character space or enter key between the two inputs. To read a string we use the function scanf or gets as follows.

```
scanf("%s", string_name);
or
gets(string_name);
e.g. scanf("%s", s);
or
gets(s);
```

The difference between the two is that scanf doesn't allow a space to be entered between two characters whereas gets allow space to be entered, i.e., if you are entering a single word you can use scanf. If you want to read a sentence gets is used.

Similarly, to display a string printf and puts functions are used as follows:

```
printf("%s", string_name);
or
puts(string_name);
e.g. printf("%s", s);
or puts(s);
```

Program 1.64: To read name of person and display Hello name.

```
void main( )
{
    char name[20];
    printf("Enter your name \n");
    gets(name);
    printf("Hello %s", name);
}
```

Program 1.65: To read name and age of two persons and display name of elder.

```
void main( )
{
    char name1 [20], name2[20];
    int age1, age2;
    printf("Enter name & age of first person \n");
```

```
        gets(name1);
        scanf("%d", &age1);
        printf("Enter name & age of second person \n");
        gets(name2);
        scanf("%d", &age2);
        if(age 1 > age2)
                printf("Elder is % s", name1);
        else
                printf("Elder is % s", name2);
}
```

1.4.10 String Functions

Manipulating string means changing, modifying or adding characters in a given string. Manipulation of strings is required very often, e.g. to combine two words, to reverse the words, to find substring, conversion into upper or lower case etc. C provides inbuilt functions for string manipulation. It is necessary to include string.h file for using these functions.

1. **Strlen:** It gives length of string i.e. number of characters in a string.

    Usage: int_var = strlen(string_name);

    e.g.   l=strlen(s);

Program 1.66: To illustrate use of strlen.

```
void main( )
{
        char s[ ]="abcd";
        int l;
        l=strlen(s);
        printf("%d", l);
}
```

Output: 4

2. **Strcpy:** It assigns one sting to another i.e. copies one string to another.

    Usage: strcpy (target_string, source_string);

    e.g.   strcpy (s2, s1);

Program 1.67: To illustrate use of strcpy.

```
void main( )
{
    char s[20], t[20];
    strcpy(s, "abcd");
    strcpy(t, s);
    printf("%s \n", s);
    printf("%s", t);
}
```

Output: abcd

            abcd

3. Strcat: It concatenates (combines) two strings. This will attach second string to first string.

    Usage: strcat (string_name1, string_name2);
    e.g.   strcat (s1, s2);

Program 1.68: To illustrate use of strcat.

```
void main( )
{
    char s1[20], s2[20];
    strcpy(s1, "abc");
    strcpy(s2, "xyz");
    strcat(s1, s2);
    printf("s1 = %s \n", s1);
    printf("s2 = %s\n", s2);
}
```

Output: s1 = abcxyz

            s2 = xyz

4. strcmp: It compares two strings. Comparison is on the basis of ASCII value of the characters in the two strings.

    Usage: int_var = strcmp(string_name1, string_name2);
    e.g.   c = strcmp (s1, s2)
    if   s1 and s2 are same   c = 0
              s1 > s2 then   c > 0
              s1 < s2 then   c < 0

Program 1.69: To illustrate use of strcmp.

```c
void main( )
{
    char s1[20], s2[20];
    int c1, c2, c3;
    strcpy(s1, "abc");
    strcpy(s2, "xyz");
    c1 =strcmp(s1, s2);
    c2=strcmp(s2, s1);
    c3=strcmp(s1, s1);
    printf("%d \n %d \n % d", c1, c2, c3);
}
```

Output: 23

                 −23

                 0

5. **strrev:** This will reverse a string.

   Usage: **strrev (string name);**

   e.g.   **strrev (s);**

Program 1.70: To illustrate use of strrev.

```c
void main( )
{
    char s[20];
    strcpy(s, "abcd");
    strrev(s);
    printf("%s \n", s);
}
```

Output: dcba

Now let us write a program which makes use of all the above functions.

Program 1.71: To check whether a given string is palindrome or not.

Note: A string is called palindrome if we read it in reverse order it will be same. For this, we have to reverse the string and compare with original. But when we reverse a string, the original string is lost hence we have to copy it in another string and then reverse.

```c
void main( )
{
    char s[80], t[80];
    int c;
    printf("Enter a string \n");
    gets(s);
    strcpy(t, s);
    strrev(s);
    c = strcmp(s, t);
    if(c==0)
        printf("Palindrome");
    else
        printf("Not palindrome");
}
```

1.4.11 String Manipulation Character by Character

Although string functions for most of the operations are available, the user might have his own requirement. Since string is an array of characters, it is possible to manipulate the string by operating on it character by character. In short we are going to see how to play with the characters in a string.

We know that when we declare a string we have to specify the size of string. We may not be using all the locations reserved for storing the string e.g. if string s is declared as char s[80]; and we store "abc" in it, we are using only 3 locations. How do we know where the string is ending? One way of finding it is to use strlen function which counts number of characters. If strlen function is not to be used, there is one more way. Each string terminates with a character called as NULL character denoted as "\0". It has ASCII value zero. We can check this character to detect end of string.

s[0]	s[1]	s[2]	s[3]	s[4]	s[5]	s[6]
b	a	n	a	n	a	\0

Fig. 1.30: Characters in string

It means extra character '10' is used to store a string.
Let us write a simple program to display all characters, each on new line using these methods.

Method I: Using strlen

Program 1.72: To display characters in a string (version 1).

```
void main( )
{
    int l, i;
    char s[80];
    printf("Enter a string \n");
    gets(s);
    l = stren(s);
    for(i=0;i<1;i++)
    {
        printf("%c \n", s[i]);
    }
}
```

Note that the control character %c is used to display the characters.

Method II: Without using strlen

Program 1.73: To display characters in a string (version 2).

```
void main( )
int l, i;
char s[80];
printf("Enter a string \n");
gets(s);
i=0;
while(s[i]!='\0')
{
    printf("%c \n", s[i]);
    i++;
}
```

Explanation:

1. The string is accepted and stored in a variable s.

2. Start from location i=0 and go till the end of string displaying each character in the string, i.e., s[i].

Method I: Using strlen

Program 1.74: To count number of a's in a string (version 1).

```c
void main( )
{
    int l, c, i;
    char s[80];
    printf("Enter a string \n");
    gets(s);
    c=0;
    l = stren(s);
    for(i=0;i<l;i++)
    {
        if(s[i]='a'||s[i]=='A')
            c++;
    }
    printf("Number of a's are %d \n", c);
}
```

Method II: Without using strlen

Program 1.75: To count number of a's in a string (version 2).

```c
void main( )
{
    int i, c;
    char s[80];
    i=0;
    while(s[i]!="\0")
    {
        if(s[i]=='a'||s[i]=='A')
            c++;
    }
    printf("Number of a's are %d \n", c);
}
```

Explanation:

3. The string is accepted and stored in a variable s.
4. Start from location i=0 and go till the end of string checking if the character at each location s[i] is 'a' or not. If yes, increment the counter c.
5. Display the count c.

1.4.12 String Pointers

We have seen that an array can be replaced by a pointer. A single pointer variable can access the consecutive locations in memory. We can also have pointer to a string. A character type pointer can be used to store address of string.

Suppose we have a variable char *p; it will reserve a location for p to store address of character or address of first character in string.

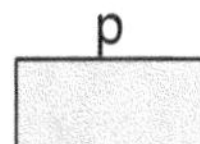

Fig. 1.31: Char type pointer

Normally, we need to allocate memory to a pointer to store data in the location pointed by it. We use malloc function for this purpose. In case of strings, the string functions do this job for you. It means you don't need malloc function here.

To read a string and store it in a location pointed by p, you can directly write

        gets(p); or scanf("%s", p);

To display the string pointed by p, you can use

        puts(p) or printf("%s", p);

Let us write a program.

Program 1.76: To illustrate use of string pointer.

```
void main( )
{
    char *p;
    printf("Enter your name \n");
    gets(p);
    printf("Hello %s", p);
    getch( );
}
```

Explanation:

1. The string is accepted and stored in memory and address of first character is stored in p as shown in figure 6.19, i.e. p is a pointer to the string:

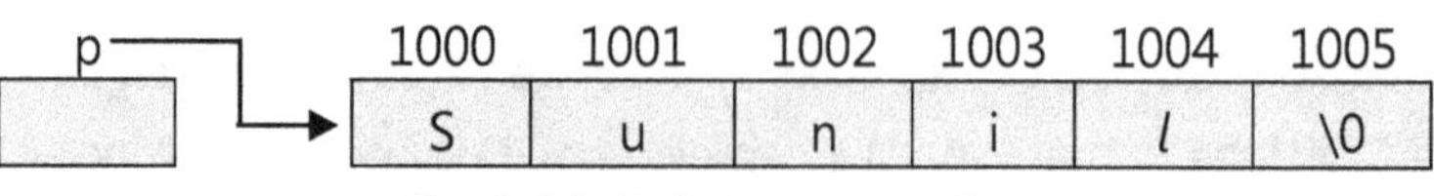

Fig. 1.32: Pointer to a string

2.   Output will be Hello Sunil

Program 1.77: To illustrate use of string pointer.

```c
void main( )
{
    char *s
    strpy(s, "abcde");
    printf("%s \n", s);
    printf("%s \n", s + 1);
    printf("%s \n", s + 3);
}
```

Explanation:
1.   The string "abcde" is stored in memory and address of first character is stored in s, i.e., s is a pointer to the string.
2.   s will be address of string hence first printf displays the string "abcde" starting at this address location.
3.   s+1 will be address of second character in string hence second printf displays the string "bcde" starting at this address location.
4.   s+2 will be address of third character in string hence third printf displays the string "cde" starting at this address location.
5.   Output will be
         abcde
         bcde
         cde

Here is a modification to above program.

Program 1.78: To illustrate use of string pointer.

```c
void main( )
{
    char *s;
    strcpy (s, "abcde");
    while (*s!='\0')
```

```
        {
            printf("%s \n", s);
            s++;
        }
    }
```

Output: abcde

                 bcde

                 de

                 e

1.4.13 Array of Strings

What if we want to store a list of names or number of sentences and words to manipulate them? We can store one name / sentence / word in a string variable. We will require number of string variables to store list persons / sentences / words. We can declare an array of strings as

$$char\ s[50][80];$$

It means we are reserving space for storing 50 strings (rows) of 80 characters (columns) each as shown in Fig. 1.33.

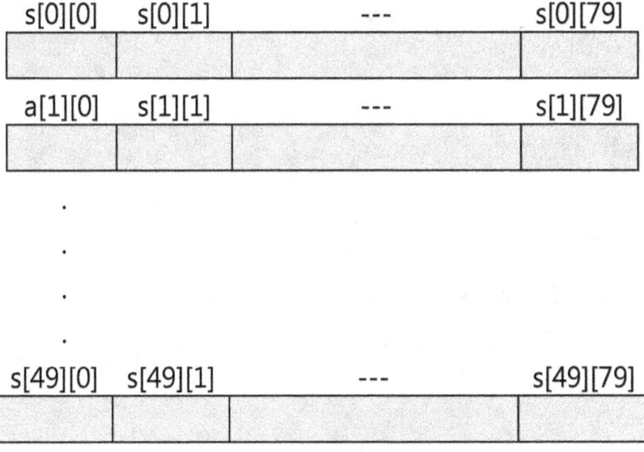

Fig. 1.33: Array of string

If we want to read and store the strings we have to use for loop as:

```
for(i=0;i<n;i++)
    gets(s[i]);
```

Note that we are specifying only row number in gets which is nothing but address of each string and that is what gets requires.

Similarly to display the strings we can write:

```
for(i=0;i<n;i++)
    printf("%s \n", s[i]);
```

Any string can be accessed by specifying the row number.

Now let us write a program to read a list of names of persons and sort it in alphabetical order.

Program 1.79: To sort the list of names.

```
void main( )
{
    char name[50][20], temp [20];
    int i, j, n;
    printf("How many names? \n");
    scanf("%d", &n);
    printf("Enter the names \n");
    for(i=0;i<n;i++)
        gets(name[i]);
    for(i=0;i<n-1;i++)
    {
        for(j=i+1;j<n;j++)
        {
            if(strcmp(name[i],name[j])>0)
            {
                strcpy(temp, name[i]);
                strcpy(name[i], name[j]);
                strcpy(name[j], temp);
            }
        }
    }
    printf("Sorted list is \n");
    for(i=0;i<n;i++)
        printf("%s \n", name[i]);
}
```

1.4.14 Passing an Array to Function

Elements in the array are stored in continuous locations. To verify this you can write a simple program as:

Program 1.80: To display address of array elements.

```
void main( )
{
    int a[10], i;
    for(i=0;i<10;i++)
        printf("%u \n", &a[i]);
}
```

A simple int array a of size 10 is defined. Addresses of the locations a[0], a[2], a[3], ... a[9] are displayed. The output will be addresses of continuous locations.

Now here is another program which will illustrate how you can access these locations with the help of single pointer.

Program 1.81: Pointer to array.

```
void main( )
{
    int a[ ]={10,20,30,40,50};
    int i, *p;
    p= &a[0];
    for (i=0;i<5;i++)
        printf("%d \n", *(p+i));
}
```

The address of first element in the array is stored in p(p= &a[0]). p+1 will be address of second element, p+2 will be address of third and so on.

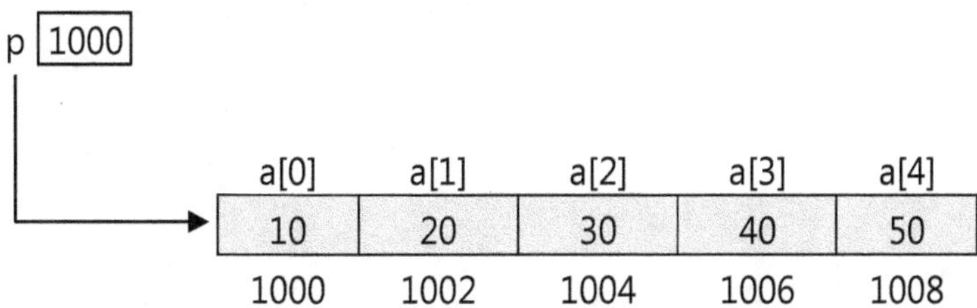

Fig. 1.34: Pointer to an array

Hence, we can access the values stored in the array using *p, *(p+1), *(p+2) and so on. Thus, with the help of single pointer p, we can access all the elements in the array. This fact is made use of in passing array to a function.

We have seen that, we can pass data to the function in two ways: by value and by address. It is called passing parameters to a function. The data passed to a function are called parameters and the data is accepted by the function through its arguments.

Now imagine a situation in which we would like to pass all the elements of an array to a function. If the array has 100 elements we would require 100 arguments in the function (note that we cannot have, array as an argument). This is impractical.

But as seen above, we can make use of the fact that the elements in an array are stored in continuous locations. It means the addresses of the elements in an array are continuous, so if we pass the address of first element in the array we will be able to access the addresses of all the elements and in turn the values stored in the array.

Let us write a simple function to display all the elements in an int array. Since we are going to pass address to the function, the function argument should be pointer. This particular function returns nothing hence it will be void function and its prototype will be void disp(int*); the function along with main program is written as follows.

Program 1.82: Function to display elements in array.

```
    void disp(int*);
    void main( )
    {
        int a[ ] = {10, 20, 30, 40, 50};
        disp (&a[0]);
    }
    void disp (int *p)
    {
    int i;
    for (i=0;i<5;i++)
        printf("%d \n *(p + i));
    }
```

Explanation:

1. The array a[ ] stores 5 fixed elements in it.
2. The address of first element in the array will be &a[0]. Hence, the function call disp(&a[0]).
3. The function has argument p which is int type pointer. When the function is called, p gets the address of first element in the array, i.e., &a[0]. Hence address of first element is p, second will p + 1, third will be p + 2 and so on. Hence values stored in the array will be accessed by using * operator.
4. When i = 0, the function will display value stored at location pointed p means *(p + 0), i.e., 10. When i = 1, it will display value stored at p + 1, i.e., 20 and so on.

The function disp can also be written as:

```
void disp (int p[ ])
{
    int i;
    for(i=0;i<5;i++)
    printf("%d \n", p[i]);
}
```

Note that the parameter here is p[ ] instead of *p and in the function the values are accessed just like we access array elements, i.e., p[i]. This kind of function writing gives better readability to the program. But note that the concept here is same as the one we had used with pointers.

The disp function above displays exactly 5 elements. If we have to generalize this function for n elements, we would require passing this value of n also to the function.

The modified function will be as follows:

```
void disp(int p[ ], int n)
{
    int i;
    for(i=0;i<n;i++)
        printf("%d \n", p[i]);
}
```

Note: The function call will be disp(&a[0], n) or disp(a, n). &a[0] and a are same, i.e., address of first element.

Program 1.83: Write a function to find sum of elements in an array.

The function sum. would require entire array to be passed to it along with number of elements (n) actually stored in the array. The function will find sum of the elements and return it. Hence, the function prototype will be,

```
int sum (int*, int);
    or
int sum (int[ ], int);
```

Hence, the program will be as follows:

```
#define MAX 100
int sum (int[ ], int);
void main( )
{
    int a[MAX];
    int i, n, s;
    printf("Enter number of elements \n");
    scanf("%d", &n);
    printf("Enter the numbers \n");
    for(i=0;i<n;i++)
        scanf("%d", &a[i]);
    s = sum (a, n);
    printf("Sum is %d", s);
    getch( );
}
int sum (int p[ ], int n)
{
    int i, s;
    s=0;
    for(i=0,i<n;i++)
        s = s+p[i];
    return(s);
}
```

Explanation:

1. Main function reads numbers into the array a. The address of array a is passed along with number of elements n to the function sum.

2. The function takes in the address of first element of the array, i.e., a in the argument p, which is a pointer to an array. The function also takes in the value of n in the argument which has same name.
3. i and s are local variables of the function.
4. The for loop in the function adds the elements at location p, p + 1, p + 2, etc. to s recursively.
5. The final sum in s is returned back to the variable s in the main function which is displayed.

1.4.15 Function and Strings

String pointers are more useful in case of functions that manipulate strings. If we have to pass a string to a function, we have to pass address of the string to the function. Therefore, the function parameter should be pointer to string. We should remember that the name of an array (whether integer, float or character) is the base address of the array.

Suppose we have a string char s[80]; s or &s[0] is the address of the string. Hence if we have to pass this string to a function, we can either pass &s[0] or s to the function. It is convenient to use s than &s[0]. The argument in the function will be char type pointer.

Let us write a function to count number of characters in string. The function requires a string to be passed to it and returns an integer hence prototype will be.

Program 1.84: Write a function to count number of characters in string.

```
int length(char *);
void main( )
{
    int l;
    char s[80];
    printf("Enter a string \n");
    gets (s);
    l = length(s);
    printf("Length is %d \n", l);
}
int length(char *p)
{
```

```
        int i=0;
        while(*(p+i)!='\0')
        i++;
        return (i);
}
```

Program 1.85: Function to copy a string into another.

```
    void copy(char*, char*);
    void main( )
    {
        char sl[80],s2[80];
        gets(s1);
        copy(s2, s1);
        printf("s2=%s\u", s2);
    }
    void copy(char*p, char*q)
    {
        int i=0;
        while(*(p+i)!= '\0')
        {
            *(q+i)=*(p+i);
            i++;
        }
        *(q+i) = '\0';
    }
```

1.4.16 Searching and Sorting Functions

Now let us revisit our programs of searching and sorting. We are now in a position to write a better program because we have learnt the art of writing functions and passing almost anything to it. We have written a menu driven program to search and sort elements using different methods.

What was the drawback of the program? We had declared the array a[ ] and n as global variables. Hence somebody who wants to use the functions we have written, has to use the name of array a and variable n in his program. Another thing is that since it is global, any function can access and modify it. Hence the programmer really has no control over such variables. He becomes helpless. It is a bad programming.

Let us rewrite the functions for searching and sorting by passing array to these functions.

The function prototypes will be:

1. Function for linear search

   int lin_search (int[ ] int, int);

   Parameters passed are:

   (i)   Address of first element in the array

   (ii) Number of elements actually stored in the array.

   (iii) Number to be searched

   Function returns:

Location number of the number in the array if found otherwise returns −1.

2. Function for binary search

   int bin_search (int[ ], int, int);

   Parameters passed are same as linear search and returned value is also same as linear search.

3. Function for bubble sort, selection sort and insertion sort

   void bubble_sort(int[ ], int);

   void sel_sort(int[ ], int);

   void ins_sort(int[ ], int);

   Parameters passed are:

   (i)   Address of first element in the array.

   (ii) Number of elements in the array.

4. Function to display the elements in the array.

   void disp(int[ ], int);

   The program will be as follows:

Program 1.86: Program for searching and sorting using functions.

```
#define MAX 100
int lin_search(int[ ],int,int);
int bin_search(int[ ], int, int);
void bubble_sort(int[ ], int);
void sel_sort(int[ ], int);
void ins_sort(int[ ], int);
void disp(int [ ], int);
void main( )
{
        int a[MAX];
```

```c
int i, n, ch, s, loc;
printf("Enter number of elements \n");
scanf("%d", &n);
printf("Enter the members \n");
for(i=0;i<n;i++)
    scanf("%d", &a[i]);
do
{
    clrscr( );
    printf(" 1. Linear_search \n 2. Binary_search \n3. Bubble sort \n 4.
    Selection_sort \n Insertion sort \n 6. Display \n 7. Exit\n");
    printf("Enter your choice \n");
    scanf("%d", &ch);
    switch(ch)
    {
        case 1:  printf("Enter number to be searched \n");
                 scanf("%d", &s);
                 loc=lin_search(a, n, s);
                 printf("Location is %d", loc);
                 break;
        case 2:  printf("Enter number to be searched \n");
                 scanf("%d", &s);
                 ins_sort(a, n);
                 loc = bin_search (a, n, s);
                 printf("Location is %d", loc);
                 break;
        case 3:  bubble_sort(a, n);
                 disp(a, n);
                 break;
        case 4:  sel_sort (a, n);
                 disp(a, n);
                 break;
        case 5:  ins_sort(a, n);
                 disp(a, n);
                 break;
    }
```

```c
                getch( );
        }while (ch!=6);
}
int lin_search(int p[ ], int n, int s)
{   int i, flag;
    flag=1;
    for(i=0;i<n;i++)
    {
        if(p[i]==s)
        {
            flag = 0;
            return(i + 1);
        }
    }
    if (flag==1)
        return(-1);
}
int bin_search(int p[ ], int n, int s)
{
    int l, u, mid, flag;
    flag = 1;
    l=0;
    u = n - 1;
    while(l<=u)
    {
        mid = (l + u)/2;
        if (p[mid]==s)
        {
            flag = 0;
            return(mid + 1);
        }
        else
        {
            if(p[mid]>s)
                u = mid-1;
            else
```

```c
                        l = mid + 1;
                }
        }
        if(flag==1)
                return(-1);
}
void bubble_sort(int p[ ], int n)
{
        int i, j, temp;
        for(i=0;i<n-1;i++)
        {
                for(j=0;j<n-1-i;j++)
                {
                        if(p[i]>p[j + 1])
                        {
                                temp = p[j];
                                p[j] = p[j+1];
                                p[j+1] = temp;
                        }
                }
        }
}
void sel_sort (int p[ ], int n)
{
        int i, j, temp, index;
        for(i=0;i<n;i++)
        {
                min=p[i];
                index=i;
                for(j=i+1;j<n;j++)
                {
                        if(p[j]<min)
                        {
                                min=p[j];
                                index=j;
                        }
```

```
                    }
                    p[index]=p[i];
                    p[i]=min;
                }
        void ins_sort (int p[ ], int n)
        {
            int i, j temp;
            for(i=1;i<n;i++)
            {
                temp = p[i];
                for(j=i-1;j>=0;j--)
                {
                    if (p[j]>temp)
                        p[j+1]=p[j];
                    else
                        break;
                }
                p[j+1] = temp;
            }
        }
        void disp (int p[ ], int n)
        {
            int i;
            for(i=0;i<n;i++)
                printf("%d \n", p[i]);
        }
```

Program 1.87: Write a program to search a name in a given list of names using: (i) linear search, (ii) Binary Search.

(i) Linear search:

```c
#define MAX 50
#include <string.h>
void main( )
{
    char names[50][20], s[20];
    int i, n, flag;
```

```c
        printf("Enter number of names \n");
        scanf("%d", &n);
        printf("Enter the names \n");
        for(i=0;i<n;i++)
        {
              flushall( );
              gets(names[i]);
        }
        printf("Enter name to be searched \n");
        gets(s);
        flag = 1;
        for(i=0;i<n;i++)
        {
              if(strcmp(name[i], s)==0)
              {
                    printf("Found at location %d", i + 1);
                    flag = 0;
                    break;
              }
        }
        if(flag == 1)
              printf("Not found");
}
```

(ii) Binary search:

```c
#define MAX 100
#include <string.4>
void main( )
{
      char names [MAX] [20], s[20];
      int i, n, /, u, mid, flag;
      printf("How many names? \n");
      scanf("%d", &n);
      printf("Enter names \n");
      for(i=0;i<n;i++)
      {
            flushall( );
            gets(names[i]);
      }
      printf("Enter name to be searched \n");
```

```
        gets(s);
        l = 0; u = n – 1; flag = 1;
        while (l<=u)
        {
                mid = (l + u)/2;
                if(strcmp(names[mid], s) == 0)
                {
                        printf("Found at location %d", mid + 1);
                        flag = 0;
                        break;
                }
                if(strcmp(name[mid], s)>0)
                        u = mid–1
                else
                l = mid = + 1;
        }
        if (flag==1)
                print("Not found");
}
```

Program 1.88: Write a program to sort the names of n persons using:
(i) Bubble sort, (ii) Selection sort, (iii) Insertion Sort
(i)   Bubble sort:

```
#define MAX 50
#include <string.h>
void main( )
{
    char name [MAX] [20], temp[20];
    int i, j, n;
    clrscr( );
    printf("How many names ?\n");
    scanf("%d", &n);
    printf("Enter the names \n");
    for(i=0;i<n;i++)
    {
        flushall( );
        gets(names[i]);
    }
    for(i=0;i<n–1;i++)
```

```c
        {
                for(j=0;j<n-1-i;j++)
                {
                        if(strcmp(name[j], name[j+1])>0)
                        {
                                strcpy(temp, name[j]);
                                strcpy(name[j], name[j+1]);
                                strcpy(name[j + 1], temp);
                        }
                }
        }
        printf("Sorted list is \n");
        for(i=0;i<n;i++)
                printf("%s \n", name[i]);
}
```

The sorting process for selection insertion is given below. The input and display `will remain as it is in above program.

(ii) Selection sort:

```c
        for(i=0;i<n-1;i++)
        {
                for(j=i+ 1;j<n;j++)
                {
                        if(strcmp(name[i], name[j])>0)
                        {
                                strcpy(temp, name[i]);
                                strcpy(name[i], name[j]);
                                strcpy(name[j], temp);
                        }
                }
        }
```

(iii) Insertion sort:

```c
        for(i=1;i<n;i++)
        {
                strcpy(temp, name[i]);
                for(j=i-1;j>=0;j--)
                {
                        if(strcmp (name[j], temp)>0)
```

```
                strcpy(name[j + 1], name[j]);
            else
                break;
        }
        strcpy(name[j + 1], temp);
}
```

SOLVED PROBLEMS

1. Write a function in 'c' to find maximum of each row for a given matrix of the order maximum having integer elements and print them.

```c
void print_max(int a[ ] [ ], int m, int n)
{
    int i, j, max;
    for(i=0;i<m;i++)
    {
        max = a[i][0];
        for(j=0;j<n;j++)
        {
            if(a[i][j]>max)
                max = a[i][j];
        }
        printf("Maximum in row %d is %d", i, max);
    }
}
```

2. Write a user defined function in 'C' using pointers for checking whether given string is palindrome or not.

```c
void check_palindrome (char *s);
{
    int i, j, l, flag;
    l = strlen (s);
    flag = 1;
    for(i=0,j=1-1;i<l/2;i++,j--)
    {
        if(*(s+i)!=*(s+j))          // or if(s[i]!=s[j])
        {
            flag = 0;
```

```
                break;
            }
        }
        if (flag ==1)
            printf("Palindrome");
        else
            printf("Not Palindrome");
    }
```

3. Write a user defined function in c to find geometric average of n numbers using formula.

$$G(Avg) = x_1 * x_2 * x_3 * ... x_n)^{\frac{1}{n}}$$

We will use an array of float to store the numbers whose geometric average is to be found.

```
    float gavg (float x int n)
    {
        float p;
        int i;
        p=1;
        for(i=0;i<n;i++)
            p = p*x[i]
        return (pow (p, 1.0/n));
    }
```

4. Write a recursive function for binary search.

```
    int bin_search(int[ ], int, int, int);
    void main( )
    {
        int a[100], i, n, s;
        printf("Enter how many numbers ?\n");
            scanf("%d", &n);
        printf("Enter the numbers \n");
        for(i=0;i<n;i++)
            scanf("%d", &a[i]);
        printf("Enter number to be searched \n");
        scanf("%d", &s);
        loc = bin_search(a, 0, n-1, s);
        if(loc!=-1)
```

```
        printf("found at %d", loc);
    else
        printf("Not found");
}
int bin_search (int a[ ], int l, int u, int s)
{
    int mid;
    if(l > u)
        return(-1);
    else
    {
        mid = (l + u)/2;
        if (a[mid]==s)
            return(mid);
        else
        {
            if(a[mid]>s)
                bin_search(a, l, mid-1, s);
            else
                bin_search(a, mid+1, u, s);
        }
    }
}
```

5. What are pointers? Are pointers fast? Justify your answer with suitable example.

Pointers give fast access to a location in the memory. If we use array to access i^{th} element a[i] in the array, we have to add i * size of data item to the base address every time. If we use pointers in place of array, the element at i^{th} location can be accessed directly using *p. We just have to advance the pointer (p++) every time.

6. Write a function in 'C' using pointers for checking whether two strings are equal or not.

```
int compare (char *s, char *t)
{
    int i, j;
    i = 0; j = 0;
    while (s[j]!='\0')
```

```
        {
            if(s[i] == t[j])
            {
                i++;
                j++;
            }
            else
                break;
        }
        return(s[i]-t[j]);
    }
```

7. Write a 'C' function using pointers to add two matrices and return the resultant matrix to calling function.

```
    int [ ][ ] add (int a[ ] [ ], int b[ ] int m, int n);
    {
        int c[10][10], i, j;
        for(i=0i<m;i++)
        {
            for(j=0;j<n;j++)
                c[i][j] = a[i][j]+b[i][j];
        }
        return (c);
    }
```

8. Find the output of following program. Justify your answer in steps. Show the output as displayed on the screen.

```
    void main( )
    {
        int n[25];
        n[0]= 100;
        n[24]= 200;
        printf("%d%d", *n, *(n+24)+*(n+0));
    }
```

Solution:

int n[25] will reserve 25 locations n[0], n[1], n[2], n[24] in memory. The first location n[0] will store JOO, last location n[24] will store 200. n is address of first location in array. Hence, *n will be value stored at location n[0] which is 100. *(n+24)+*(n+0) is equivalent to n[24]+n[0]= 100+200=300.

Hence output displayed will be,

100   300

9. What do you mean by array of pointers? Differentiate between array of pointers and pointer to array.

(i)   Array of pointer contains more than one pointer. A pointer to an array is single pointer.

(ii) Array of pointers is used for two dimensional array. Pointers to an array is used for single dimensional array.

(iii) Array of pointers is declared as

int*p[[10];

Pointer to an array is declared as

int *p;

(iv) Each element in array of pointers stores address of row. Pointer to an array stores address of first element in the array.

10. Write a 'C' function to perform following operations using pointers.

   (i) Concatenation

(i) Concatenation

```
char *concat(char s1, char s2)
{
    int i, j;
    i = strlen (s1);
    j = 0;
    while (s2[j]!='\0')
    {
        s1[i]=s2[j];
        i++;
        j++;
    }
    s1[i]='\0';
    return (s1);
}
```

11. Write output of following program.

```
void main( )
{
```

```
    int a = 10, b=20;
    int *p;
    p=&a;
    printf("%d \n", *p);
    p=&b;
    printf("%d \n", *p);
    b=a+b;
    *p=a+b;
    printf("%d \n", *p);
}
```

Solution:

(a) Since p stores address of a, *p will be 10. Hence, first output will be 10.

(b) Then p stores address of b, *p will be 20. Hence, next output will be 20.

(c) b=a+b will make b=30. Then *p=a+b will make b=10+30=40. Hence, the third printf will print 40. Thus, the output of the program will be,

```
10
20
40
```

12. Write a function to combine two strings.

Solution:

```
void combine(char s1[ ],char s2[ ])
{
    int i, j, l;
    l=strlen(s1);
    j=l;
        for(i=0;i<strlen(s2);i++)
        {
            s1[j]=s2[i];
            i++;
            j++;
        }
        s1[j]='\0';
}
```

1.5 Introduction of Structure

Storage of complex data item is an important task a programmer has to perform. Complex data items involve set of records having variety of information. This calls for a data type that can manage this variety at ease. C provides a constructed data type known as structures. We can combine different data types of our choice using structures. These structures help to organize complex data in a more meaningful way. Thus, structure is constructed or user defined data type which can group together different data types.

1.5.1 Structure in C

It is a user defined data type. We have seen basic data types like int, float and char. We can store only one type of value in these variables. But in case we want to store a record containing name, age and income of person, we need to store it in three different variables viz. char, int and float. Also, if we have to store a list of persons having name, age and income then we need three arrays of same types. It is going to be very difficult to manage the different arrays. As an example, Let us see a program which can store a list of persons have name, age and income and sorts it age-wise. We need to declare 3 arrays char name[50][20], int age[50], float income[50] (the size is assumed to be 50).

Program 1.89: List of employees using arrays

```c
void main( )
{
    char name[50] [20], temp1 [20];
    int age[50], temp2;
    float income [50], temp3;
    int i, j, n;
    printf("Enter how many persons\n");
    scanf("%d", &n);
    for(i=0;i<n;i++)
    {
        printf("Enter name \n");
        fflush(stdin);
        gets(name [i]);
```

```c
        printf("Enter age\n");
        scanf("%d", &age [i]);
        printf("Enter income \n");
        scanf("%f' , &income[i]);
    }
    for(i=0;i<n-1;i++)
    {
        for(j=i+1;j<n;j++)
        {   if(age[i] > age[j])
            {
                strcpy(temp1, name[i]);
                strcpy(name[i], name[j]);
                strcpy(name[j], temp1);
                temp2 = age[i];
                age[i] = age[j];
                age[j] = temp2;
                temp3 = income[i];
                income[i] = income[j];
                income[j] = temp3;
            }
        }
    }
    printf("The list is \n");
    for(i=0;i<n;i++)
        printf("%s \t %d \t %f \n"; names[i], age[i], income[i]);
}
```

Note that in above program while sorting the records, in the list, we had to handle each array separately as these records are stored using 3 different arrays. The program also becomes lengthy. Therefore we are structure type variables to store the record, which allows us to store different data types in one variable making manipulation of records easier.

1.5.2 Defining Structure

There is a difference between structure declaration and definition. The declaration tells the compiler about prototype of structure, whereas definition creates the structure variable. The definition allocates space in memory for structure variable.

Structure is declared as,

```
struct <name>
{
    data_type member1;
    data_type member2;
        :
    data_type membern;
};
```

where member1, member2, ..., membern etc. can be int, char, float, array, struct itself. Also note that the declaration ends with semicolon. The structure declared is called structure template.

For example,

```
struct person
{
    char name[20];
    int age;
    float income;
};
```

The fields name, age and income are called structure members.

Thus, we have declared a variable type or template called as struct person which is capable of storing name, age and income of one person. To store data items, variables of type struct person are to be defined.

For example, struct person p, q, r;

This will reserve space for storing 3 records in p, q, r as follows:

	name	age	income
p			
q			
r			

The structure declaration and variable definition can be done together as follows:

```
struct person
{
    char name[20];
    int age;
    float income;
}   p, q, r;
```

Storing data in structure variables

Once we have declared the structure type variable, we can store the values in these variables. We have to store the values in the individual fields. This is done using dot(·) operator.

For example,

```
strcpy(p.name, "abc");
p.age = 30;
p.income = 30000.00
```

Consider following program which stores a record in a structure type variable and copies into another variable of same type.

Program 1.90: To store and display data in structure variable.

```
void main( )
{
    struct person
    {
        char name[20];,
        int age;
        float income;
    };
    struct person p, q;
    strcpy(p.name, "abc");
    p.age = 25;
    p.income = 5000.00;
    q = p;
    printf("%s \t %d \t %f \n", q.name, q.age, q.income);
}
```

Output of above program will be

```
abc   25   5000.00
```

Thus, we see that the different types of data can be handled by structure type variables and it becomes very easy to manage this data.

1.5.3 Array of Structures

An array of records is used to store number of records, for example, a list of persons having name, age and income. In the previous Section, we had defined a structure for the same. Now, we can have a variable declaration as.struct person p[100]. It will reserve 100 locations as shown below to store list of 100 persons.

	name	age	income
p[0]			
p[1]			
p[2]			
:			
:			
p[99]			

To access or store data into these locations, we can use dot operator.

For example, p[0].name is the name field of first record, p[0].age is the age field of first record, etc.

To read data into this array, we can use for loop. Similarly, to process data sequentially and display, a for loop can be used. Any record or field can also be randomly accessed.

Program 1.91: To store a list of persons and display the names of persons whose age is above 40.

```
void main( )
{
    struct person                          // Structure declaration
    {
        char name[20];
        int age;
    };
    int i, n;
    struct person p[100];                  // Array of structure
    printf("Enter number of persons \n");,
    scanf("%d", &n);
    for(i=0;i<n;i++)                       // Read n records
    {
        printf("Enter name \n");
```

```c
            gets(p[i].name);
            printf("Enter age \n");
            scanf("%d", &p[i].age);
        }
        print("Persons above 40 years are \n");
        for (i=0;i<n;i++)                          // Display records
        {
            if(p[i].age>40)                        // if age > 40
            printf("%s \t %d \n", p[i].name, p[i].age);
        }
}
```

Program 1.92: To prepare a list of persons having name, age and salary and sort the list age wise.

```c
    void main( )
    {
        struct person                              // Structure definition
        {
            char name[20];
            int age;
            float sal;
        };
        int i, j, n;
        struct person p[100], temp;,               // temp and array of structure
        printf("Enter how many persons \n");
        scanf("%d", &n);
        for(i=0;i<n;i++)                           // Read n records
        {
            printf("Enter name \n");
            gets(p[i].name);
            printf("Enter age \n");
            scanf("%d", &p[i].age);
            printf("Enter salary \n");
            scanf("%f", &p[i]sal);
        }
        for(i=0;i<n-1;i++)                         // sort the records age wise
        {
            for(j=i+1;j<n;j++)
```

```
            {
                if(p[i].age>p[j].age)
                {
                    temp = p[i];
                    p[i] = p[j];
                    p[j] = temp;
                }
            }
        }
    printf("Sorted listed is \n");                 // Display records
    for(i=0;i<n;i++)
        printf("%s \t %d \t %f \n", p[i].name, p[i].age, p[i].sal);
}
```

Program 1.93: To read a list of students having roll number, name and marks in 3 subjects. Find total and percentage. Sort the list in descending order of percentage.

```
void main( )
{
    struct student                          // Define structure
    {
        int rollno;
        char name[20];
        int m1, m2, m3, total;
        float per;
    };
    struct student s[100], temp;            // temp and array of structure
    int i, j, n;
    printf("Enter number of students \n");
    scanf("%d", &n);
    for(i=0;i<n;i++)                        // Read roll no, name and marks in 3 subjects
    {
        printf("Enter rollno \n");
        scanf("%d", &s[i].rollno);
        printf("Enter name \n");
        flushall( );
        gets(s[i].name);
        printf("Enter marks in subjects \n");
```

```c
        scanf("%d %d %d", &s[i].m1, &s[i].m2, &s[i].m3);
        s[i].total = s[i].m1 + s[i].m2 + s[i].m3    // Calculate total
        s[i].per = s[i].total/3.0;                   // Calculate percentage
    }
    for(i=0;i<n-1;i++)
    {
        for(j=i+1;j<n;j++)                   // Sort records in descending order
        {
            if(s[i].per<s[j].per)
            {
                temp = s[i];
                s[i] = s[j];
                s[j] = temp;
            }
        }
    }
    printf("Sorted list is \n");
    for(i=0;i<n;i++)
    printf("%d \t %s \t %d \t %d \t %d \t %f \n", s[i].rollno, s[i].name, s[i].m1,
    s[i].m2, s[i].m3, s[i].total, s[i].per);
}
```

Initializing structure variables

Just like initialization of other variables can be done at the time of declaration [For example, int a = 10], structure variables can also be initialized.

For example,   struct person p = {"abc", 20, 2000};

or   struct person p[ ] = {"abc", 20,1000, "pqr", 30, 3000, "xyz", 40, 4000};

Rules for initializing structure variables:

1. Structure members cannot be initialized inside structure declaration or template.
2. The structure can be partially initialized like struct person p = {"abc", 20};
3. The order of the values inside braces should be same as order of definition.
4. Default initial values will be 0 for int and float members and '\0' for char type member.

Program 1.94: To store a list of items having items number, item name, rate. Search an item in the list if item number is entered.

```c
void main( )
{
    struct item
    {
        int item_no;
        char name[20];
        float rate;
    };
    struct item lst[ ] = {10, "Rin", 15.50, 11, "Lux", 10.50, 12, "Surf", 50.60};
    int s, i, flag = 1;
    printf("Enter item number \n");
    scanf("%d", &s);
    for(i=0;i<n;i++)
    {
        if(lst[i].item_no==s)
        {
            flag = 0;
            printf("%s \t %f \n", lst[i].name, lst[i].rate);
            break;
        }
    }
    if (flag==1)
    printf("Not available");
}
```

1.5.4 Structure and Pointers

Just like we can have pointer variable of int, float or character type, we can also have pointer variable of structure type. For example, if we have structure declared as,

```c
struct person
{
    char name[20];
    int age;
    float sal;
}
```

Now, let us have two variables as:

struct person p = {"abc", 25, 6000};

struct person *ptr;

two locations in the memory will be reserved as:

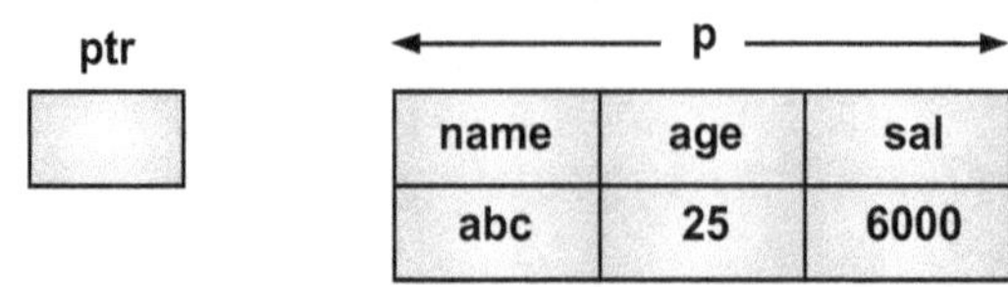

p is simple structure variable and ptr is structure type pointer variable.

Let us store address of p in ptr.

ptr = &p;

This will store address of.p say 1000 in ptr.

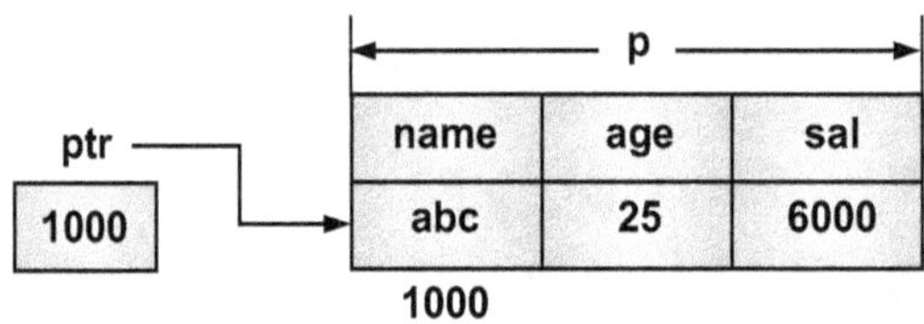

To access data stored in p, dot operator can be used.

p.name will give "abc".

p.age will give 25.

p.sal will give 6000.

Since ptr is a pointer to p, we can access the data through ptr also. An arrow operator (->) is used to access the fields through the pointer type structure variable.

ptr ->name will be same as p.name i.e., "abc".

ptr ->age will be same as p.age i.e., 25.

ptr -> sal will be same as p.sal i.e., 6000.

To access entire structure variable through ptr we can use * operator, i.e., *ptr is same as p. We can also access the fields through ptr using . operator as

(*ptr). name will be same as p.name i.e., "abc".

(*ptr). age will be same as page i.e., 25.

(*ptr). sal will be same as p.sal i.e., 6000.

Now let us write a simple program to illustrate this.

Program 1.95: Use of structure type pointer.

```
void main( )
{
    struct person
    {
        char name[20];
        int age;
        float sal;
    }
    struct person p = {"abc", 25, 6000}
    struct person *ptr, temp;
    ptr = &p;
    printf("%s \t %d \t %f \n", ptr->name, ptr->age, ptr->sal);
    temp = *ptr;
    printf("%s \t %d \t %f \n", temp.name, temp.age, temp.sal);
}
```

Explanation:
1. ptr is pointer to p. hence, output of first printf will be,
   abc   25   6000
2. temp = *ptr will store a value (entire record in p) pointed by ptr in temp. Hence, the output of second printf will also be same.

1.5.5 Array of Structure and Pointer

A pointer variable can be used to store address of an array of records. We can extend this idea for array of structure also. If we have single pointer variable

```
struct person *p;
```

This declaration will reserve only two byte of memory for p at the time of compilation. This variable can be allocated memory block, to store an array of records using malloc as:

```
p = (struct person *)malloc(n*sizeof (struct person));
```

The function malloc will allocate memory block for storing n records of the size of struct person, i.e., 26*n bytes and the address of first record will be stored in p. p+1 will be address of 2nd record, p+2 will be address of 3rd record and so on. In general, p+i will be address of i+1th record. We can use -> operator to access the locations pointed by p, p+1, p+2 etc.

    i.e., (p+i) -> name will access name in i+1th record.

(p+i) -> age will access age in i+1th record.

(p+i) -> sal will access sal in i+1th record.

Let us write a program to illustrate these concepts.

Program 1.96: To store a list of n persons and sort it on the basis of age.

```c
void main( )
{
    struct person
    {
        char name[20];
        int age;
        float sal;
    };
    struct person *p, temp;
    int i, j, n;
    clrscr( );
    printf("Enter number of persons \n");
    scanf("%d", &n);
    p=(struct person *)malloc(n*sizeof(struct person));
    for(i=0;i<n;i++)
    {
        printf("Enter name \n");
        gets ((p+i)->name);
        printf("Enter age \n");
        scanf("%d", &(p+i)->age);
        printf("Enter salary \n");
        scanf("%f ", &(p+i)->sal);
    }
    for(i=0;i<n-1;i++)
    {
        for(j=i+1;j<n;j++)
        {
            if((p+i)->age>(p+j)->age)
```

```
            {
                    temp = *(p+i);
                    *(p+i) = *(p+j);
                    *(p+j) = temp;
            }
        }
    }
    printf("Sorted list is \n");
    for(i=0;i<n;i++)
            printf("%s \t %d \t.%t \n", (p+i)->name, (p+i)->age, (p+i)->sal);
}
```

Explanation:

1. p=(struct person *)malloc(n*sizeof(struct person)); will allocate memory for storing n records, where n will be known at run time. Thus, depending on value of n, memory is allocated to the pointer variable ptr. If we have 10 records to store, memory for 10 records (260 bytes) will be allocated.
2. The first for loop runs for n times accepting every time name, age and salary and it is stored in the locations whose addresses are p, p+1, p+2, …, .
3. The second nested for will sort the records age wise using selection sort. Here, *(p+i) refers to the record pointed by p+i which is equivalent to p[i]. *(p+j) refers to the record pointed by p+j which is equivalent to p[j].
4. The third for loop displays all the sorted records.

1.5.6 Nested Structure

We can have another structure variable as a part of a structure. Consider that we want to store name and date of birth of a person. Date of birth can contain 3 fields day, month and year. Hence, we declare it as another structure as shown below:

```
struct dob
{
    int dd, mm, yy;
}
struct person
{
    char name[20];
    struct dob d;
};
```

Thus, we have name and d as two fields in struct person where d is a structure type variable nested inside struct person. If we define

    struct person p;

p will be allocated memory as:

<table>
<tr><td rowspan="2">Name</td><td colspan="3">p
d</td></tr>
<tr><td>dd</td><td>mm</td><td>yy</td></tr>
<tr><td></td><td></td><td></td><td></td></tr>
</table>

If we want to access name we write p.name. If date of birth is to be accessed, we can use p.d.dd, p.d.mm and p.d.yy.

Let us write a simple program which stores name and date of birth of n persons and displays list of person whose date of birth is in the month of June.

Program 1.97: To store name and date of birth and display list of persons whose birthday is in June.

```
void main( )
{
    struct dob
    {
        int dd, mm, yy;
    };
    struct person
    {
        char name [20];
        struct dob d;
    };
    struct person p[100];
    int i, j, n;
    printf("Enter number of persons \n");
    scanf("%d", &n);
    for(i=0;i<n;i++)
    {
        printf("Enter name \n");
        gets(p[i].name);
```

```
            printf("Enter data of birth in dd:mm:yy format");
            scanf("%d : %d : %d", &p[i].d.dd, &p[i].d.mm, &p[i].d.yy);
                                    //Note that there is : in between two %ds
                                    // You should use : while giving input
        }
        printf("List of persons whose date of birth in June is \n");
        for(i=0;i<n; i++)
        {
            if(p[i].d.mm == 6)
            printf("%s \t %d:%d:%d \n", p[i].name, p[i].d.dd, p[i].d.mm, p[i].d.yy);
        }
        getch( );
    }
```

1.5.7 Passing Structures to Functions

A function can be passed parameter of type int, float, char etc. We can also pass structure type data to a function and a function can return a structure. We can pass

1. Structure members individually,
2. Structure variables by value,
3. Structure variables by address,
4. An array of structure.

Let us see how we can do these:

1. Passing structure members individually: Consider following program.

Program 1.98: Passing structure member to function

```
    void cal_bonus(float);
    void main( )
    {
        struct person
        {
            char name[20];
            int age;
            float sal;
        };
        struct person p = {"aaa", 20, 2000}
        cal_bonus (p.sal);
    }
```

```
    void cal_bonus(float salary)
    {
        float bonus;
        bonus = salary * 0.5;
        printf("Bonus is %f", bonus);
    }
```

In program 7.9, we have passed salary of the person and calculated bonus in the function. The parameter is a float, hence the function argument is also float.

2. Passing structure by value:

Consider following program.

Program 1.99: Passing structure variable by value.

```
    void disp(struct person);
    void main( )
    {
        struct person p = {"abc" 20, 2000};
        disp (p);
    }
    void disp(struct person p)
    {
        printf("%s \t %d \t %f \n", p.name, page, p.sal);
    }
```

Output: abc 20   20000

Here, we are passing. the variable p to the function and all the fields will be available to the function which can be displayed.

Typedef:

Whenever one writes function that requires passing of structure, we have to repeatedly write the word struct and name of structure. In order to avoid this, we can create a short cut or alias for this using keyword typedef as:

```
    typedef struct person
    {
        char name [20];
        int age;
        float sal;
    }PER;
```

This means PER is an alias (another name) for struct person.

3. Passing structure by address:

Read the given program and find what will be its output.

Program 1.100: Passing structure by value.

```c
typedef struct person
{
    char name s[20];
    int age;
    float sal;
} PER;
void disp(PER);
void modify(PER);
void main( )
{
    PER p={ "abc", 20,20000};
    disp(p);
    modify(p);
    disp(p);
}
void disp(PER p)
{
    printf("%s \t %d \t %f \n", p.name, page, p.sal);
}
void modify(PER p)
{
    p.age=p.age+1;
    p.sal=1.1 *p.sal;
}
```

Output: abc 20   20000
            abc 20   20000

Explanation:

1. There are two functions disp and modify to which structure variable is passed by value.
2. When disp is called for the first time, main will pass the contents of p in main to p in disp and the records get displayed.

3. When modify is called, main will pass the contents of p in main to p in modify. The function modify will change age field of p to 21 and sal field to 22000; but these changes will be made in local variable p of modify and not of main. Hence, when control is back in main, its p is unchanged.

4. When disp is called second time, main will pass the contents of p in main to p in disp and they get displayed.

    Now, what if I want the function to modify the contents of structure variable passed to it? The answer is, we have to pass it by address as shown in program 7.12.

Program 1.101: Passing structure by address.

```c
typedef struct person
{
    char name 2[0];
    int age;
    float sal;
}PER;
void disp(PER);
void modify(PER *);
void main( )
{
    PER p={"abc",20, 20000};
    disp(p);
    modify(&p);
    disp(p);
}
void disp(PER p)
{
    printf("%s \t %d \t %f \n", p.name, page, p.sal);
}
void modify(PER *ptr)
{
    ptr->age-ptr->age+1;
    ptr->sal=1.1 *ptr->sal;
}
```

Output: abc 20   20000
            abc 21   22000

Explanation:

1. There are two functions disp and modify to which structure variable is passed by value and by address respectively.
2. When disp is called for the first time, main will pass the contents of p in main to p in disp and they get displayed.
3. When modify is called, main will pass the address of p in main to pointer ptr in modify. Hence, ptr is a pointer to location p. The function modify will change age field of p to 21 and sal field to 22000. Note that we have used operator -> to access the members of p. Hence, when control is back in main, its p has changed values.
4. When disp is called second time, main will pass the modified contents of p in main to p in disp and they get displayed.

4. Passing structure type array to function:

As we know if we have to pass an array to a function, we have to pass address of first element in the array to the function. Function argument should be pointer type variable. In this case, it should be pointer to structure. Let us consider a program to read a list of persons and sort it on the basis of age. We will write separate function for reading, sorting and displaying the records.

Program 1.102: Program to sort list of persons using separate functions for read, sort and display.

```c
typedef struct person
{
    char name [20];
    int age;
    float sal;
}PER;
void read_recs(PER *);
void disp_recs(PER *);
void sort_recs(PER *);
int n;
void main( )
{
    PERSON p[100];
    int i;
    printf("How many persons? \n");
    scanf("%d", &n);
```

```c
    read_recs(p);                       // Call read records function
    sort_recs(p);                       // Call sort records function
    disp_recs(p);                       // Call display records function
}
void read_recs(PER *ptr)
{
    int i;
    for(i=0;i<n;i++)
    {
        printf("Enter name \n");
        gets((ptr+i) -> name);
        printf("Enter age \n");
        scanf("%d", &(ptr+i) -> age);
        printf("Enter salary \n");
        scanf("%f", &(ptr+i) -> sal);
    }
}
void sort_recs(PER *ptr)
{
    int i, j;
    PER temp;
    for(i=0;i<n;i++)
    {
        for(j=i+1; j<n; j++)
            if(ptr+i)->age>(ptr+j)->age)
            {
                temp *(ptr + i);
                *(ptr+i) = *(ptr+i);
                (ptr+j) = temp;
            }
    }
}
void disp_recs (PER *ptr)
{
    int i, j
    for(i=0;i<n;i++)
        printf("%s \t %d \t %f \n", (ptr+i)->name, (ptr+i)->age, (ptr+i)->sal);
}
```

Explanation:
1. The main function has array p[100]. Its address p is passed to each function.
2. The function accepts the address in pointer variable ptr. Thus, ptr has address of first record, ptr+1 is address of second record. In general, i+1th record can be accessed through ptr+i.

1.5.8 Returning a Structure from Function

Individual structure members or entire structure can be returned back via a return statement at the access point in the calling function. If individual structure member is returned, return type of the function will be the same as type of structure member. If structure is returned, the return type of the function is same as that of structure type.

Consider following example of addition of two rational numbers represented as struct type.
Program 1.103: Addition of two rational numbers.

```
typedef struct rational
{
    int num, den;
} RAT;
RAT add(RAT, RAT)
void main( )
{
    RAT r1 = {2,3}, r2 {4,5}, r3;
    r3 = add(r1, r2);
    printf("%d /%d", r3.num, r3.den);
}
RAT add(RAT rl, RAT r2)
{
    RAT r3;
    r3.num = r1.num r2.den + r1.den r2.num;
    r3.den = r1.den r2.den;
    return(r3);
}
```

Explanation:
1. The num and den are numerator and denominator of rational numbers.
2. The function add accepts two struct type(RAT) variables r1, r2; calculates numerator and denominator of resultant rational number r3 and returns it.

1.5.9 Arrays as an ADT Insertion, Deletion and Traversals of Array

An ordered or Linear List is most simple and common data object. A Linear List consists of set of elements. It is represented as,

$$L = \{e_1, e_2, e_3, ..., e_n\}$$

where e_1, e_2, e_3, ..., etc. are elements in the List. Here, e_1, e_2, e_3, etc. can be integers, real numbers, characters, strings or records. They can be even enumerated data items also. An example of list is shown below:

(i)   List of integers:

   $L_1 = \{10, 20, 30, 40, 50\}$

(ii)   List of real numbers:

   $L_2 = \{2.5, 7.5, -8.3, 3.8, 11.57\}$

(iii)   List of characters:

   $L_3 = \{'a', 'b', 'c', 'd', 'e'\}$

(iv)   List of names:

   $L_4 = ("Sunil", "Anil", "Nitin", "Seema", "Rima"\}$

(v)   List of records:

   $L_5 = \{\{"abc", 20\}, \{"xyz", 25\}, \{"pqr", 30\}\}$

(vi)   List of days:

   $L_6 = \{Monday, Tuesday, Wednesday, Thursday\}$

The data structure that we can use for storing these lists is array. For example, the list L_1 can be stored in an array of integers, L_2 can be stored in an array of float, etc. There are number of operations that can be done on these lists. These operations are:

1.   Display the list.
2.   Search an element.
3.   Find length of the list.
4.   Modifying an element.
5.   Insert an element in the list.
6.   Delete an element in the list.
7.   Sort the list.
8.   Reverse the list.

We might require to perform all these operations or part of these operations on the list. The efficiency of these operations will depend on the way in which the data is stored i.e., data structure. Since, the only data structure we know now is an array. Let us implement a list of records using array.

Program 1.104: Write a program to implement list of employees having empno, name and age and perform following operations:

(i)   Display,

(ii) Search,

(iii) Insert,

(iv) Delete,

(v) Sort,

(vi) Append.

Let we write a menu driven program. For each of the operation specified eve need to write separate functions.

```c
#include<conio.h>
#include<stdio.h>
typedef struct employee
{
    int empno;
    char name[20];
    int age;
}   emp;
#define max 100
void disp( );
void search( );
void insert( );
void delete( );
void sort( );
void append( );
EMP e[MAX];
int n;
void main( )
{
    int i, ch;
    printf("Enter number of number of records\n");
    scanf("%d", &n);
    for(i=0;i<n;i++)
    {
        printf("Enter empno \n");
```

```c
            scanf("%d", & e[i].&empno);
            printf("Enter name \n");
            gets(e[i].name);
            printf("Enter age \n");
            scanf("%d", &e[i].age);
    }
    do
    {
        clrscr( );
        printf("1. Disp \n 2. Search \n 3. Insert \n 4. Delete \n 5. Sort \n 6.
        Append \n 7. Exit\n");
        printf("Enter your choice \n");
        scanf("%d", & ch);
        switch (ch)
        {
            case 1:  disp( );
                    break;
            case 2:  search( );
                    break;
            case 3 : insert( );
                    break;
            case 4:  delete( );
                    break;
            case 5:  sort( );
                    break;
            case 6:  append( );
            getch( );
    } while (ch!=7);
}
void disp( )
{
    int i;
    for(i=0;i<n;i++)
        printf("%d \t %s \t %d \n", e[i].empno, e[i].name, e[i].age); ·
}
```

```c
void search( )
{
    int i, s;
    printf("Enter employee number \n");
    scanf("%d", &s);
    flag = 1;
    for(i=0;i<n;i++)
    {
        if (e[i].empno==s)
        {
            printf("%s \t %d \n", e[i].name, e[i].age);
            flag=0;
            break;
        }
    }
    if (flag==1)
        printf("Not found");
}
void insert( )
{
    int i, loc;
    printf("Enter location for new record (location starts from 0) \n");
    scanf("%d", &loc);
    for (i=n-1;i>=loc;i--)
        e[i+1] = e[i];
    printf("Enter empno \n");
    scanf("%d", &e[loc].empno);
    printf("Enter name \n");
    gets(e[loc].name);
    printf("Enter age \n");
    scanf("%d", &e[loc].age);
    n++;
}
void del( )
{
    int i, loc;
```

```c
        printf("Enter record number to be deleted (location starts from 0) \n");
        scanf("%d", &loc);
        for(i=loc;i<n;i++)
            e[i-1] = e[i];
        n--;
}
void sort( )                          // namewise sorting
{
    int i, j;
    Emp temp;
    for(i=0;i<n;i++)
    {
        for(j=0;j<n-1-i;j++)
        {
            if (strcmp(e[j].name, e[j+1].name)>0)
            {
                temp = e[j]
                e[j] = e[j+1]
                e[j+1] = temp;
            }
        }
    }
}
void append( )
{
    printf("Enter empno \n");
    scanf("%d", &e[n].empno);
    printf("Enter name \n");
    gets(e[n].name);
    printf("Enter age \n");
    scanf("%d", &e[n].age);
    n++;
}
```

Note:

1. We have declared array e[ ] globally, so that it will be available to all functions and we need not pass it to them.

2. The variable n which stores number of records is also global. Since it gets changed in insert and delete, it should be made available to these functions.

3. In insert function, we have shifted all the records down from the location onwards, so that there is a space created to insert new record and since one record is added n is incremented by 1.
4. In delete function, the records are shifted up from the location onwards. Since one record is deleted, n is decremented by 1.
5. The sort function sorts the records namewise. Bubble sort is used.
6. Append function adds one records at the nth position because, last record is at $(n-1)^{th}$ position.
7. If the array e[ ] and n declared local as variables in main function, we need to pass these to the function. We may require to pass n by address wherever it gets changed otherwise it can be passed by value.

1.6 Storage Class in C

(i)   Automatic variables
(ii)   External variables
(iii) Static variables
(iv)   Register variables
(v)   Scopes and longevity of above types of variables.

1.6.1 Few Concept about the Storage Classes

1. **Scope:** The scope of a variable determines over what part(s) of the program a variable is actually available for use (active).
2. **Longevity:** It refers to the period during which a variables retains a given value during execution of a program(alive)
3. **Local(internal) variables:** Are those which are declared within a particular function.
4. **Global (external) variables:** Are those which are declared outside any function.

Automatic Variables:
•   Are declare inside a function in which they are to be utilized.
•   Are declared using a keyword auto.
    e.g. auto intnumber;
•   Are created when the function is called and destroyed automatically when the function is exited.
•   This variable are therefore private(local) to the function in which they are declared.
•   Variables declared inside a function without storage class specification is, by default, an automatic variable.

Example Program of the Automatic Variables:

```c
int main( )
{
    int m=1000;
    function2( );
    printf("%d\n", m);
}
function1( )
{
    int m=10;
    printf("%d\n", m);
}
function2( )
{
    int m=100;
    function1( );
    printf("%d\n", m);
}
```

Output:

```
10
100
1000
```

Few observation about auto variables

- Any variable local to main will normally live throughout the whole program, although it is active only in main.
- During recursion, the nested variables are unique **auto** variables.
- Automatic variables can also be defined within blocks. In that case they are meaningful only inside the blocks where they are declared.
- If automatic variables are not initialized they will contain garbage.

External Variables

- These variables are declared outside any function.
- These variables are active and alive throughout the entire program.
- Also known as global variables and default value is zero.
- Unlike local variables they are accessed by any function in the program.

- In case local variable and global variable have the same name, the local variable will have precedence over the global one.
- Sometimes the keyword externused to declare these variable.
- It is visible only from the point of declaration to the end of the program.

Example program of the external variable:

```
int number;                          int count;
float length = 7.5;                  main( )
main( )                              { count=10;
{ . . .
                                          . . .
    . . .
}                                         . . .
function1( )                         }
{ . . .                              function( )
                                     { int count=0;
    . . .
}                                         . . .

                                          . . .

                                     count=count+1;
```

The variable number and length are variable for use in all three function

When the function refernces the variable count, it will be referencing only its local variable, not the global one

Example of the Global Variable:

```
int x;                               int fun3( )
int main( )                          {
{                                        x=x+10;
    x=10;                                return(x);
    printf("x=%d\n",x);              }
    printf("x=%d\n",fun1( ));
    printf("x=%d\n",fun2( ));
    printf("x=%d\n",fun3( ));
}
int fun1( )
{   x=x+10;
    return(x);
```

Once a variable has been declared global any function can use it and change its value. The subsequent functions can then reference only that new value

```
}
int fun2( )
{    int x
     x=1;
     return(x);
}
```

Output:
```
x=10
x=20
x=1
x=30
```

External declaration:

- As far as main is concerned, y is not defined. So compiler will issue an error message.
- There are two way out at this point.
    1. Define y before main.
    2. Declare y with the storage class extern in main before using it.

Example of the External Declaration:

```
int main( )
{
    extern inty;
    . . .
    . . .
}
func1( )
{
    extern inty;
    . . .
    . . .
}
int y;
```

Note that extern declaration does not allocate storage space for variables.

Multifile Programs and External Variables:

file1.c	file2.c
`int main( )`	`int ;`
`{`	`function2( )`
`   extern int m;`	`{`
`   int i`	`   int i`

```
        . . .

        . . .

}
function1( )
{
    int j;

        . . .

        . . .

}
```

```
        . . .

        . . .

}
function3( )
{
        int count;

        . . .

        . . .

}
```

Multifile Programs and Extern Variables:

```
file1.c
int m;
int main( )
{
    int i;

        . . .

        . . .

}
function1( )
{
    int j;

        . . .

        . . .

}
```

```
file2.c.
extern int m;
function2( )
{
        int i

        . . .

        . . .

}
function3 ( )
{
        int count;

        . . .

        . . .

}
```

Static Variables:

- The value of static variables persists until the end of the program.
- It is declared using the keyword staticlike

    ```
    static intx;
    static float y;
    ```

- It may be of external or internal type depending on the place of there declaration.
- Static variables are initialized only once, when the program is compiled.

Internal static variable

- Are those which are declared inside a function.
- Scope of Internal staticvariables extend uptothe end of the program in which they are defined.
- Internal staticvariables are almost same as autovariable except they remain in existence (alive) throughout the remainder of the program.
- Internal staticvariables can be used to retain values between function calls.

Example program of the internal static variable:

- Internal static variable can be used to count the number of calls made to function. e.g.

```c
int main( )
{
    int I;
    for(i=1;i<=3;i++)
        stat( );
}
void stat( )
{
    static intx=0;
    x = x+1;
    printf("x= %d\n",x);
}
```

Output:

```
x=1
x=2
x=3
```

External Static Variables

- An external static variable is declared outside of all functions and is available to all the functions in the program.
- An external static variable seems similar simple external variable but their difference is that static external variable is available only within the file where it is defined while simple external variable can be accessed by other files.

Static function

- Static declaration can also be used to control the scope of a function.
- If you want a particular function to be accessible only to the functions in the file in which it is defined and not to any function in other files, declare the function to be static. e.g.
  static intpower(intx inty)

```
{
. . .
. . .
}
```

Register Variable

- These variables are stored in one of the machine's register and are declared using register keyword.

  e.g. register intcount;
- Since register access are much faster than a memory access keeping frequently accessed variables in the register lead to faster execution of program.
- Since only few variable can be placed in the register, it is important to carefully select the variables for this purpose. However, C will automatically convert register variables into non-registervariables once the limit is reached.
- Don't try to declare a global variable as register. Because the register will be occupied during the lifetime of the program.

SUMMARY

- Functions are independent programs which do a specific task.
- The function consists of function header with argument, local variables and body of function.
- A function can be called in any function of the program.
- The variables or values which we pass to the function are called as parameters.
- The function accepts parameters in the variables which are called as function arguments.
- The function parameters and arguments should match in number, type and order.
- A function can return only one value. The return type of the function is the type of value returned by the function.
- A function that does not return a value and can have its return type void.

- Every function should have function prototype declaration.
- A function which calls itself is called recursive function. The repetitive process represented by loops in the function can be replaced by recursion.
- The address operator (&) is used to find address of a variable stored in memory.
- The value operator (*) is used to access value stored at the specified address location.
- Pointer variable stores address of a location in the memory.
- Value stored at a particular address location can be accessed through pointer variable using * operator.
- We can pass parameters to the function in two different ways.
  1. By value,
  2. By address or reference.
- The parameters which are passed to the function are not affected by the modifications made by the function in corresponding arguments.
- The parameters which are passed by address can be modified by the function as the function has access to the locations where the parameters are stored.
- A pointer can be used to store address of a location in the memory and it can access all the successive locations also.
- A malloc function is used to allocate a block memory to a pointer variable which can access data stored in the block. In other words, a single pointer variable can be used to replace one dimensional array variable.
- An array of pointers can be used to represent a two dimensional array. Each element in the array of pointers will store the address of each row.
- String is an array of characters, used to store group of characters such as words, names, sentences etc.
- In built string functions are used to manipulate characters in a string.
- A char type pointer can be used to access characters stored in a string.
- An array of strings is used to store number of separate strings.
- An array can be passed to a function by passing address of first element in the array or name of array.
- Structure is a user defined or constructed data type which can combine different data types. So that the collection of data can be represented using single name.
- A structure definition consists of structure name and structure members called fields.
- A dot (·) operator is used to access structure members.
- An array of structure is used to store records which are nothing but collection of related fields.
- We can have a structure type pointer variable which can store address of structure variable.

- An arrow ($\rightarrow$) operator is used to access members of structure through structure type pointer variable.
- We can declare structure variable inside another structure definition which is called nested structure.
- A structure variable can be passed to a function by address or by value.
- Unions are similar to structures except that the members of union share the same memory location, whereas each member of structure is allocated separate memory.
- Bit wise operator &, |, ^, ~, <<, >> are used to manipulate individual bits stored in memory.
- The sequential representation of data elements is called ordered list. We can do various operations on the list such as display, insert, delete, modify etc.
- A polynomial in single variable can be represented using two techniques:
  (i)   Simple array,
  (ii) Array of structures.

SOLVED PROBLEMS

1. Write a program to add two complex numbers.

Solution:

```c
void main( )
{
    struct complex
    {
        float real, image;
    };
    struct complex c1, c2, c3;
    printf("Enter first complex number's real and imag part \n");
    scanf("%f%f", &c1.real, &c1.imag);
    printf("Enter second complex number's real and imag part \n");
    scanf("%f%f", &c2.real, &c2.imag);
    c3.real = c1.real + c2.real;
    c3.imag = c1.imag + c2.imag;
    printf("The addition is %.2f + %.2f \n", c1.real, c3.imag);
}
```

2. Define a structure called cricket that will describe following information:
   (i)   Player name,
   (ii) Team name,
   (iii) Batting average.

Using this, declare an array player with 50 elements. Write a function in 'C' to print the player name, team name and batting average for that player having highest batting average.

Solution:

```
struct cricket
{
    char pname[20];
    char tname[20];
    float avg;
};
struct cricket player[50];
void display (struct cricket player[ ], int n)
{
    int i, pos=0; float max;
    max = player[0].avg;
    for(i=1;i<n;i++)
    {
        if(player[i].avg>max)
            pos = i;
    }
    printf("%s \t %s \t %f \n", player[pos].pname, player[pos].tname, player[pos].avg);
}
```

3. What will be output of following program?

Solution:

```
void main( )
{
    int a = 10, b = 20, c, d, e;
    c = a & b;
    d = a | b;
    e = ~a;
    printf("%d %d %d", c, d, e );
}
```

a = 10 ⇒ 0000000000001010
b = 20 ⇒ 0000000000010100
Hence,
c = a & b ⇒ 0000000000000000 ⇒ 0
c = a | b ⇒ 0000000000011110 ⇒ 30
e = ~a ⇒ 1111111111110101 ⇒ −11

Hence output will be,

0 30 −11

4. **Database of 100 students is required to be stored. Each student record contains fields such as roll no, name, total marks. Write a program in 'c' to input the database with above fields mentioned above. Using:**

   (i) arrays,

   (ii) Array of structure. Display record of students who scored maximum marks.

Solution:

(i) Program using arrays:

```c
void main( )
{
    int m[100];
    char name[100][20];
    int marks [100];
    int i, max, index;
    for(i=0;i<100;i++)
    {
        printf("Enter roll no \n");
        scanf("%d", &rn[i]);
        printf("Enter name \n");
        gets(name[i]);
        printf("Enter marks \n");
        scanf("%d", &marks[i]);
    }
    index = 0;
    max = marks[0];
    for(i=1;i<100;i++)
    {
        if (marks[i])>max)
        {
            max = marks[i];
            index = i;
        }
    }
    printf("%d %s %d", rn[index], name[index], marks[index]);
}
```

(ii) Program using structure:

```c
void main( )
{
    struct student
    {
        int m;
        char name[20];
        int marks;
    }s[100];
    int i, max, index;
    for(i=0;i<100;i++)
    {
        printf("Enter roll no \n");
        scanf("%d", &s[i].rn);
        printf("Enter name \n");
        gets(s[i].name);
        printf("Enter age \n");
        scanf("%d", &s[i].marks);
    }
    max = s[0].marks;
    index = 0;
    for (i=1;i<100;i++)
    {
        if(s[i].marks>max)
        {
            max = s[i].marks;
            index=i;
        }
    }
printf("%d %s %d \n", s[index].rn, s[index].name, s[index].marks);
}
```

EXERCISE

1. What is recursive function? Explain how it works with a proper example.
2. What is recursion? How does the recursion works? Generate the nth terms of Fibonocci number with recursion.
3. What is recursive function? Explain how it works using proper example.
4. Write a recursive function to find factorial of number.
5. What is recursive function? Write a recursive function to find x^n.
6. Write a C function to calculate X^n using recursion.
7. Explain the term recursive function. Write a function in 'C' to find a factorial of a number which is greater than zero.
8. Define the following terms.
    (i) Data structure
    (ii) ADT.
9. What is pointer and how it is initialized?
10. Illustrate the following parameter passing techniques with suitable example.
    (i) Call by value.
    (ii) Call by reference.
11. What are the different parameter passing techniques in 'C' functions. Explain each of them with suitable example.
12. Write 'C' function to interchange two numbers using pointers.
13. What do you mean by function call by value and function call by reference? Write a pseudo code to explain the difference between function call by value and function call by reference.
14. Differentiate between function call by value and call by reference with the help of suitable example.
15. What are different parameter passing techniques? Explain each technique with suitable example.
16. Explain with suitable example, a function call be reference and function call by value.
17. With the help of suitable example, explain call by value and call by reference.
18. Write a C function to interchange two numbers using pointers.
19. Explain the malloc function.
20. What is static and dynamic allocation?
21. Explain how a pointer can be used to replace an array.
22. Explain with example how pointer variable can be used to access elements in contiguous locations.
23. Explain how array of pointers can be used to replace 2-D array.
24. What do you mean by array of pointers? Differentiate between array of pointers and pointer to array with the help of suitable example.
25. Explain different methods of storage representation in 2-D array.

26. Explain different methods of storage representation in two-dimensional array. Explain address calculation.
27. Explain different methods of storage representation in two-dimensional array. Explain address calculation.
28. Explain row major order and column major order representation of 2-dimensional arrays.
29. What is string variable? Explain how it is used.
30. What is string? Explain the usage of string function strlen and strcmp.
31. Explain how an array is passed to function.
32. Explain any four string functions.
33. Write recursive and non-recursive functions for binary search.
34. Write a propram to count number of alphabets in a given string.
35. Write a program to count number of vowels and consonants in a string.
36. Write a program to count number of words in a string.
37. What is the purpose of structure in 'C'? Can we define the structure into structure? Give suitable examples.
38. What is purpose of structure in 'C'? Can we define the structure into structure? Give suitable example.
39. What are structures? Explain its use. Define structure having name, age and salary.
40. Explain structure and union in 'C' in detail with suitable example.
41. What is union? Explain with some suitable examples. How union is declared and used in C?
42. Compare structure and union in 'C'.
43. Differentiate between structure and union
44. Explain structure and union in 'C' in detail with suitable example.
45. Write difference between union and structure with example.
46. Write a program to print whether the bit 2nd, 4th and 6th are set or not in a given number.
47. With example explain any one bit wise operators.
48. What is meant by an ordered list?
49. What is meant by an ordered list? Explain with example how a polynomial in a single variable can be represented as an ordered list. Mention at least two ways and compare their representations.
50. Explain how a polynomial can be represented using array of int or float.
51. Explain how a polynomial can be represented using array of structure.
52. Write algorithm to find addition of two polynomials using array of structure.
53. How a polynomial in a single variable can be represented in an array? Write C function to add two polynomial represented in an array?
54. Mention two different ways of representing a polynomial in array. Given a 'C' declaration for the same.

✱✱✱

Unit II

STACKS AND QUEUES

2.1 Introduction

Stack is a linear data structure where the element which is inserted last can only be taken out first. Thus, it is called LIFO (Last In First Out) type of data structure.

Stack is also defined as a data structure where all addition and deletion are made only at one end called top. It is similar to a real life situation of stack of things. If we keep things stacked one on to the another, we can take out the thing at the top. Similarly, we can keep a new thing on the top.

Stack can be implemented using:

1. Arrays,
2. Linked lists.

Following four operations can be done on a stack.

1. **Push operation:** In this, an element is stored at a location indicated by top.
2. **Pop operation:** In this operation, the element at the top is removed.
3. **Stack Full:** When all the locations reserved for stack are occupied, we can't insert any more elements. This condition is stack full condition.
4. **Stack empty:** When there is no element left on a stack, we can't pop any element. This condition is called as stack empty condition.

2.2 Stack as an Abstract Data Type (ADT)

The ADT for stack can be given as follows:

Definition: A stack is a restricted list in which entries are added and removed from the same end, called the top. This strategy is known as last-in-first-out (LIFO) strategy.

Operations (methods) on stacks:

push(item)	Inserts item on the top of the stack
pop( )	Removes the top item
size( )	Returns the number of items in the stack
empty( )	Returns true if the stack is empty
full( )	Returns true if the stack is full
ontop( )	Returns the top element without removing it from the stack

Multiple stacks using single array:
We have seen that multiple stacks can be implemented using multiple arrays. We can use single array also to implement multiple stack. For this we can divide the array into number of parts. Each part will be used as one stack. The top of each stack will be initialized to the starting index of each part in the array. For implementing stack full or stack empty condition, we can use a counter for each stack. The counter will be incremented when push operation is done and decremented when pop operation is done. Stack full condition occurs when the counter reaches maximum value (size of each stack). Stack empty condition occurs when counter becomes starting index of each stack.

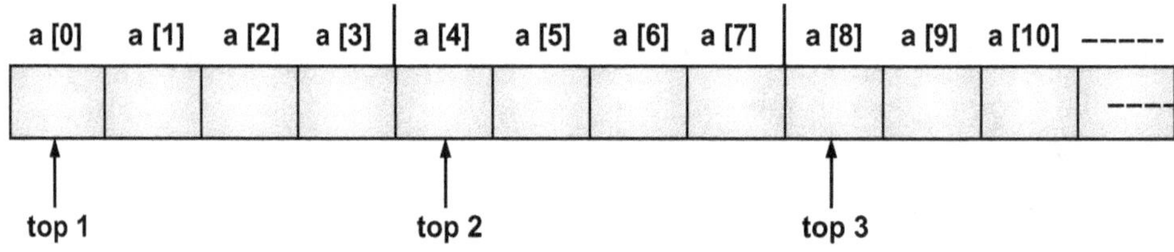

Fig. 2.1: Multiple stacks using single array

Two stacks can be efficiently implemented using single array by using the upper part of the, array for first stack and lower part for second array, The top of first stack will be initialized to −1, it will be incremented when push operation is done and decremented in pop operation. The top of the second stack is initialized to MAX (size of the array). It is decremented in push operation and incremented in pop operation.

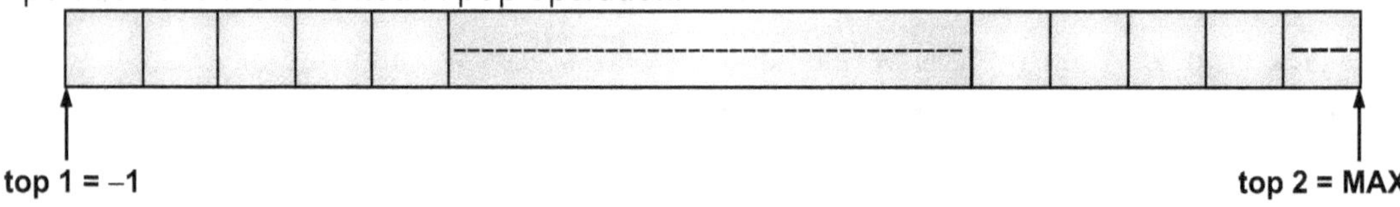

Fig. 2.2: Two stacks using single array

2.3 Stack Using Array

To represent a stack using array, we require an array of some size to be declared say int a[4]. This will create a space for storing elements on stack. The size of the stack is 4. We will require one more variable say top which will be an index to the top element of the stack. Initially, the stack is empty. The variable top will be initialized to −1.

Push operation:
Now, if we want to store a number 10 on the stack, we can increment top and the element 10 will be stored at location a[0].

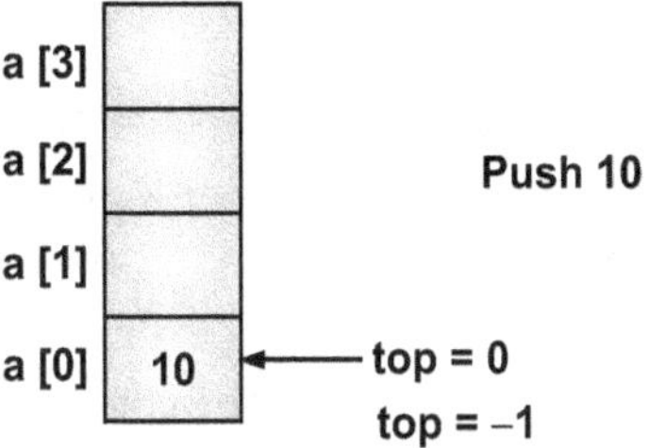

Fig. 2.3(a): Push (10)

Next, we store a number 20 on the stack, top will be incremented to 1 and element 20 will be stored at location a[1].

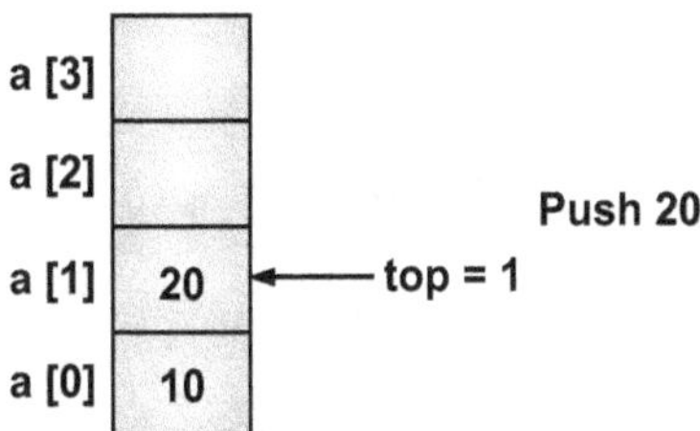

Fig. 2.3(b): Push (20)

Next, we store a number 30 on the stack, top will be incremented to 2 and element 30 will be stored at location a[2].

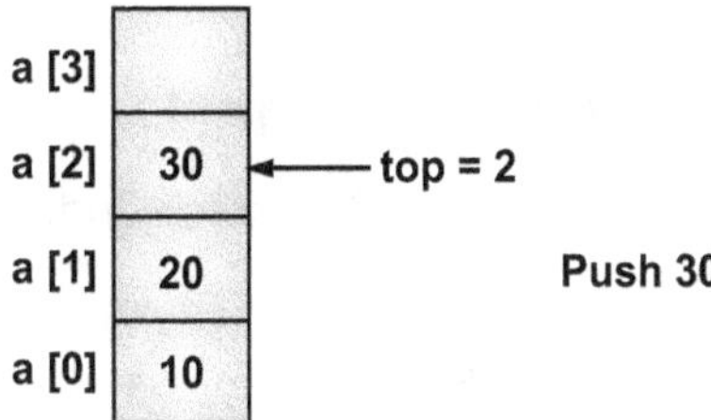

Fig. 2.3(c): Push (30)

Next, we store a number 40 on the stack, top will be incremented to 3 and element 40 will be stored at location a[3].

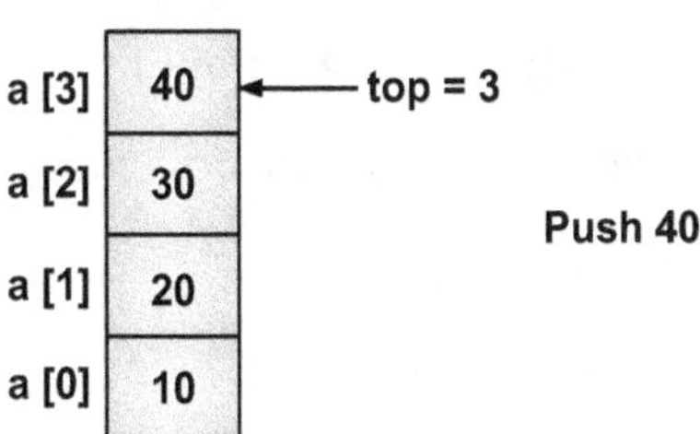

Fig. 2.3(d): Push (40)

Now there is no space left on the stack, hence, the stack is full. The condition for stack full is top becomes equal to maximum size of array −1.

Pop Operation:

Now, suppose we want to remove an element from the stack, we can access element at the top which is given by the index value in top. Consider the stack where we have already pushed four elements. If we carry out pop operation, the element at the top i.e., 40 will be accessed and top is decremented to 2.

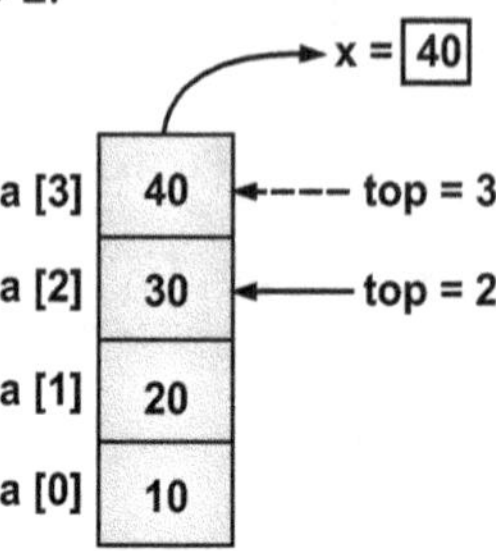

Fig. 2.4(a): x = pop( )

The next pop operation will remove 30 from the stack and top will be decremented to 1.

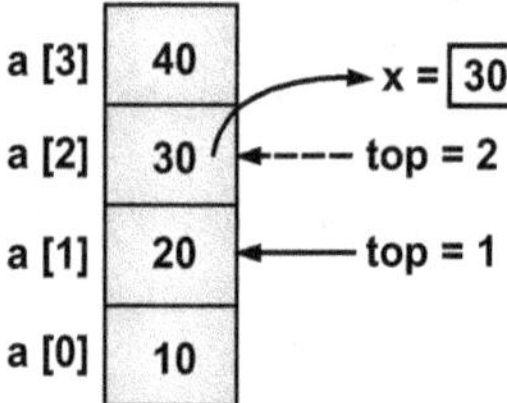

Fig. 2.4(b): x = pop( )

Another pop operation will remove 20 from the stack and top will be decremented to 0.

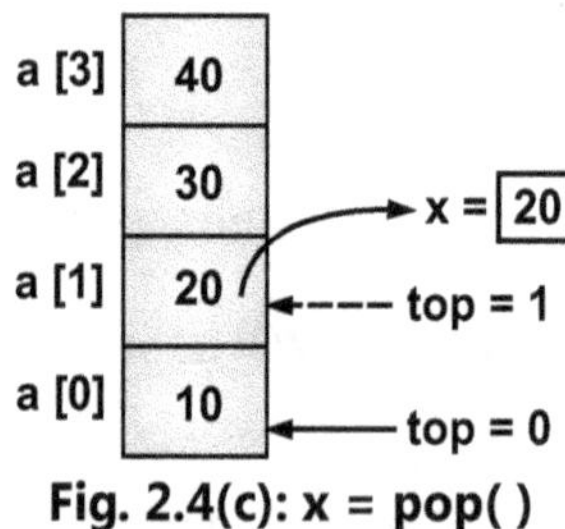

Fig. 2.4(c): x = pop( )

If the operation is carried out again, element 10 will be removed and top becomes −1.

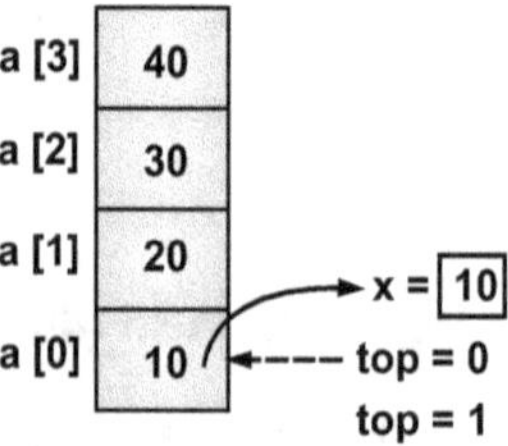

Fig. 2.4(d): x = pop( )

Then we can't remove any more elements because stack is empty. The condition for stack empty is top == −1. The program for implementation of stack will require two functions push and pop whose algorithms areas follows:

1. **Push (x):**
   (i)   If top == MAX −1
              print "stack full";
   (ii) else
              top ++;
              a [top] = x;
   (iii) Return.

Every time we do a push operation, we need to increment top and store the data at the location given by top in the array. But before we do this operation, we have to check whether the stack is full or not. Hence, the condition top ==MAX −1.

2. **x = pop( )**
   (i)   If top=−1
              print "stack empty";
              return −9999;
   (ii) else
              x = a [top]
              top −−;
              return x;

Every time we do a pop operation, we remove an element and then decrement top. But before we do this, we have to check whether the stack is empty or not. Hence, the condition top == −1. Note that we are returning −9999 when stack is empty. This is an indication for the calling function, so that it takes appropriate action when the stack is empty. The complete program for stack implementation is as follows:

Program 2.1: To implement stack using array. (Version 1)

```
#define MAX 5
int a [MAX];
int top = -1;
void push (int x)
{
       if (top == MAX - 1)
```

```c
        printf("Stack is full");
    else
    {
    top ++;
    a[top]=x;
    }
}
int pop( )
{
    int x;
    if (top == -1)
    {
        print("Stack is empty \n");
        return (-9999);
    }
    else
    {
        x = a[top];
        top --;
        return (x);
    }
}
main( )
{
    int ch, x;
    do
    {
        clrscr( );
        printf(" 1. Push \n. 2. Pop \n. 3. Exit \n");
        printf("Enter your choice \n");
        scanf("%d", &ch);
        switch (ch)
        {
            case 1: printf("Enter a number \n");
                    scanf("% d", &x);
                    push (x);
```

```
                        break;
            case 2: x = pop( );
                    if (x!= -9999)
                        printf("% d", x);
        }
        getch( );
    } while (ch!=3);
}
```

We can implement separate functions for stack full and stack empty conditions as follows:

```
int stk_full( )
{
    if (top == MAX -1)
    {
        printf("Stack full");
        return (1);
    }
    else
        return (0);
}
```

The function returns 1 when stack is full otherwise 0.

```
int stk_empty( )
{
    if (top == -1)
    {
        print ("Stack is empty");
        return (1);
    }
    else
        return (0);
}
```

The function returns 1 when stack is empty otherwise 0.
These functions can be used in functions 'push' and 'pop' as follows:

```
void push (int x)
{
    if (!stk_full( ))
    {
        top ++;
        a[top] = x;
    }
}
int pop( )
{
    if (!stk_empty( ))
    {
        int x;
        x = a[top];
        top --;
        return x;
    }
    else
        return (-9999);
}
```

The stack consists of an array and top. If multiple stacks are to be implemented in single program, we need to define separate arrays and tops for each stack. Instead, we can define a stack variable for a stack which combines array and top together.

```
typedef struct stack
{
    int a[4];
    int top;
} STK;
```

Now if we declare a variable STK s1; it consists of an array and top as shown in Fig. 2.5.

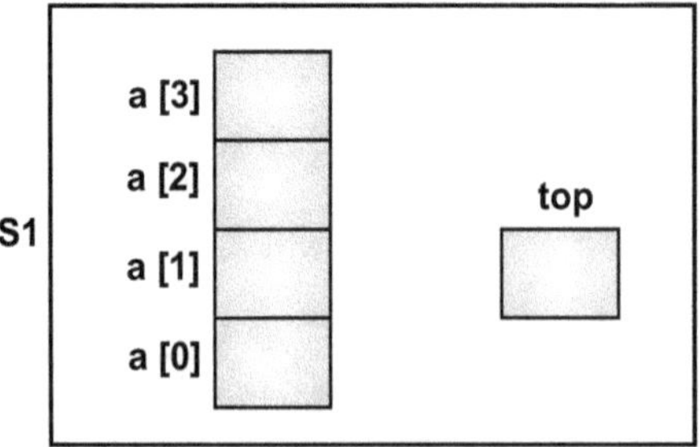

Fig. 2.5: Stack using structure

The elements in the stack can be accessed using dot operate, e.g., if top of the stack is to be initialized, we can write s1.top = −1 or if 10 is to be stored at the top of the stack; we can write s1.a [s1.top] = 10. But the major advantage of this struct type stack will be when more than one stack is to be implemented. The push and pop functions require the stack variable to be passed to them. Since these functions are going to modify the contents of the stack variable, we have to pass it by address. Hence, the function parameter will be pointer to a structure.

The push function will have prototype as,

void push (STK*, int)

The first argument is the pointer to the stack in which we are going to store the element and second argument is the integer number to be stored on the stack.

The pop function will have prototype as,

int pop (STK *)

The argument is the pointer to the stack from which number returns will be popped. A complete program using this is given as follows:

Program 2.2: Implementation of stack

```c
#define MAX 5
typedef struct stack
{
    int a[MAX];
    int top;
} STK;
void push (STK*, int);
int pop (STK *);
main( )
{
    STK s1, s2;
    s1.top = -1;
    s2.top = -1;
    push (&s1, 10);
    push (&s1, 20);
    push (&s2, 100);
    push (&s2, 200);
    x = pop (&s1);
    printf("%d", x);
    x = pop (&s1);
    printf("%d", x);
```

```c
        x = pop (&s2);
        printf("%d", x);
        x = pop (&s2);
        printf("%d", x);
}
void push (STK *s, int x)
{
    if (s->top == MAX -1)
        printf("Stack is full");
    else
    {
        (s->top) ++;
        s->a [s->top] = x;
    }
}
int pop (STK *s)
{
    int x;
    if (s->top == -1)
    {
        printf("Stack is empty");
        return (-9999);
    }
    else
    {
        x=s->a [s->top];
        (s->top) --;
        return (x);
    }
}
```

Explanation:

1. The main function has two variables s1 and s2 which are stacks.
2. The functions push and pop are passed addresses of stack. It is because the functions are going to change the contents of stack. Since we are passing the structure variable by address, the structure members are accessed using -> operator, e.g., top of stack is accessed through s as s -> top.

3. Note that though we are using two stacks, we have only one structure declaration and same functions push and pop for both the stacks.

4. We can modify the menu driven program we had written earlier for implementation of stack.

Program 2.3: To implement stack using array (version 2).

```
void push (STK *, int);
int pop (STK*);
void main( )
{
    STK s1;
    int ch, x;
    s1.top = -1;
    do
    {
        clrscr( );
        printf(" Push \n 2, Pop \n 3. Exit \n");
        printf("Enter your choice");
        scanf("%d", &ch);
        switch (ch)
        {
            case 1:  printf("Enter data \n");
                     scanf("%d", &x);
                     push (&s1, x);
                     break;
            case 2:  x = pop (&s1);
                     if (x! = -9999)
                         printf ("%d \n", x);
                     break;
        }
        getch( );
    } while (ch!=3);
}
```

2.3.1 Stack Using Linked List

The array implementation of stack is not efficient from the point of view of memory utilization. The fixed size of array is required and it remains allocated for the entire duration of the program. Linked list implementation will have advantage over the array implementation because we can allocate memory as and when it is required.

The stack using linked list consist of nodes having data and address of next node. The node definition will be,

```
typedef struct node
{
    int data;
    struct node *next;
} NODE;
```

A pointer called top can be declared (NODE *top) which will always point to the top of the stack. The operations push and pop will be implemented as follows:

Push Operation:

Step 1: Create a node.
Step 2: Store the data in the node.
Step 3: Link the next field of the node to the node where top is pointing.
Step 4: Point top to the recently created node.
Following figures show this operation.

Push (10):

Fig. 2.6(a): Stack using linked list push (10)

Push (20):

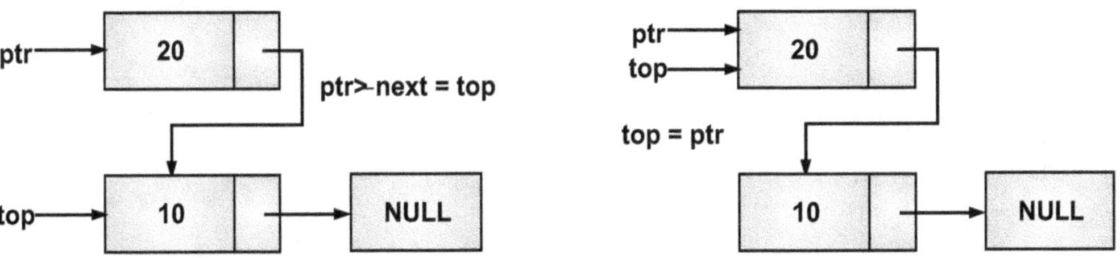

Fig. 2.6(b): Stack using linked list push (200)

Pop Operation:

Steps:

1. Make a pointer temp point to the top of the stack.
2. If it is NULL, then stack is empty.
3. If not, remove the data from this node then advance top.
4. De-allocate memory pointed by temp.

Following figures show this operation.

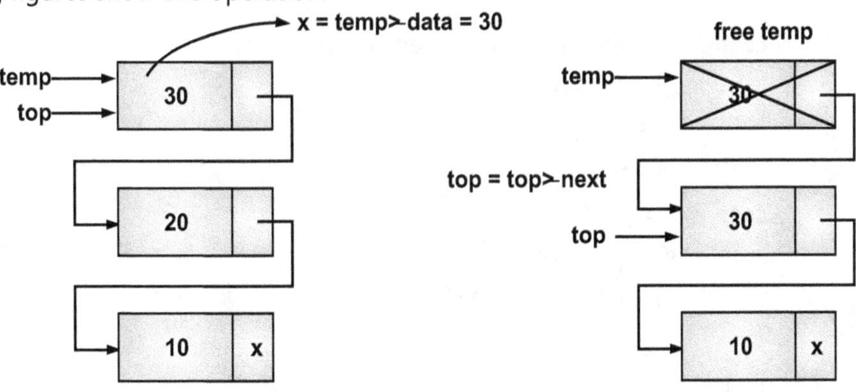

Fig. 2.7: Pop operation in stack using linked list

Following program implements stack using linked list. It has the function push and pop which has the-same prototype as that used in case of array. The function push accepts data, creates a node and puts it into a linked list. The function pop removes an element from the linked list and returns it.

Program 2.4: To implement stack using linked list.

```c
typedef struct node
{
    int data;
    struct node * next;
} NODE;
NODE *top = NULL;
void push (int);
int pop( );
void main( )
{
    int ch, x;
    do
    {
        clrscr( );
        printf(" 1. Push \n 2. Pop \n 3. Exit \n");
        printf("Enter your choice");
        scanf("%d", &ch);
        switch (ch)
        {
            case 1: printf("Enter a number \n");
                    scanf("%d", &x);
                    push (x);
                    break;
            case 2: x = pop( );
                    if (x!= -9999)
                        printf ("%d \n", x);
        }
        getch( );
    } while (ch!=3);
}
void push (int x)
{
    NODE *ptr;
    ptr = (NODE *) malloc (size of (NODE));
    if (ptr == NULL)
```

```c
            printf("Insufficient memory");
        else
        {
            ptr->data = x;
            ptr->next = top;
            top = ptr;
        }
    }
    int pop( )
    {
        NODE *temp; int x;
        temp = top;
        if (temp == NULL),
        {
            printf ("Stack empty");
            return (-9999);
        }
        else
        {
            x = temp->data;
            top = top->next;
            free (temp);
            return (x);
        }
    }
```

2.4 Application of Stack

Stack can be used in number of applications such as:

1. Conversion of expression.
2. Evaluation of expression.
3. Processing function calls.
4. Handling recursive function or removal of recursion.
5. Reversing a string.
6. Syntax checking e.g., parenthesis check.

2.5 Arithmetic Expression : Polish Notation

This is the most important application of stack. When we write a program, we write number of expressions (arithmetic, logical, etc.) in it. The compiler has to interpret and convert these expressions into machine language.

An expression consists of operands and operators, e.g., the expression a + b has two operands a and b and one operator +. This is a very simple expression. Expression can be very complex consisting of number of operands and operators. While converting an expression into correct machine language format, compiler has to take care of the priority of the operators. It is very difficult to directly produce a code for evaluation of expression. The solution to this is, convert the expression into a form which will not require priority of operators and the expression can be directly evaluated.

An expression can be written in three different forms:
1. **Infix Expression:** Operator is in between the two operands, e.g., a + b.
2. **Postfix Expression:** Operator is after the two operands, e.g., ab+. It is called Reverse polish notation.
3. **Prefix Expression:** Operator is before the two operands, e.g., +ab. It is called Polish notation.

Suppose we have an expression in infix format a + b * c.
Its postfix is abc * +
and prefix is + a * be

If you observe postfix and prefix expression, we find that these expressions can be evaluated directly without knowing the priority of operators. Whereas for infix expression we have to find out priority and then evaluate.

Before we learn how to evaluate the postfix expression let us see how to convert an infix expression to postfix or prefix.

If we are given an infix expression the a + b * c steps for conversion will be as follows:
1. Write the expression with full parenthesized as per the priority of operators as
   e.g. (a + (b * c))
2. Replace the innermost parenthesized expression with e_1 as:
   exp = (a + e_1) where e_1 = b * c
3. Replace the next innermost parenthesized expression with e_2.
   i.e. exp = e_2 where e_2 = a + e:
   Continue till you get a single expression.

4. Now go in reverse direction replacing each expression with postfix or prefix.

e.g., exp = ae_1 + or exp = + ae_1

exp = abc* +   exp = + a * bc

Hence the postfix expression is abc * +

and the prefix expression is + a * be.

Example 1: Convert following expressions into postfix and prefix expressions.

1. a * b + c
2. a * b + c * d
3. a + b + c + d
4. a * b/c* d − e/f
5. a ** b * c ** d

Solution:

1.   exp = ((a * b) + c)

= (e_1 + c) e_1 = a * b

= e_2 e_2 = e_1 + c

Postfix   **Prefix**

exp = e_2 exp = e_2

= e_1c +   = +e_1c

= ab * c+   = +* abc

2.   exp = ((a *b) + (c * d))

= (e_1 + e_2) e_1 = a * b e_2 = c * d

= e_2 e_2 = e_1 + e_2

Postfix   **Prefix**

exp = e_2 exp = e_2

= e_1 e_2 +   = +e_1 e_2

= ab * cd * +   = + * ab * cd

3.   exp = (((a + b) + c) +d)

= ((e_1 + c) + d) e_1 = a + b

= (e_1 + d) e_2 = e_1 + c

= e_3 e_3 = e_2 + d

Postfix   **Prefix**

exp = e_3 exp = e_3

= e_2d +   = +e_2d

= e_1c + d+   = ++$e_1$cd

= ab + c + d+   = +++ abcd

4.   exp $= a * b/c * d - e/f$

$= ((((a * b)/c) * d) - (e/f)$

$= (((e_1/c) * d) - e_2)$ $e_1 = a * b$ $e_2 = e/f$

$= ((e_3 * d) - e_2)$ $e_3 = e_1/c$

$= (e_4 - e_2)$ $e_4 = e_3 * d$

$= e_5$ $e_5 = e_4 - e_2$

Postfix   **Prefix**

exp $= e_5$ exp $= e_5$

$= e_4e_2 -$ $= -e_4\ e_2$

$= e_3d * e_2 -$ $= - * e_3de_2$

$= e_1c/d * e_2 -$ $= - * /e_1cd\ e_2$

$= ab * c/d * ef/ -$ $= - * / * abcd / ef$

5.   exp $= a**b*c**d - e$

where $**$ is raised to operator

$= (((a**b)*(c**d)) -e)$

$= ((e_1 * e_2) - e)$ $e_1 = a ** b$ $e_2 = c ** d$

$= (e_3 - e)$ $e_3 = e_1 * e_2$

$= e_4$ $e_4 = e_3 - e$

Postfix   **Prefix**

exp $= e_4$ exp $= e_4$

$= e_3\ e -$ $= -e_3\ e$

$= e_1\ e_2 * e -$ $= - e * e_1\ e_2$

$= ab**cd***e-$ $= -e***ab**cd$

2.5.1 Evaluation of Postfix Expression

Now let us see how we can evaluate a postfix expression. If we are given a postfix expression the expression is scanned from left till we come across an operator. The operator corresponds to previous two operands hence operate on the operand and result is an operand for next operator. Like this go on scanning till the end of the expression.

e.g. Suppose we have the expression 456 * +

1.   The first operator is *. It will operate on 5 and 6 to give 30. The resultant expression is 430 +.

2.   Next operator is +. It will operate on 4 and 30 to give the result is 34.

When we scan the expression and come across an operator we take latest two operands hence we can use a stack to store the operands, so that latest two operands can be accessed. Hence, the procedure for evaluation of postfix expression will be as follows:

1. Scan the expression.
2. In case of operand.
        push the operand on stack.
3. In case of operator
    Pop two operands from stack
    Do the operation
    Push the result on stack.
4. Repeat 2 and 3 till the end of expression.

The expression can be stored in a string and can be scanned character by character. The procedure is illustrated with example below:

Suppose we have the expression 456 * +.

Expression character	Action	Stack content
4	push	4 ...
5	push	4 5 ...
6	push	4 5 6 ...
*	pop 6	
	pop 5	
	push (5 * 6)	4 30 ...
+	pop 30	
	pop 4	
	push (30 + 4)	34 ...

Fig. 2.8: Evaluation of postfix expression 456*+

The detailed algorithm and program is:

Algorithm 2.1:
1. Read expression in string expr[ ]
2. i=0
3. while (expr [i] !='\0')   // while it is not end of string
    {
        if(expr[i] is operand)
            push (expr[i])

```
        else
        {
            op1 = pop( )
            op2 = pop( )
            v = op1 (operator in expr[i]) op2
            push (v)
        }
        i++;
    }
4.  result = pop( )
5.  print result
```

Program 2.5: To evaluate postfix expression.

```c
#define MAX 10
int stk [MAX];
int top = -1;
void push (int);
int pop( );
void main
{
    char expr[40];
    int i, op1, op2;
    clrscr( );
    printf("Enter expression \n");
    gets (expr);
    i=0;
    while (expr[i] != '\0')
    {
        if (isdigit(expr[i]))
            push (expr[i] -'0');
        else
        {
            op2 = pop( );
            op1 = pop( );
            switch (expr[i])
            {
                case '+':  push (op1 + op2);
                           break;
                case '-':  push (op1 - op2);
```

```c
                                break;
                case '*':    push (op1 * op2);
                                break;
                case '/':    push ((op1 / op2));
                                break;
            }
        }
        i++;
    }
    result=pop( );
    printf("The result is %d", result);
    getch( );
}
void push (int x)
{
    if (top == MAX -1)
        printf("Stack is full")
    else
    {
        top ++;
        stk [top] = x;
    }
}
int pop( )
{
    int x;
    if (top == -1)
    {
        print("Stack is empty \n");
        return (-9999);
    }
    else
    {
        x = stk [top];
        top --;
        return (x);
    }
}
```

2.5.2 Conversion of Infix Expression to Postfix

The evaluation of postfix expression requires stack and the priority of operators need not be considered for evaluating the expression. Normally, we write the expression in infix format. It needs to be converted into postfix format. The procedure for conversion is as follows.

A stack is used this time to store operators. The infix expression is scanned from left to right. Incase of operands, the operands are directly copied to postfix expression. In case of operators, either of two decisions is taken.

(i)   If priority of operator is greater than operator on top of stack, the operator is pushed on stack.

(ii) If priority of operator is less than operators on stack, the operators on stack are popped and copied into the output expression and the operator is pushed on to the stack.

Following examples illustrate the process of conversion of infix to postfix.

Example 1: a+b*c

Incoming character	Action	Postfix	Stack Contents
a	Copy to output	a	
+	Push	a	`+ | | | ...`
b	Copy to output	ab	
*	Priority more than +, Push *	ab	`+ | * | | ...`
c	Copy to output	abc	
c	Pop all operators copy to output	abc* +	

Fig. 2.9: Conversion of infix to postfix

Example 2: a*b+c

Incoming character	Action	Postfix	Stack Contents
a	Copy to output	a	
*	Push	a	`* | | ...`
b	Copy to output	ab	
+	Priority less than *, pop *, copy to output, push +	ab*	`+ | | ...`
c	Copy to output	ab*c	
End of expression	Pop all operators copy to output	ab*c+	

Fig. 2.10: Conversion of infix to postfix

Example 3: a +b * c / d - e

Incoming character	Action	Postfix	Stack Contents
a	Copy to output	a	
+	Push	a	+ | | | ...
b	Copy to output	ab	
*	Priority more than +, push	ab	+ | * | | ...
c	Copy to output	abc	
/	Priority equal to *, pop*, copy to output, push /	abc*	+ | | | ...
d	Copy to output	abc*d	
-	Priority less than /, pop /, copy to output	abc*d/	
	priority equal to +, pop +, copy to output, push -	abd*d/+	- | | | ...
e	Copy to output	abc*d/+e	
End of expression	Pop all operations copy to output	abc*d/+e-	

Fig. 2.11: Conversion of infix to postfix

The algorithm for conversion of infix to postfix is:

Algorithm 2.2: To convert infix expression to postfix.

```
1.  Read infix expression
2.  i=0, j=0
3.  while (infix[i] != '\0')
    {
        if (infix[i] is operand)
        {
            postfix[j] = infix[i];
            j++;
        }
        else
        {
            if (stack empty)
                push (infix[i]);
            else
```

```
        {    if (priority (infix [i])>priority (stack[top]))
                    push (infix[i]);
            else
            {
                do
                {
                    postfix[j] = pop( );
                    j++;
                } while (priority (infix[i]))<=priority(stk[top])&& (!stack_empty);
                push (infix[i]);
            }
        }
    }
    i++;
}
4. while (!stack_empty)
   {
        postfix[j] = pop( );
        j++;
   }
5. postfix[j] = '\0';
6. print postfix
7. stop.
```

For implementation of above algorithm following consideration are required.

1. A stack of characters need to be defined along with the operations push and pop.
2. A function called priority needs to be defined which will return address of operator passed to it.
3. Two string variables will be required one for storing infix expression and other for postfix expression.
4. So as to make the program simple, the stack is implemented using array and it is declared globally along with the top of stack, so that we can directly access it in main function.
5. Only four operators +, −, *, / are taken for the conversion. Otherwise the program will be bit complex since apart from priority; associativity of operators also plays an important role in the conversion.
6. The expression is assumed to have variable with single character or digit e.g. a + b * c and not like sum = n1 + n2.

Program 2.6: To convert infix expression to postfix

```c
#define MAX 50
char stk[MAX];
int top = -1;
void push (char);
char pop( );
int priority (char);
void main( )
{
    char infix[MAX], postfix[MAX];
    int i, j;
    clrscr( );
    printf("Enter infix expression \n");
    gets (infix);
    i=0; j=0;
    while (infix [i]!='\0')
    {
        if (isalpha(infix[i]) || isdigit(infix [i]))
        {
            postfix [j] = infix [i];
            j++;
        }
        else
        {
            if(top == -1 || priority(infix[i])>priority(stk[top]))
                push (infix[i]);
            else
            {
                do
                {
                    postfix[j] = pop( );
                    j++;
                } while (priority (infix [i])<=priority(stk[top]) && top!=-1);
                push (infix[i]);
            }
        }
        i++;
    }
```

```c
        while (top!=-1)
        {
            postfix[j] = pop( );
            j++;
        }
        postfix[j] = '\0';
        printf("%s", postfix);
}
void push (char x)
{
    if(top!=MAX-1)
    {
        top ++;
        stk [top] = x;
    }
}
char pop( )
{
    char x;
    if (top!=-1)
    {
        x = stk[top];
        top --;
    }
    return(x);
}
int priority (char ch)
{
    switch (ch)
    {
        case '*' :
        case '/' :  return (2);
                    break;
        case '-' :
        case '+':   return (1);
    }
}
```

Note: If at all you want to include the raised to operator ($ or ^) you can assign priority 3 (highest) to it.

2.6 Introduction of Queue

Queue is a linear data structure in which the first element inserted is taken out first. Thus, Queue is a first in first out (FIFO) type of a list where all insertions are made at one end called rear end and all deletions-are made at other end called front end. It is just like queue for railway reservation or buses. The first person in the queue will be first to go out.

Queue can be implemented using:

1. Arrays.

2. Linked lists.

Following four operations can be done on a queue.

1. **Insert operation:** In this, an element is stored at a location indicated by rear.

2. **Delete operation:** In this operation, the element at the front is removed.

3. **Queue Full:** When all the locations reserved for queue are occupied, we can't insert any more elements. This condition is queue_full condition.

4. **Queue empty:** When there is no element stored in a queue, we can't delete any more element. This condition is called as queue_empty.

2.7 Queue Using Array

To represent a queue using array we require an array of some size to be declared say int a[4]. This will create a space for storing elements of queue. The size of the queue is 4. We will require two more variables say front and rear which will be indices to the front and rear element of the queue. Initially, the queue is empty. The variables front and rear will be initialized to −1.

Insert operation:

Now if we want to store a number 10 on the queue, we can increment rear and the element 10 will be stored at location a[0].

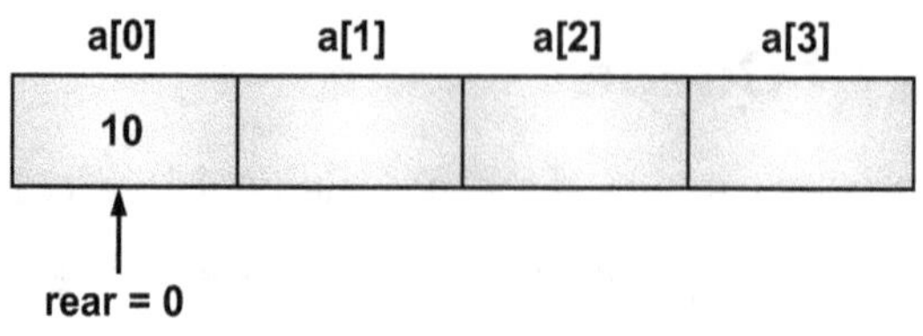

Fig. 2.13(a): Insertq (10)

Next we store a number 20 on the queue, rear will be incremented to 1 and element 20 will be stored at location a[l].

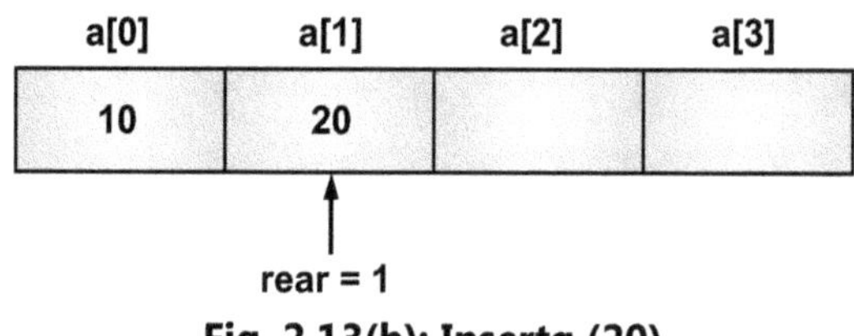

Fig. 2.13(b): Insertq (20)

Next we store a number 30 on the queue, rear will be incremented to 2 and element 30 will be stored at location a[2].

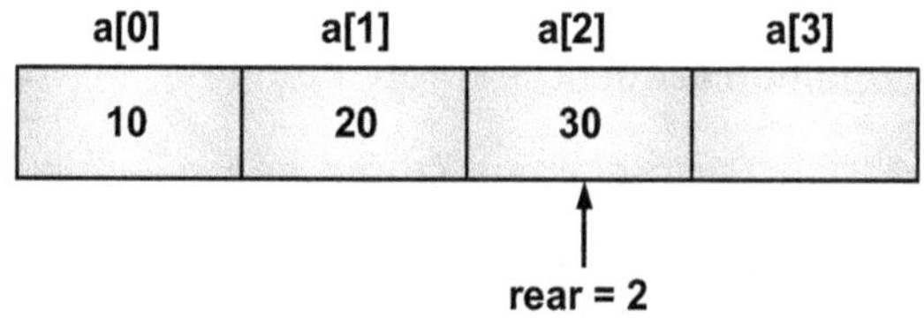

Fig. 2.13(c): Insertq (30)

Next we store a number 40 on the queue, rear will be incremented to 3 and element 40 will be stored at location a[3].

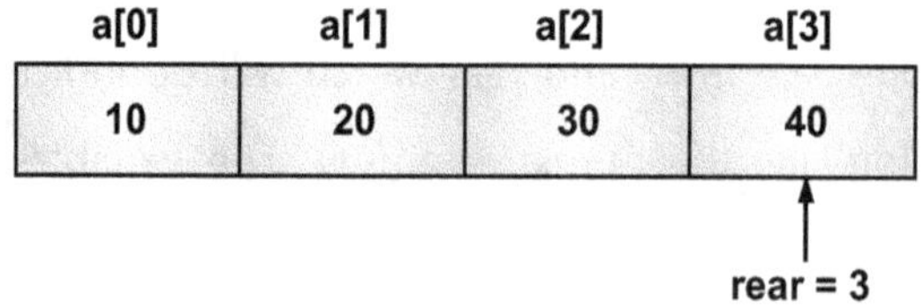

Fig. 2.13(d): Insertq (40)

Now there is no space left on the queue hence, the queue is full. The condition for queue_full is rear becomes equal to maximum size of array −1.

Delete operation:

Now suppose we want to remove an element from the queue. We can access element at the front which is given by the index value in front. Consider the queue where we have already inserted four elements. If we want to carry out delete operation, front is incremented to 0 and element at the front 10 will be accessed.

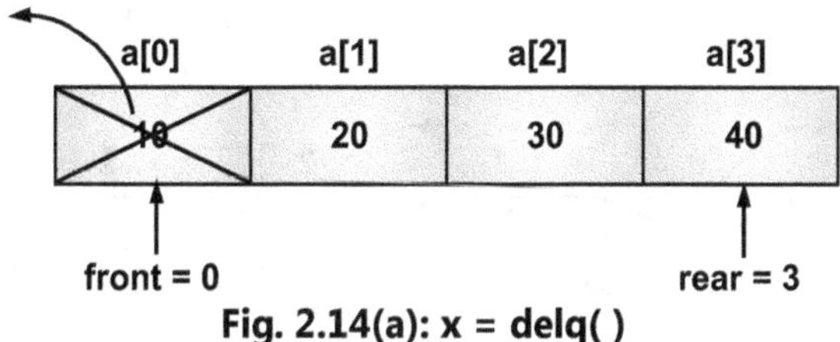

Fig. 2.14(a): x = delq( )

The next delete operation will increment front to 1 and remove 20 from the queue.

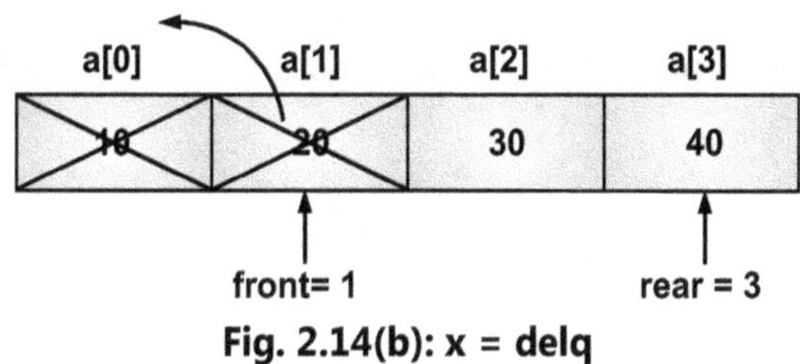

Fig. 2.14(b): x = delq

Another delete operation will increment front to 2 and remove 30 from the queue.

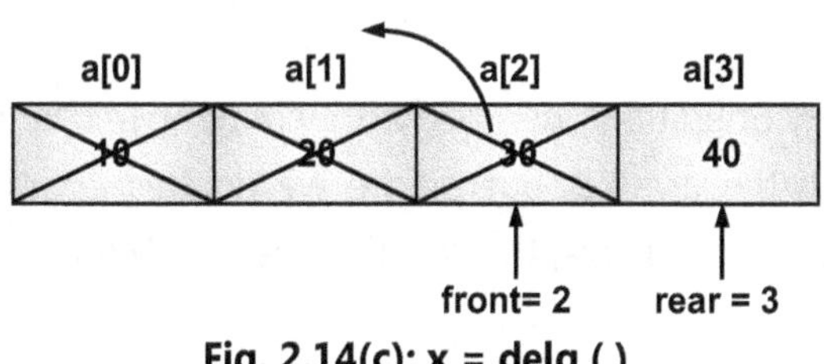

Fig. 2.14(c): x = delq ( )

If the operation is carried out again, element 40 will be removed and front becomes 3 equal to rear.

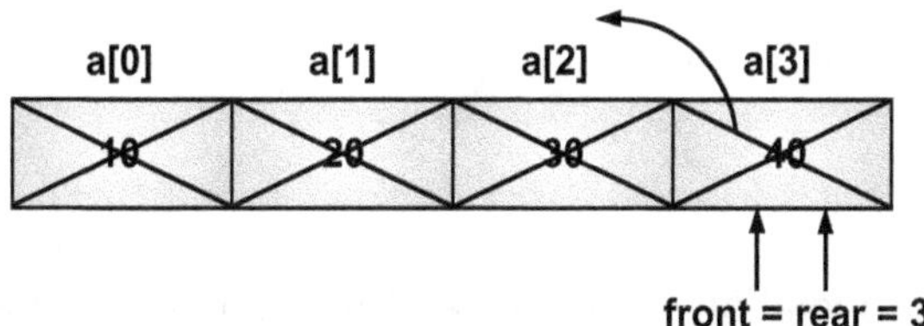

Fig. 2.14(d): x = delq( )

Then we can't remove any more elements because queue is empty. The condition for queue_empty is front == rear.

The disadvantage of linear queue is when rear reaches the value MAX-1, queue full condition occurs. Now if we remove some elements from front end of the queue, we will not be able to store or insert element in these locations as rear remains MAX-1.

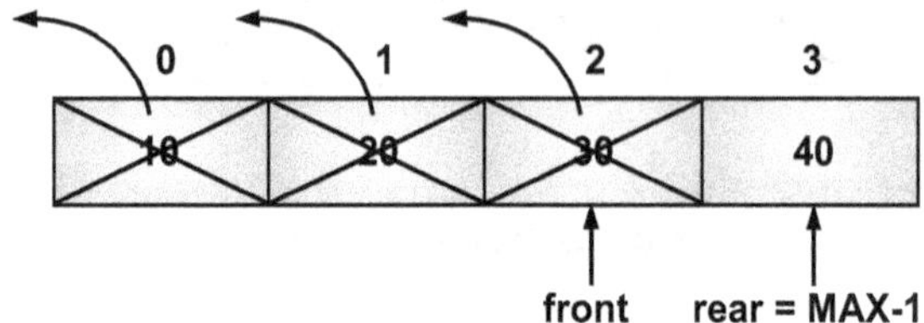

Fig. 2.15: Problem with insert operation even if queue is not full

The program for implementation of queue will require the two functions insertq and delq whose algorithms are as follows:

1. Insertq (x)

    1.   If rear == MAX –1

            print "queue full"

    2.   else

            rear ++;

            a [rear] = x;

    3.   stop.

Every time we do insertq operation, we need to increment rear and store the data at the location given by rear in the array a. But before we do this operation, we have to check whether the queue is full or not. Hence, the condition rear==MAX-1.

II. x = delq( )

    1.   If front == rear

            return –9999

    2.   else

            front++

            x = a [front]

            return x

Every time we do a delq operation, we increment front and remove an element. But before we do this operation, we have to check whether the queue is empty or not. Hence the condition front == rear. Note that we are returning −9999 when queue is empty. This is an indication for the calling function so that it takes appropriate action when the queue is empty. The complete program for queue implementation is as follows:

Program 2.7: To implement queue using array.

```c
#define MAX 4
int a[MAX];
int front = -1, rear = -1;
void insertq(int);
int delq( );
void main( )
{
    int ch;
    do
    {
        clrscr( );
        printf 1. Insert \n 2. Delete \n 3. Exit \n");
        printf ("Enter your choice");
        scanf ("%d", &ch);
        switch (ch)
        {
            case 1 :  printf ("Enter data \n");
                      scanf ("%d", &x);
                      insertq (x);
                      break;
            case 2 :  x = delq( );
                      if (x!=-9999)
                          printf ("%d \n", x);
                      break;
        }
        getch( );
    } while (ch!=3);
}
void insertq (int x)
{
    if (front == MAX -1)
```

```c
            front = rear = (-1);
        if (rear == MAX -1)
            printf ("Queue full");
        else
        {
            rear ++;
            a[rear] = x;
        }
}
int delq( )
{
    int x;
    if (front ==rear)
    {
        printf ("Q is empty");
        return (-9999);
    }
    else
    {
        front ++;
        x=a[front];
        return (x);
    }
}
```

We can implement separate functions for queue_full and queue_empty conditions as:

```c
int q_full( )
{
    if (rear==MAX -1)
    {
        printf("Queue full");
        return (1),
    }
    else
        return (0);
}
```

The function returns1, when queue is full; otherwise 0.

```c
int q_empty( )
{
    if (front == rear)
    {
        printf("Quede is empty");
        return (1);
    }
    else
        return (0);
}
```

The function returns 1, when queue is empty, otherwise 0.

These functions can be used in functions 'insertq' and 'delq' as:

```c
void insertq (int x)
{
    if (front == MAX –1)
    front = rear = –1;
    if(!q_full( ))
    {
        rear ++;
        a[rear] = x;
    }
}
int delq( )
{
    int x;
    if (!q-empty( ))
    {
        front ++;
        x = a[front];
        return (x);
    }
}
```

The queue consists of an array, front and rear. If multiple queues are to be implemented in single program, we need to define separate arrays, font and rear for each queue. Instead, we can define a structure variable for a queue which combines array, front and rear together. The structure definition for queue is

```
typedef struct queue
{
    int a[MAX];
    int front, rear;
} Q;
```

Now if we declare a variable Q q1; it consists of an array, front and rear as:

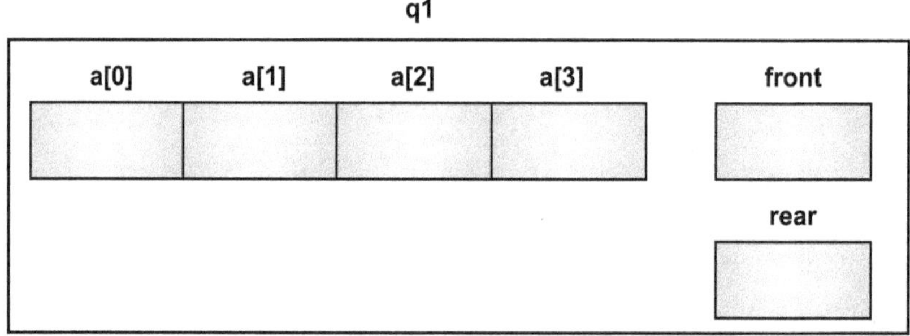

Fig. 2.16: Queue using structure

The elements in the queue can be accessed using dot operate, e.g., if front of the queue is to be initialized we can write q1.front = −1 or if 10 is to be stored at the rear end of the queue we can write q1.a [q1.rear] = 10. But the major advantage of this struct type queue will be, when more than one queue is to be implemented. The insertq and delq. functions require the queue variable to be passed to them. Since, these functions are going to modify the contents of the queue variable; we have to pass it by address. Hence, the function parameter will be pointer to a structure.

The insertq function will have prototype as,

void insertq (Q*, int)

The first argument is pointer to the queue in which we are going to store the element and second argument is the integer number to be stored on the queue.

The delq function will have prototype as,

int delq (Q *)

The argument is pointer to the queue from which number returned will be popped. A complete program using this is given as follows:

Program 2.8: Implementation of queue using structure

```c
#define MAX 5
typedef struct queue
{
    int a[MAX];
    int front, queue;
} Q;
void insertq (Q*, int);
int delq (Q*
main( )
{
    Q q 1, q2;
    q1.front = q1.rear = q2.front = q2.rear=(-1);
    insertq(&q1, 10);
    insertq(&q1, 20);
    insertq(&q2, 100);
    insertq(&q2, 200);
    x = delq(&q1);
    printf("%d \n", x);
    x = delq(&q1);
    printf ("%d \n", x);
    x = delq (&q2);
    printf ("%d \n", x);
    x = delq (&q2);
    printf ("%d \n", x);
}
void insertq (Q *q, int x)
{
    if (q->front == MAX-1)
        q->front = q->rear=-1;
    if (q->rear == MAX-1)
        printf("Queue is full");
    else
```

```
        {
            (q->rear) ++;
            q->a[q->rear]=x;
        }
    }
    int delq (Q *q)
    {
        int x;
        if (q->front == q->rear)
        {
            printf("Queue empty");
            return (-9999);
        }
        else
        {
            (q->front) ++;
            x = q->a [q->front];
            return (x);
        }
    }
```

2.7.1 Queue Using Linked List

The array implementation of queue is not efficient from the view point of memory utilization. The fixed size of array is required and it remains allocated for the entire duration of the program. Linked list implementation will have advantage over the array implementation because we can allocate memory as and when it is required and memory can be deallocated (free) when not in use.

The queue using linked list consist of nodes having data and address of next node.

The node definition will be

```
    typedef struct node
    {
        int data;
        struct node *next;
    } NODE;
```

Two pointers called front and rear can be declared (NODE *front, *rear) which will point to the front and rear end of the queue. The operations insert and delete will be implemented as follows:

Steps for insert operation:

1. Create a node and store data in the node.
2. Link rear node to new node, if it is not first node.
3. Point rear to the recently created node.
   Following figures show this operation.
   Initially, front = rear = NULL

1. Insertq (10)

Fig. 2.17(a): Insertq (10) in queue using linked list

2. Insertq (20)

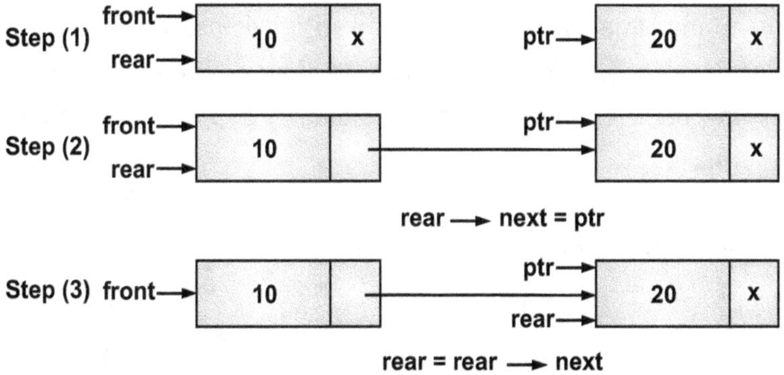

Fig. 2.17(b): Insertq (20) in queue using linked list

Steps for delete operation:

1. Make a pointer temp point to the front end of the queue.
2. If it is NULL, then queue is empty..
3. If not, remove the data from this node and advance front.
4. De-allocate memory pointed by temp.

Following figures show this operation.

1. x = delq

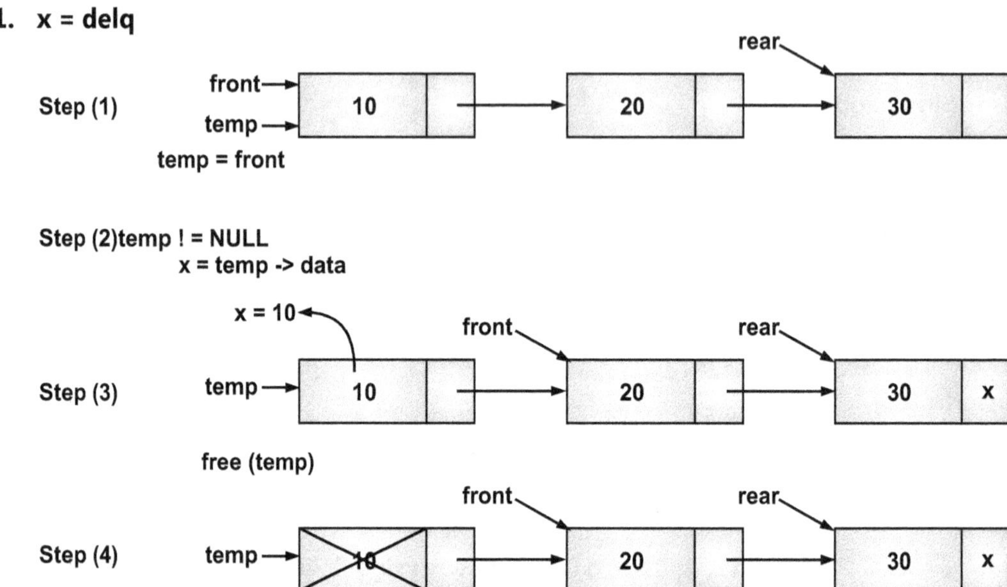

Fig. 2.18: Delete operation in queue using linked list

Following program, implements queue using linked list. It has the function push and pop which have the same prototype as that used in case of array. The function push accepts data, creates a node and puts it into linked. list. The function pop removes an element from the linked list and returns it.

Program 2.9: Implementation of queue using linked list.

```
typedef struct node
{
    int data;
    struct node*next;
} NODE;
NODE*front=NULL, rear=NULL;
void insertq (int x)
{
    NODE*ptr;
```

```
    ptr = (NODE.*)malloc(sizeof(NODE));
    if (ptr == NULL)
        printf("Insufficient memory");
    else
    {
        ptr->data = x;,
        ptr->next = NULL;
        if (rear == NULL)
            front = rear = ptr;
        else
        {
            rear->next = ptr,
            rear = ptr;
        }
    }
}
int delq
{
    NODE = temp, int x;
    temp = front;
    if (temp == NULL)
    {
        printf("Queue empty");
        return(-9999);
    }
    else
    {
        x = temp->data;
        front = front->next;
        free (temp);
        return (x);
    }
}
```

In order to implement queue using linked list you can use two pointers front and rear. Front will point to first node and rear to the last node. Whenever insert operation is done a new node is created, it is attached to the last node in the list and the pointer rear points to this new node. Whenever delete operation is done an element from front end is accessed, front is advanced to next node and the node is deleted.

2.8 Queue as an Abstract Data Type (ADT)

```
//Queue data definition
typedef struct queue
{
    <datatype> data;
    struct queue*front, *rear;
}Q;


//Operation definition
initializeq(Q);              // Initialize front and rear
insertq(Q, x);               // Insert into Q
x = delq(Q);                 // Remove x from Q
int qempty(Q)                // If Q is empty return 1 else return 0
int qfull(Q)                 // If Q is full return 1 else return 0


The above data definition can be written as
typedef struct queue
{
    <data type> data [size]
    int front, rear;
} Q;
```

2.9 Circular Queue

The disadvantage of linear queue is that, even if some locations are available for storage, we will not be able to use them when rear becomes MAX −1. Hence, when rear reaches MAX −1, we should be able to come back to location 0 in case it is empty. Hence, rear ++ can be replaced by rear = (rear + 1) % MAX.

Similarly, when front reaches MAX-1 we should be able to come back to location 0 which is done using front = (front + 1) % MAX. This implementation is called circular queue. In order to handle queue full and queue empty conditions, one more variable called counter will be required. The counter c is incremented whenever insert operation is performed and decremented when delete operation is performed. The program for circular queue is as follows:

Program 2.10: To implement circular queue.

```
#define MAX 5
int a[MAX];
int front = 0, rear = -1, c = 0;
void insertq (int);
int delq( );
void main( )
{
    int ch;
    do
    {
        clrscr( );
        printf ("1. Insert \n 2. Delete \n 3. Exit \n");
        printf ("Enter your choice");
        scanf("%d", &ch);
        switch (ch)
        {
            case 1 : printf ("Enter data \n");
                     scanf ("% d". &x),
                     insertq (x);
                     break;
            case 2 : x = delq( );
                     if (x!=-9999)
                         printf ("%d \n", x);
                     break;
        }
        getch( )
    }while (ch!=3);
}
void insertq (int x)
{
    if (c==MAX)
```

```c
            printf("Q is full");
    else
    {
        rear = (rear + 1) % MAX;
        q[rear] = x;
        c++;
    }
}
int delq( )
{
    int x;
    if (c == 0)
    {
        printf("Q is empty"),
        return(-9999);
    }
    else
    {
        x = q[front];
        front = (front + 1) % MAX;
        c --;
        return (x);
    }
}
```

Explanation:

1. Let us assume queue size 5. Initially when queue is empty

    front = 0   rear = −1   c = 0

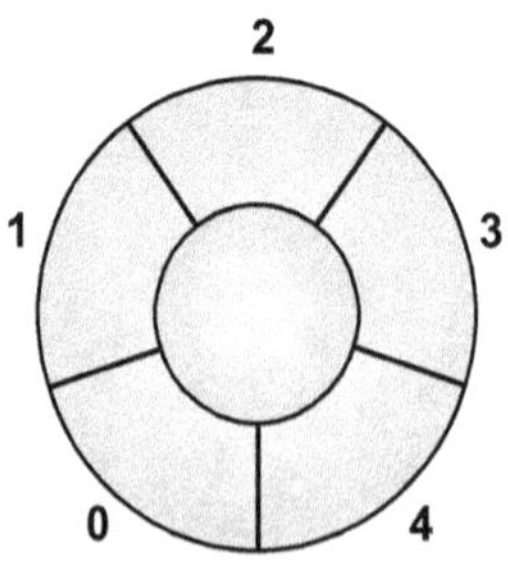

Fig. 2.19(a): Circular queue

2. Insert(10) operation
    front 0
    rear = 0   c = 1

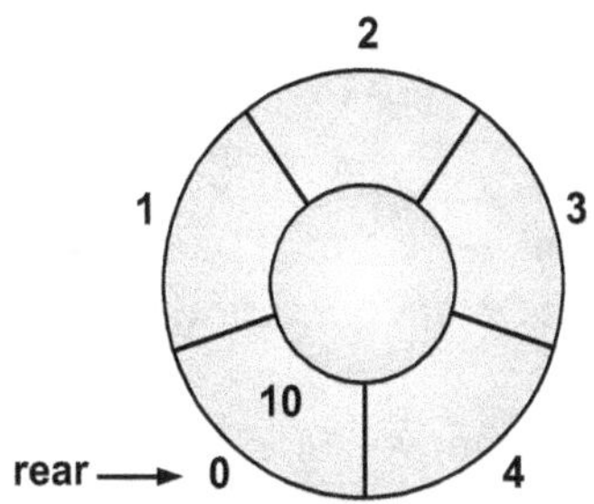

Fig. 2.19(b): Insert (10)

3. Insert(20) operation
    front = 0   rear = 1   c = 2

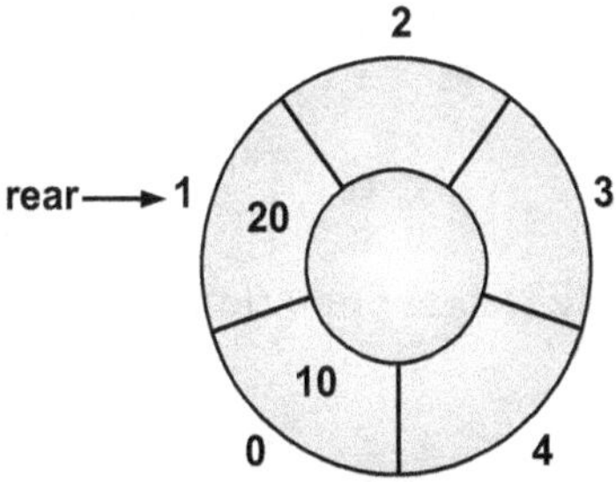

Fig. 2.19(c): Insert (20)

4. Like this if we insert 30, 40, 50
    front = 0   rear = 4   c = 5
    The queue is full i.e., c=MAX=5

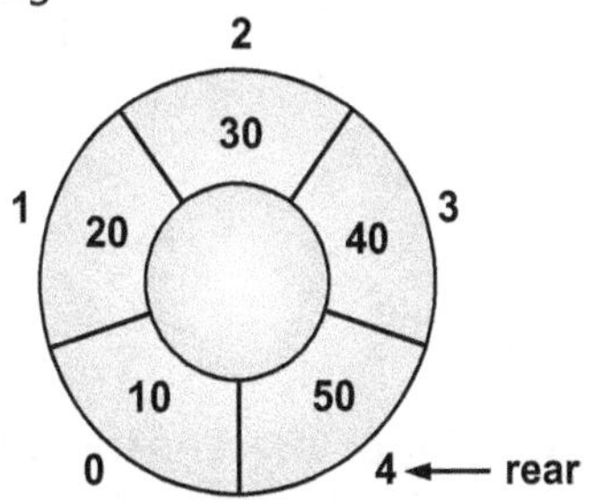

Fig. 2.19(d): Insert (30), Insert (40), Insert (50)

5. Now if delete operation is performed, 10 will removed,
    Before delete, front = 0   rear = 4   c = 5
    After delete,   front = 1   rear = 4   c = 4

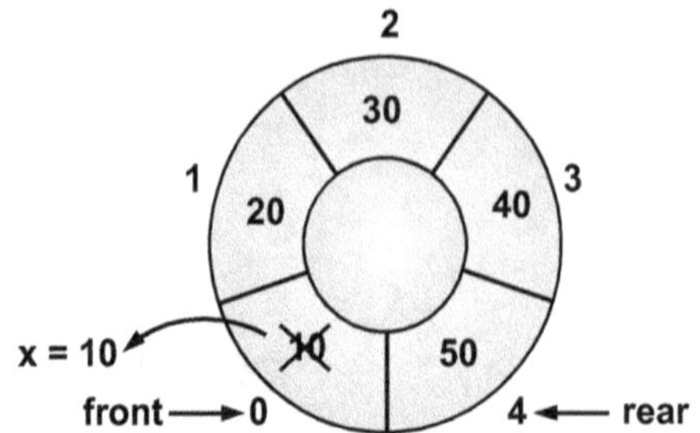

Fig. 2.19(e): Delete operation in circular queue

6. One more delete operation will remove 20
    Before delete; front = 1   rear = 4   c = 4
    After delete,   front = 2   rear = 4   c = 3

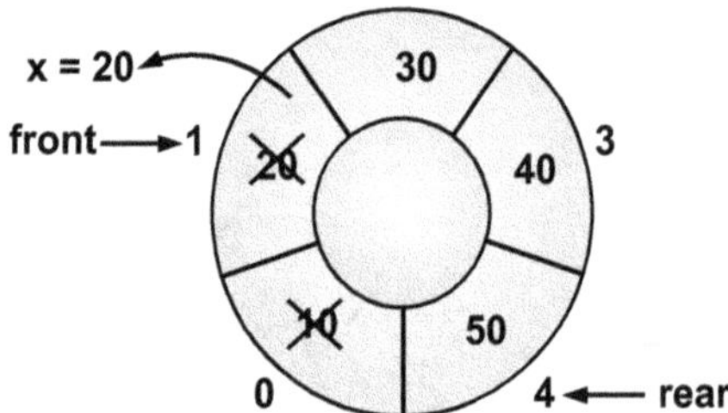

Fig. 2.19(f): Delete operation in circular queue

Now if we want to insert say 60,

rear = (rear + 1)% MAX.= (4 + 1)% 5 = 0 and we can store/insert the element at location 0.

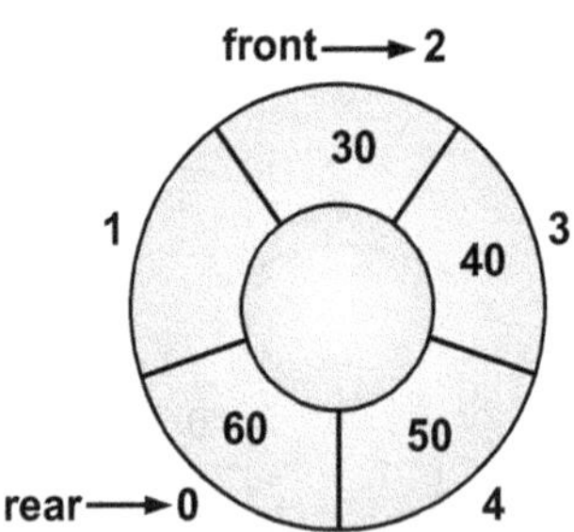

Fig. 2.19(g): Insert operation

Thus, we are able to insert the element in the queue at location 0 even if rear has reached value MAX−1.

Note: If we don't use counter, the implementation becomes slightly complex, we have to keep one location empty in the queue.

Circular queue using linked list

A circular queue can also be implemented using circular linked list. This implementation will most efficient than array implementation. We can use two pointers front and rear. In fact a single pointer to last element will also be sufficient. We can access the front element with this pointer as list is circular.

2.10 Priority Queue

The priority queue is a data structure in which the ordering of elements decides the two operations insert and delete. The elements from the priority queue are removed as per their priority. There are two types of priority queues:

1. Ascending order Priority Queue,
2. Descending order Priority Queue.

1. **Ascending order Priority Queue:** It is collection of elements into which the elements are stored or inserted in any order but the smallest element can be removed.
2. **Descending order Priority Queue:** It is collection of elements into which elements are inserted at any order but only larger element can be removed. The other operations on priority queue will be queue empty and queue full. There are several implementations of priority queues.

The priority queue can be implemented in number of ways. One method can be:

(i)   When insert operation is done, the element is stored in an array in the continuous locations.
(ii) But when the element is removed, we have to search for maximum in case of descending priority queue or minimum in case of ascending priority queue.
(iii) In place of deleted element an invalid element (say −1) is stored.

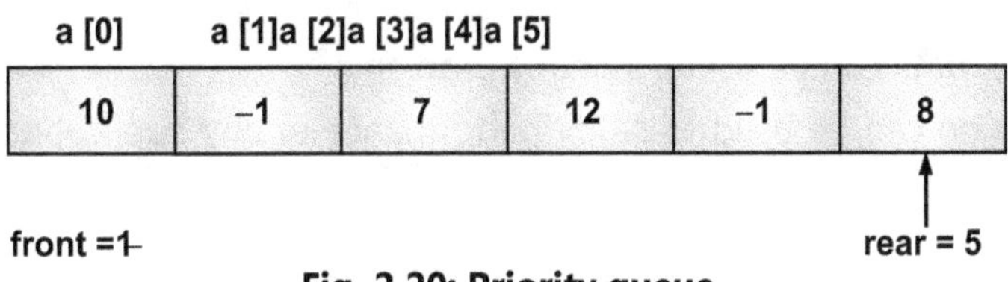

Fig. 2.20: Priority queue

(iv) When an element is inserted, we can increment rear but if rear reaches maximum size, we can do compaction i.e. rearrange the array to remove invalid elements as shown in Fig. 2.21.

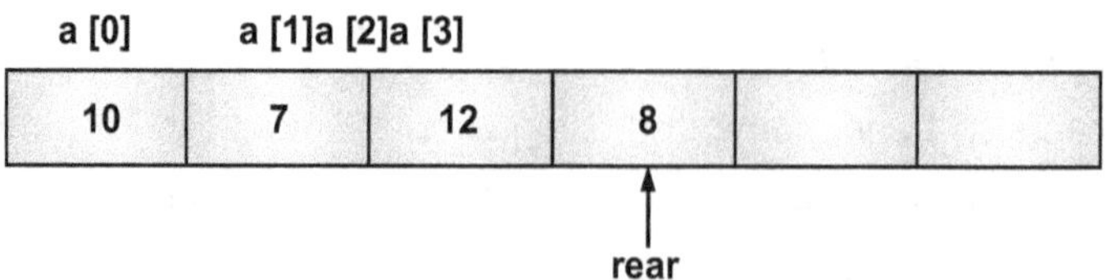

Fig. 2.21: Priority queue after compaction

Second method can be

(i) Instead of maintaining the priority queue as an unordered list of elements, we can maintain it as an ordered (sorted) list of elements but then this will require more work while inserting the element in the queue.

(ii) The delete operation will be simple as the minimum or maximum element is available as front end of queue.

The priority queue is used for scheduling of jobs by operating system programs. The priority queue can be used in job scheduling where the execution of job is required to be done based on the priorities. The jobs will be kept in a queue along with their priority numbers. Whenever a new job is to be executed, the job with highest priority will be taken up from the queue.

2.11 Applications of Queue

Applications of Queues:

There are several applications of queues in real world. Some of these applications are:

(i) Railway/Bus/Airplane Reservations.

(ii) Processing of customer requests.

(iii) Processing of online applications.

(iv) In a computer system processing of jobs such as print spool (printing of multiple files/pages).

(v) In a operating system scheduling of jobs as per their priority in multitasking operating system.

(vi) Categorizing of data can be useful in many problems.

(vii) Queue simulation can be used to study performance of any application involving queue like situation.

Categorizing Data:

We need to organize the data into groups. For example, if we have a list records having empno, name and age and we may want to group them as per their age as 21-30, 31-40, 41-50, 51-60 etc. While rearranging these records into groups, the original order is to be maintained.

The following algorithm implements categorizing of data into four groups of 1-10, 11-20, 21-30 and 31-40.

Algorithm 2.3: The algorithm reads integers between 1-40 and inserts them into four queues.

```
Step 1: Read n                          // Number of data items
Step 2: i=1
Step 3: while(i<n)
        {
                Read x                          // Enter data
                if(x<=10)
                        insertq (&q1, x)
                if(x>10 && x<=20)
                        insertq(&q2, <=30)
                if(x>21, &&xx<=30)
                        insert(&q3, x)
                if(x>31 && x<=40)
                        insert(&q4, x)
                j=x+1
        }
Step 4: Stop
```

The complete program is given below.

/*Program for categorizing data
Input is a list of integers between 0-39
output is four groups (queues)*/

```
#include <stdio.h>
#include <conio.h>
#include <stdlib.h>
#define MAX 5
typedef struct queue
{
    int ar [MAX];
    int front, rear;
}Q;
void insertq (Q*, int);
```

```c
int deleteq (Q*);
void main( )
{
    Q q[4];
    int x, i, n;
    clrscr( );
    for(i=0;i<4;i++)
        q[i].front=q[i].rear=-1;
    printf("How many numbers\n");
    scanf("%d",&n);
    i=0;
    randomize( );
    while(i<n)
    {
        //printf("Enter number between 1-40\n");
        //scanf("%d",&x);
        x=rand( )%100;
        if (x>=0 && x<40)
        {
            insertq(&q[x/10],x);
            i++;
        }
        else
            printf("Invalid number\n");
    }
    printf("\nThe categorised data is\n");
    i=0;
    while(i<4)
    {
        printf("\nData between %d to %d is \n", 10*i, 10*i+9);
        while (1)
        {
            x=deleteq(&q[i]);
            if(x!=-9999)
                printf("%d\t",x);
            else
                break;
```

```c
        }
        printf("\n");
        i++;
    }
}
void insertq (Q *q, int x)
{
    if(q->front == MAX-1)
        q->front = q->rear = -1;
    if (q->rear == MAX-1)
        printf("queue is full");
    else
    {
        (q->rear) ++;
        q->ar[q->rear] = x;
    }
}
int deleteq (Q *q)
{
    int x;
if (q->front == q->rear)
{
    //printf("queue empty"); return (-9999);
}
else
{
    (q->front) ++;
    x = q->ar [q->front];
    return (x);

}
}
```

Simulation of Queues:

Any real life application involving queue like activity can be simulated and the performance of the system can be analysed under different conditions. Thus, we can create a model of the real life application.

Suppose a shop is open for 8 hours a day for 6 days in a week. The shop activity can be studied in different situations i.e. busy day, average day, busy hours etc. We need to simulate the activities of the shop as queue. The events that can take place are as below:

(i)   A customer arrives.

(ii) The counter is free.

(iii) The customer is served.

When the customer arrives and counter is not free he waits in a queue. Hence, we need to create a queue of customers.

When the counter becomes free to serve next customer, we need to start a timer to find out how much time is taken by each customer. When a customer is served we should count time taken by the server, waiting time for the customer in queue etc. This can be used to find average taken to serve each customer, average waiting time for each customer etc.

We can use random numbers to generate the inputs such waiting time for a customer, time taken to serve a customer etc.

Job Scheduling:

The operating system programs like Window, Unix etc, which are multitasking operating systems, execute number of programs simultaneously. It is required to do scheduling of executions of these programs. There are number of techniques for scheduling some of them are:

    (i)   First Come First Serve (FCFS)

    (ii) Round - Robin Technique.

Both these technique uses queues for the implementation of scheduling program execution.

First Come First Serve (FCFS): The FCFS technique stores the programs in the queue on first come first serve basis. The program which comes first will be executed first. This technique is useful for scheduling of print jobs in a print server.

The disadvantages is, if one of the job in queue takes more time the other jobs have to wait for a long time.

Round Robin Technique: In this technique, the programs to be executed are stored in a queue. But each program is given a fix time slot for execution. If execution is over in time slot allotted, the program is removed otherwise the program is kept in the rear end of queue so that it gets another turn. The next program in the queue will be given its turn of execution for the next time slot as shown in Fig. 2.22.

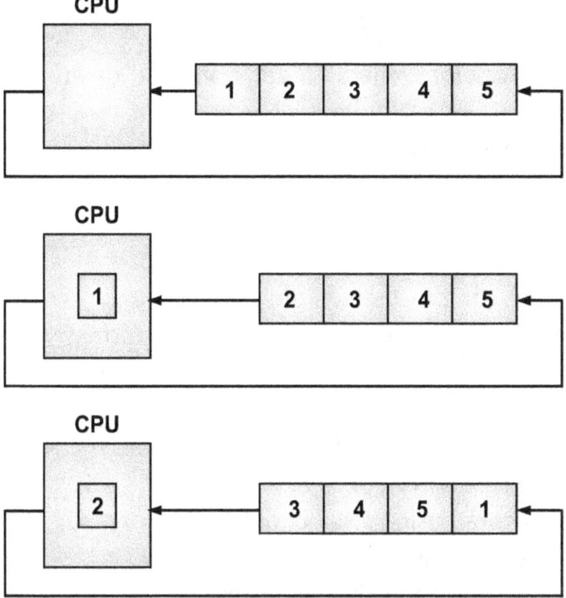

Fig. 2.22 (a): Round Robin technique

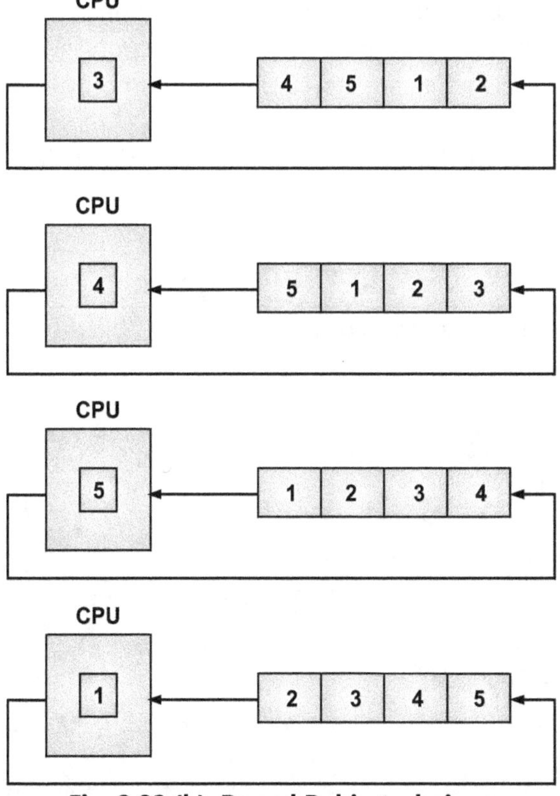

Fig. 2.22 (b): Round Robin technique

SUMMARY

- Stack is a linear data structure where all additions and deletions are made only at one end called top.
- The operations performed on stacks are:
  (i) Push, (ii) Pop, (iii) Stack-empty, (iv) Stack full.
- Stack can be implemented using array or linked list.
- Stack can be used for expression conversion and evaluation, handling recursion, reversing a string, language processing applications, etc.
- An expression can be written in infix, postfix and prefix format.
- Postfix and prefix expressions are easier to evaluate than infix since priority of operators need not be considered.
- Queue is a linear data structure in which all insertions are made at rear end deletions are made at the other end called front end.
- Queue can be' implemented using array or linked list.
- The four operations done on queue are:
  (i) Insert, (ii) Delete, (iii) Queue full, (iv) Queue empty.
- Linear queue has the advantage that when queue becomes full, rear reaches end of queue and even if we remove some elements we cannot insert elements in it.
- Circular queue is used to avoid disadvantage of linear queue stated above. We can go to the front end of queue and insert the elements if it is empty in circular queue.
- In priority queue, the elements are stored as per the priority. The priority queue can be ascending or descending.
- Queue can be used in scheduling techniques like First Come First Serve or Round Robin Technique.

SOLVED PROBLEMS

1. Write a program to reverse string using stack.

Solution:

```
#define MAX 80
int top=-1;
char stk[MAX];
void main( )
{
    char s [MAX];                  // String variable
    int i;
    printf("Enter a string \n");
    gets(s);                       // Accept a string
    i=0;
    while(s[i] !='\0')             // while it is not end of string
```

```c
    {
        push(s[i]);                     // Push character on stack
        i++;
    }
    i=0;
    while(top!=-1)                      // while stack is not empty
    {
        s[i]=pop( );                    // Pop a character from stack
        i++;
    }
    printf("Reversed string is %s", s);
}
void push (char x)
{
    if(top!=MAX-1)
    {
        top ++;
        stk [top] = x;
    }
}
char pop( )
{
    char = x;
    if(top!=-1)
    {
        x = stk [top];
        top --;
    }
}
```

2. Write necessary 'C' functions to implement stack of characters using array.
Solution:

```c
    #define MAX 10
    char s[MAX];
    int top=-1;
    void push (char x)
    {
        if(top == MAX-1)
            printf("Stack full");
        else
```

```
        {
            top ++;
            s[top] = x;
        }
    }
    char pop( )
    {
        char x;
        if(top == -1)
            printf("Stack full");
        else
        {
            x = s[top];
            top --;
        } return (x);
    }
```

3. Modify program 2.6 to incorporate bracketed expression e.g. (a*(b+c)).

Hint: Assign lowest priority (say 0) to opening bracket`('. Whenever there is opening bracket push it on the stack. Whenever there is closing bracket pop all the operators and copy them in output, till you get an opening bracket in the stack. The procedure for expression (a + (b * c / d) − e) is as follows:

Incoming character	Action	Postfix	Stack Contents
(	Push		(
a	Copy to output	a	
+	Priority more than (, push)		(+
(	Push		(+(
b	Copy to output	ab	
*	Priority more than (, push	ab	(+(*
c	Copy to output	abc	
/	Priority equal to *, pop*, copy to output, push/		
d	Copy to output	abc*d	
)	Pop /, copy to output, Pop (	abc*d/	(+
-	Priority equal to +, pop +, copy to output push-	abc*d/+	(−
e	Copy to output	abc*d/+e	
)	Pop-, Copy to output	abc*d\+e-	
End of expression		abc*d\+e-	

4. Evaluate the following postfix expression using stack.

623 +− 382/+*2$3+

Incoming character	Action	Stack
6	Push	6
2	Push	6, 2
3	Push	6, 2, 3
+	Pop 3, 2 Push 2 + 3 = 5	6, 5
−	Pop 5, 6 Push 6 − 5 = 1	1
3	Push	1, 3
8	Push	1, 3, 8
2	Push	1, 3, 8, 2
/	Pop 2, 8 Push 8/2 = 4	1, 3, 4
+	Pop 4, 3 Push 3 + 4 = 7	1, 7
*	Pop 7, 1 Push 1 * 7 = 7	7
2	Push	7, 2
$	Pop 2, 7 Push 7^2 = 49	49

3	Push	49, 3

+	Pop 3, 49	
	Push 49 + 3 = 52	52

$$\therefore \text{result} = 52$$

5. Convert following expression into prefix and infix.

(a + b * c) / (x + y / z)

Solution:

$$
\begin{aligned}
\text{Postfix} \ &= (a + b * c) \ (x + y/z) \ / \\
&= (a + (bc \ *)) \ (x + (yz/))/ \\
&= abc*+xyz/+/ \\
\text{Infix} \ &= / \ (a + b * c) \ (x + y/z) \\
&= / \ (a + (* \ bc) \ (x + (/ \ yz)) \\
&= / + a * bc + x / yz
\end{aligned}
$$

6. What is stack? Explain how stack is used to check validity of parenthesis with suitable example.

Solution: (Refer Section 2.1 for definition of stack)

Validity of parenthesis using stack:

1. Stack can be used to check validity of parenthesis.
2. For example, if you are given an expression ((a + (b + c / d)) – e), we can scan the expression from left to right.
4. We can create a stack of characters and as- and when we came across a (opening parenthesis) we push it on stack and whenever we get (closing parenthesis)) an opening parenthesis w be popped!
5. At the end of the expression, if the stack is empty it means we have equal number of opening and closing parenthesis otherwise the expression is invalid.

   The algorithm for the same is given as follows:

1. Input exp
2. i=0;
3. while (exp[i]!='\0')
   {   65
       if(exp[i] == '(')
           push('(')
       if(exp[i] == ')')
           pop( );
   }
4. if(stack_empty( ))
       print "Valid expression"
   else
       print"Invalid expression"

7. Consider infix expression.

a + (c / d) * (e * f)

Convert it into postfix and prefix. Evaluate postfix expression for a = 2, c = 4, d = 2, e = 3, f = 5.

Solution:

Given: a + (c / d) * (e * f)

$$\text{expr} = (a + ((c/d) \quad * \quad (e * f)))$$
$$\downarrow \qquad\qquad \downarrow$$
$$= a \quad cd\backslash \quad ef ** +$$

Hence, postfix is acd \ef ** +

$$\text{expr} = (a + ((c/d) * (e * f)))$$
$$= +a * / cd * ef$$

Prefix is a * / cd * ef

Evaluation: acd \ ef ** +

Incoming character	Action	Stack
a	Push a = 2	2
c	Push c = 4	2, 4
d	Push d = 2	2, 4, 2
/	Pop 2, 4 Push 4/2 = 2	2, 2
e	Push e = 3	2, 2, 3
f	Push f = 5	2, 2, 3, 5
*	Pop 5, 3 Push 3 * 5 = 15	2, 2, 15
*	Pop 15, 2 Push 15 * 2 = 30	2, 2, 15 2, 30
+	Pop 30, 2 Push 2 + 30 = 32	32

$$\therefore \text{result} = 32$$

8. Convert the following expression in other two forms where $ stands for unary minus.

    (i) ab + cd - *   **(ii) $a + (b − c) ↑ d**

    (iii) /- * abc + ef   **(iv) $a + p ↑ q ↑ r**

Solution:

(i) ab + cd - *

The expression is postfix.

$$exp \rightarrow ((ab +) (cd -) *)$$
$$\rightarrow (((a + b) * (c − d)) \qquad \text{Infix}$$
$$\rightarrow * + ab − cd \qquad \text{Prefix}$$

(ii) $a + (b − c) ↑ d

The expression is infix.

$$exp \rightarrow \$a + (b − c) ↑ d$$
$$\rightarrow (\$a) + ((b − c) ↑ d)$$
$$\rightarrow + \$a ↑ − bc\ d \qquad \text{Prefix}$$
$$\rightarrow a\$\ bc − d ↑ + \qquad \text{Postfix}$$

(iii) /- * abc + ef

The expression is prefix.

$$expr \rightarrow (/ (− (* a b) c) + (ef))$$
$$\rightarrow ((a * b) − c) / (e + f) \qquad \text{Infix}$$
$$\rightarrow ab * c − ef +/ \qquad \text{Postfix}$$

(iv) $a + p ↑ q ↑ r

The expression is infix.

$$expr \rightarrow \$a + p ↑ q ↑ r$$
$$\rightarrow (\$a) + ((p ↑ q) ↑ r)$$
$$\rightarrow a\$\ pq ↑ r ↑ + \qquad \text{Postfix}$$
$$\rightarrow + \$a ↑↑ pqr \qquad \text{Prefix}$$

9. Explain the necessity of representing expression in prefix and postfix. Evaluate the following expression. Show stepwise stack contents.

$$ABC * DEF ^ \backslash G * - H +$$

A= 6, B = 1 C = 4, D = 16, E = 2, F = 3, G = 2, H = 5.

Solution:

Incoming character	Action	Stack
A	Push A = 6	6
B	Push B = 1	6, 1
C	Push C = 4	6, 1, 4
*	Pop 4, 1 Push 4	6, 4
D	Push D = 16	6, 4, 16
E	Push E = 2	6, 4, 16, 2
F	Push F = 3	6, 4, 16, 2, 3
^	Pop 3, 2 Push 2 ^ 3 = 8	6, 4, 16, 8
/	Pop 8, 16 Push 16/8 = 2	6, 4, 2
G	Push 4 = 2	6, 4, 2, 2
*	Pop 2, 2 Push 2 * 2 = 4	6, 4, 4
-	Pop 4, 4 Push 4 − 4 = 0	6, 0
H	Push 5	6, 0, 5
*	Pop 5, 0 Push 5 * 0 = 0	6, 0
+	Pop 0, 6 Push 6 + 0 = 6	6

Result = 6

10. Convert the following expression into postfix. Show all steps.
Solution:

a + b * c / d – e

Incoming character	Action	Stack	Output
a	Print		a
+	Push	+	
b	Print	+	ab
*	Push	+ *	a
c	Print	+ *	abc
/	Pop Push /	+ /	abc*
d	Print	+ /	abc*d
-	Pop / Pop + Push	-	abc*d/+
e	Print		abc*d/+e
\0	Pop -		abc*d/+e–

Postfix is abc*d/+e-

11. Explain the application of stack to check the validity of parentheses in the expression. Also write the pseudo code for the same.
Solution:

(a) We can use stack to check validity of parentheses.

(b) The opening parentheses can be pushed into stack and as soon as a closing parenthesis comes, one parenthesis is popped. In the end, if the stack is empty there will be equal number of opening and closing parentheses.

(c) Pseudo-code will be as below:

1. Read expr
2. i=0
3. while expr[i] != '\0'

```
    {
        if(expr [i] == '(')
            push('(');
        if(expr [i] == ')')
            pop( );
    }
```

4. if(stack_empty( ))
      print "Valid"
    else
        print "Invalid"

---

12. Write a program to reverse a queue using stack.

Solution:

```
#define MAX 5
int q[MAX];
int front = 1, rear = -1;
void insertq (int);
int delq( );
int front -1, rear -1;
int stk[MAX]
int top =-1;
void main( )
{
    int i, x, n;
    printf ("Enter n \n")
    scanf("%d", &n);
    for(i=0; i<n; i++)
    {
        scanf("%d", &x);
        insertq(x);
    }
    while(front!=rear)
```

```c
        {
            x=delq( );
            push(x);
        }
        while(top!=-1)
        {
            x=pop( );
            insertq(x);
        }
    }
    void insert q (int x)
    {
        if (front == MAX -1)
        front = rear = -1;
        if (rear = MAX -1)
            printf ("Queue full");
        else
        {
            rear ++;
            q[rear] = x;
        }
    }
    int delq( )
    {
        int x;
        if (front == rear)
        {
            printf ("Q is empty");
            return (-9999);
        }
        else
        {
            front ++;
            x = q [front];
            return (x);
        }
```

```
      }
      void push (int x)
      {
          if(top == MAX-1)
              printf("Stack is full");
          else
          {
              top ++;
              stk [top] = x;
          }
      }
      int pop( )
      {
          int x;
          if (top == -1)
          {
              print ("Stack is empty \n");
              return (-9999);
          }
          else
          {
              x = stk [top];
              top- -;
              return (x);
          }
      }
```

13. Differentiate between circular and linear queue.

Solution:

No.	Linear queue	Circular queue
1.	When rear becomes MAX −1, we cannot insert elements at front end even if space is available.	When rear becomes MAX −1, we can continue adding elements at front end if space is available.
2.	Counter is not required to check Q full or Q empty.	Counter is required to check Q full or Q empty.
3.	Easy implementation.	Difficult implementation.

EXERCISE

1. Write 'push' and 'pop' functions in C to implement stack in an array.
2. Explain the of stack with the help of suitable example. Also write the pseudo-code for the operations performed cm stack.
3. Write necessary 'C' functions to implement stack using array.
4. Write functions in 'C' for push, pop is empty for stack using linked list. Give declaration in 'C' for implementing above functions for stack.
5. Write a program to perform following operations:
   (i)   Push 10 and 20 on first stack.
   (ii) Push 100 and 200 on second stack.
   (iii) Pop all elements from both stacks one by one and display.
6. Write an ADT for stack.
7. What do you mean by ADT? Write an ADT for stack.
8. Define ADT. Write down ADT of stack.
9. Write necessary 'C' functions to implement stack using linked list.
10. Write all the necessary functions to represent stack using linked list. Write a C function using stack to determine whether the given string is palindrome or not.
11. Give a 'C' declaration to define a node structure for a stack using linked list.
12. Write function in 'C' to 'push' and 'pop' an item from a stack using linked list.
13. Explain how stack is implemented using linked list.
14. Write a 'C' function for push, pop, is stack empty using linked list.
15. Explain the necessity of representing expression in prefix and postfix notation. For the given postfix expressions, evaluate it for the values given. Show stepwise stack contents.

$$A\ B\ C * D\ E\ F \wedge / G * -1 * +$$
$$A = 61\ B = 1,\ C = 4,\ D = 16,\ E = 2,\ F = 3,\ G = 2,\ 1+= 5$$

where $\wedge$ = exponential operator
16. Write pseudo C algorithm for postfix evaluation.
17. Give an algorithm for evaluation of a postfix expression.
18. Write a function in 'C' to evaluate postfix expression and explain with suitable example.
19. Write pseudo C algorithm for infix to postfix conversion.
20. Write an algorithm to convert infix expression to postfix. Convert the following infix expression to postfix using stack.

   A / B $ C + D * E – A * C where $ is an exponentiation. Show stepwise conversion.
21. Write pseudo-C algorithm to convert infix expression to postfix using stack.
22. Write an algorithm to convert infix expression to postfix.
23. Give the postfix and prefix forms of the infix expression given below. Also write an algorithm or pseudo 'C' code to evaluate a postfix expression.
   infix expression - (a + b * c) / (x + y/2).

24. Convert the following expressions into other two forms:
    (i)   ((A – (B + C)) * D) $ (E + F) where $ = exponentiation
    (ii) /m n $ q p $ y $ /-r s * +
25. Convert following infix expression into postfix using stack. Show all steps.
    A/B**C+D*E-A*C where ** is exponentiation.
26. Explain the concept of queue with suitable example. Also explain any one application of queue with Pseudo-Code.
27. What is queue? Explain circular queue and priority queue with suitable example.
28. Explain concept of queue with suitable example. Also explain any one application of queue with pseudo code.
29. Write a menu driven program for implementation of queue using structure.
30. Write necessary 'C' functions to implement Queue using array.
31. Write necessary functions to implement queue using array.
32. How can queue be implemented using array and linked list? Explain.
33. Explain array and linked list implementation of queue.
34. Explain array and linked list implementation of queue.
35. Write necessary 'C' functions to implement Queue using linked list.
36. Write 'insert' and 'delete' operations to implement a linked queue.
37. Compare linear and circular queue representations using arrays. Give a node structure in 'C' to define a queue using linked list. Also write a function to add an item into a queue using linked list.
38. Write necessary 'C' functions to implement Circular Queue using array.
39. Write necessary functions in C to implement circular queue in all array. Assume rear=front=0 initially.
40. How circular queue is advantageous over sequential queue? Explain with an example.
41. Differentiate between linear and circular queue when represented using array.
42. Implement the following functions in 'C' to implement circular queue using array.
    (i)   Insert an element,
    (ii) Delete an element,
    (iii) Queue full,
    (iv) Queue empty.
    Assume data elements to be integer.

43. Explain advantages of circular queue over linear queue.

44. What is circular queue? Explain insert and delete operations in circular queue.

45. Explain the concept of priority queue with suitable example. Explain one application of Priority queue.

46. Explain the concept of priority queue with suitable example.

47. What is Priority Queue? Write Pseudo 'C' function to insert and delete item from Priority Queue.

48. Why do we need priority Queue? Explain with appropriate data structure, the implementation of priority queue.

49. What do you mean by priority queue? Explain any one application of priority queue with suitable example.

50. Explain priority queue and give application for the same.

51. What do you mean by priority queue? Explain any one application in detail.

52. Explain the term priority queue and give the application for the same.

53. What is priority queue? What are the applications of priority queue? Write a 'C' function to perform insertion and deletion on priority queue.

54. What is priority queue? Explain how insert and delete operations are implemented in it.

55. Compare circular and linear queue.

56. Write applications of queue.

Unit III

LINKED LISTS

3.1 Introduction

A list consists of set of data items. Storage, retrieval, processing of the list is a major task required to be performed on computer. In the previous chapter, we have seen how can we store and process these lists using array. Though, it is easy to use array for storing the lists, there are two disadvantages of arrays.

(i)   We cannot increase or decrease the size of the array as per our requirement during program execution.

(ii) The insert and delete operations are computationally complex.

Another way of storing a list is using linked organisation. We can store the data items alongwith address or link to the next data items. It is called linked list. Since linked lists allow us to allocate memory dynamically, we can increase or decrease the size of the list as per the number of elements to be stored. The linked lists make it easy to insert or delete the elements.

We summarize below the difference between arrays and linked lists.

Arrays	**Linked Lists**
1. Size of array needs to be mentioned while writing program. Hence fixed memory location are assigned for storage of data items.	1. Memory is allocated as and when it is required for storing data items in the linked list.
2. Data items are stored in contiguous (adjoining) memory locations.	2. Data items not in contiguous memory locations.
3. No overhead of storing address of another node.	3. Overhead of storing address of another node/structure.
4. Element in the array is difficult to insert or delete.	4. It becomes very easy to insert or delete.
5. Random access of any data element in an array is possible.	5. To access an element in linked list we have to traverse the list from beginning.
6. When an items is not required its space cannot be utilised by another variable.	6. When an item is no longer needed its space can be returned to the system which can be used by another variable.

Thus, the advantages of using linked lists are:

1. Linked list is a dynamic data structure which allows usage of memory as per requirement.

2. It is easy to perform insert and delete operations.

3. The deleted data items memory can be de-allocated.

The disadvantages are:

1. It is complex to implement.

2. Extra memory required for next field.

3. Random access not possible.

3.2 Singly Linked List: Concept

A singly linked list (SLL) is a linear collection of nodes, which consists of data item and the address of next node. Thus, each node is the SLL consists of two parts, data field and link field. Fig. 3.1 shows a linked list of integers.

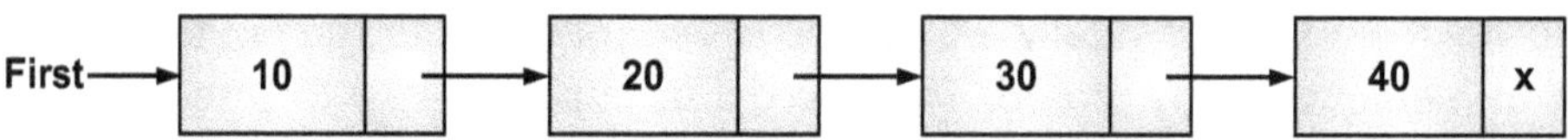

Fig. 3.1: Linked list of integers

Similarly, we can have a list of real numbers, list of names, list of records represented in Fig. 3.2.

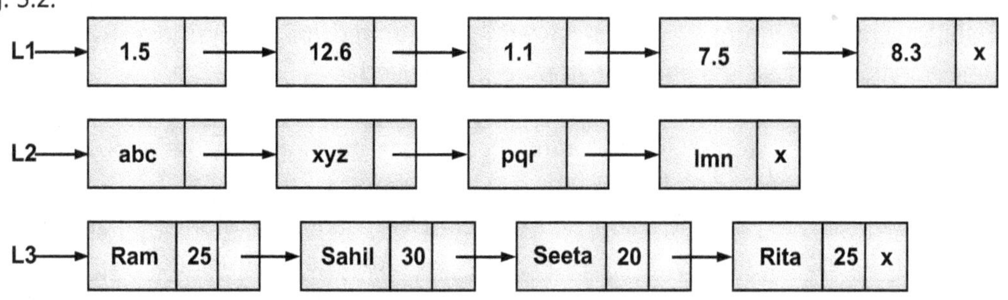

Fig. 3.2: Linked lists

It can be seen that the last node's link field contains nothing, hence it is filled with NULL (denoted as X). The first node in the list is the access point of the list, hence its address is stored in a variable called list pointer variable (For example, first L1, L2, L3 shown in the figures).

Example 3.1:

Suppose, we have a list of numbers to be stored using linked list. We want the numbers to be stored in sorted order, then the storage of number can be done alongwith its address of successor as below.

Location number	Data	Next
0	-	-
1	20	6
2	40	4
3	10	1
4	50	NULL
5	-	-
6	30	2

Linked list of numbers

It can be seen that the address (location number) of first element in the list is in first. The address of second number is next field of 10 i.e. 1 and so on. The next field of last element is NULL.

3.2.1 Linked List as ADT List

Linked list can be used to implement an ADT list. Linked list can be used to implement a linear or non-linear structures.

A linear list consists of link to every element except the last node which has NULL pointer.

A non-linear list can have two or more links.

A list can be empty list with NULL which is called NULL list pointer.

3.3 Representation of Linked List in Memory

To maintain a linked list in memory two linear arrays will be required. One array contains information and second array will store links to the next node. A list will also have a variable say first which stores location of first node in the list. The last node in the list will have NULL or in its link field.

Suppose we want to store two lists in memory consisting of students having two elective subjects SUB1 and SUB2. Then the list can be maintained in memory as shown below.

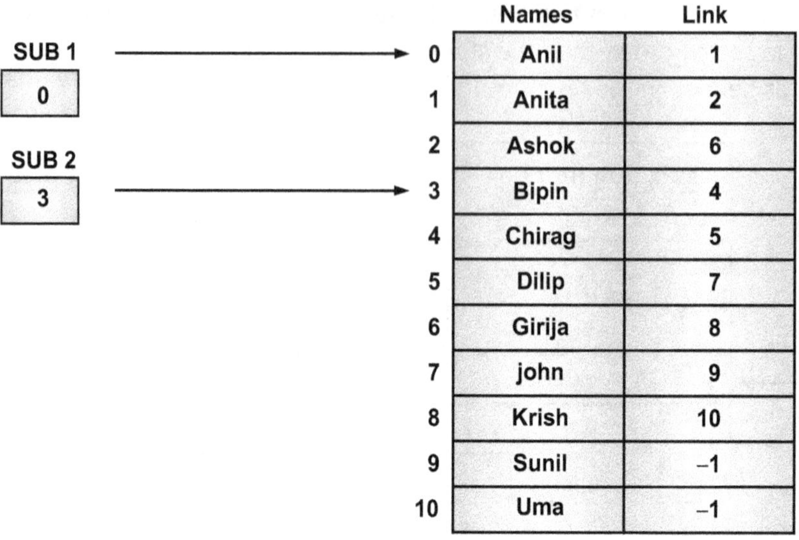

Fig. 3.3

Logically, the two lists will be represented as below:

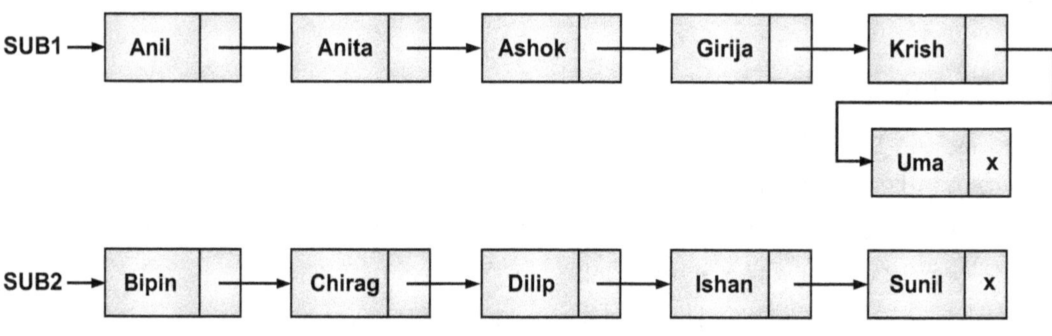

Fig. 3.4

The linked list can be implemented using static representation i.e. array or using dynamic representation i.e. pointer. Let us first see how can we store the linked list using array and traverse.

Let us consider a list shown in Fig. 3.3.

Two arrays namely DATA[ ] and NEXT[ ] will be used. A variable FIRST will store location number of first element in the list. A variable PTR will be used to store the location of mode currently being processed. Thus, we have,

FIRST=3

DATA[1]=20   NEXT[1]=6

DATA[2]=40   NEXT[2]=4

DATA[3]=10   NEXT[3]=1

DATA[4]=50   NEXT[4]=NULL

DATA[6]=30   DATA[6]=2

Note: The location number 0 and 5 are not used.

The algorithm for traversal of the linked list will be as below.

Algorithm 3.1: Traversing a linked list

Step 1:   Set PTR=FIRST

Step 2:   Repeat steps 3 and 4 while PTR != NULL

Step 3:   Display DATA[PTR]

Step 4:   Set PTR=NEXT [PTR]

Step 5:   Stop.

Similarly, we can write algorithms to perform various operations on the list such as insert, delete, search etc. The above implementation uses static memory allocation and hence is not efficient. The same concept can be used in implementation using dynamic memory allocation. Hence, we will discuss in detail the implementation of linked list using self-referential structure and pointers.

3.4 Singly Linked List Operations

Linked list is a set of structures (called nodes) having one of the fields as pointer to similar structure. (nodes)

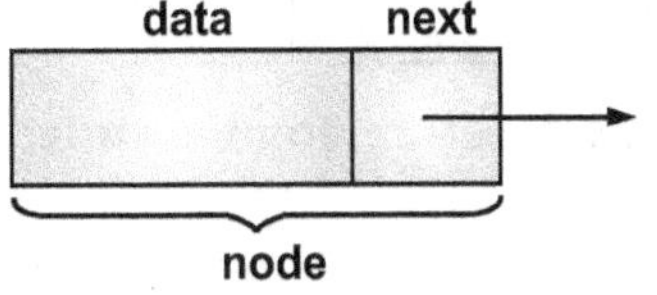

Fig. 3.5: Node in a linked list

The data field can be integers/real/string/record and next field is a pointer containing address of similar node.

A linked list is represented as:

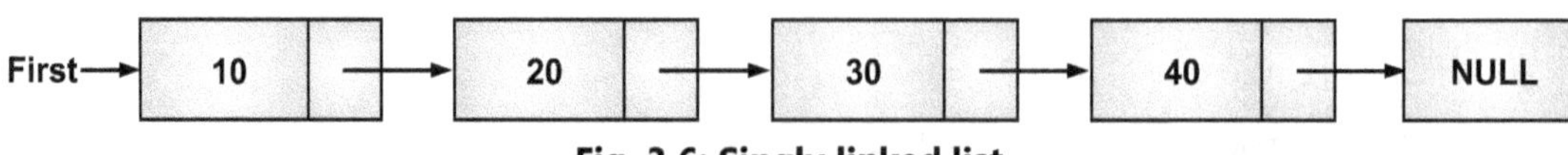

Fig. 3.6: Singly linked list

Here, first is a pointer containing address of first node of the linked list.

Also note that the last node has next field pointing to NULL means it is referring nowhere.

Before we go into details of linked list we discuss some basic concepts.

1. **Static Variable:** These variables are declared and named while writing program For example,

    int a, b;

    the space allotted to these variables exists as long as program is running.

2. **Dynamic Variables:** They are created during program execution as and when required. These variables are accessed using pointers. They can be destroyed when they are not required.

3. **Defining a node in linked list:** Suppose that we have to store a list of integer numbers in a linked list following structure variable can be defined.

```
struct node
{
    int data;
    struct node *next;
};
```

Here we are declaring a structure called as node. It has two fields data and next; data to store integer number and next to store address of another similar structure. (This is called as self referential structure),

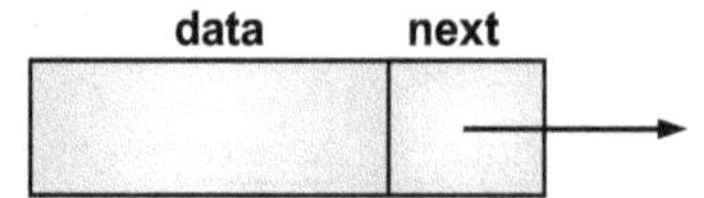

Fig. 3.7: Self referential structure

If we declare a pointer variable

struct node *ptr;

It means a pointer called ptr is declared which is of type struct node i.e. ptr can store address of a variable of type struct node.

If we want to store a list of persons having name and age. The node can be defined as

```
struct node
{
        char name [25];
        int age;
        struct node *next;
};
```

4. How to Allocate and Deallocate Memory?

To allocate memory to a dynamic variable we use malloc function as

```
ptr = (struct node*) malloc (sizeof (struct node));
```

when we do this a block of memory of the size of struct node is allocated to ptr. i.e. ptr starts pointing to the node as shown in Fig. 3.8.

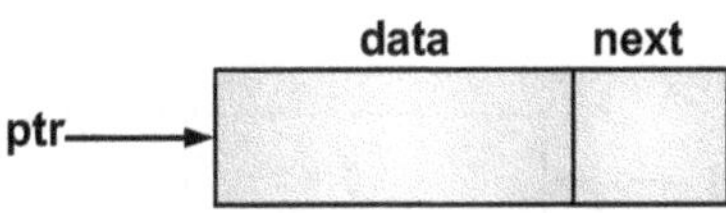

Fig. 3.8: Pointer to a node

Thus, ptr has address of the node.

If we have to assign the data to this structure pointed by ptr, we can write

```
ptr->data=x;
```

where, x is an integer number.

To de-allocate the memory allocated to ptr we can write

```
free (ptr);
```

The memory allocated to ptr will be returned back to system so that system can reuse it.

Note: When malloc fails to allocate memory, it returns NULL.

5. Some linked list related statements: Let us consider that we have pointers,

*ptr1, *ptr2, *ptr3 of the type struct node

The following statements will result into the 3 pointers pointing to 3 locations (Structures) as shown in Fig. 3.8.

```
ptr1=(struct node*)malloc(sizeof (struct node));
ptr2=(struct node*)malloc(sizeof (struct node));
ptr3=(struct node*)malloc(sizeof (struct node));
```

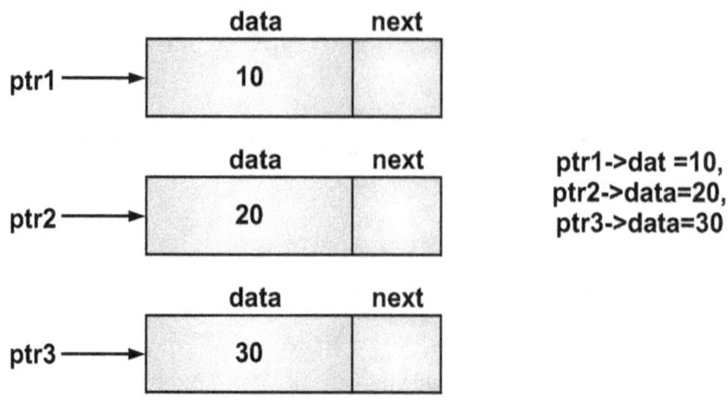

Fig. 3.9: Memory allocation and data storage

Now if we write

(a) ptr1->next=ptr2

We are storing address of second node (pointed by ptr2) in the next field of first node (pointed by ptr1). You can read this as ptr1's next will start pointing to a place where ptr2 is pointing.

i.e.

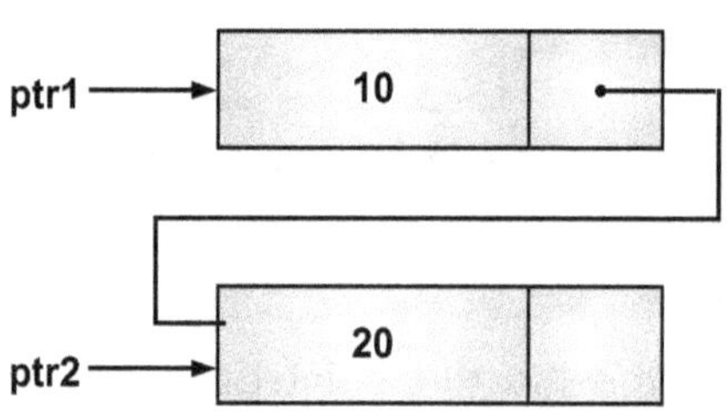

Fig. 3.10: Linking two nodes

(b) temp=ptr1;
temp will no longer point to current location. It will start pointing to a node pointed by ptr1. You can read this as temp will start pointing to a place where ptr1 is pointing

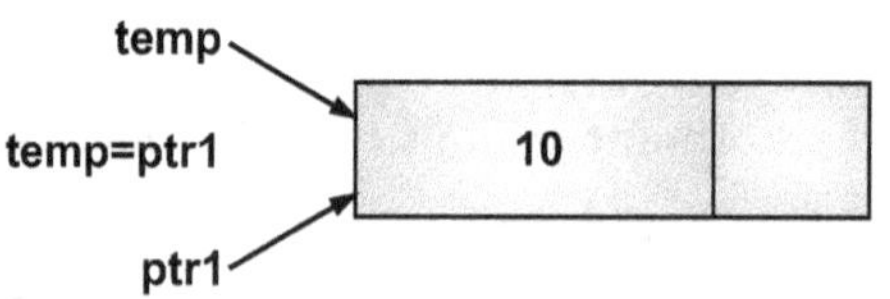

Fig. 3.11: Another pointer to a node

(c) The following statements will result in creation of a linked list.
    1.   ptr1->next=ptr2;
    2.   ptr2->next=ptr3;

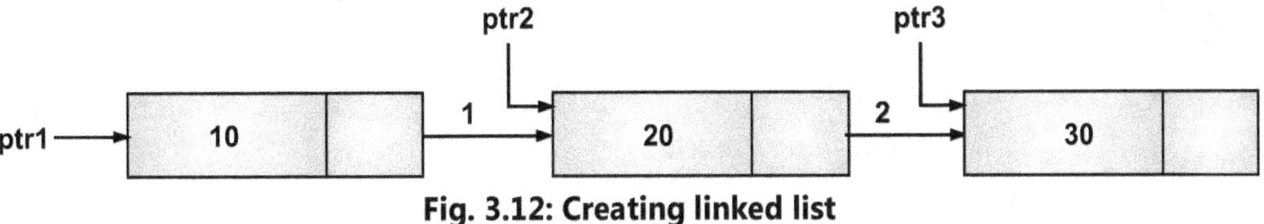

Fig. 3.12: Creating linked list

(d) If we write temp=ptr1->next, temp will start pointing to a place where ptr1-> next is pointing.

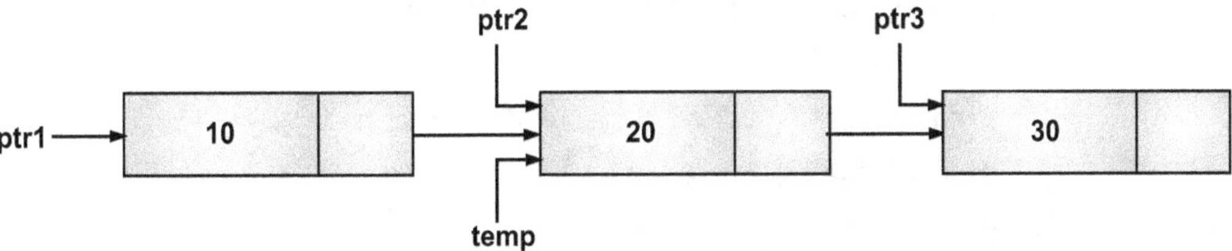

Fig. 3.13: Pointer to a next node

(e) ptr1->next=ptr->3

It will make ptr1->next point to the node pointed by ptr2->next. It will stop pointing to the node pointed by ptr2.

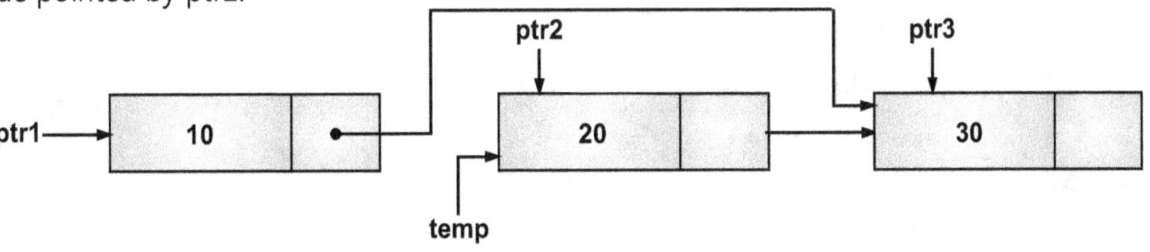

Fig. 3.14: Eliminating a node

Now let us write a simple program to create a linked list and display the elements in it.

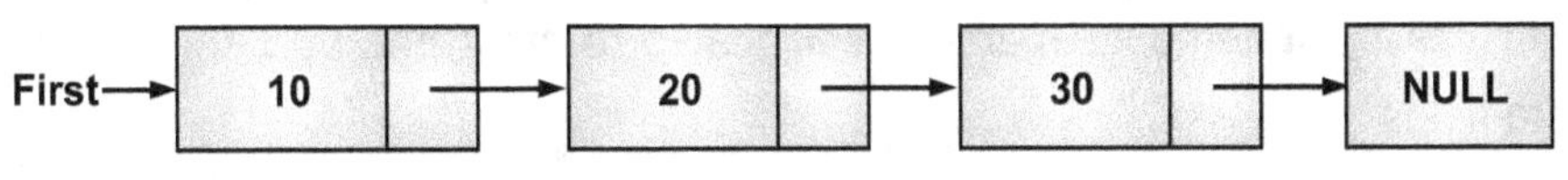

Fig. 3.15: Singly linked list

Program 3.1: A linked list of three elements.

```
#include<stdio.h>
#include<conio.h>
void main( )
{
        struct node
```

```
            {
                    int data;
                    struct node *next;
            };
            struct node *ptr1, *ptr2, *ptr3, *temp;
            ptr1=(struct node*)malloc(size of (struct node));
            ptr1->data=10;
            ptr2=(struct node*)malloc(size of (struct node));
            ptr2->data=20;
            ptr3=(struct node*)malloc(size of (struct node));
            ptr3->data=30;
            ptr1->next=ptr2;
            ptr2->next=ptr3;
            ptr3->next=NULL;
            temp=ptr1;
            while (temp!=NULL)
            {
                    printf("%d\n", temp->data);
                    temp=temp->next;
            }
    }
```

Explanation:

1. In the first seven statements, memory is allocated to ptr1, ptr2, ptr3 and data is stored in the data fields.

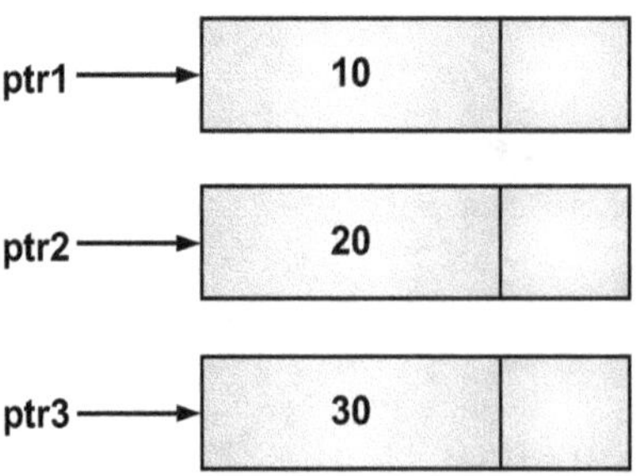

Fig. 3.16: Memory allocation and storage in nodes

2.   ptr1->next=ptr2

  and ptr2->next=ptr3

        ptr3->next=NULL;

will create a linked list and the various pointers will be pointing as below.

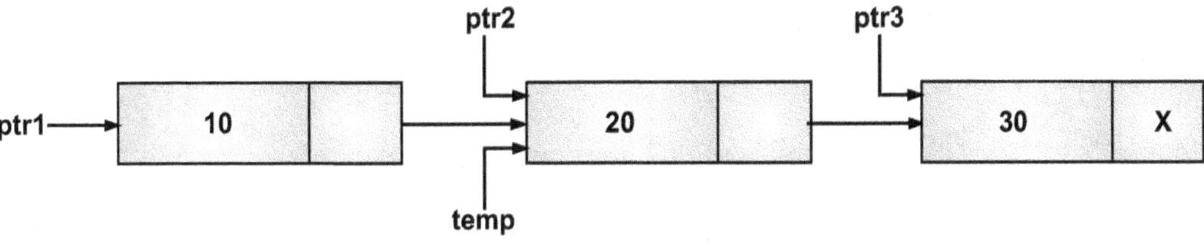

Fig. 3.17: Linking nodes

3.   Next, to display the elements in the list we point temp to ptr1 and go on advancing the pointer while displaying the data in each node.

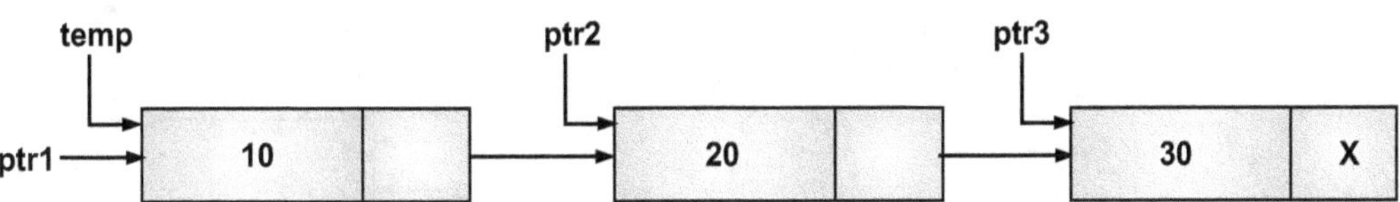

Fig. 3.18: Pointer to a first node

Above program is very elementary. Now let us write a program to create a linked list of n elements (i.e. generalized linked list). To create a list of integer numbers, we first read number of elements in the list. Then we go on allocating memory for each node and establishing link between them. Following is the program which creates and displays the linked list.

Program 3.2: To create and display a linked list.

```c
#include<stdio.h>
#include<conio.h>
void main( )
{
    struct node
    {
        int data
        struct node *next;
```

```c
};
struct node *first, *temp, *ptr;
int i, n, x;
clrscr( );
printf("Enter how many elements\n");
scanf("%d", &n);
for(i=1;i<=n;i++)
{
    printf("Enter data\n");
    scanf("%d", &x);
    ptr=malloc(size of (struct node));
    ptr->next=x;
    ptr->next=NULL;
    if (first==NULL)
    {
        first=ptr;
        temp=ptr;
    }
    else
    {
        temp->next=ptr;
        temp=ptr;
    }
}
temp=first;
while (temp!=NULL)
{
    printf("%d->", temp->data);
    temp=temp->next;
}
printf("NULL");
getch( );
}
```

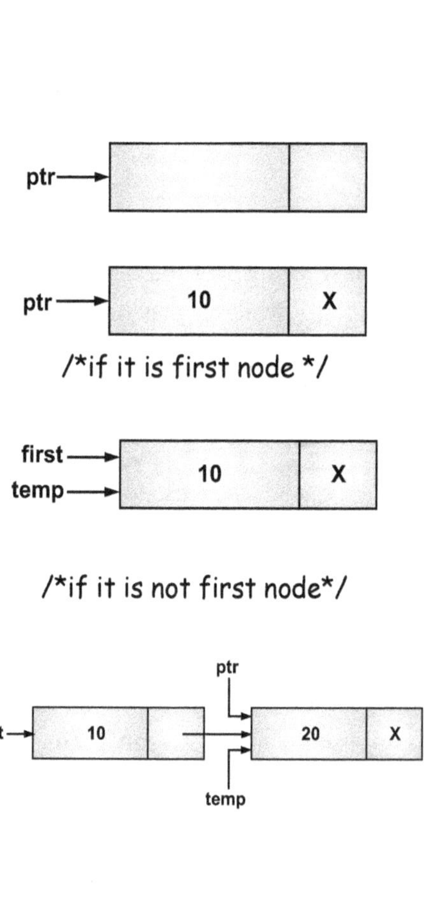

Explanation:

1. We read number of elements in the list in variable n.
2. We go on reading data in x. Allocate memory for ptr, store the data in x in the data field of ptr. If we are storing first element the condition first==NULL will be true. We should point the pointer first to this node (if part).
   Otherwise we link previous node with current and advance the pointer temp (else part).
3. To display the elements in the linked list we first point the pointer temp to first node. Access data and advance temp to next node. We continue this till temp doesn't reference to NULL.

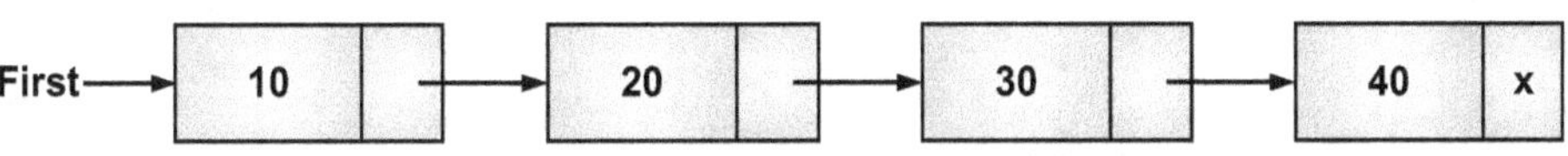

Fig. 3.19: Singly linked list

Now let us write separate functions for create and display the linked list:

Program 3.3: To create linked lists.

```c
NODE *create( )
{
        NODE *first, *ptr, *temp;
        int i, x, n;
        printf("Enter number of elements \n");
        scanf("%d", &n);
        first=NULL;
        for(i=1;i<=n;i++)
        {
                printf("Enter data \n")
                scanf("%d"; &x);
                ptr=(NODE *)malloc(size of (NODE));
                ptr->data=x;
                ptr->next=NULL;
                if(first==NULL)
                        first=ptr;
                else
                        temp->next=ptr;
```

```
                    temp=ptr;
        }
        return(first);
}
void disp(NODE *temp)
{
        while (temp!=NULL)
        {
                printf("%d->", temp->data);
                temp=temp->next;
                printf("NULL \n");
        }
}
void main( )
{
        NODE *l1, *l2;
        l1=create( );
        l2=create( );
        disp (l1);
        disp (l2);
}
```

Explanation:

1. The create function when called from main function creates a linked list which is pointed by first pointer. The address in linked list in pointer first is return back in the main function to a pointer variable say *l1* or *l2*. The pointer variable *l1* and *l2* in a main function now as address of linked list created by the create function.
2. The function disp displays the elements in the linked list, it required the address of linked list to be passed to it. The pointer variable temp collects this address and traverses the list sequentially.

3.4.1 Insert Operation

To insert an element in the linked list, the pointer (say temp) is advanced to the node after which the new element is to be inserted. A new node is created and it is inserted with the help of the pointer temp. The procedure is shown in Fig. 3.20.

(1)   Get a pointer (temp) to a node after which element is to be inserted.

(2)   Create a new node store the data.

(3)   ptr->next=temp->next;

(4)   temp->next=ptr;

It means we have to establish two new links and one link will be removed during insert operation in SLL. If the node is to be inserted before first node, then following steps will be performed.

(1) ptr->next=first

(2) first=ptr

In this case only one new link will be established.

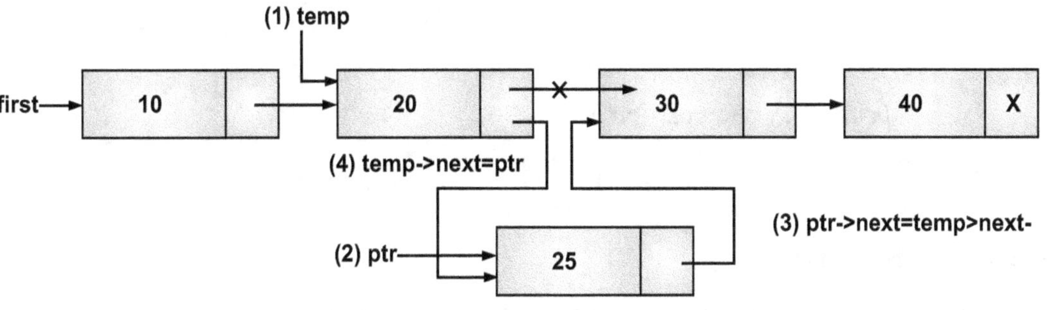

Fig. 3.20: Insert operation in SLL

The detailed algorithm is given as follows.

Algorithm 3.2: Insert an element in SLL

The detailed algorithm is given as follows:

```
(1)   Read position p;
(2)   temp=first;
(3)   i=1;
(4)   while (i<p&&temp!=NULL)
      {
            temp=temp->next;
            i++;
      }
(5)   if (temp!=NULL)
      {
            ptr=malloc(sizeof(NODE));
```

```
            ptr->data=x;
            if(p==0)                        // inserting before first node;
            {
                    ptr->next=first;
                    first=ptr;
            }
            else                            // otherwise insert after any node
            {
                    ptr->next=temp->next;
                    temp->next=ptr;
            }
        else
            printf("Invalid position");
(6)  stop.
```

3.4.2 Delete Operation

To delete an element in the linked list, the pointer (say temp) in advanced to the node which is to be deleted. One more pointer (say prev) is required just before the node to be deleted. The procedure is shown in Fig. 3.21.

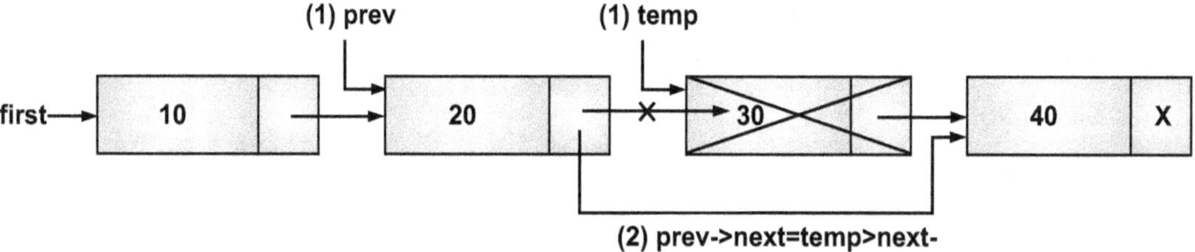

Fig. 3.21: Delete operation

(1)   Let a pointer temp point the node to be deleted and pointer prev to the previous node.

(2)   prev->next=temp->next.

(3)   free (temp)

It means one new link will be established and two links will be removed during delete operation in SLL.

If the node to be deleted is the first node in the linked list, first has to be advanced to the second position and then it is deleted.

   (1)   first=first->next.

   (2)   free (temp);

In this case only one link will be removed.

Algorithm 3.3: Delete an element in the linked list.

```
(1)   Read position p;
(2)   i=i; temp=first;
(3)   while (i<p&&temp!=NULL)
      {
            prev=temp;
            temp=temp->next;
            i++;
      }
(4)   if (temp!=NULL)
      {
            if(p==1)                        // node to be deleted is first node
            {
                  first=first->next;
                  free (temp);
            }
            else                            // any other node than first
            {
                  prev->next=temp->next;
                  free (temp);
            }
      }
      else
            printf("Invalid position");     //list is empty or p specified is more
(5)   stop.
```

3.4.3 Search Operation

To search an element in the linked list, we start with a pointer (say temp) to the first node and keep on advancing it till we find the required data in the linked list at a particular node. The algorithm will be as below.

Algorithm 3.4: Search an element in the linked list.

    (1)   Input x. (data to be searched)

    (2)   temp=first

    (3)   while(temp->data!=x&&temp!=NULL)

         temp=temp->next;

    (4) if (temp==NULL)

         printf("Found");

    else

         printf("Not found");

3.4.4 Implementation of SLL

Now we can write a complete menu driven program to implement operations viz. create, display,   search, insert, delete in a linked list. For this we have to write separate function for these operations.

Program 3.4: Implementation of singly linked list with operations create, display, insert, delete and search.

```c
#include<stdio.h>
#include<conio.h>
typedef struct_node
{
    int_node;
    struct node *next;
} NODE;
NODE *create( );
void disp (NODE *);
int search (NODE*, int);
```

```c
NODE *insert (NODE*, int, int);
NODE *del (NODE *, int);
void main( )
{
    NODE *first=NULL;
    int x, p, ch
    do
    {
        clrscr( );
        printf ("1.create\n, 2. Display\n, 3. search\n, 4. Insert\n,
        5. Delete\n, 6. Exit \n");
        printf("Enter your choice\n");
        scanf("%d", &ch);
        switch(ch)
        {
            case 1:  first=create( );
                        break;
            case 2:  disp (first);
                        break;
            case 3:  printf("Enter number to be searched \n");
                        scanf("%d", &x);
                        p=search (first, x);
                        if (p>0)
                            printf("found at %d", p);
                        else
                            printf("Not found");
            case 4:  printf("Enter data & position \n");
                        scanf(%d %d", &x, &p);
                        first=insert (first, x, p);
            case 5:  printf("Enter node number \n");
                        scanf("%d", &p);
                        first=del (first, p);
```

```c
            }
            getch( )
        } while (ch!=6);
}
NODE *create( )
{
    NODE *first, *ptr, *temp;
    int i, x, n;
    printf("Enter number if elements \n");
    scanf("%d", &n);
    first=NULL;
    for(i=1;i<=n;i++)
    {
        printf("Enter data \n");
        scanf("%d", &x);
        ptr=(NODE*)malloc(sizeof(NODE));
        ptr->data=x;
        ptr->next=NULL;
        if(first==NULL)
            first=ptr;
        else
            temp->next=ptr;
        temp=ptr;
    }
    return(first);
}
void disp (NODE *temp)
{
    while (temp!=NULL)
    {
        printf("%d->", temp->data);
        temp=temp->next;
```

```c
        }
}
int search (NODE *first, int x)
{
    Node *temp;
    int c=1;
    temp=first;
    while (temp->data!=x&&temp!=NULL)
    {
        temp=temp->next;
        c++;
    }
    if (temp!=NULL)
        return (c);
    else
        return (-1);
}
NODE *insert (NODE *first, int *x, int p)
{
    NODE *temp, *ptr;
    int i;
    temp=first; i=1;
    while (i<p&&temp!=NULL)
    {
        temp=temp->next;
        i++;
    }
    if (temp!=NULL)
    {
        ptr=(NODE *)malloc(sizeof (NODE));
        ptr->data=x;
        ptr->next=NULL;
```

```c
                if (p==0)
                {
                        ptr->next=first;
                        first=ptr;
                }
                else
                {
                        ptr->next= temp->next;
                        temp->next=ptr;
                }
        }
        else
                printf("Invalid position");
        return (first);
}
Node *del (NODE*first, int p)
{
        NODE *temp, *prev;
        int i;
        temp=first; i=1;
        while (i<p&&temp!=NULL)
        {
                prev=temp;
                temp=temp->next;
                i++;
        }
        if (temp!=NULL)
        {
                if (p==1)
                {
                        first=first->next;
                        free (temp);
```

```c
            }
            else
            {
                    prev->next=temp->next;
                    free (temp);
            }
        }
        else
            printf ("Invalid position");
        return (first);
}
void insert (NODE *first, int p, int x)
{
        NODE *ptr, *temp;
        temp=first;
        i=1;
        while (i<p&&temp!=NULL)
        {
                temp=temp->next;
                i++;
        }
        if (temp!=NULL)
        {
                ptr==(NODE *)malloc(sizeof (NODE));
                ptr->data x;
                if (p==0)                           // inserting before the first node;
                {
                        ptr->next=first;
                        first=ptr;
                }
                else                                // otherwise
                {
                        prev->next=temp->next;
```

```
                    temp->next=ptr;
            }
        }
        else
            printf ("Invalid position");
        return (first);
    }
```

3.5 Memory Allocation; Garbage Collection

The insert operation in linked list requires new memory location to be allocated and the delete operation makes the nodes free. The operating system has to allocate memory to new nodes when malloc requests for it. For this the operating system should know which location is available for allocation. For this system has to detect and reclaim the free nodes. This process is called garbage collection. Since these memory locations are scattered, the system has to maintain a list of available free nodes. For this the system has to periodically collect all the deleted locations free nodes.

The garbage collection is performed in two steps through a operating system routine called garbage collector.

(I)   The system finds out all the nodes/cells which are currently in use and tags them. This phase is called marking phase.

(II) The entire memory is scanned and all the untagged spaces are collected and maintained under free storage list. This phase is called collection phase.

The garbage collection takes place under following circumstances.

(i)   When there is minimum amount of space or no space available in the free storage list.

(ii) When CPU is idle and has time to do the garbage collection.

Whenever garbage collector is called, all user processing is stopped therefore, garbage collector has to be called under above circumstances.

3.5.1 Overflow and Underflow

When insert operation is performed and there is no space available, i.e. the free storage list is empty, overflow occurs. For example, during insert operation if malloc function fails to allocate memory, it returns NULL value. The programmer can display an error message indicating the overflow.

Similarly, during delete operation if there is no data in the list, it is called underflow. The programmer can print an error message when the pointer "first" is NULL.

3.5.2 Garbage Compaction

Though the method of garbage collection makes efficient use of memory, the available free list may not be usable, this is because the available memory is fragmented and may exist in the blocks of different sizes. If a programmer requires memory in large block sizes then some of the locations in the available free list may not be useful. For example, suppose all the even locations in memory are occupied and request for storing records of size more than one comes. This request will be rejected because the odd numbered location are of size one unit. The solution to this problem is to move all used (tagged) nodes to one end of memory and all the free nodes to the other. This process is called compaction.

The process of compaction requires all the pointers to be updated whenever a block is moved. This is required because the next element of the current node will be moved to a new location and this happens for every node.

3.6 Header Linked List

Sometimes it is desirable to keep an extra node in front or at the end of a linked list. This node will not store any data but it will be a dummy node and it is called as 'header node' or 'list header'. The data field can be used to store some information about the list, For example, number of nodes in the list. A list with header node is shown in Fig. 3.22.

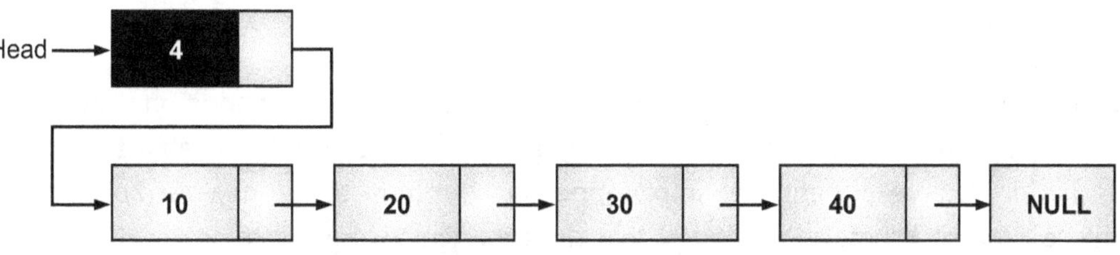

Fig. 3.22: Header node in linked list

This kind of head node will be useful in circular linked list where there is no fixed first node. Instead of a pointer to last node we can have a header node at the front end. The algorithms will be required to be modified to accommodate this change.

3.7 Applications of Link List Manipulation

3.7.1 Polynomial Manipulation

A polynomial can be represented in an array or in a linked list by simply storing the coefficient and exponent of each term. However, for any polynomial operation, such as addition or multiplication of polynomials, you will find that the linked list representation is easier to deal with. First of all note that in a polynomial all the terms may not be present, especially if it is going to be a very high order polynomial. Consider,

$$5x^{12} + 2x^9 + 4x^7 + 6x^5 + x^2 + 12x$$

Now this 12th order polynomial does not have all the 13 terms (including the constant term). It would be very easy to represent the polynomial using a linked list structure, where each node can hold information pertaining to a single term of the polynomial. Each node will need to store the variable x, the exponent and the coefficient for each term. It often does not matter whether the polynomial is in x or y. This information may not be very crucial for the intended operations on the polynomial. Thus we need to define a node structure to hold two integers, viz. exponent and coefficient, For example, a polynomial $3x^4 + 5x^3 + 6x$ is represented in a linked list as,

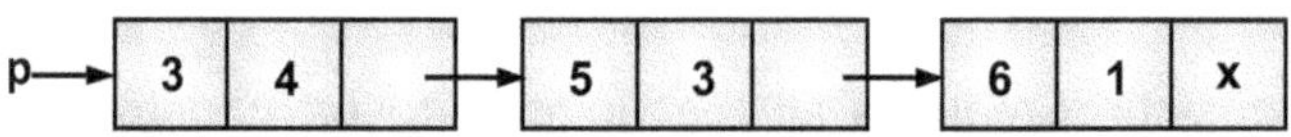

Fig. 3.23: Polynomial representation using SLL

3.7.2 Addition of Two Polynomials
Consider addition of the following polynomials,
$$5x^{12} + 2x^9 + 4x^7 + 6x^6 + x^3$$
$$7x^8 + 2x^7 + 8x^6 + 6x^4 + 2x^2 + 3x + 40$$

The resulting polynomial is going to be,
$$5x^{12} + 2x^9 + 7x^8 + 6x^7 + 14x^4 + 6x^4 + x^3 + 2x^2 + 3x + 40$$

Now notice how the addition was carried out. Let us say the result of addition is going to be stored in a third list. We started with the highest power in any polynomial. If there was no item having same exponent, we simply appended the term to the new list and continued with the process. Wherever we found that the exponents were matching, we simply added the coefficients and then stored the term in the new list. If one list gets exhausted earlier and the other list still contains some lower order terms, then simply append the remaining terms to the new list. Now we are in a position to write our algorithm for adding two polynomials. Let a, b and c represent the pointers of the three lists under consideration. Let each node contain two integers exponent and coefficient. Let us assume that the two linked lists already contain relevant data about the two polynomials. Also assume that we have got a function insert to insert a new node at the end of the given list. Let us consider two polynomials as,
$$3x^3 + 5x^2 + 7$$
$$3x^4 + 5x^3 + 6x$$
Following linked list pointed by a and b will be created using create function. The terms in a polynomial can be stored sequentially using a linked list as shown. The coefficient and power of each term is stored in -the nodes of linked list. The process of addition of two polynomials consists of testing each term power sequentially. The resultant polynomial will be pointed by c and is shown in Fig. 3.24.

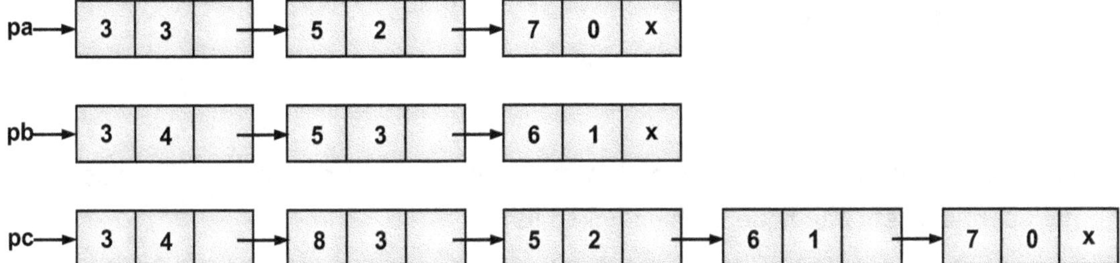

Fig. 3.24: Additional of two polynomials

Algorithm 3.4:

The algorithm to add two polynomials using linked list will be as follows:

1. Create first polynomial. Let, a be pointer to it.

> a=create( )

2. Create second polynomial. Let, b be pointer to it.

> b=create( )

3. Let, pa=a pb =b pc=NULL

4. while (pa !=NULL&&pb!=NULL)

```
{
     if(pa->power==pb->power)
     {
          c=pa->coeff + pb->coeff;
          p=pa->power;
          pa=pa->next; ph=pb->next;
     }
else
     if(pa->power>pb->power)
     {
          c=pa->coeff;
          p=pa->power;
          pa=pa->next;
     }
     else
     {
          c=pb -> coeff;
          p=pb -> power;
```

```
        pb=pb -> next;
            }
        }
```

insert (pc, c, p); i.e. create new node with c and p (coeff and power of terms to be added) and insert the node in third linked list pc.

```
    }
```

5. while (pa!=NULL)   // Remaining terms of first polynomial.
    ```
    {
        c=pa->coeff;
        p=pa->power;
        insert (pc, c, p);
    }
    ```

6. while (pb!=NULL)   // Remaining terms of second polynomial
    ```
    {
        c=pb->coeff;
        p=pb->power;
        insert (pc, c, p);
    }
    ```

7. Display third polynomial terms.

    To write a program for addition of two polynomials we require four functions viz.

1. create( )
2. disp( )
3. addpoly( )
4. insert( )

Program 3.5: Addition of two polynomials using linked list.

```
typedef struct node
{
    int coeff, pow;
    struct node *next;
}   NODE;
NODE *create( );
void disp(NODE *);
```

```c
NODE *addpoly (NODE NODE *);
NODE *insert(NODE *, int, int);
void main( )
{
    NODE *a, *b, *c;
    a=create( );
    b=create( );
    c=addpoly(a, b);
    disp (c);
}
NODE *create( )
{
    int i, n;
    NODE *first, *temp, *ptr;
    int c, p;
    printf("Enter number of terms \n");
    scanf("%d", &n);
    first=NULL;
    for(i=1;i<n;i++)
    {
        printf ("Enter coefficient and power \n");
        scanf("%d %d", &c, &p);
        ptr=(NODE *) malloc (sizeof (NODE));
        ptr->coeff=c;
        ptr->pow=p;
        ptr->next=NULL;
        if (first==NULL)
            first=ptr;
        else
            temp->next=ptr,
        temp=ptr;
    }
```

```c
            return (first);
}
void disp (NODE*first)
{
    NODE *temp;
    temp=first;
    while (temp!->next=NULL)
    {
        printf ("%dx^ %d+", temp->coeff, temp->power);
        temp=temp->next;
    }
    if(temp->power!=0)
        printf("%dx^ %d+", temp->coeff, temp->power);
    else
        printf("%d", temp->coeff);
}
NODE *addpoly(NODE *pa, NODE *pb)
{
    NODE *pc=NULL;
    int c, p;
    while (pa!=NULL&&pb!=NULL)
    {
        if (pa->power==pb->power)
        {
            c=pa->coeff + pb->coeff;
            p=pa->power;
            pa=pa->next; pb=pb->next;
        }
        else
        {
            if(pa->power > pb->power)
            {
```

```c
                    c=pa->coeff;
                    p=pa->power;
                    pa=pa->next;
            }
            else
            {
                    c=pb->coeff;
                    p=pb->power;
                    pb=pb->next;
            }
        }
        pc=insert (pc, c, p);
    }
    while (pa!=NULL)
    {
        c=pa->coeff;
        p=pa->power;
        pa=pa->next;
        pc=insert (pc, p, c);
    }
    while (pb!=NULL)
    {
        c=pb->coeff;
        p=pb->power;
        pb=pb->next;
        pc=insert (pc, p, c);
    }
    return (pc);
}
NODE *insert (NODE *first, int c, int p)
{
    NODE *temp; *ptr;
```

```
        ptr=(NODE*) malloc(sizeof (NODE));
        ptr->coeff=c;
        ptr->power=p;
        ptr->next=NULL;
        if(first==NULL)
                first=ptr;
        else
        {
                temp=first;
                while (temp->next!=NULL)
                        temp=temp->next;
                temp->next=ptr;
        }
        return (first);
}
```

Explanation:

1. The function create( ) creates a linked list of polynomial and returns address of the linked list. The create function is called twice in main to create and store two polynomials in linked lists a and b.

2. The addpoly( ) function adds the two polynomials and returns the address of third polynomial. For this we take three pointers pa, pb and pc; each points to the three linked lists of polynomials a, b and c (initially pc will be NULL). We start comparing the terms of first and second polynomial copy the terms in third polynomial as per the conditions mentioned and advance the pointers to next terms. To copy the term in third polynomial insert function is used.

3. The disp( ) function displays the polynomial stored in the linked list.

3.8 Circular Linked List (CLL)

In singly linked list we can access the data only in forward direction. Given a pointer to a node in a singly linked list, we can access all the node which follow that node. But we can not access the previous node.

In circular linked list, we store the first node's address in the next field of last node, so that the list becomes circular. In this case, given a pointer to any node we can access all the nodes in the list.

Truly speaking circular linked list does not have first or last node. Any node can be treated as a first node and the node before it can be last. But as a convention and convenience we can have pointer to last node and the next will be first node.

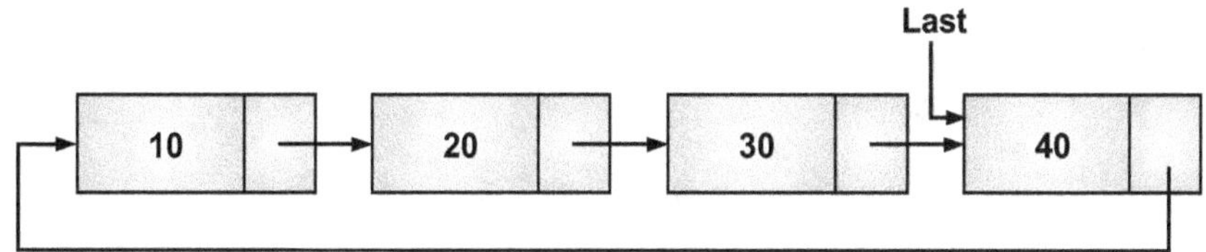

Fig. 3.25: Circular Linked List

Some of the algorithms where we need to frequently move in the forward or backward direction are easily implemented using circular linked list.

There can be different ways of implementation of CLL

Following program implements a circular linked list. The circular linked list is created in such a way that at every stage, the list will be circular, i.e., right from insertion of first node, the list will be circular. The rest of the operations insert, delete, search etc. will be similar to singly linked list.

Program 3.6: To implement Circular Linked List.

```
typedef struct node
{
    int data;
    struct NODE *next;
}   NODE;
NODE *create( )
{
    NODE *last, *ptr, *temp;
    int i, x, n;
    printf("Enter number of elements \n");
    scanf("%d", &n);
```

```c
        last=NULL;
        for(i=1;i<n;i++)
        {
            printf("Enter data");
            scanf("%d", &x);
            ptr=(NODE *) malloc(sizeof (NODE));
            ptr->data=x;
            ptr->next=NULL;
            if(last==NULL)
                last=ptr;
            else
                last->next=ptr;
            ptr->next=last;
                last=ptr;
        }
        return (last);
}
void disp (NODE *last)
{
    NODE *temp;
    temp=last->next;
    while (temp!=last)
    {
        printf ("%d->", temp->data);
        temp=temp->next;
    }
    printf("%d", temp->data);          // Last element
}
void main( )
{
    NODE *last;
    last=create( )
    disp (last);
}
```

Explanation:

1. The pointer 'last' points to the last node in the list.

2. To create a list we start with last=NULL.

   Data is accepted stored in a node ptr.

   If it is first element last will point to it.

   Second element onward the node is linked to last and the next field is linked to first node which is nothing but

   last->next and the new node is made last.

3. To display, we start with first node (i.e. last->next) and advance till we reach the last node.

3.9 Doubly Linked List

A doubly linked list is a set of linked nodes in which each node stores data as well as address of next and previous nodes. In singly linked list we can move only in forward direction. Doubly linked list allows us to move in both directions. Hence, given pointer to a node we can access any element which is either after the node or before the node. Some of the algorithm can be implemented with better time complexity using doubly linked list. But this list requires additional space in each node for storing previous node address. The implementation of the list is complex compared to singly linked list.

A node in the doubly linked list can be defined as below:

```
typedef struct node
{
    int data;
    struct node *next, *prev;
} NODE;
```

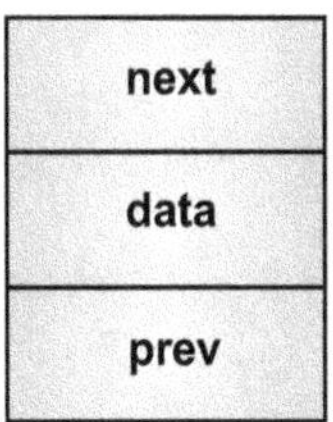

Fig. 3.26: NODE in a doubly linked list

The field data stores data element. The field next stores address of the next node and the field prey stores address of the previous node. A doubly linked list of integers is shown in Fig. 3.27.

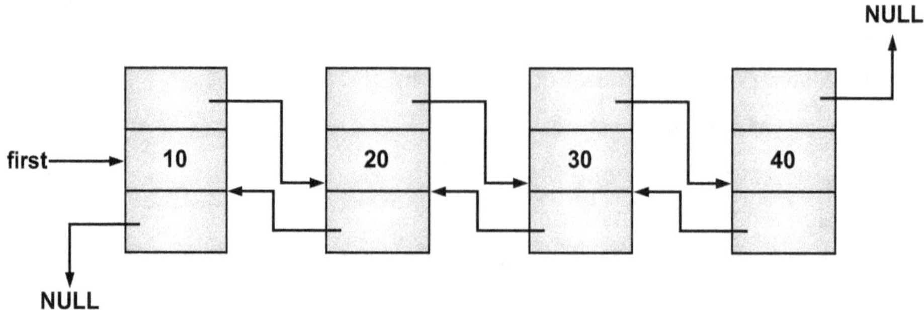

Fig. 3.27: Doubly linked list

Now let us discuss various operations on doubly linked list.

The node definition will be as follows:

```c
typedef struct node
{
    int data;
    struct node *next, *prev;
}   NODE;
```

1. Create:

```c
NODE *create( )
{
    NODE *first, *temp, *ptr;
    int i, n, x;
    first=NULL;
    printf("How many elements \n");
    scanf("%d", &n);
    for(i=1;i<=n;i++)
    {
        printf("Enter data \n");
        scanf("%d", &x);
        ptr=(NODE*)malloc(sizeof (NODE));  // Create a node
        ptr->next=ptr->prev NULL;
        ptr->data=x;  // Store data in node
        if (first==NULL)
            first=ptr;                              // if it is first node point first to it
```

```
            else
            {
                    temp->next=ptr;        // Link previous node with new node (forward link)
                    ptr->prev=temp;        // Link new node with previous node (backward link)
            }
            temp=ptr;                      // Advance temp
      }
      return (first);
}
```

The process is shown in Figure 3.28.

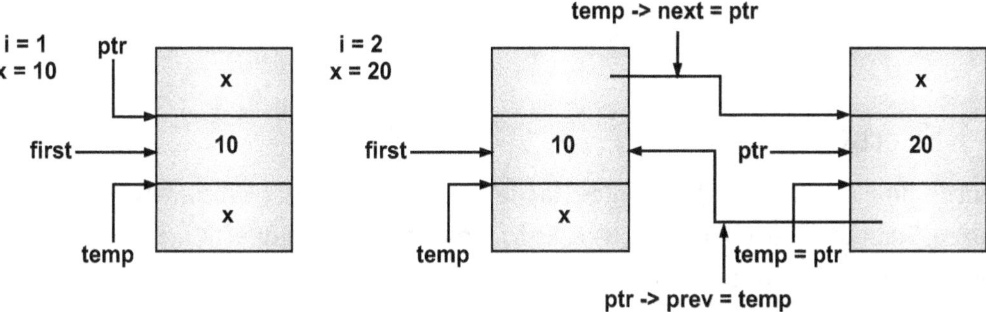

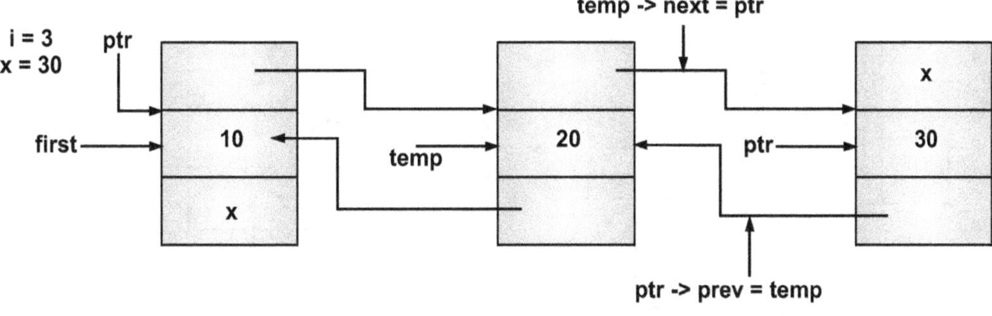

Fig. 3.28: Create procedure of DLL

2. Display:

```
void disp (NODE *first)
{
      NODE *temp;
      temp=first;
      printf("DLL in forward direction \n");
      while (temp->next!=NULL)
      {
```

```
        printf("%d->", temp->data);
        temp=temp->next;
}
printf("%d \n", temp->data);
printf("DLL in reverse direction \n");

while (temp!=NULL)
{
        printf("%d<-", temp->data);
        temp=temp->prev;
}
}
```

3.9.1 Insert Operation

To insert an element we get a pointer (say temp) to a node after which new element to be inserted. Then the new node (say ptr) links to temp in backward direction and the next node after temp in forward direction. It is shown in figure 3.29, where 30 is inserted in between 20 and 40.

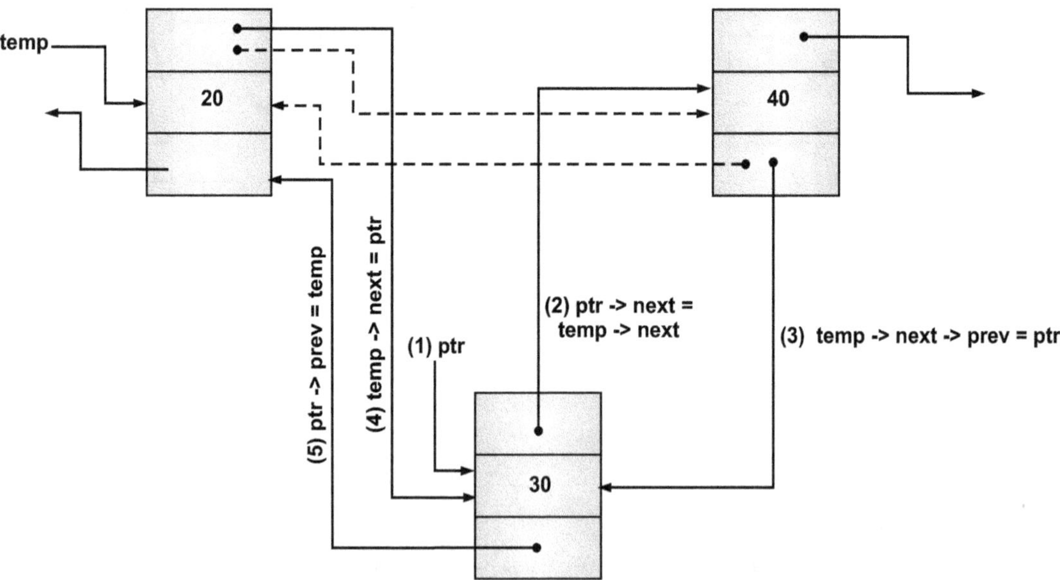

Fig. 3.29: Insert operation in DLL

It means during insert operation in DLL, four new links are created and two links are deleted. If we are inserting before first node, only two new links are established.

Algorithm 3.5: To insert a node in DLL.

```
1.  Read p position where new node is to be inserted.
2.  i=1;
3.  temp= first;
4.  while (i<p&&temp!= NULL)
    {
          temp=temp->next;
          i++;
    }
5.  if (temp!=NULL)
    {
          Read x;
          ptr=malloc (sizeof (NODE))
          ptr->data=x;
          ptr->next=ptr->prev=NULL;
          if (p==0)                          // Insertion before first node
          {
                ptr->next=temp;
                temp->prev=ptr;
                first=ptr;
          }
          else                               // Insertion after first node
          {
                ptr->next=temp->next;
                temp->next->prev=ptr;
                temp->next=ptr;
                ptr->prev = temp;
          }
    }
    else
          printf("Invalid position");
6.  stop.
```

3.9.2 Delete Operation

To delete node in DLL we get a pointer (say temp) to a node to be deleted. With the help of this pointer a node previous to temp and next to temp are linked to each other and temp is eliminated from the list. The operation is shown in figure 3.30.

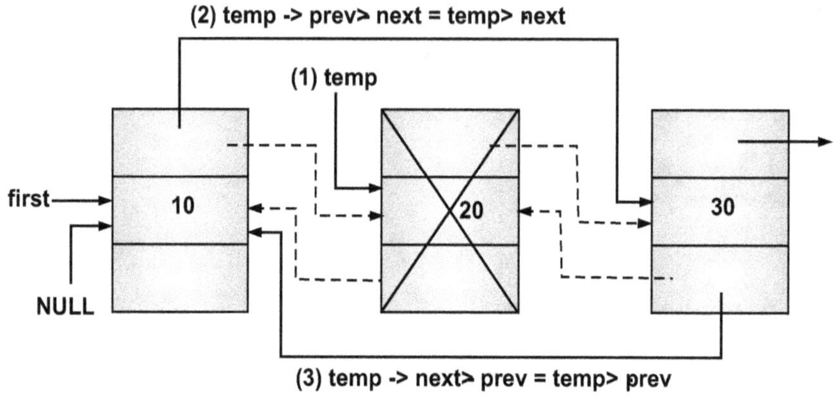

Fig. 3.30: Delete operation

It means during delete operation in DLL, two new links are established and four links are removed. If we are deleting first node, only two links are deleted.

Algorithm 3.6: To delete a node in DLL.

1. Read p
2. i=1.
3. temp=first
4. while (i<p&&temp!= NULL)
    {
        temp=temp->next;
        i++;
5. if (temp!==NULL)
    {
        if (p==1)   // First node
        {
            first=first->next;
            first->prev=NULL;

```
            free (temp);
    }
    else                                  // Any other node after first
    {
            temp->prev->next=temp->next;
            temp ->next->prev=temp->prev;
            free (temp);
    }
}
else
    printf("Invalid position");
```
6. stop.

3.9.3 Search Operation

To search an element, we start from the first node and keep on advancing in the list till we get the data at a particular node.

Algorithm 3.7: To search data in DLL.

1. Read s (data to be searched)
2. temp=first;
3. while (temp->data!=s&&temp!=NULL)
           temp=temp->next;
4. if (temp!=NULL)
           printf("Found");
    else
           printf("Not found");

3.9.4 Implementation of DLL

Now let us write a complete program to implement a DLL. The functions used in the program are:

1. **Create:** Creates a DLL and returns the address of first node.
    node *create_dll( );

2. **Display:** Displays the list in forward and reverse direction.
    void disp_dll(NODE*);
3. **Insert:** Inserts a new node in DLL and returns the address of first node.
    NODE *insert_dll(NODE*, int, int);
4. **Delete:** Deletes a node in DLL and returns the address of first node.
    NODE *del_dll(NODE*, int);
5. **Search:** Finds a node with given data and returns position of the node.
    int *search_dll(NODE*, int);

Program 3.7: To implement various operations on DLL.

```c
typedef struct node
{
    int data;
    struct node *next, *prev;
}    NODE;
NODE *create_dll( );
void disp_dll(NODE *);
int search_dll(NODE*, int);
NODE *insert_dll (NODE*, int, int);
NODE *del_dll (NODE*, int);
void main( )
{
    NODE *first;
    int ch, x, p;
    do
    {
        clrscr( );
        printf 1. Create \n 2. Display \n 3. Search \n 4. Insert \n 5. Delete \n 6.
        Exit \n");
        printf ("Enter your choice \n");
        scanf("%d", &ch);
        switch (ch)
        {
            case 1:  first=create_dll( );
                     break;
            case 2:  disp_dll (first);
                     break;
```

```c
            case 3:  printf("Enter number to be searched \n");
                     scanf("%d", &x);
                     p=search_dll (first, x);
                     if (p>0)
                         printf(Found at %d", p);
                     else
                         printf("not found");
            case 4:  printf("Enter data and position \n");
                     scanf("%d %d", &x, &p);
                     first=insert_dll (first, x, p);
            case 5:  printf("Enter node number \n");
                     scanf("%d", &p);
                     first=del_dll (first, p);
        }
        getch( );
    }    while (ch!=6);
}
NODE *create_dll( )
{
    NODE *first, *temp, *ptr;
    int i, n, x;
    first=NULL;
    printf("How many elements? \n");
    scanf("%d", &n);
    for(i=1;i<=n;i++)
    {
        printf("Enter data \n"),
        scanf("%d", &x);
        ptr=(NODE*) malloc(sizeof (NODE));
        ptr->data=x;
        if (first==NULL)
            first=ptr;
        else
        {
            temp->next=ptr;
            ptr->prev=temp;
```

```c
            }
            temp=ptr;
        }
        return (first);
}
void disp_dll(NODE *first)
{
    NODE *temp;
    temp=first;
    printf("DLL in forward direction \n");
    while (temp->next!=NULL)
    {
        printf("%d->", temp->data);
        temp=temp->next;
    }
    printf("%d \n", temp->data);
    printf("DLL in reverse direction \n")
    while (temp!=NULL)
    {
        printf("%d<-", temp->data);
        temp=temp->prev;
    }
}
int search_dll(NODE *first, int x)
{
    NODE *temp;
    int i=1;
    temp=first;
    while (temp->data!=x&&temp!=NULL)
    {
        temp=temp->next;
        i++;
    }
    if (temp!=NULL)
        return (i);
    else
```

```c
            return (-1);
}
NODE *insert_dll(NODE first, int p, int x)
{
    NODE *temp, *ptr;
    int i;
    i=1;
    temp=first;
    while (i<p&&temp!=NULL)
    {
        temp=temp->next;
        i++;
    }
    if (temp!=NULL)
    {
        ptr=(NODE*) malloc (sizeof (NODE));
        ptr->data=x;
        ptr->prev=ptr->next=NULL;
        if (p==0)
        {
            first->prev ptr;
            ptr->next=first;
            first=ptr;
        }
        else
        {
            ptr->next=temp ->next;
            temp->next->prev=ptr;
            temp->next=ptr;
            ptr->prev=temp;
        }
    }
    else
        printf("Invalid position");
    return (first);
}
```

```c
NODE *delete_dll(NODE *first, int p)
{
    NODE *temp, *ptr;
    int i;
    i=1;
    temp=first;
    while (i<p&&temp!=NULL)
    {
        temp=temp->next;
        i++;
    }
    if (temp!=NULL)
    {
        if (p==1)
        {
            first=first->next;
            first->prev=NULL;
        }
        else
        {
            temp->prev->next=temp->next;
            temp->next->prev=temp->prev;
            free (temp);
        }
    }
    else
        printf("Invalid position");
    return (first);
}
```

3.10 Comparison of Singly Linked, Circularly Linked and Doubly Linked List

Singly linked list	Doubly linked list	Circular linked list
1. It consist of nodes having single link to next data.	1. It consist of nodes having double link one to next node and other to previous node.	1. It consists of last node whose next field stores address of first node.
2. Given a pointer p to a node one can only traverse in forward direction.	2. Given a pointer p to a node one can traverse in both forward and backward direction.	2. Given pointer P to a node one can access node.
3. Implementation is simple.	3. Implementation is complex.	3. Implementation is complex compared to SLL.
4. Delete operation requires two pointers.	4. Delete operation requires one pointer.	4. Delete operation requires two pointers.
5. Used in application where you need to access elements sequentially.	5. Used in application where traversal in both direction is required.	5. Used in application where nodes may be traversed frequently.

SUMMARY

- Linked list is linear, dynamic data structure in which elements are stored in nodes which are connected to each other. Each node in the linked list consists of data field and address field.

- Singly linked list (SLL) consists of set of nodes which have single address field which stores the address of next node. SLL can be traversed in forward direction only.

- Doubly linked list (DLL) consists of set of nodes with two address fields for string address of previous and next node. The DLL can be traversed in both directions.

- A polynomial can be stored in linked list with coefficient and power of each term being stored in each node along with address of next node.

- Addition of two polynomials stored in two linked lists can be carried out by accessing each term in the linked lists sequentially.

- A Circular Linked List (CLL) stores address of first node in the next field of last node.
- Linked list can be used for information storage and retrieval, storage management and implementation of stacks and queues etc.
- A Generalized Linked List (GLL) consists of elements which themselves can be sub-list.
- A Generalized Linked List (GLL) can be used to store polynomial with multiple variables.

SOLVED PROBLEMS

1. Write a function to reverse a Singly Linked List without creating new node or swapping data.

Solution:

```c
NODE *reverse(NODE *first)
{
    NODE *p1,*p2,*p3;        // Take three pointers to point to 3 successive nodes
    p1=NULL;
    p2=first;                // Initialize
    p3=first->next;
    while(p2!=NULL)          // while it is not end of list
    {
        p2->next=p1;         // link middle's next to first
        p1=p2;               // advance first to middle.
        p2=p3;               // advance middle to last
        if(p3!=NULL)
            p3=p3->next;     // advance p3 to next node
    }
    return(p1);
}
```

2. Write a function to merge two Singly Linked Lists.

Solution:

```c
NODE *merge(NODE *p, NODE *q)
{
    NODE *pc NULL, *temp;
    if(p!=NULL)
    {
        temp=pc=p;
        p=p->next;
```

```c
        }
        else
        {
            if(q!=NULL)
            {
                temp=pc=q;
                q=q ->next;
            }
        }
        while (p!=NULL&&q!=NULL)
        {
            temp->next=q;
            q=q->next;
            temp=temp->next;
            temp->next=p;
            p=p->next;
            temp=temp->next;
        }
        while (p!=NULL)
        {
            temp->next=pa;
            p=p->next;
            temp=temp->next;
        }
        while (q!=NULL).
        {
            temp->next=q;
            q=q->next;
            temp=temp->next;
        }
        return(pc);
    }
```

3. Write a C function to delete a node in DLL pointed by P.

Solution:

```c
    NODE *delete_dll(NODE *first, NODE *p)
    {
        NODE *temp;
        temp=p;
        if(temp!=NULL)
```

```
        {
            if (temp==first)          // For first nude
            {
                first=first->next;
                first->prev=NULL;
            }
            else
            {
                temp->prev->next=temp->next;
                temp ->next->prev=temp ->prev;
                free (temp);
            }
        }
        else
            printf("List empty");
        return (first);
    }
```

4. Write a C function to delete a node in DLL with value x.   **[May 09]**
Solution:

```
    NODE *delete-dil(NODE *first, int x)
    {
        NODE *temp;
        temp=first;
        while(temp->data!=x&&temp!=NULL)
            temp=temp->next;
        if(temp!=NULL)
        {
            if (temp==first)                        // For first node
            {
                first=first->next;
                first->Prev=NULL;
            }
            else
            {
                temp->prev->next=temp->next;
                temp->next->prev=temp->prev;
                free (temp);
            }
```

```
        }
        else
            printf("Data not found");
        return (first);
    }
```

5. Create a linked list of person having name, age and salary.

Hint: The node definition will be as follows:

```
    typedef struct node
    {
        char name [20];
        int age;
        float sal;
        struct NODE*next;
    }   NODE;
    NODE *first;
```

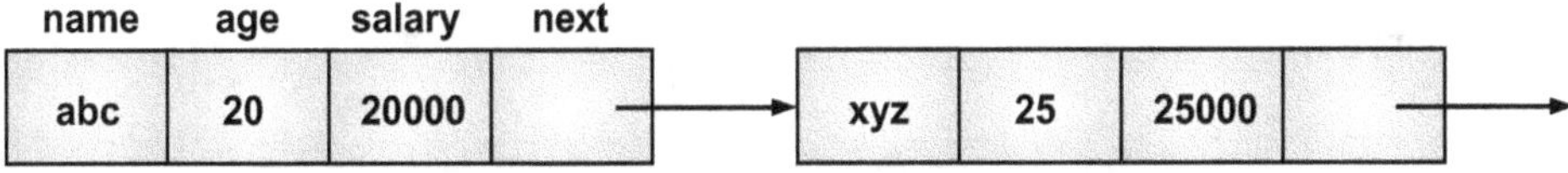

Fig. 3.31: Nodes in a linked list of records

6. Write a C function to delete all nodes in a SLL.

Solution:

```
    void del_all(NODE *first)
    {
        NODE *temp;
        temp=first;             // Start with first node
        while (temp!=NULL)      // not end of list
        {
            first=first->next;  // Advance first
            free (temp);        // delete node
            temp=first;         // Advance temp
        }
    }
```

7. Write a 'C' function to add two binary numbers using doubly linked list (DLL).

Solution:

```
NODE *add(NODE *l1, NODE *l2)
{
    int d1, d2, d3, c, r;
    NODE *l3=NULL, *ptr;
    while (l1->next!=NULL)          // go to LSB next;
        l1=l1->next;
    while (l2->next!=NULL)          //go to LSB
        l2=l2->next;
    c=0,
    while (l1 != NULL&&l2!= NULL)
    {
        d1=l1->data;
        l1=prev;
        d2=l2->data;
        l2=l2->prev;
        r=(d1 + d2 + c)/2;
        c=(d1 + d2 + c)/2;
        ptr=(NODE *)malloc(size of (NODE));
        ptr->data=r;
        ptr->next=ptr->prev=NULL;
        if(l3==NULL)
            l3=ptr;
        else
        {
            temp->prev=ptr;
            ptr->next=temp;
        }
        temp=ptr;
    }
    return (l3);
}
```

Explanation:

(a) The two binary numbers are stored in two DLL's $l1$ and $l2$.

(b) The two DLL's are traversed from last to first node adding each binary digit and storing the result in third DLL which gets created the same way a DLL is created but in reverse order (last node to first node).

(c) $l3$ points to the last node that is LSB.

---

8. Write a 'C' function to sort doubly linked list (DLL). Explain with example.

Solution:

```c
NODE *sort(NODE *first)
{
    NODE *temp, *last;
    int t
    temp=first;
    while(temp->next!=NULL)
        temp=temp->next;
    last=temp;
    while(last!=first)
    {
        temp=first;
        while(temp!=last)
        {
            if(temp->data>temp->next->data)
            {
                t=temp->data,
                temp->data=temp->next->data
                temp->next->data=t;
            }
            temp temp->next;
        }
        last last->prev;
    }
    return (*first);
}
```

9. Write a function in 'C' to delete the node of DLL with data value x.

Solution:

```c
NODE *del(NODE *first, int x)
{
    NODE *temp;
    temp=first;
    while(temp->data!=x&&temp NULL)
        temp=temp->next;
    if(temp != NULL)
    {
        temp->prev->next=temp->next;
        temp->next->prev=temp->prev;
        free(temp);
    }
    else
        printf("Not found");
}
```

10. Give a node structure for singly linked list. Write a function in 'C' to add a node in SLL which is maintained in ascending order of numeric value. Function should handle:

(i)   Insertion at the beginning.

(ii) Insertion at the end.

(iii) Insertion in the middle.

Solution:

```c
NODE structure
typedef struct node
{
    int data;
    struct node *next;
}   NODE;
NODE *insert(NODE *first, int x)
{
    NODE *temp, *ptr, *prev;
    temp=first;
```

```
        while(temp->data <- x)
        {
            prey=temp;
            temp=temp->next;
        }
        ptr=(NODE *)malloc(size of (NODE));
        ptr->data=x;
        ptr->next=NULL
        if(temp==first)                    // Insert at beginning
        {
            ptr->next=temp;
            first=ptr;
        }
        else                               // Insert in middle for end
        {
            ptr->next temp->next;
            prev->next=ptr
        }
        return(first);
}
```

11. Write a function to delete a node pointed by p from DLL. Also write a function in 'C' to insert a new node after a node which is pointed by p.

Solution:

```
void insert(NODE *p, NODE *q)
{
    q->next p->next;
    p->next->prey=q;
    p->next q;
    q->prev p;
}
```

12. Write a recursive function to count number of nodes in DLL or SLL.

Solution:

```
int count(NODE *first)
{
```

```
        if(first==NULL)
            return (0);
        else
            return(1+count (first->next));
    }
```

13. Write a C program to sort a given linked list and display the sorted linked list.

Solution:

```
    typedef struct node
    {
        int data;
        struct node *next;
    } NODE;
    void main( )
    {
        NODE *first, *temp, *ptr;
        int i, n, x;
        printf("Enter number of elements \n");
        scanf("%d", &n);
        first=NULL;
        for(i=1; i<n; i++)
        {
            printf("Enter data \n");
            scanf("%d", &x);
            ptr=(NODE *)malloc(size of (NODE));
            ptr->data=x;
            ptr->next=NULL;
            if(first==NULL)
                first=ptr;
            else
                temp->next=ptr;
            temp=ptr;
        }
        temp=first;
        for(i=1;i<=n-1;i++)
        {
            temp1=temp->next;
            for(j=i+1;j<=n;j++)
            {
```

```c
            if(temp->data > temp1->data)
            {
                    t=temp->data;
                    temp->data=temp1->data;
                        temp1->data=t;
            }
                temp1=temp1->next;
        }
        temp=temp->next;
    }
    printf("Sorted list is \n");
    temp=first;
    while(temp != NULL)
    {
        printf("%d->", temp->data);
        temp=temp->next;
    }
}
```

14. Compare Singly liked list with Doubly linked list and Circular linked list.

Solution:

Singly linked list	Doubly linked list	Circular linked list
1. It consist of nodes having single link to next data.	1. It consist of nodes having double link one to next node and other to previous node.	1. It consists of last node whose next field stores address of first node.
2. Given a pointer p to a node one can only traverse in forward direction.	2. Given a pointer p to a node one can traverse in both forward and backward direction.	2. Given pointer P to a node one can access node.
3. Implementation is simple.	3. Implementation is complex.	3. Implementation is complex compared to SLL.
4. Delete operation requires two pointers.	4. Delete operation requires one pointer.	4. Delete operation requires two pointers.
5. Used in application where you need to access elements sequentially.	5. Used in application where traversal in both direction is required.	5. Used in application where nodes may be traversed frequently.

15. Write a C function to delete all nodes in SLL.
Solution:

```
void del_all(NODE *first)
{
    NODE *temp;
    temp=first;
    while(temp!=NULL);
    {
        first=first->next;
        free(temp);
        temp=first;
    }
}
```

16. Write a C function to delete all nodes in SLL after the node pointed by p.
Solution:

```
void del(NODE *p)
{
    NODE *temp;
    temp=p;
    while(temp!=NULL);
    {
        p=p->next;
        free(temp);
        temp=p;
    }
}
```

17. Write a function in 'C' to insert a node in sorted singly linked list, so that after insertion the list remains sorted. Consider all cases of insertion.
Solution:

```
NODE *insert(NODE *first, int x)
{
    NODE *ptr, *temp, *prey;
    ptr=(NODE *)malloc(size of(NODE));
    ptr->data=x;
    ptr->next=NULL;
    temp=first;
    if(temp==NULL)              // If the list is empty
        first=ptr;
    else                        // not empty
```

```c
    {
        if(temp->data>x)   // if data at current node is greater
        {
            ptr->next=temp;
            first=ptr;                          // Insert
        }
        else
        {
            while(temp->data<=x)                // If data at current node is smaller
            {
                prev=temp;                      // move forward
                temp=temp->next;
            }
            prev->next=ptr;                     // Insert
            ptr->next=temp;
        }
    }
    return(first);
}
```

EXERCISE

1. Write a program to count number of nodes in a link list.

2. Write a program to sort the elements in a linked list.

3. Write a program to reverse a linked list.

4. Write difference between array and linked list.

5. What is the need of linked list? Explain any one application of DLL with suitable example.

6. Write a function for following operations in SLL.

   (i) Display the elements.   (ii) Search an element.

7. Write a C function to add a node in doubly linked list at any position.

8. Write a C function to delete a node from doubly linked list from any position.

9. Give a 'C' declaration for a node structure for declaring a DLL.

10. Write a function for following operations in DLL.

    (i) Display the elements.   (ii) Search an element.

11. Write a C function to delete a node from doubly linked list from any position.

12. Write a pseudo-code to delete a node in DLL at any position.

13. Write a function in 'C' to delete a node from DLL without using any additional pointer.

14. What are the different ways to represent polynomial in single variable?

15. Write a C function for insertion of a node in circular linked list at any position.

16. Explain what do you mean by circular linked list.

17. What is CLL? Explain any one application of CLL.

18. What is circular linked list? Explain any one application of CLL.

19. What is circular linked list? What are advantages of CLL?

20. What is CLL? Write a function to create a circular linked list.

21. Write a pseudo-c code for addition of two polynomials using SLL.

22. Write a function in 'C' to invert the singly linked list.

23. Write a C function to reverse a singly linked list.

24. Write a function in 'C' to invert SLL without creating new node and without swapping data. Assume the list contains numerical data.

25. Consider a linked list which is pointed by pointer P having nodes P_1, P_2, ... P_n. Consider another linked list pointed by pointer Q having nodes Q_1, Q_2, ... Q_n. Write a function in 'C' to merge the above two linked lists in the third list having nodes P_1, Q_1, P_2, Q_2, ... P_n, Q_n.

No additional memory allocation should be done while merging. Size of 2 linked lists could be different.

26. Let p be a pointer to head node of one SLL and q be a pointer to head node of second SLL. Write a function in 'C' to merge the two SLL's as shown below.

$$p_1 \rightarrow q_1, p_2 \rightarrow q_2, ..., p_n \rightarrow q_n$$

27. Write a function to merge two sorted, linked lists.

28. Write a C function to insert a node in DLL after the node pointed by p.

29. Write a function in 'C' to delete a node of doubly linked list where 'P' denotes the pointer to the node to be deleted.

30. Write a function in 'C' to delete a node of doubly linked list where 'P' denotes the pointer to the node to be deleted.

31. Write a function to delete a node in DLL pointed by p.

32. Write a non-recursive function in 'C' to delete all nodes in SLL pointed by p.

33. Write a function to create sorted linked list.

34. Write a program to sort the elements in a linked list.

35. Write a C function to create a SLL for storing list of persons with name and age. State the node structure also.

Unit IV

GRAPHS

4.1 Introduction

Graph is a nonlinear data structure used in many applications. These applications include finding shortest path in a network analysis of electrical circuits, project planning, genetics, identification of chemical compounds etc. Many problems can be modeled as graph and solved.

4.2 Graph Theory and Terminology

Definition: A graph can be defined as set of nodes or vertices or points (V) and set of arcs or edges (E), such that each edge e is identified with unique ordered pair [u, v] of nodes in V.

A graph is denoted as $G \equiv (V, E)$ where V is set of vertices and E is set of edges.

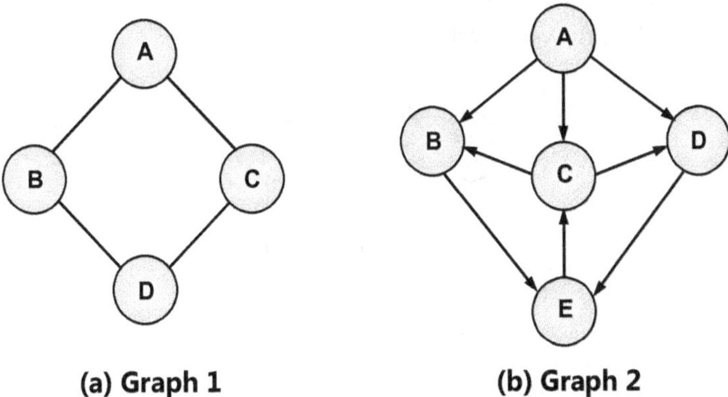

(a) Graph 1   **(b) Graph 2**

Fig. 4.1: Example of graph

Graph 1 consists of vertices {A, B, C, D} and edges {(A, B) (A, C), (B, D), (C, D) }

Graph 2 consists of set of vertices {A, B, C, D, E} and set of edges {<A, B>, <A, D>, <A, C>, <C, D>, <C, B>, <B, E>, <E, C>, <D, E>}

If e = [u, v] is an edge, then the nodes u and v are called end points of e. Also u and v are said to be adjacent nodes or neighbours.

A graph can be of two types.

1.   Directed graph or digraph

2.   Undirected graph.

Directed graph is a graph in which each edge has direction or we say that the pair of vertices in the graph is ordered Fig. 4.1 (b) is a directed graph.

The set of edges in such graph are written in <> sign.

Suppose G is directed graph with edge e = <v, u>, then e is also called an arc.

Following terminology is used.

(i)   e begins at u and ends at v.

(ii)   u is origin and v is destination of e.

(iii) u is predecessor and v is successor or neighgour of e.

(iv) u is adjacent to v and v is adjacent to u.

Undirected graph is a graph in which the edges do not have direction. The flow between two edges can be in both directions. In undirected graph, the set of edges are written in ( ) sign. Fig. 4.1 (a) is an undirected graph.

The vertices in undirected graph are said to be unordered. If (v, u) is an edge and (u, v) represents same edge.

A graph sometimes has weight or cost specified for each edge as shown in Fig. 4.2. Such graph is said to be labelled or weighted graph.

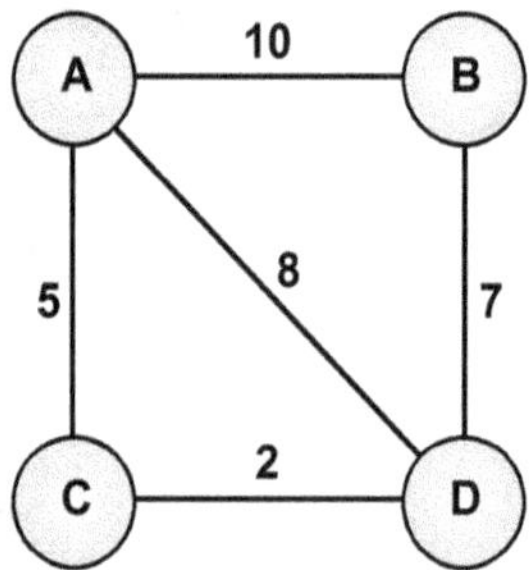

Fig. 4.2: Weighted graph

Tree also can be termed as graph as it has set of edges and vertices.

There are some terms used with graph. Let us understand them.

1.   A graph is said to be complete if it has n(n − 1)/2 number of district unordered pairs, where n is number of vertices. For a directed graph maximum number of edges will be n(n − 1).

2.   If (u, v) is an edge of graph, we say that u and v are adjacent (vertices) and we say that edge (u, v) is incident on vertices u and v.

3.   A graph G1 is a subgraph of Graph G, in which all vertices of G1 belong to G and all edges of G1 belong to G.

Following Fig. 4.3 show graph G and its sub-graph.

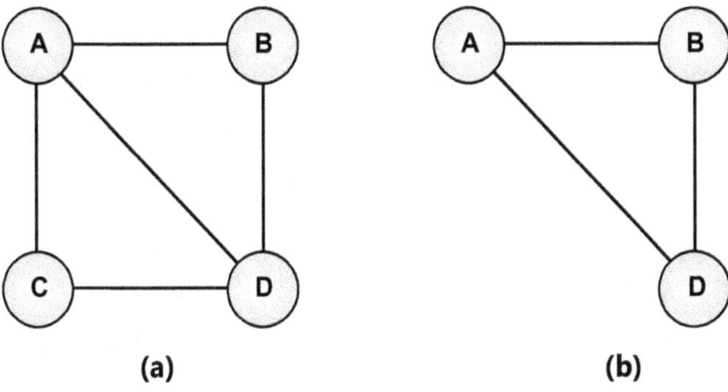

(a)   (b)

Fig. 4.3

4.   A path in a graph (G) is a sequence of vertices $v_1, v_2, v_3, \ldots v_m, v_n$ where (v_1, v_2) (v_2, v_3) ... (v_m, v_n) are edges in the graph.

5.   A simple path is a path such that all vertices are distinct except first and last which could be same.

6.   A graph can have an edge from a vertex to same vertex called self edge as shown in Fig. 4.4. The path from A to A is called loop.

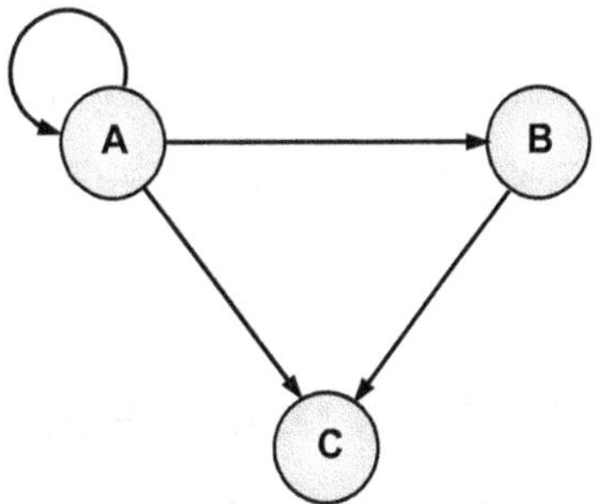

Fig. 4.4: Graph with self edge node

7.   A cycle in a directed graph is a path of length at least 1 such that $v_1 = v_n$ i.e. the first and last vertex is same.

8.   In undirected graph for a cycle, the edges are to be distinct. Otherwise edge (u, v) will also be cycle.

9. A directed graph is called acyclic if it has no cycles. It is denoted as DAG.

10. An undirected graph is said to be connected if there is path from every vertex to all other vertices.

11. A directed graph is said to be connected or strongly connected if for every pair of distinct vertices in graph G there is directed path in both direction i.e. v_i, to v_j and v_j to v_i.

12. Strongly connected component of undirected graph (G) is maximal connected sub-graph of G.

13. Indegree of vertex in a graph is number of incoming edges at that vertex.

14. Out-degree of vertex is the number of outgoing edges from that vertex.

15. Total degree of vertex is sum of indegree and outdegree.

16. A graph is said to be complete if every node in G is adjacent to every other node. A complete graph with n nodes will have n (n − 1)/2 edges.

17. A graph without any cycle is called tree graph or free tree or simply tree.

18 Distinct edges e and e' are called multiple edges if they connect same end points, that is, if e = [u, v] and e' = [u, v].

19. An edge e is called a loop if it has identical endpoints, that is, if e = [u, u].

20. A graph having multiple edges and loops is called multigraph.

21. A multigraph with finite number of edges is called finite multigraph.

22. A directed graph is said to be simple if G has no parallel edges. It means a simple graph can have loops but it cannot have more than one loop at a given node.

23. A directed Acyclic Graph (DAG) can be used to solve problems like critical path analysis, expression free evaluation etc. A sink vertex is a vertex with only single edge ending on it. A source vertex is a vertex having edges starting from it.

24. A Biconnected graph is a connected graph which cannot be broken down further by deletion of any single vertex (and incident edges).

4.3 Representation of Graph using Adjacency Matrix

A graph can be represented using two different ways:

1. Adjacency matrix

2. Adjacency list.

The choice of particular representation depends on application or function to be performed.

The adjacency matrix representation is the simplest representation in which we use a two dimensional array of integers. The elements in the two dimensional array represent the information about edges and vertices in the graph. Suppose, a graph has an edge (v_1, v_2) then the element in the matrix in row no. v_1 and column No. v_2 will be 1. If there is no edge between v_1 and v_2 the element will be 0.

Let us consider two graphs as shown in Fig. 4.5.

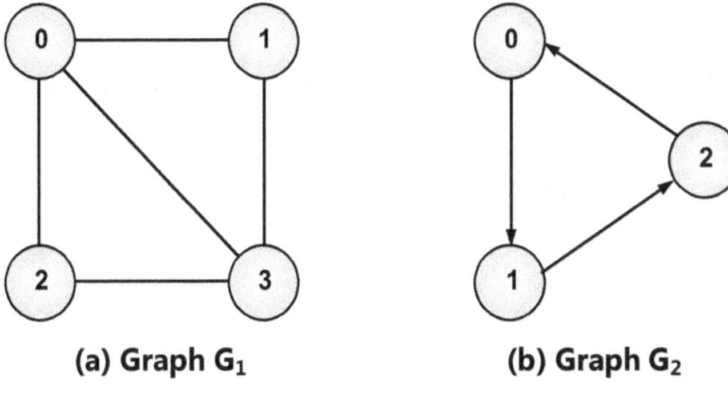

(a) Graph G₁   **(b) Graph G₂**

Fig. 4.5

The adjacency matrix for graph G_1 will have 4 rows and 4 columns as there are 4 vertices. The elements in the matrix will be as shown in Fig. 4.6.

$$
\begin{array}{c}
\begin{array}{cccc} 0 & 1 & 2 & 3 \end{array} \\
\begin{array}{c} 0 \\ 1 \\ 2 \\ 3 \end{array}
\left[
\begin{array}{cccc}
0 & 1 & 1 & 1 \\
1 & 0 & 0 & 1 \\
1 & 0 & 0 & 1 \\
1 & 1 & 1 & 0
\end{array}
\right]
\end{array}
$$

Fig. 4.6: Adjacency matrix for G₁

Note that the graph G_1 is undirected graph. Hence, the matrix is symmetric. We can store only upper or lower triangular matrix to reduce the space requirements. The adjacency matrix for graph G_2 is shown in Fig. 4.7.

$$
\begin{array}{c}
\begin{array}{ccc} 0 & 1 & 2 \end{array} \\
\begin{array}{c} 0 \\ 1 \\ 2 \end{array}
\left[
\begin{array}{ccc}
0 & 1 & 0 \\
0 & 0 & 1 \\
1 & 0 & 0
\end{array}
\right]
\end{array}
$$

Fig. 4.7: Adjacency matrix for graph G₂

From adjacency matrix we can find whether there is an edge between given two vertices or not.

We can find indegree of vertexes by counting number of 1's in corresponding column and out-degree by counting number of 1's in corresponding row.

For example, Indegree of vertex 1 in G_1 = 2

Outdegree of vertex 1 in G_1 = 2

If the cost or weight is specified on the edges of graph, we can put the cost or weight in place of 1.

The advantage of adjacency matrix representation is its simplicity but requires more space of the order of n^2.

Let us write a program to represent a graph in adjacency matrix format. The program accepts from user number of vertices and edges in the graph and prints the matrix. It also calculates indegree, outdegree and total degree of a given vertex.

Explanation:

int g[MAX] {MAX} is the 2-D array for storing matrix.

n is number of vertices.

There are three functions used

(i)   create_graph( )

It accepts the number of vertices of n. If the graph is undirected, their reverse edge corresponding to two vertices is also stored.

(ii)   disp( )

This function displays the matrix.

(iii) calc( )

This function calculates indegree, outdegree and total degree of a given vertex.

Program 4.1: To represent graph using adjacency matrix, display it and calculate indegree - outdegree of nodes.

```
#define MAX 10,
int g[MAX] [MAX];
int n;
void create_graph( );
void disp( );
void calc( );
```

```c
void main
{
    create_graph( );
    disp( );
    calc( );
}
void create_graph( )
{
    char ch, type;
    printf("How many vertices\n");
    scanf("%d", &n);
    printf("Enter type of graph directed or undirected \n");
    type = getch( );
    do
    {
        printf("Enter edge");
        scanf("%d %d", &v1, &v2);
            g[v1] [v2] = 1;
        if(type=='u'||type=='U')
        g[v2] [v1] = 1;
        printf("Do you want to continue? \n");
        ch = getch( );
    }   while (ch=='y'||ch=='y');
}
void disp( );
{
    int i, j;
    for(i=0; i<n; i++)
    {
        for(j=0; j<n; j++)
        {
            printf(%d", g[i][j]);
        }
        printf("\n");
```

```
        }
    }
    void calc( );
    {
        int c1 = 0, c2 = 0, c3 = 0, v;
        printf("Enter vertex \n");
        scanf("%d", &v);
        for (i=0; i<n; i++)
        {
            if (g[i][v]==1)
            c1++;
        }
        for(i=0, i<n; i++)
        {
            if(g[v] [i] ==1)
            c2++;
        }
        c3 = c1 + c2;
        printf("Indegree =%d\n", c1);
        printf("outdegree=%d\n", c2);
        printf("Total degree = %\n", c3);
    }
```

If A is adjacency matrix of a graph G, then the element a_{ij} in the matrix A^k will be equal to number of paths of length k between vertex v_i to v_j

Similarly, the matrix $B_r = A + A^2 + A^3 + \ldots A^r$ will have element b_{ij} equal to number of paths of length less than or equal to r from node v_i to v_j.

Consider a graph as given below.

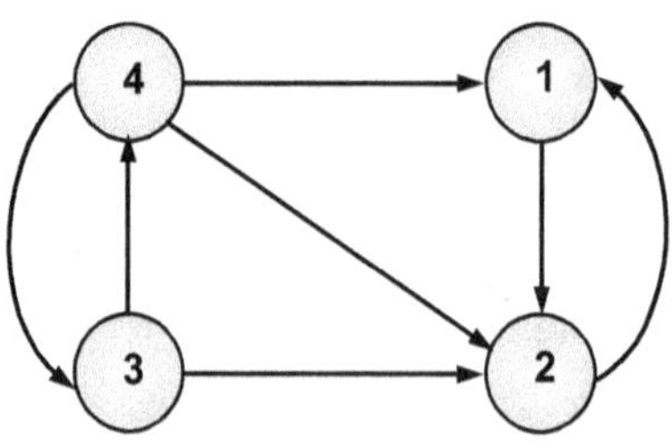

Fig. 4.8: Graph G

The adjacency matrix for the graph will be

$$A = \begin{bmatrix} 0 & 1 & 1 & 1 \\ 0 & 0 & 1 & 0 \\ 1 & 1 & 1 & 0 \\ 1 & 0 & 1 & 0 \end{bmatrix}$$

$$\therefore \qquad A^2 = \begin{bmatrix} 1 & 0 & 2 & 0 \\ 1 & 1 & 0 & 0 \\ 0 & 1 & 1 & 0 \\ 1 & 2 & 0 & 1 \end{bmatrix}$$

$$A^3 = \begin{bmatrix} 2 & 3 & 0 & 1 \\ 0 & 1 & 1 & 1 \\ 2 & 1 & 2 & 0 \\ 1 & 1 & 3 & 1 \end{bmatrix}$$

We can see from A^2 there is one path of length 2 from 0 to 0 i.e. $0 - 3 - 0$. There is no path of length 2 from 0 to 1. There are two paths of length 2 from 0 to 2. i.e. $0 - 1 - 2$ and $0 - 3 - 2$ etc.

From A^3 we can observe that there are 2 paths of length 3 from 0 to 0 i.e. $0 - 1 - 2 - 0$ and $0 - 3 - 2 - 0$. There are 3 paths of length 3 from 0 to 1 i.e. $0 - 3 - 2 - 1, 0 - 3 - 0 - 1, 0 - 1 - 2 - 1$.

Path Matrix : Let G be a simple directed graph with n vertices $v_1, v_2, \dots v_n$, then the path matrix or reachability matrix of G is $n \times n$ matrix P such that the elements P_{ij} are.

$$P_{ij} = 1 \qquad \text{if there is a path between } v_i \text{ and } v_j$$
$$= 0 \qquad \text{otherwise}$$

The path matrix can be obtained from adjacency matrix. If A is adjacency matrix of graph G than the path matrix P will have a entry $P_{ij} = 1$ if and only if there is non-zero member in the ij entry of the matrix.

$$B_{n \times n} = A + A^2 + A^3 + \dots A^n$$

Consider the graph shown in Fig 4.8. There are 4 vertices i.e. n = 4.

$$\therefore \qquad B_4 = A + A^2 + A^3 + A^4$$

$$= \begin{bmatrix} 0 & 1 & 0 & 1 \\ 0 & 0 & 1 & 0 \\ 1 & 1 & 0 & 0 \\ 1 & 0 & 1 & 0 \end{bmatrix} + \begin{bmatrix} 1 & 0 & 2 & 0 \\ 1 & 1 & 0 & 0 \\ 0 & 1 & 1 & 1 \\ 1 & 2 & 0 & 1 \end{bmatrix} + \begin{bmatrix} 2 & 3 & 0 & 1 \\ 0 & 1 & 1 & 1 \\ 2 & 1 & 2 & 0 \\ 1 & 1 & 3 & 1 \end{bmatrix} + \begin{bmatrix} 1 & 2 & 4 & 2 \\ 2 & 1 & 2 & 0 \\ 2 & 4 & 1 & 2 \\ 4 & 4 & 2 & 1 \end{bmatrix}$$

$$= \begin{bmatrix} 4 & 6 & 6 & 4 \\ -3 & 3 & 4 & 1 \\ 5 & 7 & 4 & 3 \\ 7 & 7 & 6 & 3 \end{bmatrix}$$

Since all entries in B_4 are non zero, the path matrix will also have all 1's as below.

$$P = \begin{bmatrix} 1 & 1 & 1 & 1 \\ 1 & 1 & 1 & 1 \\ 1 & 1 & 1 & 1 \\ 1 & 1 & 1 & 1 \end{bmatrix}$$

It means the graph is strongly connected i.e. for any pair of nodes u and v in G, there is path from u to v and from v to u also.

A transitive closure of graph G is a graph G' such that G' has same number of nodes as G and there is an edge (v_i, v_j) in G' whenever there is path from v_i to v_j in G. Thus, path matrix of G is adjacency matrix of its transitive closure G'.

4.4 Representation of Graph Using Adjacency List

This is linked list representation of graph. The n rows of adjacency matrix are represented as n linked lists. For each vertex there will be one list. The list contains adjacent vertices of that vertex. Let us consider two graphs and their adjacency list representations.

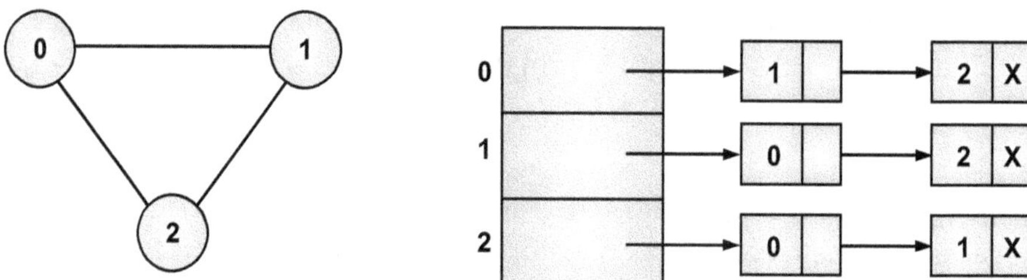

Fig. 4.9: Graph and its adjacency list

As seen in the graph, vertex 0 has adjacent vertices 1 and 2. Hence, the list corresponding to vertex 0 has two nodes with 1 and 2 in its list and list 2 has vertices 0 and 1.

Another example is directed graph.

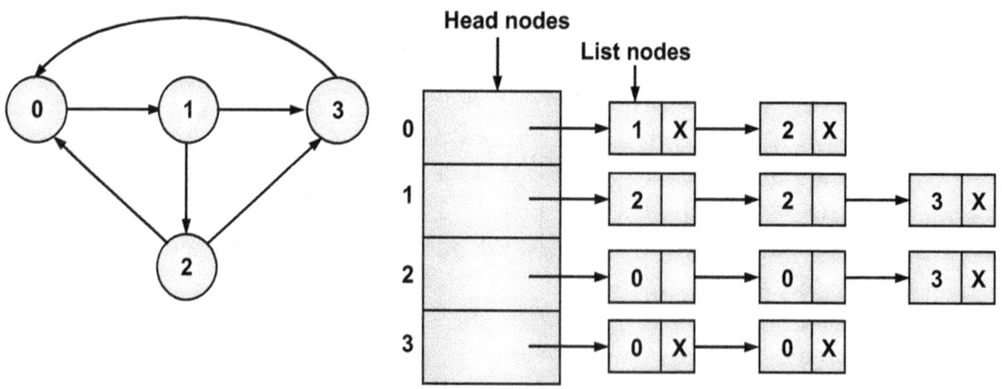

Fig. 4.10: Graph and its adjacency list

Each list has head node which stores the address of the list. For directed graph if there are n vertices and e edges, the adjacency list will have n head nodes and e list nodes.

For undirected graph if there are n vertices and e edges the list will have n head nodes and 2e list nodes.

The indegree of a vertex in undirected graph is number of nodes in the corresponding list.

The outdegree of a vertex in undirected graph is number of nodes in list.

The outdegree of a vertex in directed graph is number of nodes in the corresponding list.

The indegree of a vertex is calculated by examining the entire adjacency list. The number of nodes of that vertex in adjacency list is the indegree of that vertex.

The comparison of adjacency list with adjacency matrix is

1. The adjacency list consists of dynamic allocation hence, space requirement for adjacency list will be less compared to matrix representation.

2. The adjacency list is complex structure and difficult to implement whereas adjacency matrix is simple and easy to implement.

Operations on Graph: There are various operations such as searching, inserting and deleting nodes and edges in the graph.

Searching in a Graph: We can find the location, loc of a node N in a graph G. This can be accomplished easily with both representation that is adjacency matrix or adjacency list.

In adjacency matrix, the row number or column number responds to node. In adjacency matrix, the list address corresponds to node.

We can also find the location, loc of a edge (v_i, v_j) in the graph. In adjacency matrix if the ij^{th} entry in the matrix is 1 the edge is present otherwise absent.

In adjacency list representation, we can search the edge, (v_i, v_j) in the ith row of the list.

Inserting a Graph: To insert a node N in the graph, in adjacency matrix, we can increase row number and column number in the matrix. In the adjacency list, we can increase one more element in the list of pointers.

To insert an edge (v_i, v_j) we can enter 1 in the ith row and j^{th} column of the adjacency matrix. In case of adjacency list we can append one more node at the end (append) in the ith row of the list.

Deleting from a Graph: To delete a node from the graph, we can insert all zeros in the corresponding row and column, in case of adjacency matrix. In case of adjacency list, we can delete entire list corresponding to the node. We also have to delete all nodes in the other lists corresponding this vertex.

4.5 Traversals of Graph (DFS and BFS)

The graph can be traversed in two different ways:

(i)   Depth first search,

(ii)   Breadth first search.

Traversal means visiting each vertex in the graph once. The tree traversals were studied in chapter 5. In the starting point of the traversals, there was root node. In case of graph, starting point may be any vertex. Now traversing in case of graph means, visiting all vertices that are reachable from the starting vertex because every vertex may not be reachable from a given vertex.

4.5.1 Depth First Search (DFS) Traversal

As the name suggests, starting from a given vertex we go till the depth of the vertex and then go back to traverse another path till its depth.

Suppose we start at a vertex v1, process it, we go to its adjacent vertex say v2, process it, then we move to adjacent vertex of v2 say v3. Like this, we continue till there is no vertex left with adjacent vertex. After this we come back to the previous vertex (last but one processed). If there is any other adjacent vertex, we move to that vertex, process and keep on going forward. When we have reached a vertex with no adjacent vertices, we keep coming back. Thus, when we start with a vertex we keep on going forward to its descendants. While doing this, every vertex should be processed only once in the entire traversal.

Let us take a graph and see the DFS traversal of it.

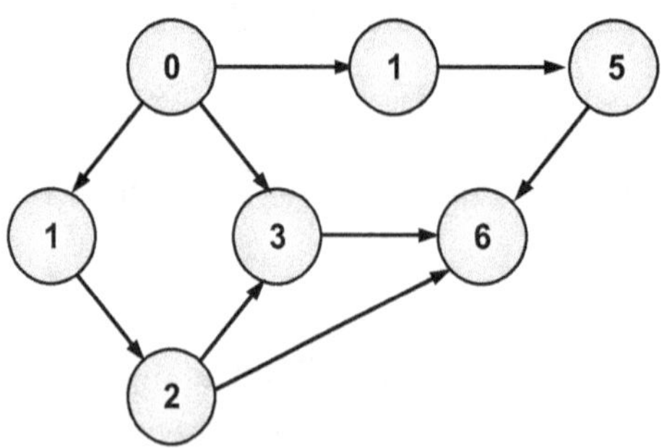

Fig. 4.11: Graph

Suppose our starting vertex is 0 (process it)

From 0 we can go to 1 or 3 or 4 (Adjacent vertex).

Let us select 1 (process it)

From 1 we can to 2 (process it)

From 2 we can go to 3 or 6.

Let us select 3 (process it).

From 3 we can go to 6 (process it)

From 6 you cannot reach any node, which is not processed or visited.

Hence, go back to 3 (previous vertex)

There is no other vertex connected to 3.

Go back to 2.

From 2 we can go to 6 but it is already processed.

Go back to 0.

From 0 we can go to 3 but it is already processed.

From 0 we can go to 4. (Process it)

From 4 we can go to 5. (Process it).

From 5 we can go to 6 but it is already processed.

Go back to 0.

There is no other vertex left out

Hence the Traversal is 0, 1, 2, 3, 6, 4, 5.

The traversal is shown in Fig. 4.12.

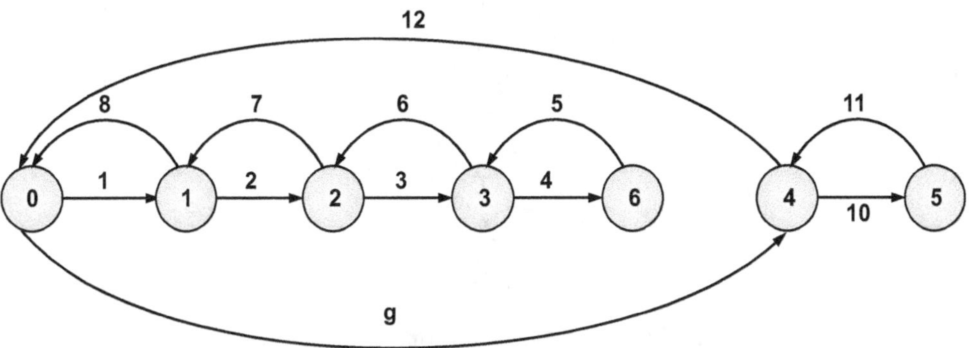

Fig. 4.12: DFS traversal of graph in Fig. 4.11

Let us take one more graph and see its DFS Traversal.

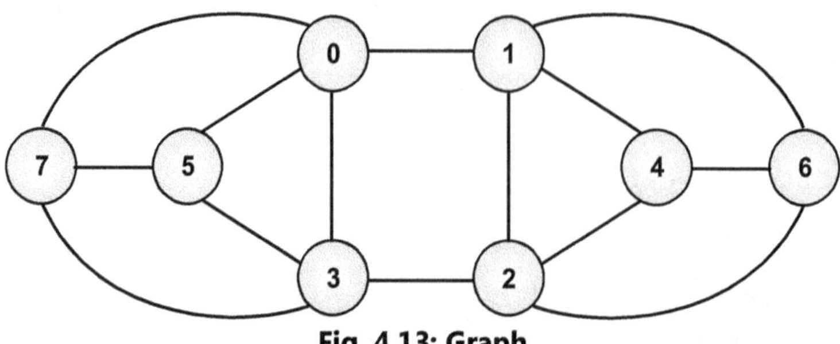

Fig. 4.13: Graph

The traversal path is shown in Fig. 4.14.

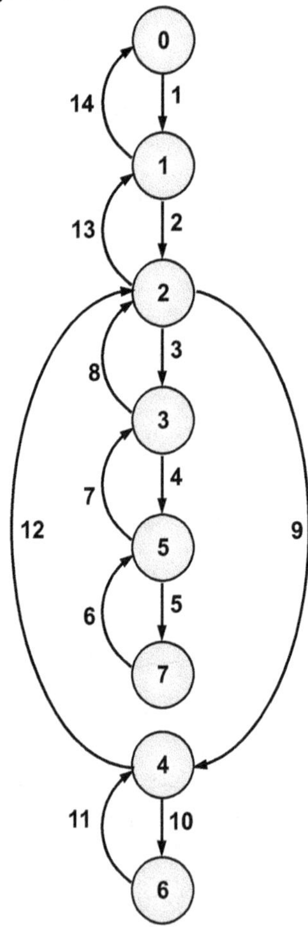

Fig. 4.14: DFS traversal of graph in Fig. 4.13

The DFS traversal is 0 1 2 3 5 7 4 6.

Algorithm for DFS Traversal:

DFS is a recursive process. We can either use recursive function or stack to implement DFS. The algorithm we are going to write is for adjacency matrix representation. The create_graph( ) function which we have already written will be used here for storing graph in the 2-D array int g[MAX] [MAX] and n is number of vertices. We require an additional array to store the information about status of each vertex whether it is visited or not. Let us have the array int visited[MAX]. Initially, the elements of this array will be 0. Whenever a vertex is visited the corresponding element will be made 1. The algorithm is as follows:

```
void dfs(int v1)
{
    print v1;                    // visit or process
    visited [v1] = 1;           // mark as visited
    for(v2=0; v2<n; v2++)       // check all adjacent vertices edge for a (v1, v2)
    {
        if (g[v1] [v2]==1)
        {
            if(visited [v2]==0)  // if not visited
                dfs (v2);        // Repeat dfs again
        }
    }
}
```

Explanation:

1. We start with source vertex v1 in the graph. It is processed (display) and marked as visited.

2. In the loop we are finding an adjacent vertex of v1 (verifying g[v1] [v2] ==) say v2 and if it is not visited yet, the function DFS will be called to process visit that node. This process continues recursively as explained in through example.

Analysis:

The total time to determine adjacent vertices of a vertex is n and for each vertex we have to do this. Hence time complexity of this algorithm is $O(n^2)$. The space required for this algorithm is the array visited and stack (of program) a part from the n × n array.

Let us consider DFS traversal of the following graph.

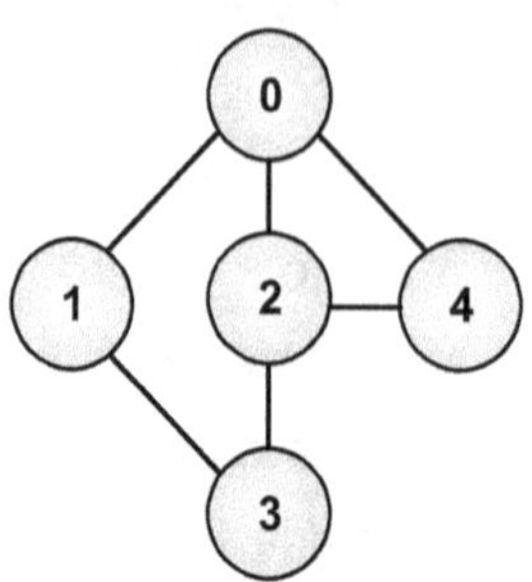

Fig. 4.15

Table

Call No.	V_1	Output	Visited array V					2
1	0	0	0	1	2	3	4	
			1	0	0	0	0	0
								1
2	1	1	0	1	2	3	4	
			1	1	0	0	0	0
								1
								2
			0	1	2	3	4	3
3	3	3	1	1	0	1	0	0
								1
			0	1	2	3	4	2
4	2	2	1	1	1	1	0	0
								1
								2
								3
			0	1	2	3	4	4
5	4	4	1	1	1	1	1	0
								1
								2
								3
								4
								5 →

After call number 5, control goes back to 4	$V_2 = 5$
Control goes back to call 3	$V_2 = 3, 4, 5$
Control goes back to call 2	$V_2 = 4, 5$
Control goes back to call 1	$V_2 = 2, 3, 4, 5$

Following is the algorithm for non-recursive traversal of DFS.

```
void dfs(int v1)
{
    push v1;                    // Store v1 in stack
    visited [v1] = 1;           // Mark it as visited
    while(stack not empty)
    {
        v1 =pop( );             // Remove the vertex in stack
        print v1;               // Process or visit
        for(v2=0;v2<n;v2++)     // Check all adjacent vertices
        {
            if (g[v1][v2]==1 && visited [v2]==0)    // If there is edge v1 - v2 and V2 is not visited
            {
                visited [v2] = 1;      // Mark it as visited
                push (v2);             // Store the vertex on stack
            }
        }
    }
}
```

4.5.2 Breadth First Search (BFS) Traversal

In BFS, we go to the breadth of the current vertex every time we come to a new vertex and then take up the next vertex.

Suppose we start with vertex v_1, process it, then we visit all the adjacent vertices of v_1 say v_{11}, v_{12}, v_{13} ... v_{1n}. Then we visit all the adjacent vertices of v_{11}, then of v_{12} so on upto v_{1n}. This is continued till there is not vertex left out to be visited. Let us consider a graph given in Fig. 4.16.

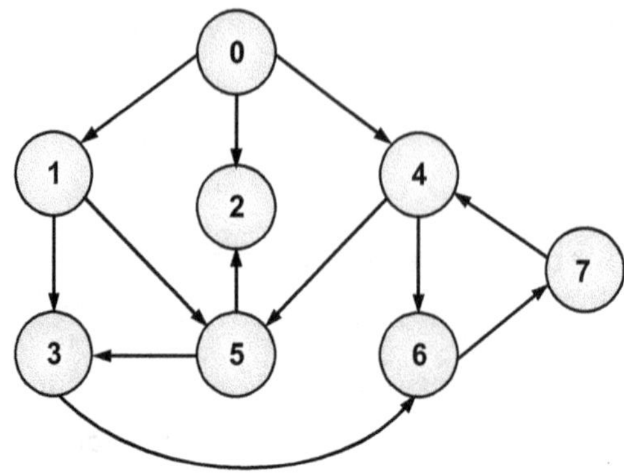

Fig. 4.16: Graph

For the graph, we start with say vertex 0.

Mark it as visited.

The adjacent vertices are 1 and 2.

Mark them as visited

The adjacent vertices of 1 are 3, 5

Mark them as visited

The adjacent vertices of 2 is 5 (already visited)

The adjacent vertices of 3 is 6

Mark it as visited.

The adjacent vertices of 5 is 2 and 3 already visited

The adjacent vertices of 6 is 7

Mark it as visited.

The adjacent vertices 7 is 4

Mark it as visited

The adjacent vertices of 4 are 0, 5 (already visited)

Hence, the BFS traversal is 0, 1, 2, 3, 5, 6, 7, 4.

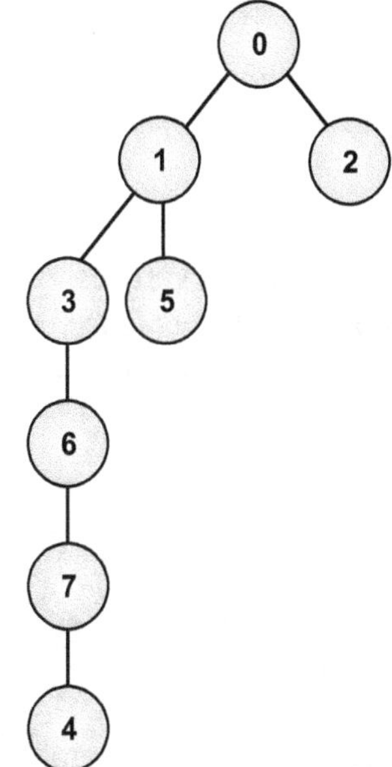

Fig. 4.17: BFS traversal of graph in Fig. 4.16

Now consider an undirected graph shown in Fig. 4.18.

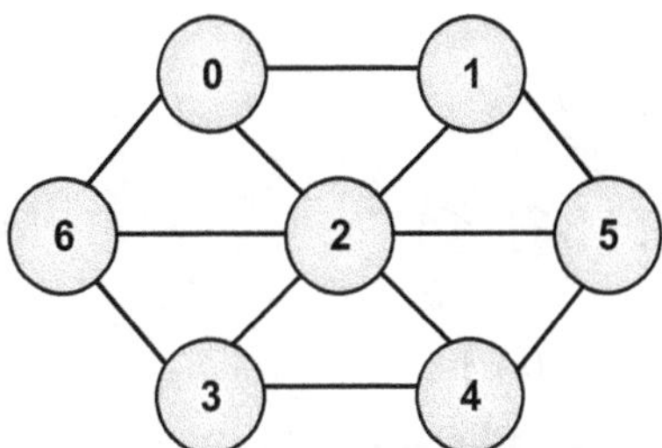

Fig. 4.18: Graph

If starting vertex is 0.

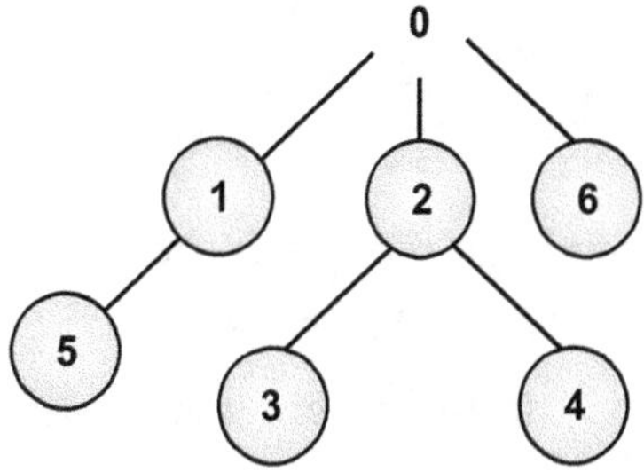

Fig. 4.19: BFS traversal of graph in Fig. 4.18

Hence, the BFS Traversal is 0, 1, 2, 6, 5, 3, 4.

Algorithm for BFS Traversal:

For implementing BFS traversal, we have to use queue for storing the adjacent vertices of current vertex being visited.

The create_graph( ) function which was written earlier will be used here for storing graph in 2-D array int g[MAX] [MAX] and n is number of vertices. An additional array int visited [MAX] is used to store the information about status of each vertex whether it is visited or not. Initially, the elements of this array will be 0. Whenever a vertex is visited corresponding element will be made 1.

The algorithm is as below.

```
void bfs(int v1)
{
    insertq(v1);
    visited[v1] = 1;
    while (Queue is not empty)
    {
        v1=delq( );
        print v1
        for(v2=0;v2<n;v2++)
        {
            if(g[v1] [v2]==1)              // If there is edge v1 – v2
            {
                if(visited [v2]==0)        // If there is not yet visited
                {
                    insertq (v2)
                    visited[v2] = 1;
                }
            }
        }
    }
}
```

Explanation:

1. In above function, it is assumed that the queue is defined with an array of int, along with two functions insertq and delq. The detailed program is given at the end of this section.

2. We start with source vertex v1 in the graph. It is inserted in the queue and marked as visited.

3. A vertex in the queue is removed and it is processed i.e. displayed.

All adjacent vertices of this current vertex are inserted in the queue and marked them as visited.

This process is repeated until the queue becomes empty.

Let us consider a graph given in Fig. 4.20.

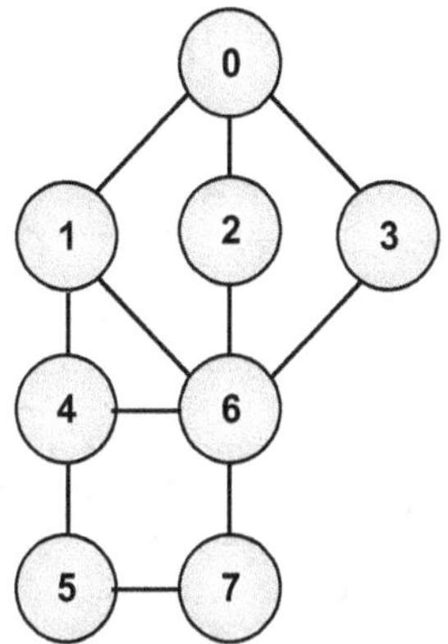

Fig. 4.20: Graph

0	Suppose our starting vertex is 0, it is inserted in queue and marked as visited.	q	0							
		visited	1	0	0	0	0	0	0	0
			0	1	2	3	4	5	6	7
1	Remove 0 from queue and display. Output is 0. Insert adjacent vertices of 0 i.e. 1, 2, 3 on queue and mark them as visited.	q	X	1	2	3				
		visited	1	1	1	1	0	0	0	0
			0	1	2	3	4	5	6	7
2	Remove 1 from queue and display. Output is 1. Insert adjacent vertices of 1 i.e. 4 and 6 on queue and mark them as visited.	q	X	X	2	3	4	6		
		visited	1	1	1	1	1	1	0	0
			0	1	2	3	4	5	6	7
3	Remove 2 from queue and display Output is 2. There is no adjacent vertex of 2 not yet visited.	q	X	X	X	3	4	6		
		visited	1	1	1	1	1	1	0	0
			0	1	2	3	4	5	6	7

4	Remove 3 from queue and display. Output is 3. There is no adjacent vertex of 3 not yet visited.	q: X X X X 4 6 [ ] [ ] visited: 1 1 1 1 1 1 0 0 (indices 0–7)
5	Remove 4 from queue and display. Output is 4. Insert 5 on queue. Mark it as visited.	q: X X X X X 6 5 [ ] visited: 1 1 1 1 1 1 1 0 (indices 0–7)
6	Remove 6 from queue and display. Output is 6. Insert adjacent vertex of 6 i.e. 7 on queue and mark it as visited.	q: X X X X X X 5 7 visited: 1 1 1 1 1 1 1 1 (indices 0–7)
7	Remove 5 from queue and display. Output is 5. There is no adjacent vertex of 3 not yet visited.	q: X X X X X X X 7 (indices 0–7)
8	Remove 7 from queue and display. Output is 7. There is no adjacent vertex of 3 not yet visited and queue is empty. The BFS traversal is 1, 2, 3, 4, 6, 5, 7	q: X X X X X X X X (indices 0–7)

Following is the menu drive program to create a given graph using adjacency matrix and display BFS and DFS traversals.

```
# define MAX 10
int g[MAX] [MAX]
int n;
void create_graph( );
void disp( );
void bfs (int);
void dfs (int);
```

```c
int q[MAX];
int rear = -1, front = -1;
void insertq (int);
int delq (int);
int visited [MAX];
void main( )
    {
        int ch, v1;
        do
        {
            for(i=0,i<n;i++)
                visited [v1] = 0;
                clrscr();
                printf("1. create\n 2. Disp\n3. DFS\n4. BFS\n5. Exit\n")
                printf("Enter your choice\n");
                scanf("%d", &ch);
                switch(ch)
                {
                    case1:   creat_graph();
                             break;
                    case2:   disp( );
                             break;
                    case3:   printf("Enter starting vertex\n");
                             scanf("%d, &v1);
                             dfs(v1);
                             break;
                    case4:   printf("Enter starting vertex");
                             scan("%d", &v2);
                             bfs(v2);
                }
                getch( );
            } while (ch!=5);
```

```c
        }
        void create_graph ()
        {
                int v1, v2, i;
                char type, ch;
                printf("Enter type of graph\n");
                type = getch( );
                printf("Enter number of vertices\n");
                scanf("%d", &n);
                do
                {
                        printf("Enter edge\n");
                        scanf("%d%d", &v1, &v2);
                        g [v1] [v2] = 1;
                        if(type=='u'||type=='u')
                                g[v2] [v1] = 1;
                        printf("Do you want to continue ?\n");
                        ch = getch( );
                }    while(ch=='y'||ch=='Y')
        }
        void disp( )
        {
                int i;
                printf("Adjacency matrix is\n");
                for(i=0;i<n;i++)
                {
                        for(j=0;j<n;j++)
                        {
                                printf("%d",g[i][j]);
                        }
                        printf("\n");
                }
```

```c
        }
    void dfs (int v1)
    {
        int i, v2;
        printf("%d\n", v1)
        visited [v1] = 1;
        for (v2=0; v2<n; v2++)
        {
            if (g[v1] [v2]==1)
            {
                if (visited [v2]==0)
                dfs (v2);
            }
        }
    }
    void bfs (int v1)
    {
        int v2;
        insertq (v1)
        visited[v1] = 1;
        while (front ! = rear)
        {
            v1 = delq ();
            printf("%d\n", v1);
            for(v2=0; v2<n; v2++)
            {
                if (g[v1] [v2]==1)
                {
                    if(visited [v2]==0)
                    {
                        insertq(v2);
                        visited [v2] = 1;
```

```c
                    }
                }
            }
        }
    }
    void insertq(int v1)
    {
        if (rear==MAX - 1)
            printf("Q full\n");
        else
        {
            rear++;
            q[rear] = v1;
        }
    }
    int delq( )
    {
        int v1;
        if (front==rear)
            printf("Q empty");
        else
        {
            front ++;
            v1 = q[front];
            return(v1);
        }
    }
```

Explanation:

1. Most of the variables in the program are declared as global because they are required in at least one of function.

2. The initialization of array visited[ ] is required because it is going to be modified in BFS and DFS functions.

3. The variables front and rear of the queue are global and can be used directly in BFS to check whether q is empty or full.

4. We can write separate functions for insertq, delq etc.

4.6 Minimal Spanning Tree

An undirected graph is said to be connected if for every pair of distinct vertices there is a path.

For a connected undirected graph if we carry out DFS traversal from any vertex as source, all the vertices in the graph can be traversed.

Hence, for a connected undirected graph we can form set of edges which will include all the vertices. Moreover it is possible to for trees with the edges that include all the vertices. A tree is a graph in which there is no cycle (closed path).

Any tree that has set of edges in the graph and includes all the vertices is called spanning Tree.

Consider a graph given in Fig. 4.21 with cost/weights.

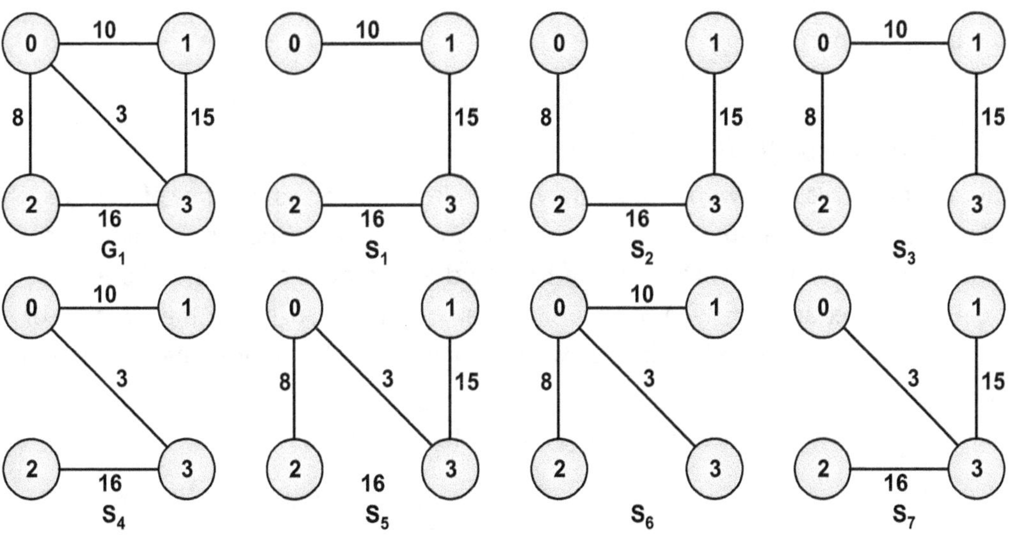

Fig. 4.21: Graph G_1 and its spanning Trees

The cost of spanning tree is total weights of all the edges in the spanning tree.

The cost of spanning trees shown in the graph of Fig. 4.21 are

$S_1 \rightarrow 41$

$S_2 \rightarrow 39$

$S_3 \rightarrow 33$

$S_4 \rightarrow 29$

$S_5 \rightarrow 26$

$S_6 \rightarrow 21$

$S_7 \rightarrow 34$

The minimum cost is 21 for spanning tree S_6. It is called as minimal cost spanning tree or minimal spanning tree.

Definition:

The spanning tree of a graph whose sum of the costs or weights is minimum is called minimum spanning tree.

There are two algorithms which are used to find minimum spanning tree.

1.   Prim's algorithm

2.   Kruskal's algorithm,

4.6.1 Prim's Algorithm

In this algorithm, we start with any arbitrary vertex in the graph as the root of the tree. Then we find the vertex adjacent to this root vertex which has an edge with minimum cost or weight. Now we have two vertices in the tree. Find all the out-going edges from these two vertices and select an edge with minimum cost among these such that the addition of this edge should not form a cycle. Like this we continue till all the vertices are included in the tree.

Let us consider an example i.e. the same graph we had in Fig. 4.22 (a).

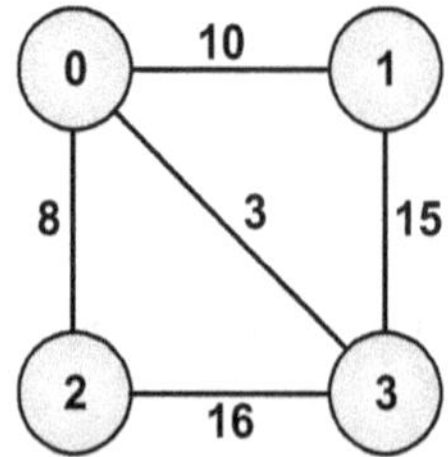

Fig. 4.22 (a): Graph

Let us start with vertex 0.

The outgoing edges from this vertex and selected vertex is shown in Fig. 4.22 (b).

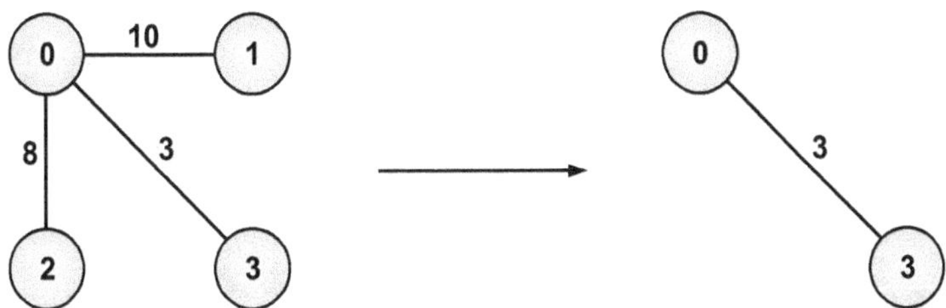

Fig. 4.22 (b): Step 1 for MST

Now find the outgoing edges of 0 and 3 and select minimum of the edges.

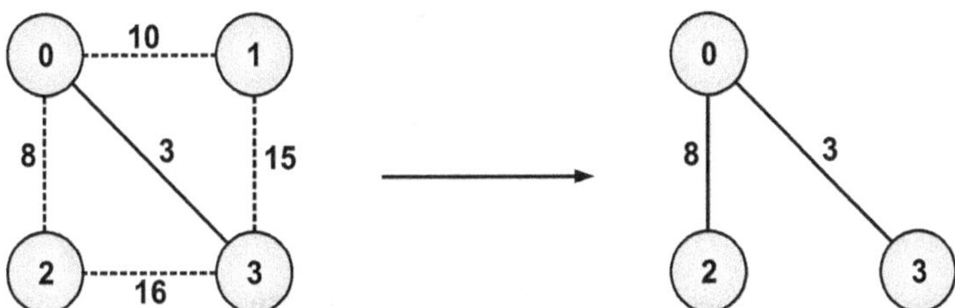

Fig. 4.22 (c): Step 2 for MST

Now find the outgoing edges of 0, 2, and 3.

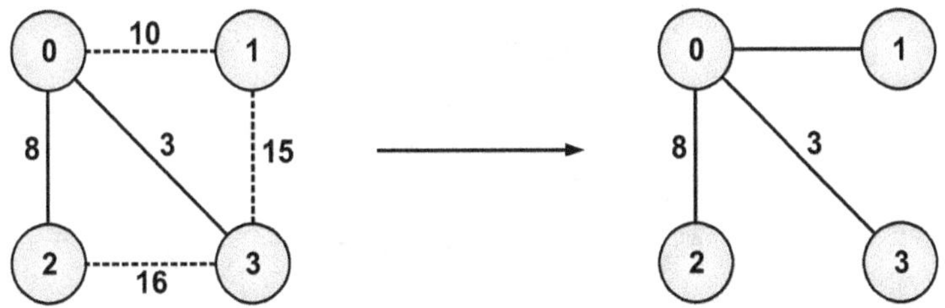

Fig. 4.22 (d): Step 3 for MST

Since above graph includes all vertices it is the MST.

Example 4.2: Show the stepwise construction of minimum spanning tree for the given graph using Prim's algorithm. [Fig. 4.23 (a)].

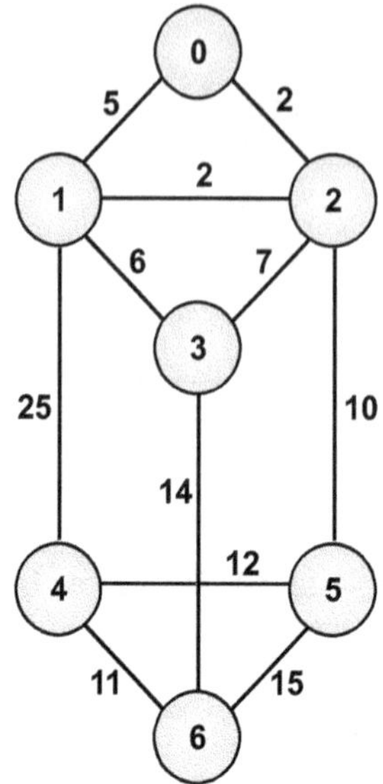

Fig. 4.23 (a): Graph

Step 1: Let us start from vertex 0

Fig. 4.23 (b): *Prim's* algorithm

Step 2: The adjacent vertices with cost are

$$0 - 1 \rightarrow 5$$
$$0 - 2 \rightarrow 2 \text{ (minimum)}$$

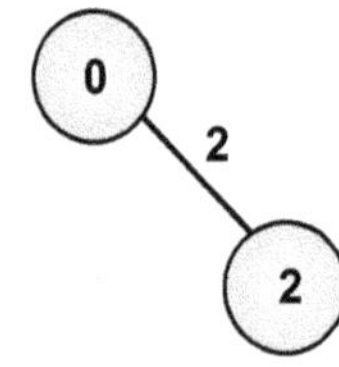

Fig. 4.23 (c): *Prim's* algorithm

Step 3: The adjacent vertex of 0 and 2 not forming cycle are

$$0 - 1 \rightarrow 5$$
$$0 - 2 \rightarrow 2 \text{ (minimum)}$$
$$2 - 3 \rightarrow 7$$
$$2 - 5 \rightarrow 10$$

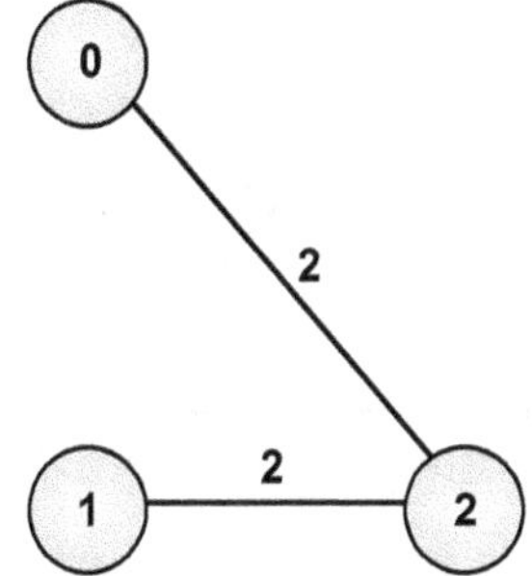

Fig. 4.23 (d): *Prim's* **algorithm**

Step 4: The adjacent vertex of 0, 1, 2 not forming cycle are

$$2 - 5 \; \text{-> } 10$$

$$2 - 3 \; \text{-> } 7$$

$$1 - 3 \; \text{-> } 6 \; (\text{minimum})$$

$$1 - 4 \; \text{-> } 25$$

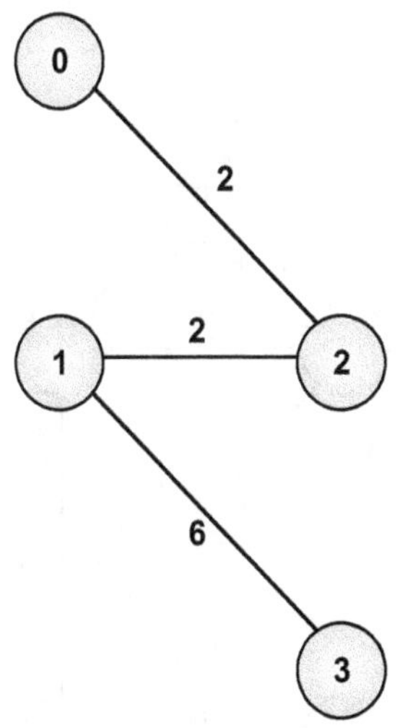

Fig. 4.23 (e): *Prim's* **algorithm**

Step 5: The adjacent vertex of 0, 1, 2, 3 are

$$2 - 5 \; \text{-> } 10 \; (\text{minimum})$$

$$1 - 4 \; \text{-> } 25$$

$$3 - 6 \; \text{-> } 14$$

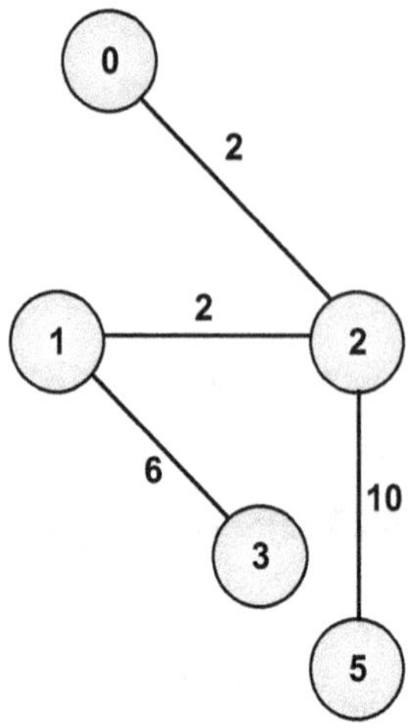

Fig. 4.23 (f): *Prim's* algorithm

Step 6: The adjacent vertex of 0, 1, 2, 3, 5 are

$$1 - 4 \ -> \ 25$$
$$5 - 4 \ -> \ 12 \quad (\text{minimum})$$
$$3 - 6 \ -> \ 14$$
$$5 - 6 \ -> \ 15$$

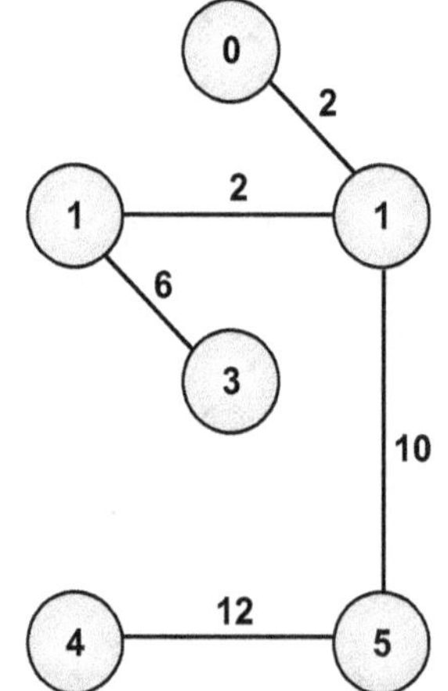

Fig. 4.23 (g): *Prim's* algorithm

Step 7: The adjacent vertex of 0, 1, 2, 3, 4, are

$$5 - 6 \ -> \ 15$$
$$4 - 6 \ -> \ 11 \ (\text{minimum})$$

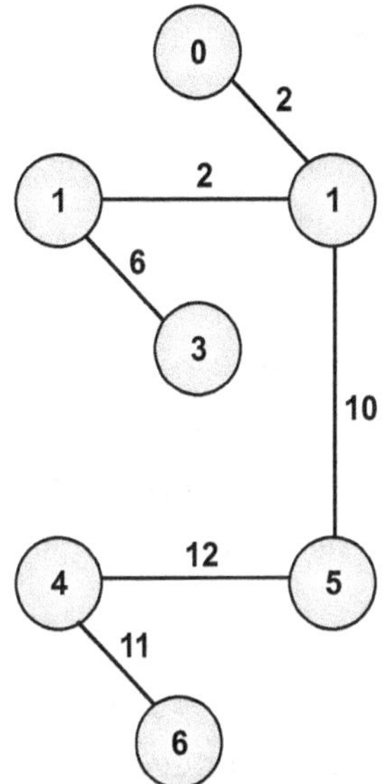

Fig. 4.23 (h): *Prim's* **algorithm**

This is spanning tree of given graph the total cost is 2 + 2 + 6 + 10 + 12 + 11 = 43.

The algorithm can be written as below.

Prim's algorithm:

      1.   T = {φ }

      2.   S = {0}

      3.   While(u≠v)

            {

                Let (u, v) be lowest cost edge such that u is in S and v is in V – S

                T = T ∪ { (c, v) }

                S = S ∪ {v}

            }

      4.   Stop

Explanation:

1.   T is the set of edges of the minimum spanning tree to be constructed. Initially, it will be empty set.

2.   S is the set of vertices of the minimum spanning tree. Initially, it will be having starting vertex say 0.

3. At each step we find shortest edge (u, v) that connects S and remaining vertices of the graph G i.e. V – S. The edge is added to T and vertex to S.

This process is continued until S becomes V (i.e. all vertices of graph are included in the tree).

Analysis:

When we start with particular vertex, we examine the edges connected to it. For this we have to check connectivity to all vertices and then select minimum cost edge. This process is repeated for all vertices. Hence, it is nested loop where outer, and inner loop will run for n times; where n is number of vertices. Hence, time complexity of algorithm will be $O(n^2)$.

4.6.2 Kruskal's Algorithm

This algorithm also finds minimum spanning tree. If we are given a graph $G \equiv (V, E)$, we start taking all vertices of the graph initially and no edges. We keep on adding the edges to the spanning tree in order of increasing cost in the MST, till all vertices are in one component.

Algorithm:

1. $G \equiv (V, E)$.
2. We start with a graph $T \equiv (V, \varphi)$ consisting of n vertices of G and no edges.
3. Examine edges from E. Repeat 4 and 5 in increasing order of cost of edges.
4. Add edge e_i to T if it connects two vertices in two different connected components of T. Otherwise discard e_i.
5. Take next edge and go to 3, if the vertices are not in one connected component.

Analysis:

A priority queue can be used to store the edges and taking them in increasing cost order. The formation of priority queue of e edges will require $O(e\log_2 e)$. Hence, there are n vertices and e edges assuming n < e. This algorithm will have time complexity $O(e\log_2 e)$.

Consider following example:

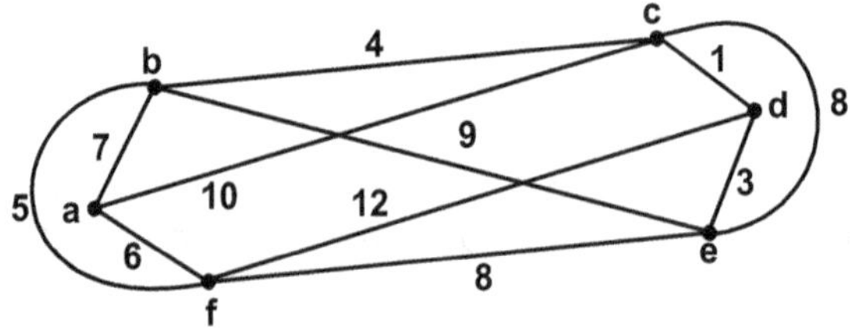

Fig. 4.24 (a): Graph

We start with all vertices in the graph a, b, c, d, e, f as follows:

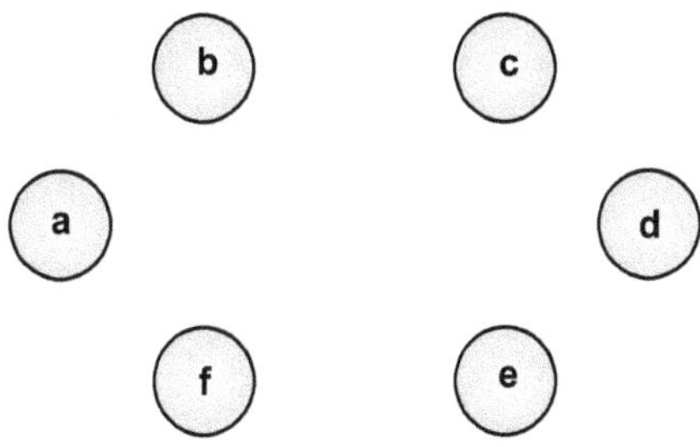

Fig. 4.24 (b): *Kruskal's* algorithm

Step 1: The edges with cost 1 are c – d include it in MST.

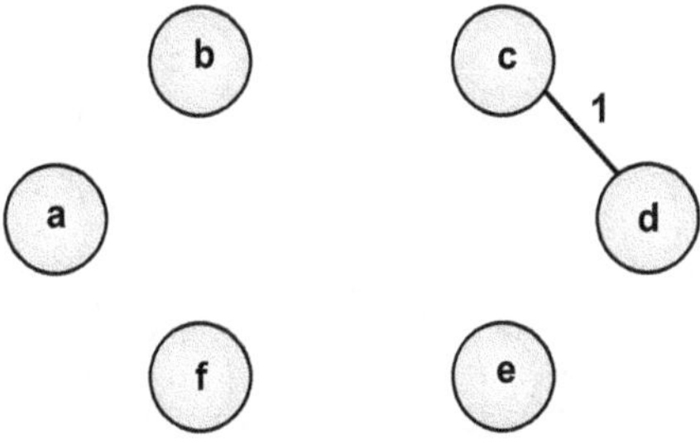

Fig. 4.24 (c): *Krushal's* algorithm

Step 2: Edges with cost 2 Nil

　　Edges with cost 3 d – e

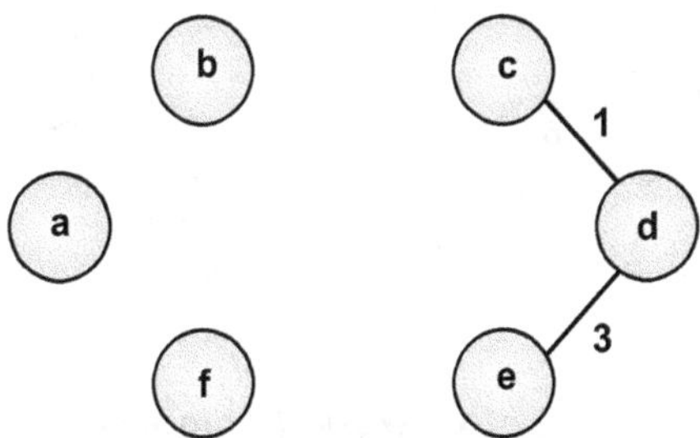

Fig. 4.24 (d): *Krushal's* algorithm

Step 3: Edges with cost 4: b – c

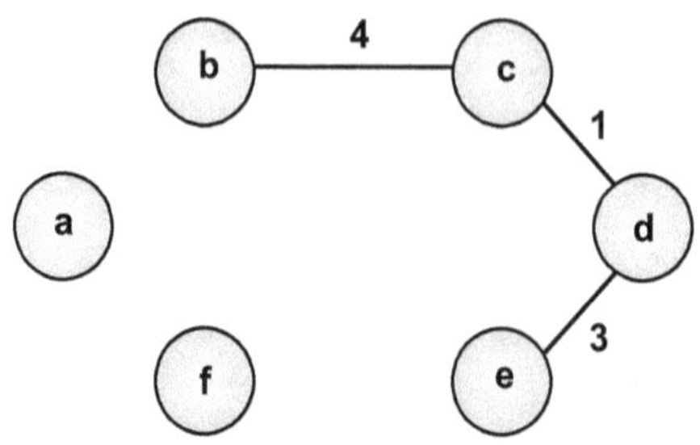

Fig. 4.24 (e): *Kruskal's* **algorithm**

Step 4: Edges with cost 5: b – f

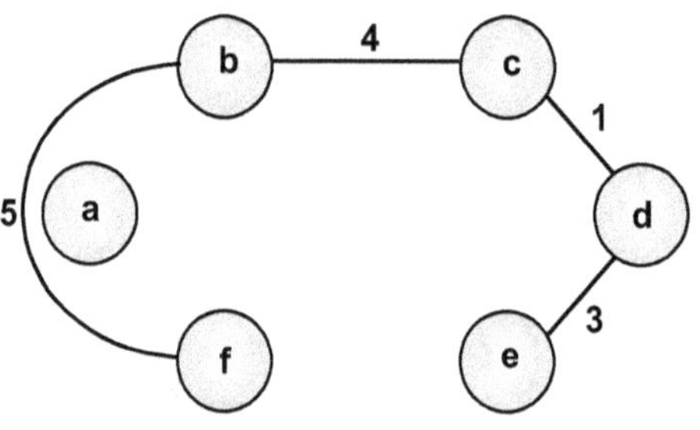

Fig. 4.24 (f): *Kruskal's* **algorithm**

Step 5: Edges with cost 6: f – a

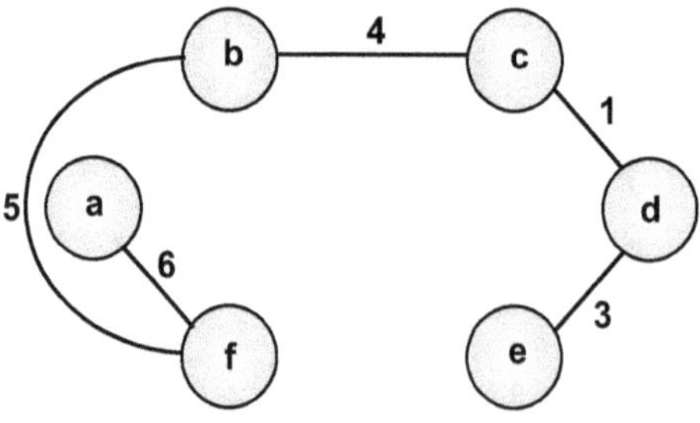

Fig. 4.24 (g): *Kruskal's* **algorithm**

This is minimum spanning tree. Total cost is 19.

Example 4.3: Find minimum spanning tree for following graph using *Kruskal's* algorithm

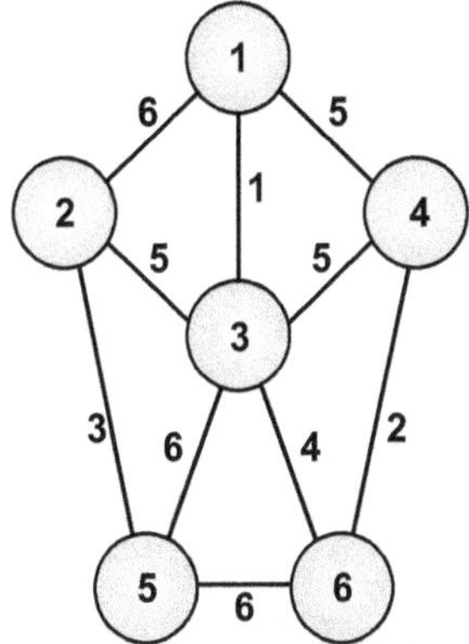

Fig. 4.25 (a): Graph

Solution:

We start with all vertices in the graph.

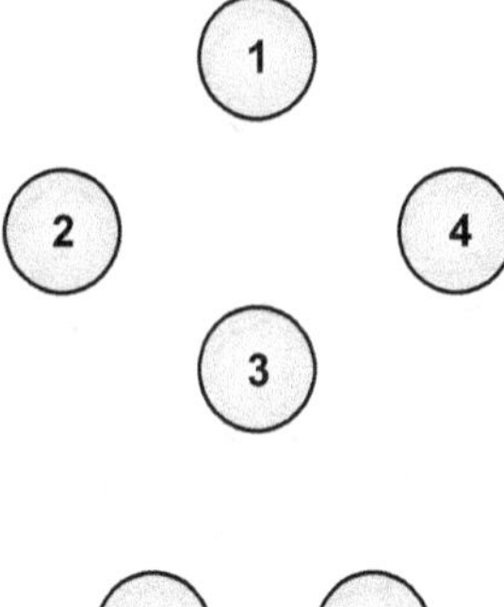

Fig. 4.25 (b): *Kruskal's* algorithm

Step 1: Edges with cost = 1 are 1 – 3

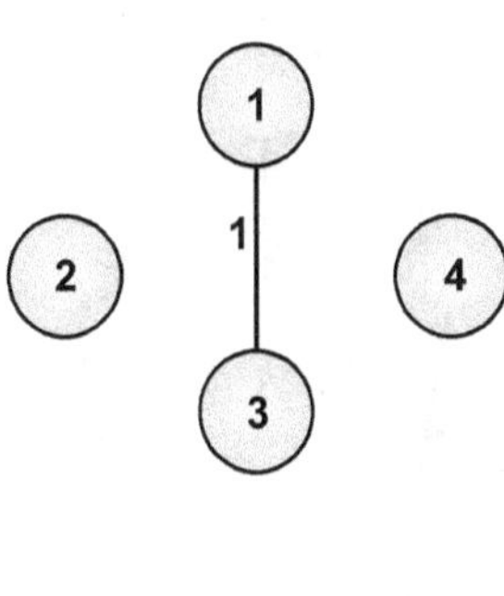

Fig. 4.25 (c): *Kruskal's* algorithm

Step 2: Edges with cost = 2 are 4 – 6

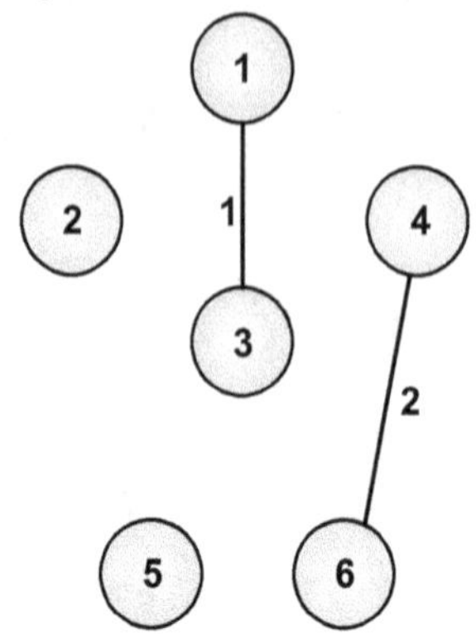

Fig. 4.25 (d): *Kruskal's* **algorithm**

Step 3: Edges with cost = 3 are 2 – 5

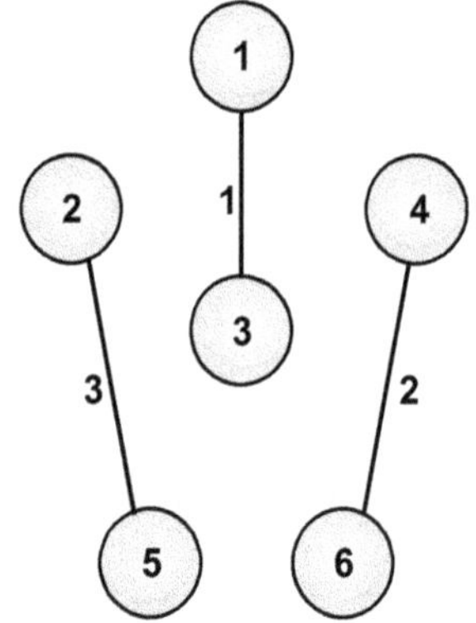

Fig. 4.25 (e): *Kruskal's* **algorithm**

Step 4: Edges with cost = 4 are 3 – 6
    Vertices are not in one component.

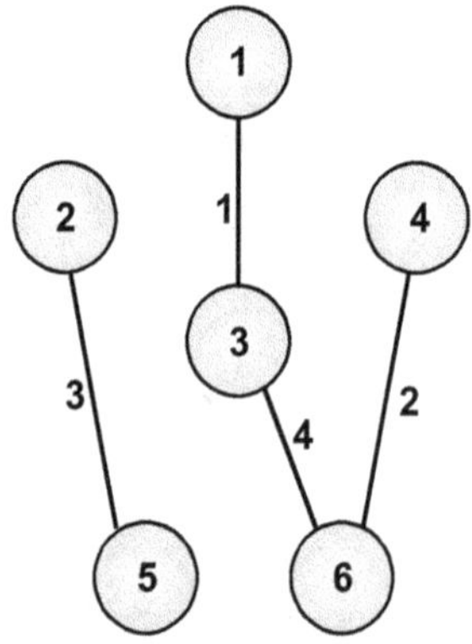

Fig. 4.25 (f): *Kruskal's* **algorithm**

Step 5: Edges with cost = 5 are 2 – 3 and 3 – 4

3, 4 are in same connected component hence include.

2, 3 are in different connected component hence include.

All vertices are in are connected component.

Hence this is minimum spanning tree.

The cost of MST is 15.

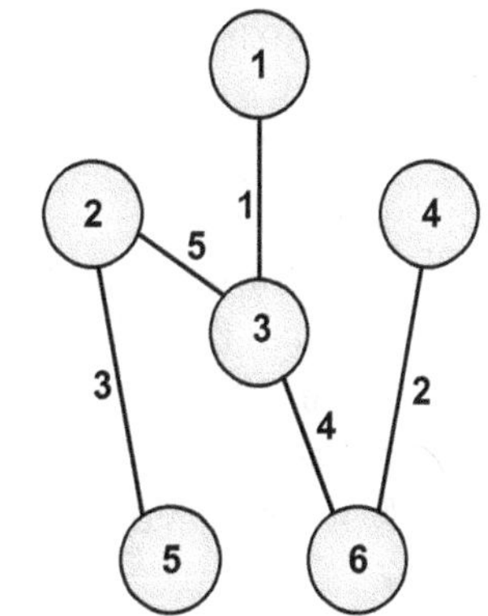

Fig. 4.25 (g): *Kruskal's* **algorithm**

4.7 Shortest Path Algorithm

One of the common applications of graph is to find shortest path between any two vertices of in a network. Suppose there are two cities A and B and there are number of paths between the two. The our aim is to find out the shortest path between the two. Another problem can be in a compaler network, suppose a packet is to be transferred between the two hosts in the network then air aim will be to find out shortest route through which the packet can be forwarded. Such problems can be ?? as graph with edges having cost or weight associated with them. The starting vertex of the path is called source and final vertex is called destination. The graph will be directed graph. In a graph we will be solving a single source shortest path problem.

Given as input a weighted graph G (V, E) and a distinguished vertex s find the shortest weighted path from S to every other vertex in G.

The algorithm for finding shortest path was given by Dijkstra. It is called Dijkstra's algorithm.

4.7.1 Dijkstra's Algorithm

We start with source vertex and find distances of all vertices viewed from this vertex. If the vertex is not adjacent its distance is taken as ?. Then we determine the minimum distance vertex. This vertex will be used to calculate the minimum distance of the next vertex.

The distance of all other vertices will be updated from source vertex with reference to this vertex whose minimum distance is already determined. The process is continued till al vertices shortest distance is determined.

1. Input n (number of vertices)
2. Input G ≡ (V, E) as cost matrix, C_{ij}
3. Input source vertex δ
4. S {s{

5. for(i=1;9<=n;i++)
    if (i ≠ s)
    $d_i = C_{si}$
6. for(i=1;i<n;i++)
    {   choose a vertex w is Y – S
        such that dw is minimum
        add ω to S.
        for each vertex v in V – S
        dv = min (dv, dv + Cwv)

    }
7. for(i=1;i<=n;i++)
    if (i ≠ s)
    print dw

Explanation:

1. The input to the program will be number of vertices n, cost matrix of the graph and source vertex 3.
2. S is a set of vertices whose shortest path is already determined. The source vertex (S) will be initial element of this sets.
3. The initial values of shortest distance of vertices d_i will be determined form cost matrix elements C_{si} where 5 is source vertex and i is vertex whose distance is calculated. If the vertex i is not directly connected to s the value of C_{si} will be ∞.
4. V is set of vertices in the graph. Hence V-S means all vertices in V excluding S.
5. Every time we determine shortest distance of a vertex (w) it is added to S. Once it is added to S it is not updated.

    Let us take an example and ?? above algorithm

Example 1: Find shortest distance of all vertices in the graph from vertex 0.1.

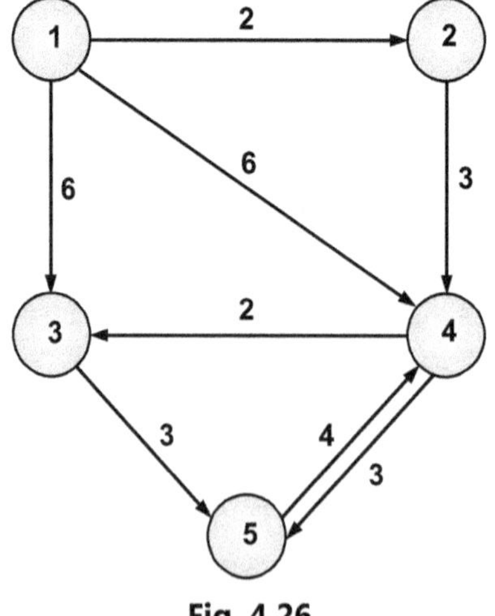

Fig. 4.26

Solution:

Here $n = 5$ Source vertex $s = 1$

∴   The set $S = \{1\}$

$$d_2 = 2$$
$$d_3 = 6$$
$$d_4 = 6$$
$$d_5 = \infty$$

Step 1: The minimum distance vertex is 2

i.e. $d_2 = 2$

Hence shortest distance of vertex 2 from 1

is 2 and Path is $1 \to 2$

$S = \{1, 2\}$

We have to update d3, d4, d5

$$d_3 = \min(d_3, d_2 + C_{23})$$
$$= \min(6, \ 2 + 3)$$
$$= 5$$
$$d_4 = \min(d_4, d_2 + C_{24})$$
$$= \min(6, 2 + \infty)$$
$$= 6$$
$$d_5 = \min(d_5, d_2 + C_{25})$$
$$= \min(\infty, 2 + \infty)$$
$$= \infty$$

Step 1 : Minimum of d_3, d_4, d_5 is $d_3 = 5$

which is updated in previous step

Hence shortest path of vertex 3 from 1

is $1 \to 2 \to 5$ and shortest dist $d_3 = 5$.

∴ $S = \{1, 2, 3\}$.

$$d4 = \min(d_4, d_2 + C_{34})$$
$$= \min(6, 5 + 2)$$
$$= 6$$
$$d5 = \min(d_5, d_3 + C_{35})$$
$$= \min(\infty, 5 + 3)$$
$$= 8$$

Step 1 :   Minimum of d_5 is single vertex left out. It was updated in step 2 where its distance from vertex 3 was calculated to be 8.

Hence shortest path of vertex 5 from 1 is $1 \to 2 \to 3 \to 5$ and shortest dist is $d_5 = 8$.

and $S = \{1, 2, 3, 4, 5\}$ which includes now all vertex.

The summary is as below.

Destination	Shortest Distance	Path
2	2	$1 \rightarrow 2$
3	5	$1 \rightarrow 2 \rightarrow 3$
4	6	$1 \rightarrow 2 \rightarrow 3 \rightarrow 4$
5	8	$1 \rightarrow 2 \rightarrow 3 \rightarrow 5$

Example 2: Find the shortest distance and path of all vertices for graph given below form vertex 1.

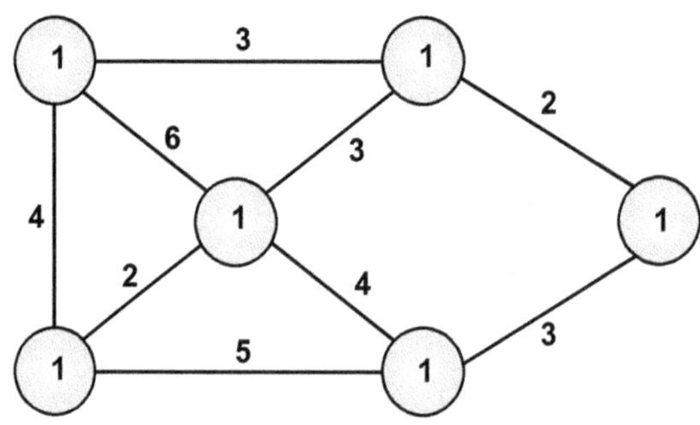

Fig. 4.27

Solution: Let node 1 be the source node.

(1) $S = \{1\}$

(2) $d2 = 4$, $d3 = 3$, $d4 = 6$, $d5 = \infty$, $d6 = \infty$.

    (Note that d5 and d6 are ∞ because they do not have direct path from node 1).

(3) $d_i = \min d_j$

           $j \notin S$

       $= d_3 = 3$

(4) Node 3 is added to S

$\therefore \quad S = \{1, 3\}$

Now,

    $d_2 = \min(d_2, d_3 + c_{32})$

        $= \min(4, 3 + \infty)$

        $= 4$

    $d_4 = \min(d_4, d_3 + c_{34})$

        $= \min(5, 3 + 3)$

        $= 5$

$$d_5 = \min(d_5, d_5 + c_{35})$$
$$= \min(\infty, \infty)$$
$$= \infty$$
$$d_6 = \min(d_6, d_3 + c_{36})$$
$$= \min(\infty, 3 + 2)$$
$$= 5$$

In the next iteration, we select minimum of d_2, d_4, d_6 which is $d_2 = 4$ and proceed on the same line as above.

Following table shows all the iterations.

Iteration Number	s	d_2	d_3	d_4	d_5	d_6
Initialize	{1}	4	(3)	6	∞	∞
1	{1, 3}	(4)	-	6	∞	5
2	{1, 3, 2}	-	-	6	8	(5)
3	{1, 3, 2, 6}	-	-	(6)	8	-
4	{1, 3, 2, 6, 4}	-	-	-	(8)	-
5	{1, 3, 2, 6, 4, 5}	-	-	-	-	-

Hence, shortest paths from node 1 are as below.

Source to Destination Path	Cost
$1 - 3$	3
$1 - 2$	4
$1 - 2 - 6$	5
$1 - 4$ or $1 - 3 - 4$	6
$1 - 3 - 6 - 5$	8

SOLVED PROBLEMS

1. **Find minimum spanning tree for following graph using Prim's algorithm.**

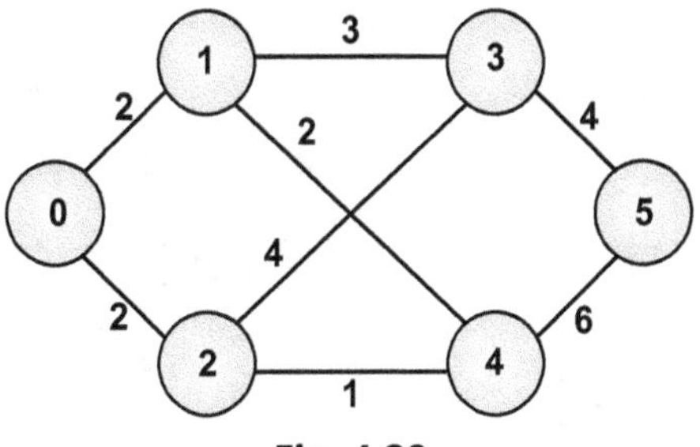

Fig. 4.28

Solution: We start with vertex 0.

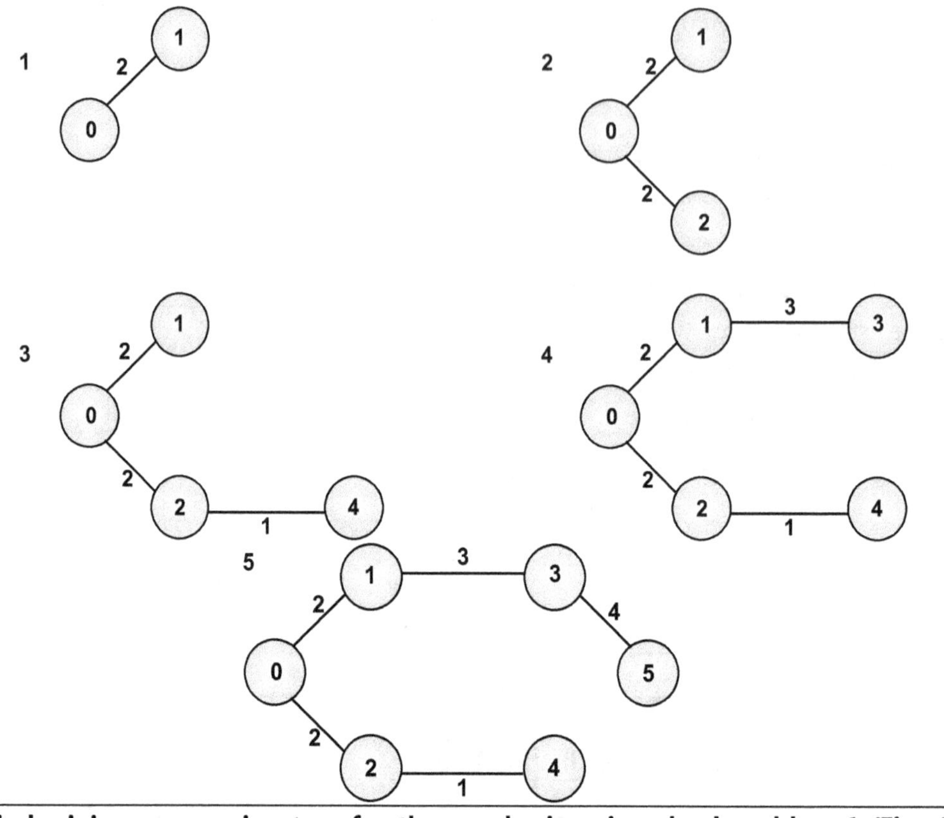

2. **Find minimum spanning tree for the graph given in solved problem 1 (Fig. 4.28) using *Krushal's* algoritm.**

Solution:

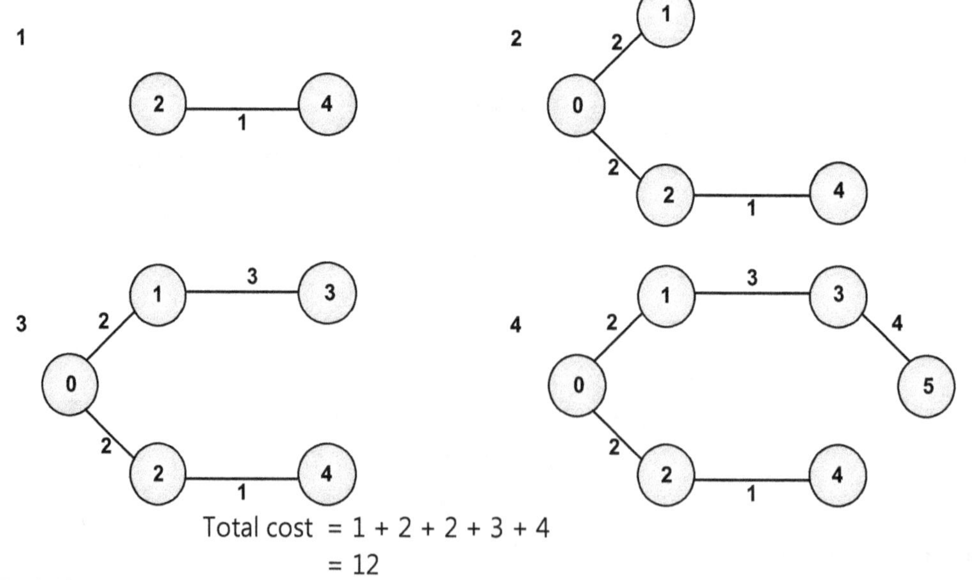

$$\text{Total cost} = 1 + 2 + 2 + 3 + 4$$
$$= 12$$

3. Represent following graph using adjacency matrix and adjacency list.

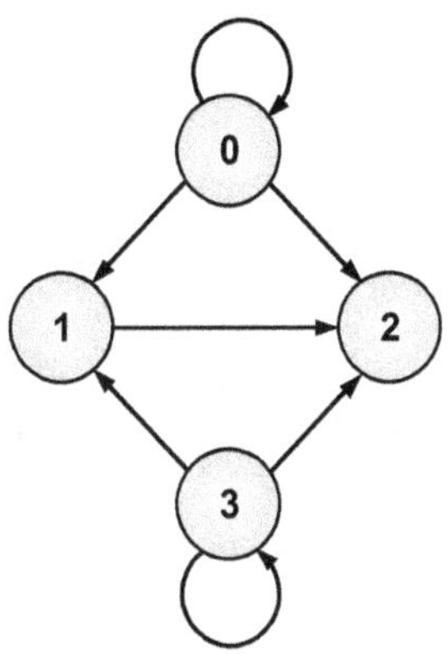

Fig. 4.29

Solution:

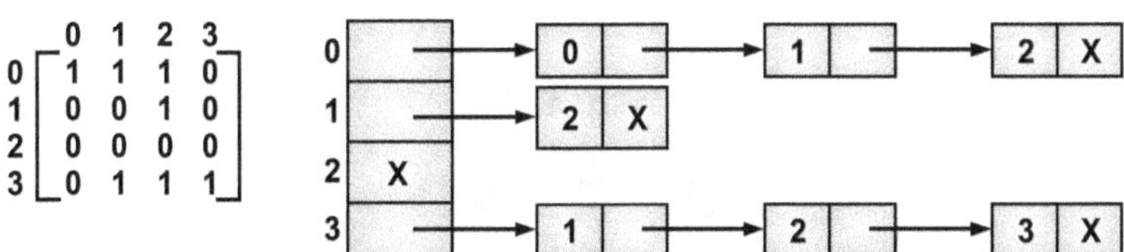

4. Write DFS and BFS traversal for given graph in solved problem 3 (Fig. 4.29)

Solution:

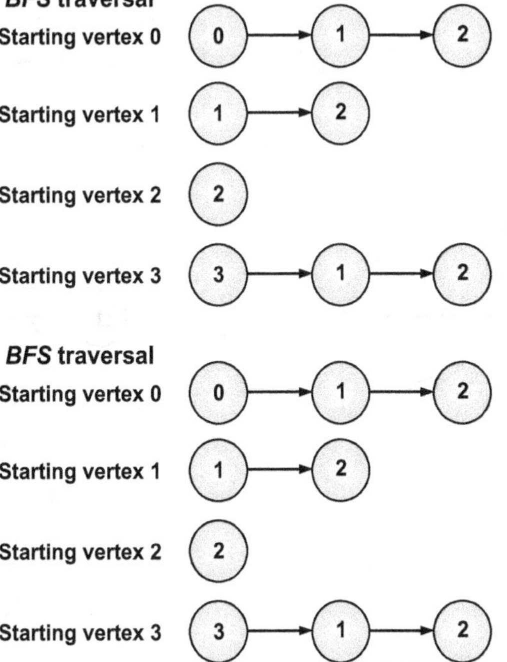

5. **What do you mean by adjacency matrix and adjacency list adjacency matrix and adjacency list of the following graph:**

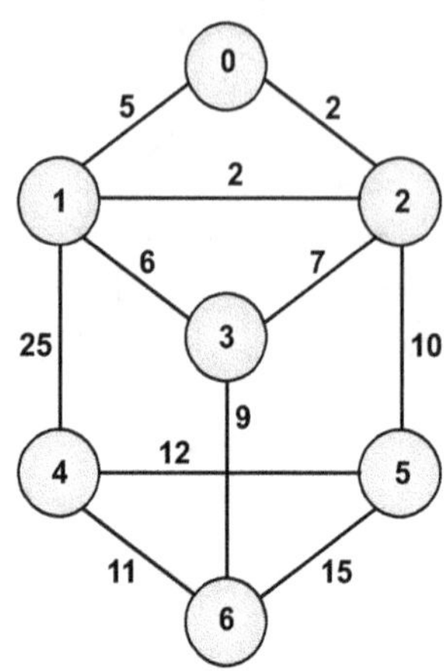

Fig. 4.30

Solution:

1 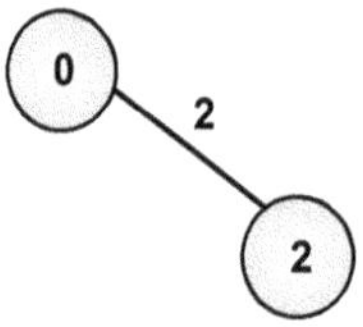 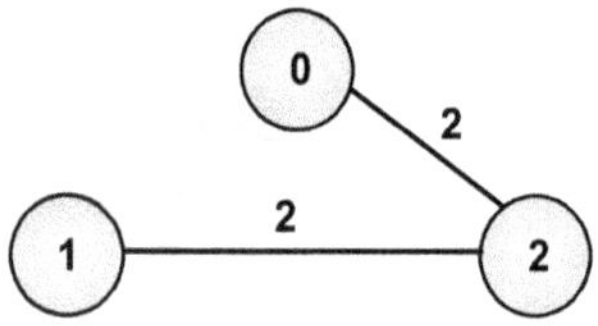	
3. 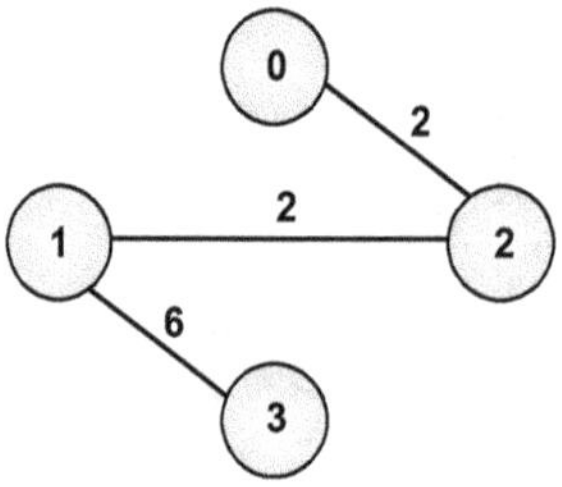 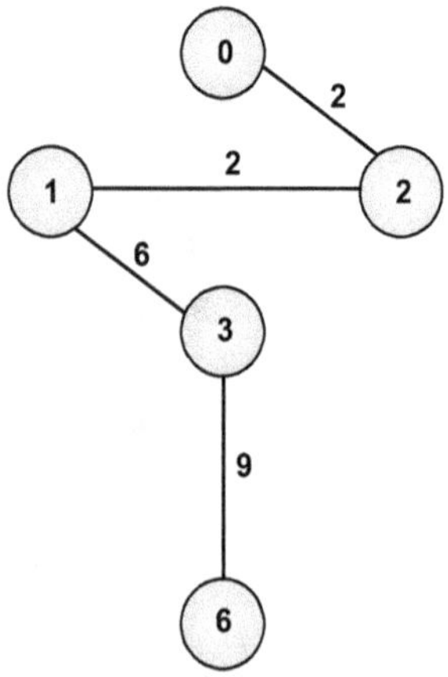	

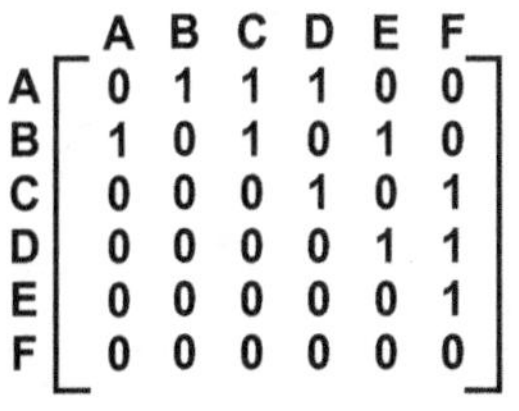

5.

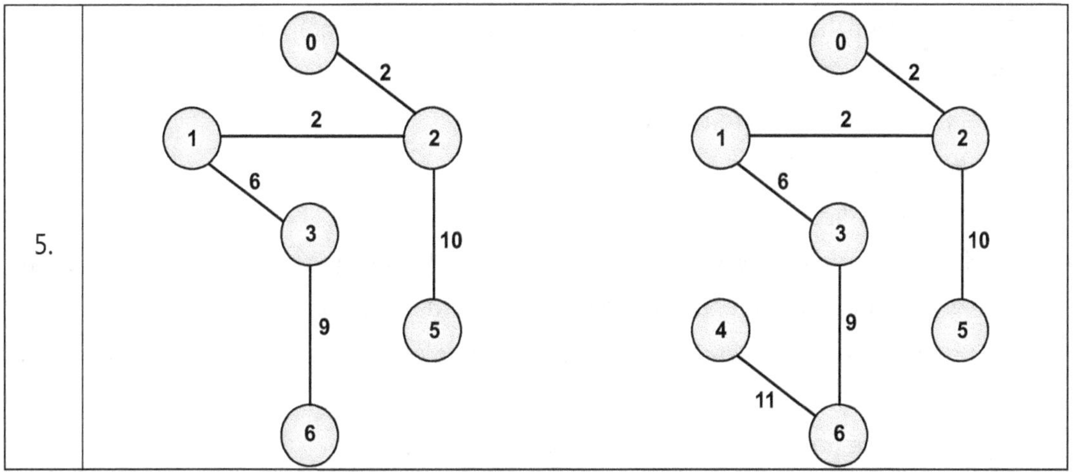

6. **What do you mean by adjacency and adjacency list adjacency matrix and adjacency list of the following graph:**

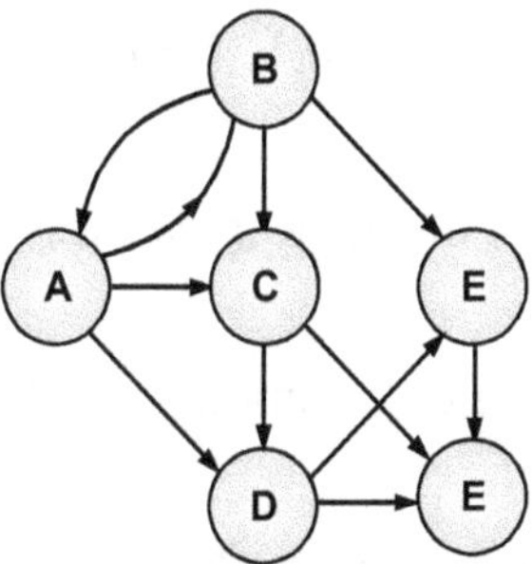

Fig. 4.31

Solution:

Adjacency matrix

	A	B	C	D	E	F
A	0	1	1	1	0	0
B	1	0	1	0	1	0
C	0	0	0	1	0	1
D	0	0	0	0	1	1
E	0	0	0	0	0	1
F	0	0	0	0	0	0

Adjacency list

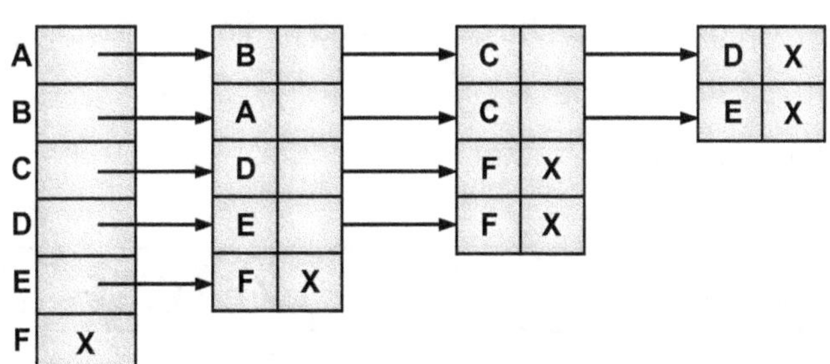

SUMMARY

- Graph is a non-linear data structure consisting of set of nodes (vertices and edges (arcs).
- A graph can be of two types:
  (i)   Directed graph,
  (ii) Undirected graph.

- Directed graph has ordered edges whereas undirected graph does not have ordered edges.
- A graph can be represented using:
  (i)   Adjacency matrix,
  (ii) Adjacency list.
- In adjacency matrix representation, if there is edge between two vertices of graph v_1 and v_2, the element in row v_1 and column v_2 is 1, otherwise it will be 0.
- In adjacency list representation, a list of nodes adjacent to each vertex is stored in an array of head nodes.
- A graph can be traversed using two ways:
  (i)   Depth First Search (DFS),
  (ii) Breadth First Search (BFS).
- DFS traversal involves visiting vertices such that every time we visit a new vertex adjacent to it.
- BFS traversal involves visiting all the adjacent vertices of current vertex then move to the next.
- Shortest path algorithm (Dijkstra's algorithm) is used to find shortest path from a vertex to all other vertices of the graph.
- A spanning tree of a graph is a tree which includes all the vertices of the graph.
- Minimum spanning tree of a graph is a spanning tree of the graph whose sum of costs is minimum.
- Two algorithm can be used to find minimum spanning tree:
  (i)   *Prim's* algorithm,
  (ii) *Kruskal's* algorithm.

EXERCISE

1. Define the term graph. With the help of suitable example give adjacency matrix representation and adjacency list representation for the same.
2. What is graph? Explain how to represent graph using adjacency list and matrix.
3. Explain how graph is represented using suitable example.
4. Describe the methods of representing graph with suitable example.
5. What are the different ways of representing graph 2. Explain with suitable example.

6. What are the different ways of representing a graph? Explain with suitable example.

7. With the help of any graph, explain the term adjacency list and adjacency matrix.

8. Take your own example of graph and represent it using matrix and adjacency linked list. Give 'C' declaration for the above mentioned representation.

9. With the help of any graph, explain the terms adjacency list and adjacency matrix.

10. How can a graph be represented? Explain with suitable example.

11. Write non-recursive pseudo-c algorithm for depth first search of a graph.

12. Write non-recursive pseudo-c algorithm for BFS of a graph.

13. Describe the following with suitable examples.

    (i)   Depth first search (Refer Section 4.5)

14. Write a non-recursive pseudo-c function for breadth first search of a graph.

15. Write a non-recursive pseudo-c function for depth-first search of a graph.

16. Write an algorithm for Depth First Search for a graph.

17. What is Depth First Search? What are the advantages and disadvantages of DFS? Give pseudo-code to implement DFS on any graph.

18. Explain what are BFS and DFS. Write a pseudo-c to traverse a graph using BFS.

19. Write necessary C functions to implement BFS of graph.

20. Define DFS and BFS for graph.

21. Write recursive C functions to find DFS of graph.

22. What is DFS? Write a function for DFS for a graph.

23. Write recursive function to find DFS of a graph.

24. Write non-recursive pseudo-c algorithm for DFS of graph and explain with suitable example.

25. Write non-recursive pseudo-c algorithm for BFS of graph and explain with suitable example.

26. What is BFS? Write a function for BFS for a graph.

27. What do you mean by spanning tree? Explain Kruskal's algorithm to find minimum spanning tree with the help of suitable example.

28. What is spanning tree? What is minimum spanning tree?

29. What is minimum spanning tree? Explain Prim's algorithm.

30. Explain Prim's algorithm.

31. What do you mean by spanning tree? Explain Kruskal's algorithm to find minimum spanning tree with suitable example.

32. Explain Kruskal's algorithm.

33. Write pseudo-c code to find minimum spanning tree using Kruskal's algorithm. Explain all steps with suitable example. What is time complexity of algorithm?

34. Explain Kruskal's algorithm.

35. Find the minimum spanning tree for the graph shown in figure 4.30 using Prim's algorithm. Show all necessary steps.

36. Construct minimum spanning tree (step-by-step) from the following graph using Kruskal's algorithm.

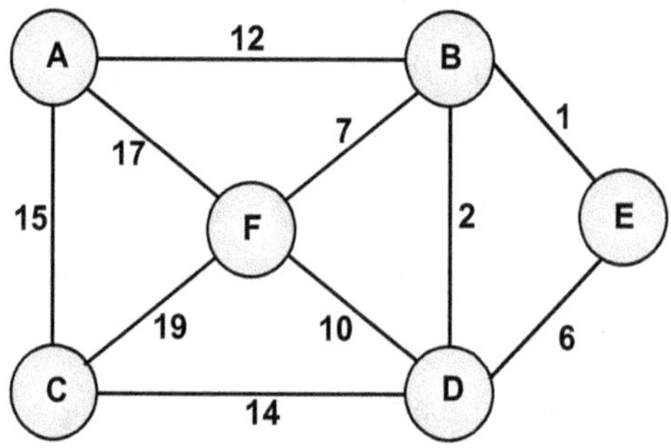

Fig. 4.32: Graph

37. Determine minimum spanning tree for the following graph using Kruskal's algorithm. Show all the steps.

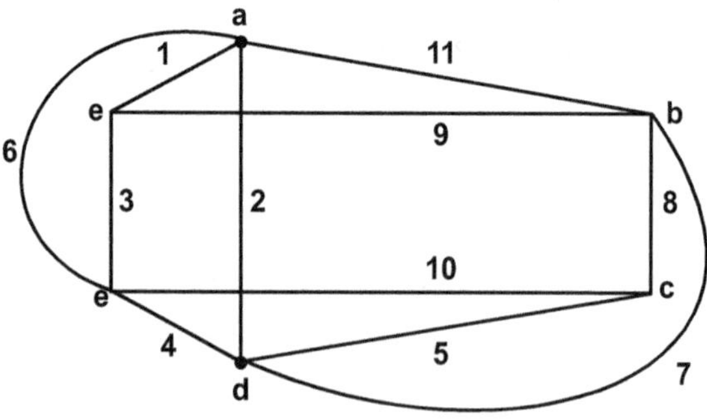

Fig. 4.33

38. Construct minimum spanning tree using Kruskal's algorithm for the following graph:

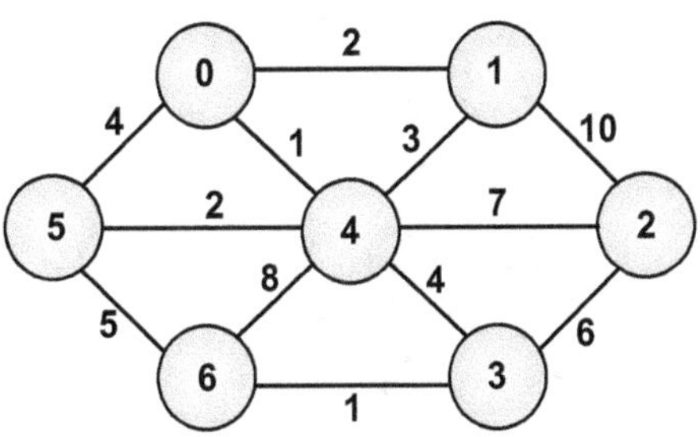

Fig. 4.34: Graph

39. What is minimum spanning tree? Find minimum spanning tree of the following graph using Kruskal's algorithm.

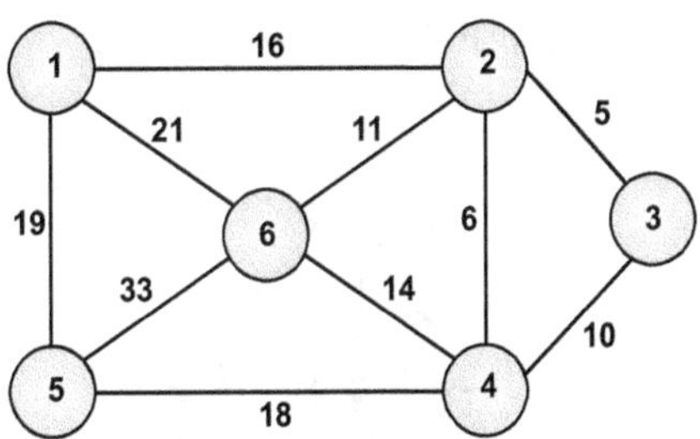

Fig. 4.35: Graph

40. What is minimum spanning tree? Find minimum spanning tree of the following graph using Kruskal's algorithm.

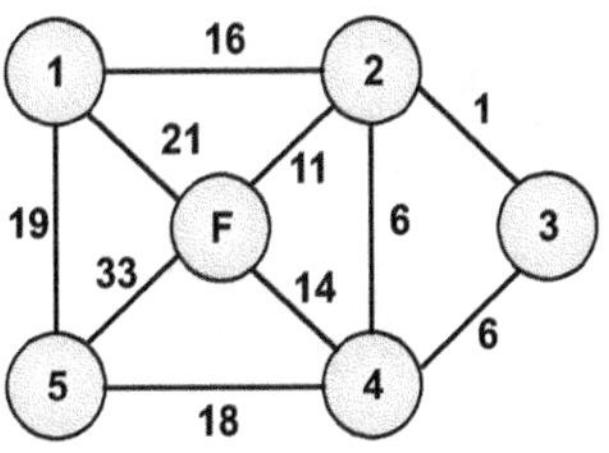

Fig. 4.36: Graph

41. Define DFS and BFS for graph. Show DFS and BFS for the graph given below:

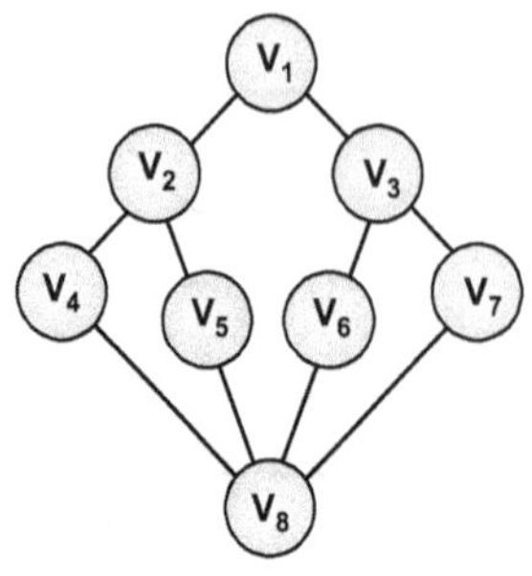

Fig. 4.37: Graph

42. Construct minimum spanning tree using Prim's algorithm for the figure 4.35.

43. What do you mean by adjacency matrix and adjacency list? Give the adjacency matrix and adjacency list of the following graph:

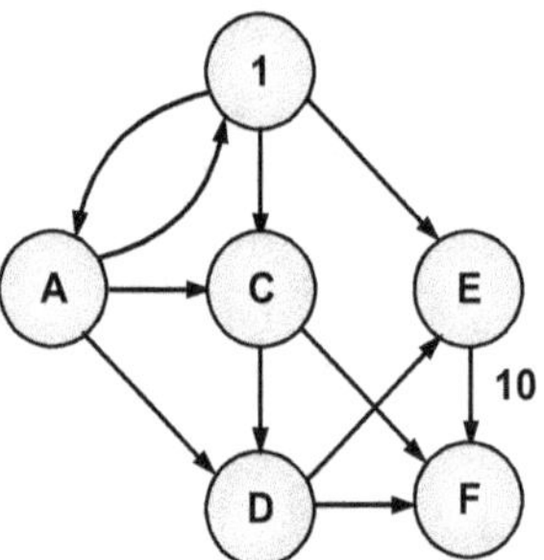

Fig. 4.38: Graph

Unit V

TREES

5.1 Introduction

Till now we have seen data structures such as arrays, linked lists, stacks, queues, etc. All these are linear data structures. The data is stored in sequential locations. In order to retrieve data, we have to traverse in sequence. For large amount of data this kind of access is not efficient because, time complexity of retrieval in such data structures will be poor, i.e. O(n).

If we arrange the data in hierarchical manner, we can have more than one successor of a data element as shown in Fig. 5.1.

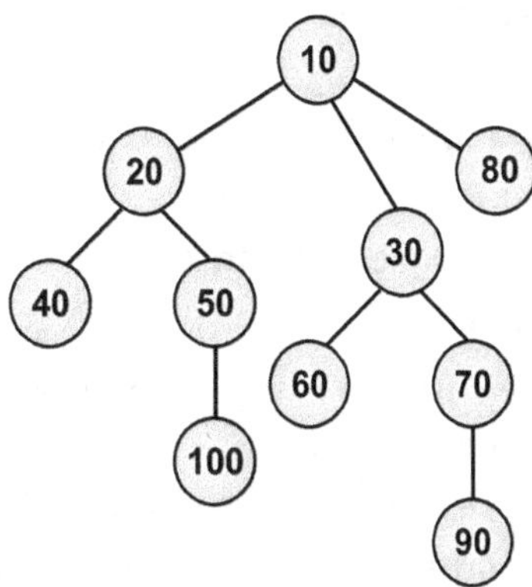

Fig. 5.1: Tree

Such a structure is called tree. There are number of applications in computer science where we can use this data structure. A tree can be defined in several ways.

Definition 1:

A tree (T) is a set of nodes. The set can be empty. If its nonempty set it consists of a specially designated node called root node and zero or more (sub) trees T_1, T_2, T_3, ..., T_n, each of whose roots are connected by a directed edge from the root of T.

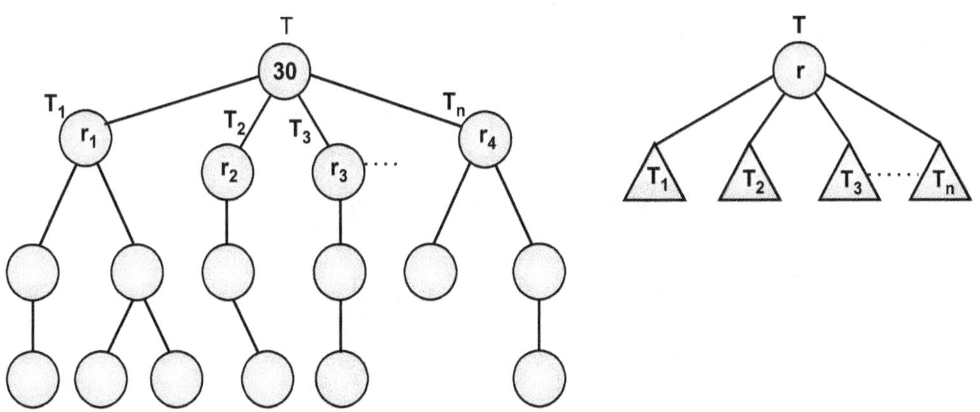

Fig. 5.2: Tree definition

Definition 2:

A tree consists of finite set of elements called nodes and a finite set of directed lines called branch edges that connect the nodes.

5.2 Basic Terminology

There are number of terms used with tree. Let us see the definition of each of them.

1. **Node:** It stands for item of information plus the branches to other items.
2. **Degree:** The total number of edges associated with a node is called degree of that node.
3. **Indegree:** The total number of edges converging a node is called indegree of the node. Root node will have indegree 0.
4. **Outdegree:** The total number of edges diverging from a node is called outdegree of the node.
5. **Leaf node or Terminal node:** The nodes that have outdegree zero are called leaf node or terminal node.
6. **Non-terminals:** The nodes which have nonzero outdegree are called nonterminals.
7. **Children:** The root nodes of the sub-tree of a node are called children of that node, i.e., they are immediate successors of node.
8. **Parent Node:** If A is child of B then B is the parent node of A, i.e., it is immediate predecessor of a node.
9. **Siblings:** Children of the same parent are called siblings.
10. **Degree of a tree:** It is maximum degree of a node in the tree.
11. **Ancestor nodes:** Ancestors of a node are all the nodes along the path from the root to that node.
12. **Level of a node:** Root node of a tree is said to be at level 1. Its children will be at level 2. In general, the node at level l will have its children at level $l + 1$.
13. **Height or depth of tree:** It is the maximum level of any node in the tree.
14. **Forest:** It is a set of disjoint trees, i.e., these trees will not have common node amongst them. Let us draw a tree and represent these terms.

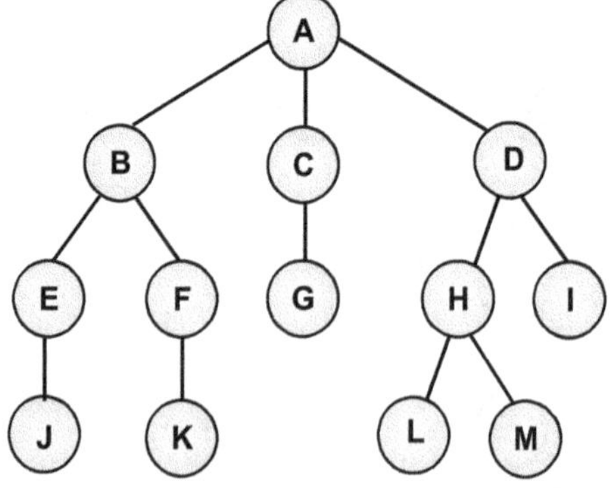

Fig. 5.3: Tree

Observation:

1. Total degree of A $\Rightarrow$ 3

2. Indegree of H $\Rightarrow$ 1

3. Out-degree of H $\Rightarrow$ 2

4. Leaf nodes $\Rightarrow$ J, K, G, L, M, I

5. Non-terminal $\Rightarrow$ A, B, C, D, E, F, H

6. Children of B $\Rightarrow$ E, F

7. Parent node of J $\Rightarrow$ E

8. Siblings $\Rightarrow$ {B, C,D}, {E, F}, {H, I} {L, M}

9. Ancestors of J $\Rightarrow$ E, B, A

10. Degree of Tree $\Rightarrow$ 3

11. Level of H $\Rightarrow$ 3

12. Height of Tree $\Rightarrow$ 4

13. Forest: if we remove root A of the tree we get set of three trees which is a forest.

The tree can be represented in a linked list format, where each node in the tree will be as:

Data	Link 1	Link 2	......	Link 4

For a general tree there are no restrictions on the number of sub-trees. The data field will store the information. The link fields will store the addresses of children of the node. Now the question is how many link fields should be defined? It is going to depend on maximum number of branches a node can have. Hence, it is very difficult to create a general tree. Binary trees are used in most of the applications where the number of branches will be fixed to 2. Hence, we will restrict our study to binary trees.

5.3 Binary Tree

A binary tree is a tree in which no node has more than two sub-trees. It means any node can have at most two branches. i.e., there is no node with degree greater than two.

Definition:

A binary tree is a finite set of nodes which is either empty or consists of root and two disjoint binary trees called left sub-tree and right sub-tree.

Following are examples of binary trees.

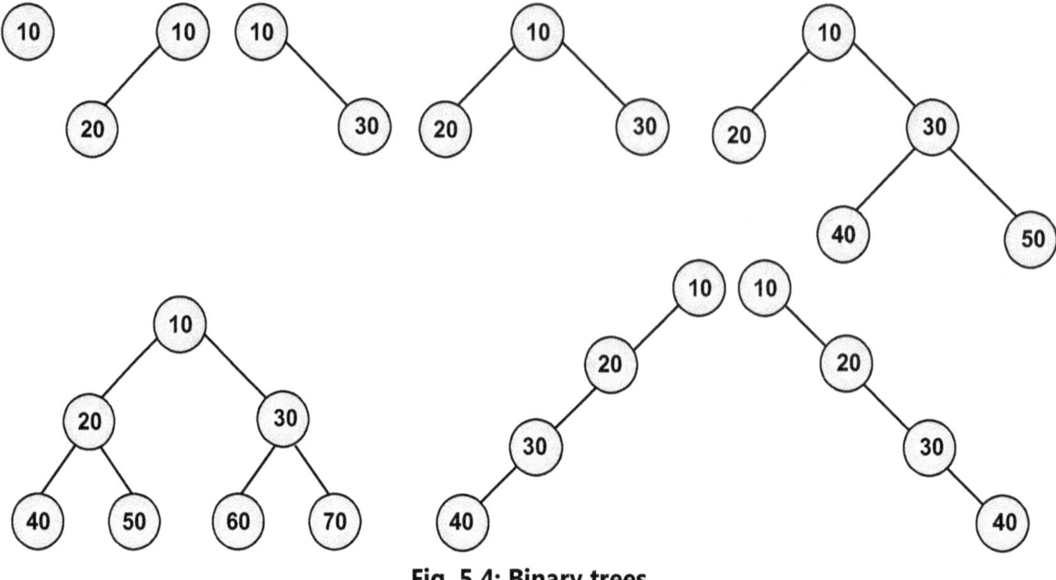

Fig. 5.4: Binary trees

The maximum number of nodes in a binary tree will be 2^h-1 where h is height of the tree. The number of leaf nodes in the binary tree will be 2^{h-1}.

Depending on how the nodes are placed in the binary, we can have following types of binary tree.

1. Complete binary tree:

If the height of binary tree is h and there are 2^{h-1} node at least level, then it is complete binary tree. Following are examples of complete binary tree. It is also called full binary tree.

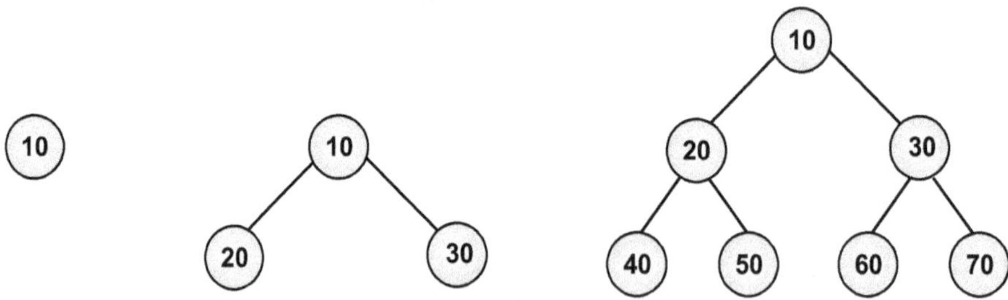

Fig. 5.5: Complete binary tree

2. Almost complete binary tree: If the height of binary tree is h, then the binary tree is said to be almost complete if

    (i)   The leaf nodes are at level h or h − 1.

    (ii) There is no leaf node at level h − 2 i.e., at h − 2 level every node has two children.

    (iii) At level h the leaf nodes are as far to the left as possible.

Following are examples of almost complete binary tree.

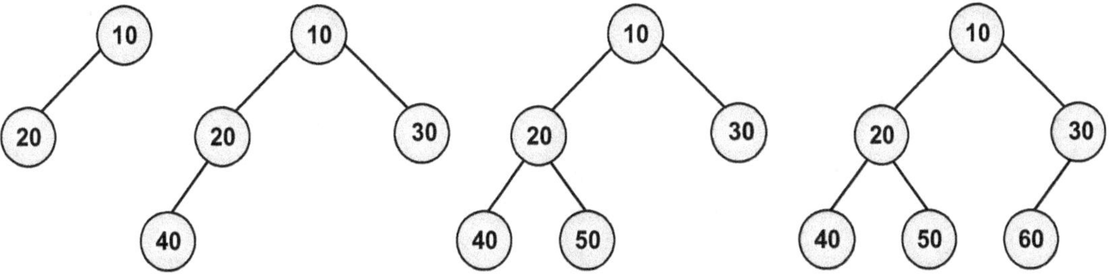

Fig. 5.6: Almost complete binary tree

3. Left skewed binary tree:

If the nodes in a binary tree have only left child it is called left skewed binary tree.

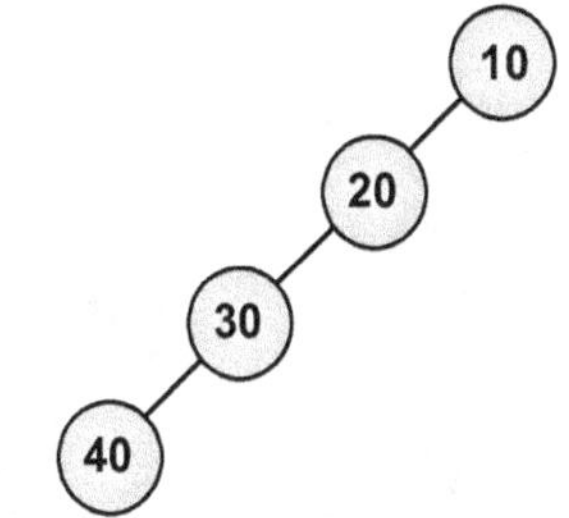

Fig. 5.7: Left skewed binary tree

4. Right skewed binary tree:

If the nodes in a binary tree have only right child it is called right skewed binary tree.

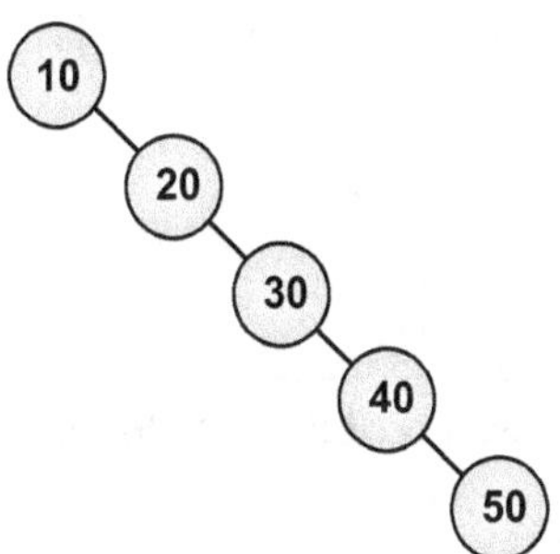

Fig. 5.8: Right skewed binary tree

5. Strictly binary tree:

It is a binary tree in which each node will have either two children or no child. Examples of strictly binary tree are shown in Fig. 5.9.

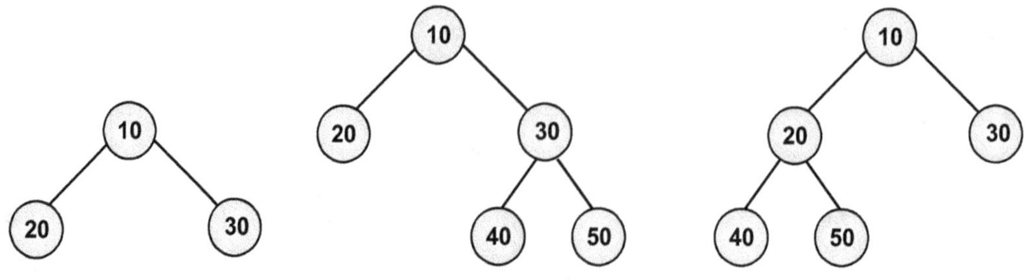

Fig. 5.9: Strictly binary tree

5.3.1 Representation of Binary Tree

A binary tree can be represented using arrays or linked lists.

The array representation of binary tree is very simple for implementations where each node in binary tree will be stored in the array sequentially. Consider a complete binary tree as shown in Fig. 5.10.

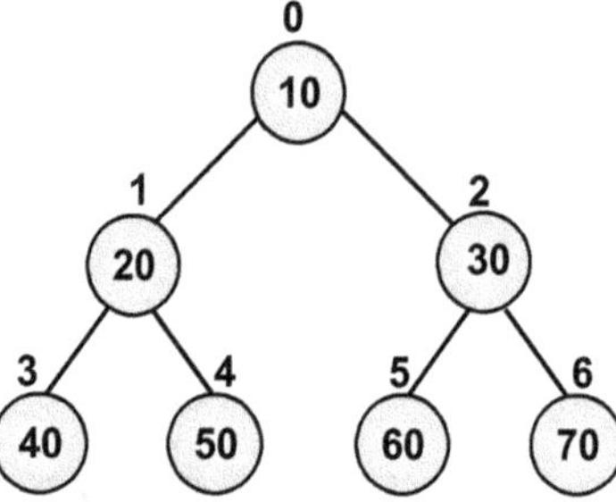

Fig. 5.10: Binary tree

The nodes are designated by numbers which can be used as location number of the element in the array for example, the element 30 will be stored a[2]. The array representation of above binary tree is shown in Fig. 5.11.

a[0]	a[1]	a[2]	a[3]	a[4]	a[5]	a[6]
10	20	30	40	50	60	70

Fig. 5.11: Array representation of binary tree in Fig. 5.10

Observe that if an element is at i^{th} location, its left child will be at $(2i+1)^{th}$ location and right child will be at $(2i+2)^{th}$ location.

But, if we have binary tree which is not complete binary tree or almost complete binary tree most of the space in the array will be unutilized. For example, if we have a binary tree as shown in Fig. 5.12.

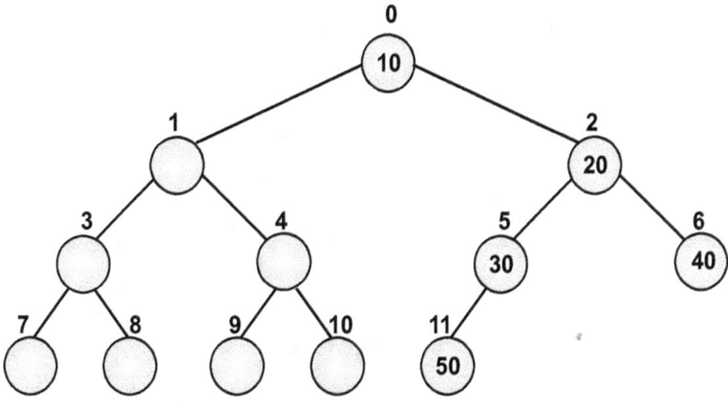

Fig. 5.12: Binary tree

Its array representation will be

a[0]	a[1]	a[2]	a[3]	a[4]	a[5]	a[6]	a[7]	a[8]	a[9]	a[10]	a[11]	a[12]
10	–	20	–	–	30	40	–	–	–	–	50	–

Fig. 5.13: Array representation of binary tree in figure 5.12

It is not only wastage of space, the insertion or deletion of node is also going to cause lot of movements. These problems can be eliminated using linked representation.

In linked representation, each node will be having three fields viz., data, lchild and rchild. The data field is information to be stored. It can be int, float, char, array or records. The two field's lchild and rchild will be pointers storing the addresses of left sub-tree and right sub-tree.

The node structure can be defined as

```
typedef struct node
{
    int data;
    struct node *lchild, *rchild;
}   NODE;
```

The node will be as shown in Fig. 5.14.

Fig. 5.14: Node in a binary tree

The binary tree in node structure will be as shown in Fig. 5.15.

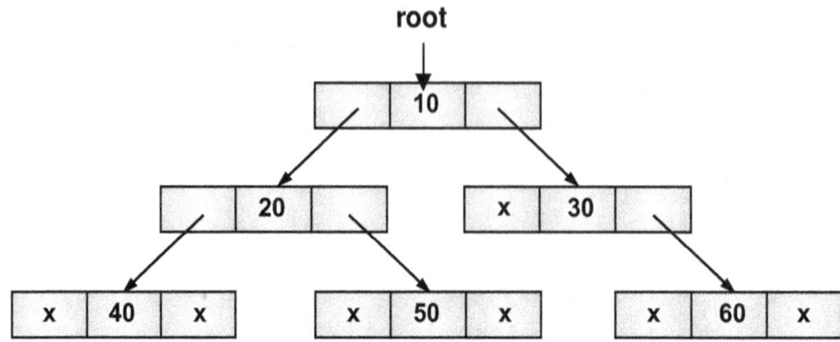

Fig. 5.15: Linked list representation of binary tree

5.3.2 Binary Tree Traversal

Once a binary tree is created the major operation that we will be required to do will be traversal of the tree. Traversing a tree means, visiting each node in the tree exactly once.

While traversing a binary tree, if we are at-a particular node there are six different ways in which we can move. They **LVR, VLR, LRV, RVL, VRL** and **RLV**. Where **V** is visit the node or access data, **L** move to left and **R**-move to right. There is a standard conversation that we should move to left first before right. Hence, there are only three standard traversals **LVR, VLR** and **LRV**.

LVR is called in order traversal where left sub-tree is processed first then root and finally right sub-tree. **VLR** is called preorder traversal where root is processed first followed by left sub-tree the right sub-tree.

LRV is called post order traversal where left sub-tree is processed first then right and finally root node.

Let us consider a binary tree.

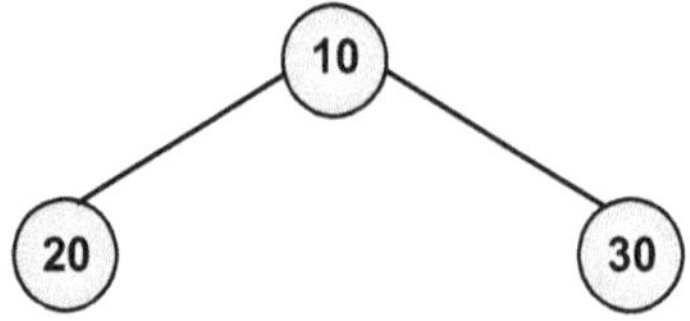

Fig. 5.16: Binary tree

Inorder traversal for Fig. 5.16, is shown in Fig. 5.17.

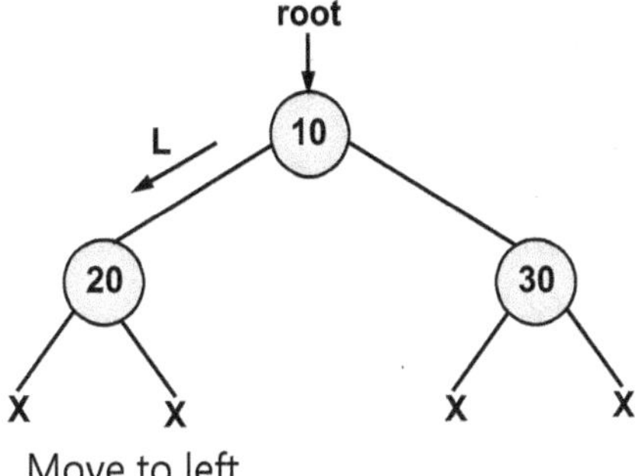

Move to left

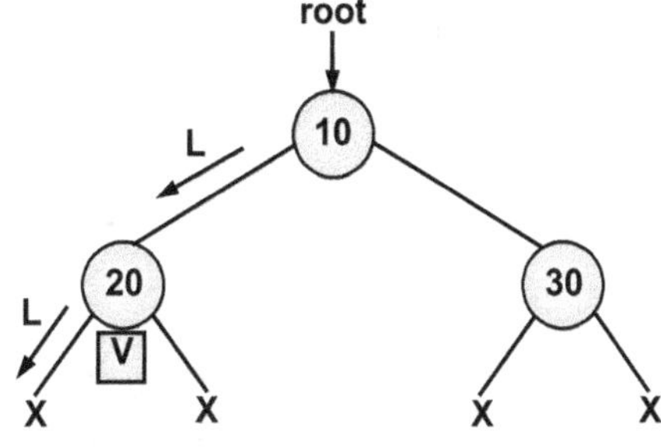

Move to left

left sub-tree of 20 is Null

Hence, visit node 20

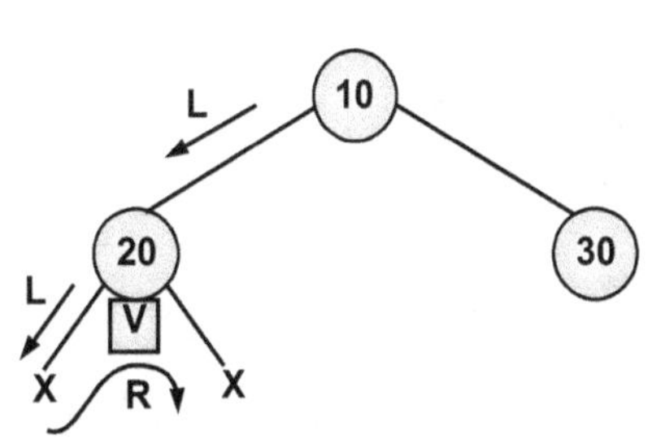

Move to right

Right sub-tree of 20 is Null

LVR for 20 is order

Go back to previous node

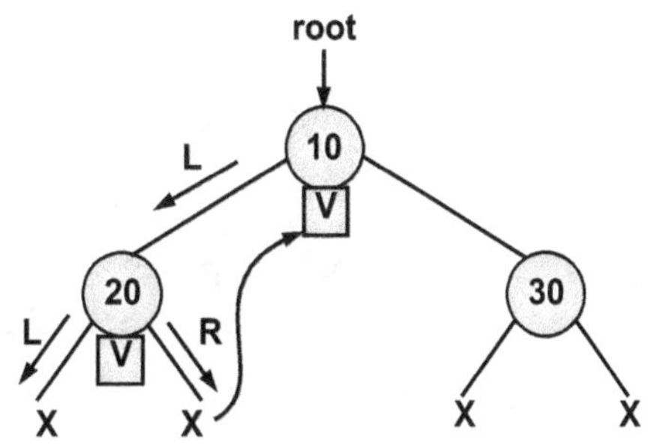

Left sub-tree of 10 is over

Visit the node 10

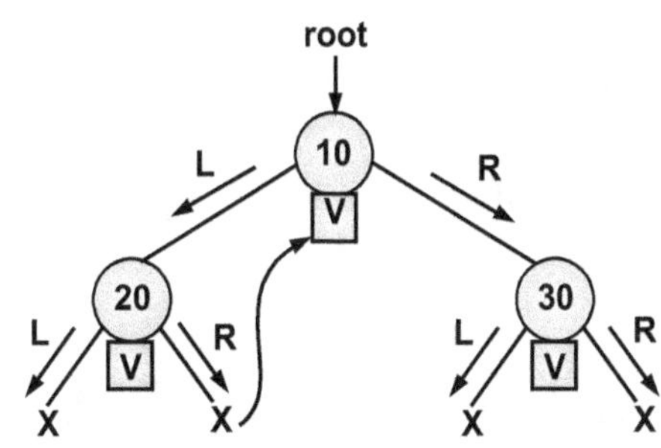

Move to right

Move to left, it is NULL

Visit 30

Move to right, it is Null

LVR for 30 is over, Go back to 30

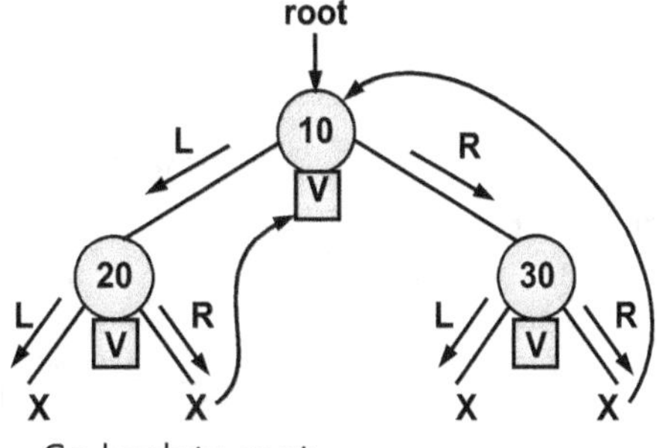

Go back to root

LVR for 10 is over

Fig. 5.17: Inorder traversal of binary tree

Hence, inorder traversal is 20 10 30.

Similarly, preorder traversal will be as shown in Fig. 5.18.

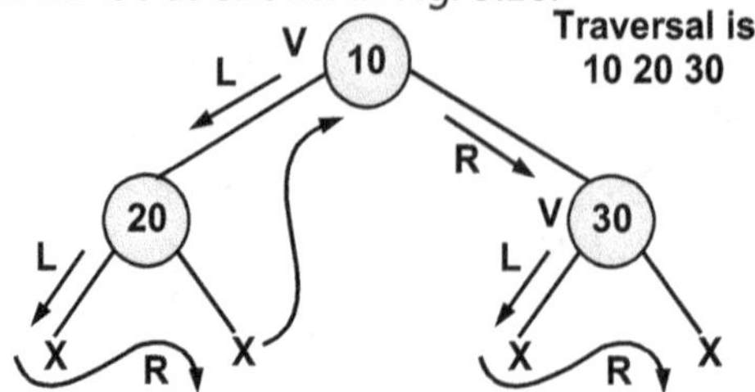

Fig. 5.18: Preorder traversal

Postorder traversal will be as shown in Fig. 5.19.

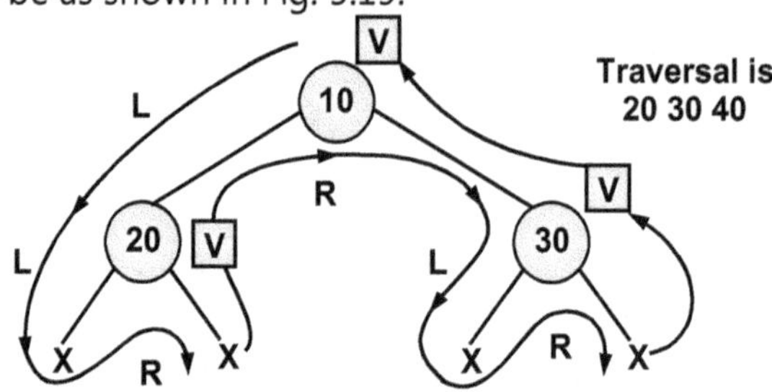

Fig. 5.19: Postorder traversal

Let us consider another example.

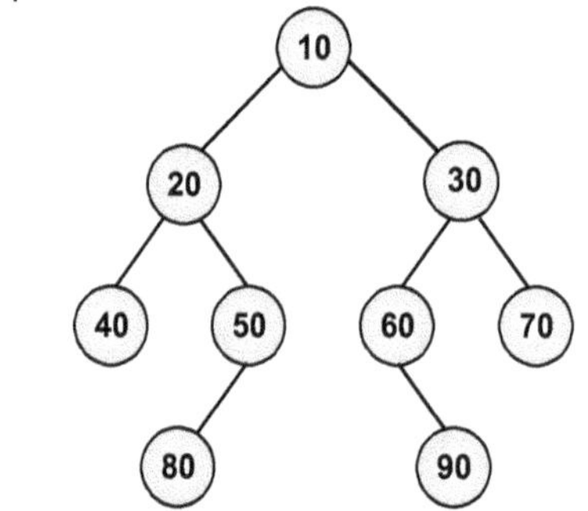

Fig. 5.20: Inorder traversal

Inorder traversal:

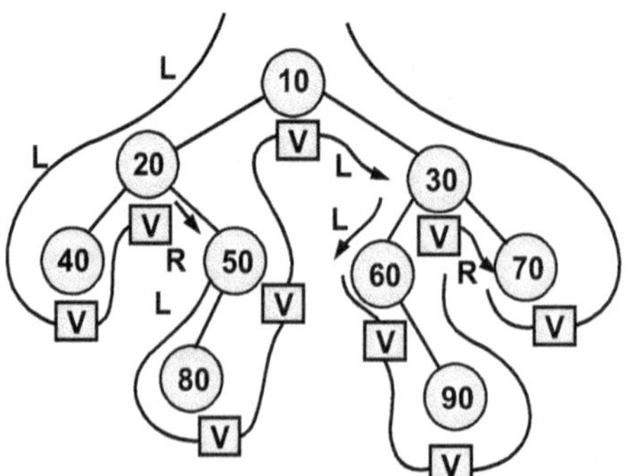

Fig. 5.21: Inorder traversal

Traversal is 40 20 80 50 10 60 90 30 70.

Preorder traversal:

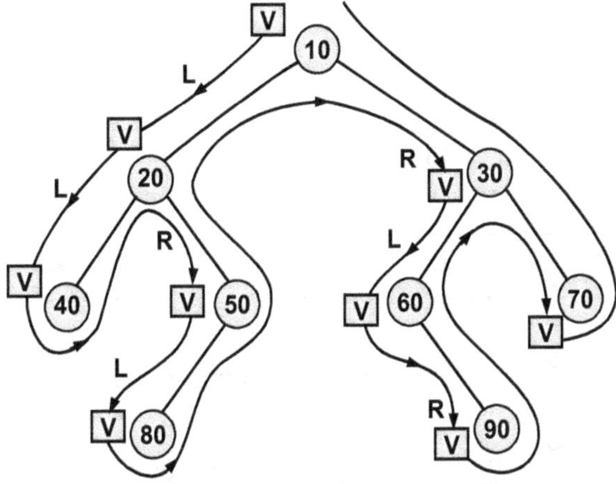

Fig. 5.22: Preorder traversal

Traversal is 10 20 40 50 80 30 60 90 70

Postorder traversal:

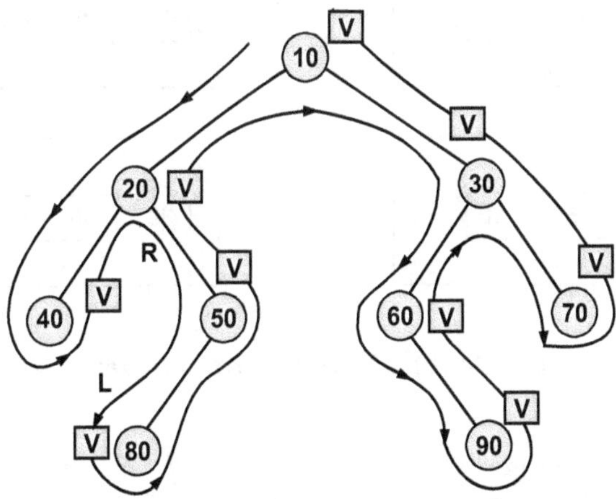

Fig. 5.23: Postorder traversal

Traversal is 40 80 50 20 90 60 70 30 10

Observation:

1. In inorder traversal, the root element is in between the left sub-tree and right sub-tree.
2. In preorder traversal, root element is at the beginning.
3. In postorder traversal, root element will be at the end.
4. If we are given any two traversals of a tree we can draw the tree diagram.

Example: Let us take up the same traversals of Figs. 5.21 and 5.22.

    Inorder: 40 20 80 50 10 60 90 30 70

    Preorder: 10 20 40 50 80 30 60 90 70

Step 1: From preorder, we find that root is 10. Hence the right and left sub-tree elements will be as shown in Fig. 5.24 (a).

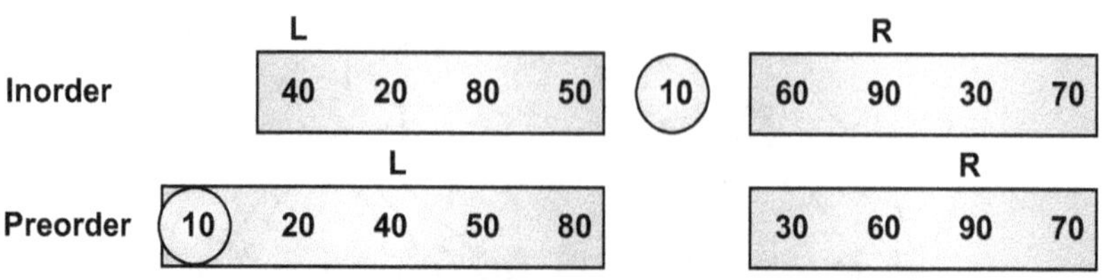

Fig. 5.24 (a): Binary tree from traversal

Step 2: Left sub-tree has root 20 (first element of pre-order).

Right sub-tree has root 30 (first element of pre-order).

Hence, the division will be as shown in Fig. 5.24 (b).

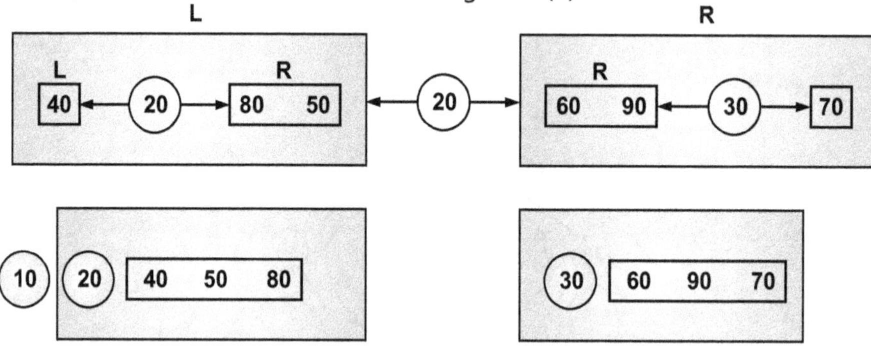

Fig. 5.24 (b): Binary tree from traversal

Step 3: Continuing on the same lines.

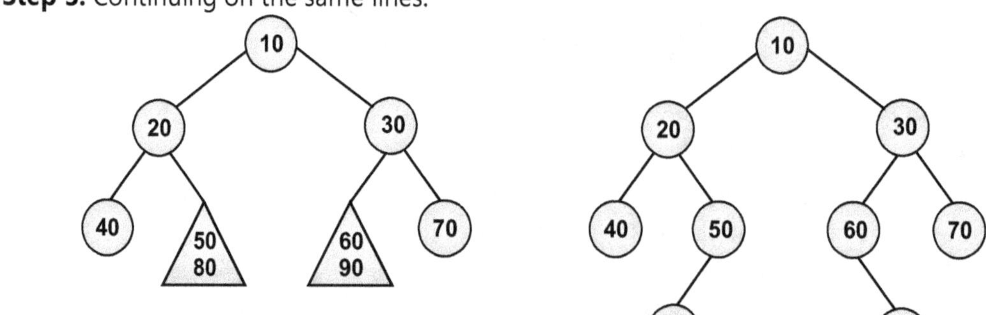

Fig. 5.24 (c): Binary tree from traversal

5.4 Binary Search Tree (BST)

Binary search tree as the name suggests, is used for storing the data mainly for searching applications. We have seen that nonlinear data structures are used for speeding up the process of searching. If we store the data in binary tree in a particular way, we will be able to improve the efficiency of searching to the order of $\log_2 n$ similar to binary search. In fact, **BST** implements the same principle as that of binary search,

Definition 1:

A binary search tree is a binary tree that is either empty or has each node that can satisfy following conditions.

(i)   All the elements in left sub-tree of the root precede the element in the root.

(ii) All the elements in the right sub-tree of the root succeed the element in the root.

(iii) Left and right sub-trees are again binary search tree.

Definition 2:

A binary search tree is a binary tree in which for each node the left sub-tree elements are less than the node element and right sub-tree elements are greater than the node element or vice versa.

The example of BST is shown in Fig. 5.25.

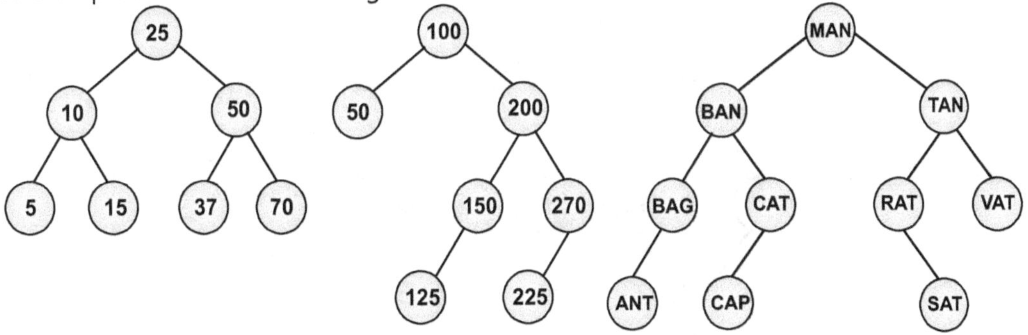

Fig. 5.25: Binary search tree

5.5 Operations on Binary Search Tree

We can use the traversals discussed earlier for the binary search trees. For example for first tree the traversals will be as:

Inorder	:	5	10	15	25	37	50	75
Preorder	:	25	10	5	15	50	37	75
Postorder	:	5	15	10	37	75	50	25

Note that inorder traversal of BST will result into ascending order.

We can store the elements in BST in reverse order also. i.e., smaller element on right side and larger element on left side of root. In that case, the inorder traversal will result into descending order of the elements in the tree.

The main operation that we need to do on binary search tree is searching an element. Consider tree as shown in Fig. 5.26.

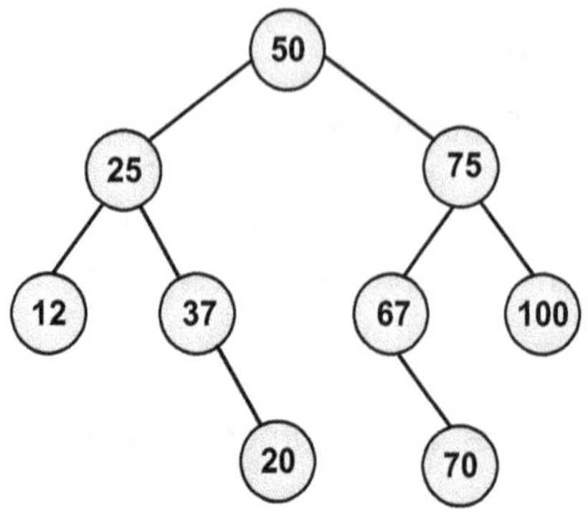

Fig. 5.26: Binary search tree

Suppose we want to search 37 in the tree. We start from the root node and move to left or right side depending on whether the number is smaller or greater.

Step 1: Compare whether element at current node is 37. The answer is no. Now since 37 < 50 we move to the left side.

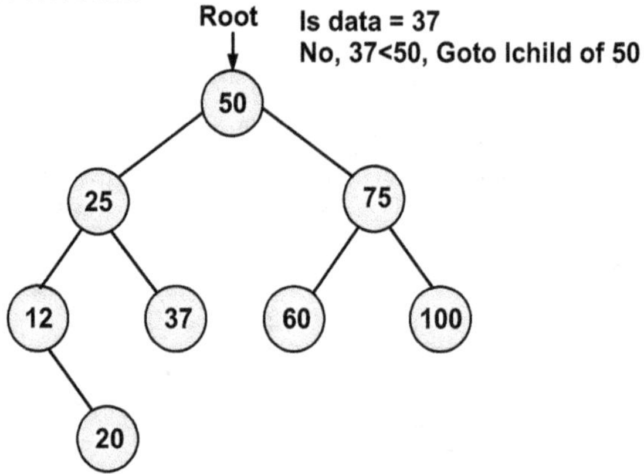

Fig. 5.27 (a): Search operation

Step 2:

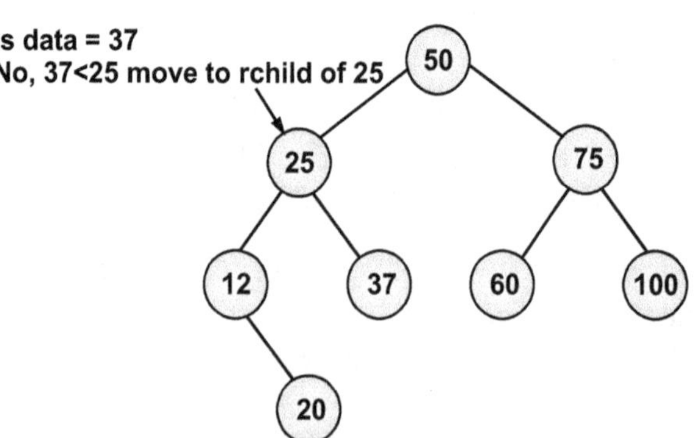

Fig. 5.27: (b) Search operation

Step 3:

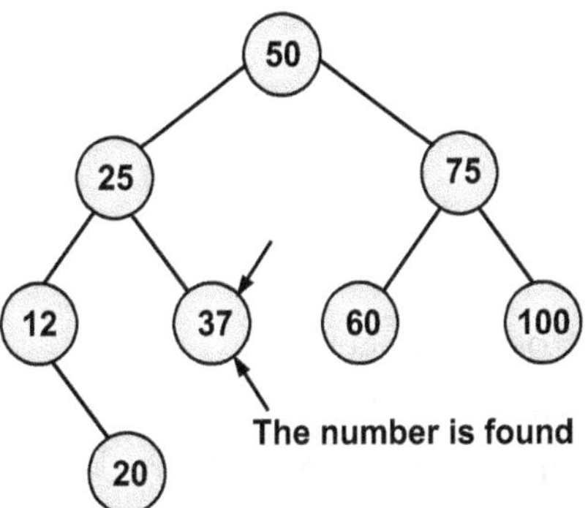

Fig. 5.27 (c): Search operation

If the number to be searched is not there in the BST, we will reach the end of BST (i.e. Leaf node).

There are various operations that can be performed on BST viz., create, search and traverse.

Let us write the algorithms for various operations on BST.

5.5.1 Creating BST

1. Read n {Number of elements}
2. root=Null
3. Repeat Steps 4 to 11 n times.
4. Read x
5. Create a node ptr
6. ptr->data=x
7. ptr->lchild=ptr->rchild=Null
8. temp = root
9. if (temp==NULL) root=ptr
10. while (temp!=NULL)

```
        {
            prev=temp;
            if (temp->data>x)
                temp=temp->lchild; flag=1;
            else
                temp= temp->rchild; flag=0;
        }
```

11.   if (flag==1)
              prev->lchild = ptr;
         else
              prev->rchild=ptr;

Explanation:
1. n is number of elements to be stored in BST.
2. The root pointer points to root node which is initially null.
3. Every time we accept the data, we create a new node ptr, store the data in it and this node is to be placed in the BST.
4. When first node is created it will be pointed by root.
5. Whenever a new node is created we start from root node and find a position for this node in BST. For this we compare the element in the tree with current element and move to right or left side. Before we move, pointer prev is kept behind so that we can connect new node to the current node, in case its lchild or rchild becomes null.
6. The movement of pointer temp before it becomes null gives location where new node is to be inserted. It is tracked with the help of flag.

5.5.2 Searching in BST

1. Read s
2. temp=root
3. while (temp!=NULL)
   {
        if (temp->data ==s)
        {
            printf("Found");
            break;
        }
        if (temp->data>s)
            temp=temp->lchild
        if (temp->data <s)
            temp=temp->rchild
   }
4. if (temp==NULL)
        printf("Not found");

Explanation:
1. The element to be searched is s.
2. We start from the root and move into the tree either on left or right side depending on data at current node,
3. If we find the data at a particular node, we exit.
4. If we don't find the data, temp will finally become null.

5.5.3 Tree Traversal Operations

We can use recursive functions as:

Inorder (temp)
1. {
2.   if(temp!=NULL)
         {
3.   inorder (temp- >lchild)
4.   print temp->data
5.   inorder (temp->rchild).
         }
     }

Explanation:

Let us take a BST as shown in figure 5.28 for this.

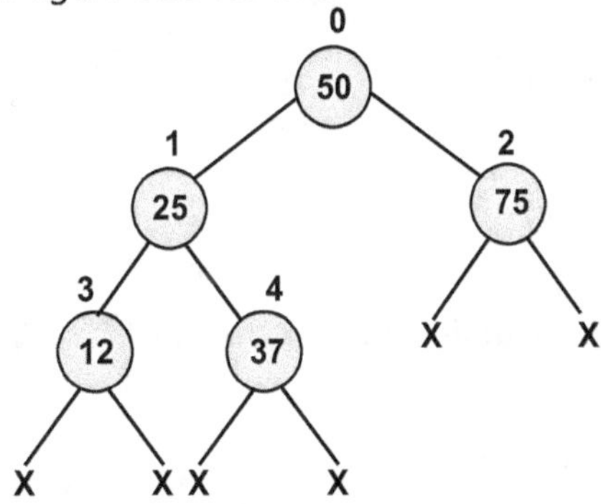

Fig. 5.28: Binary search tree

Let 0, 1, 2, 3, 4 be the addresses of there nodes.

The function will be called as

    inorder (root)

The function gets address of root which is assumed to be 0. Temp is assigned this address. The following table shows how the function gets called recursively. Follow the numbered lines in that sequence.

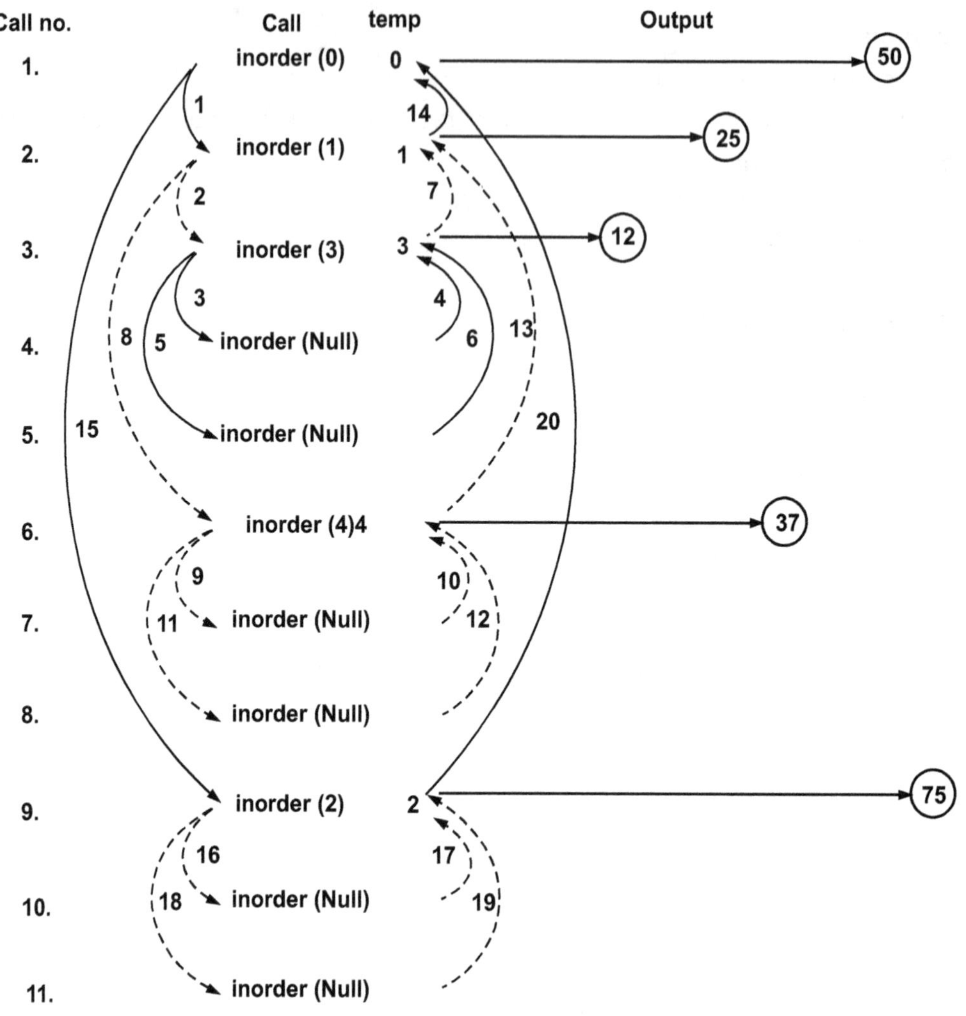

Fig. 5.29: Recursive inorder traversal function trace

The other two traversal functions are as follows:

```
preorder (temp)
{
    if (temp!=Null)
    {
        print temp->data
        preorder(temp->lchild)
        preorder(temp->rchild)
    }
```

```
}
postorder (temp)
{
    if(temp!=Null)
    {
        postorder(temp->lchild)
        postorder(temp->rchild)
        print temp->data
```

5.5.4 Delete Operation

Deleting a node in BST is a complex operation because we need to readjust the nodes in the tree. There are four different situations in the BST for deleting a node. They are,

(i)   The node to be deleted is leaf node.

(ii) The node has right child only.

(iii) The node has left child only.

(iv) The node has both children.

Let us find out how to deal with these four cases with example

Case 1:

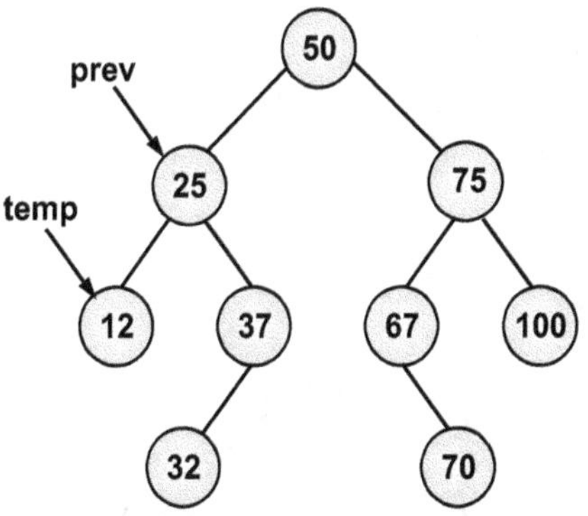

Fig. 5.30 (a): Delete operation leaf node

Suppose, the node to be deleted is 12, we need two pointers one at 12 (temp) other at its parent node i.e. 25 (prev). We need to check whether the node to be deleted (temp) is connected to lchild or rchild of prev.

    if   prev->lchild=temp make prev-lchild=Null

    if   prev->rchild=temp make prev->rchild=Null

    and then free (temp)

Case 2:

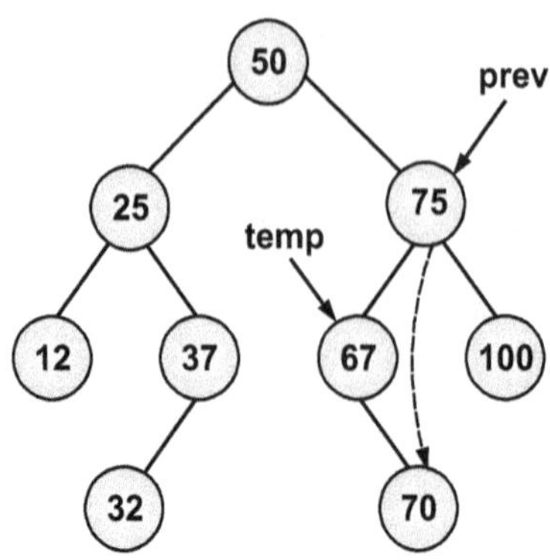

Fig. 5.30 (b): Delete operation node with rchild

Suppose, the node to be deleted has right child as shown in Fig. 5.30 (b). In this case, since 67 is to be deleted, its successor 70 is to be made *lchild* of its parent i.e. 75. The node to be deleted might be right child of its parent or left child. Hence, we have to determine this first. The code will be:

```
if (temp->rchild != NULL &&temp->lchild == NULL)
{
    if(prev-lchild==temp)
        prev-lchild=temp->rchild
    else
        prev->rchild=temp->rchild;
}
```

Case 3:

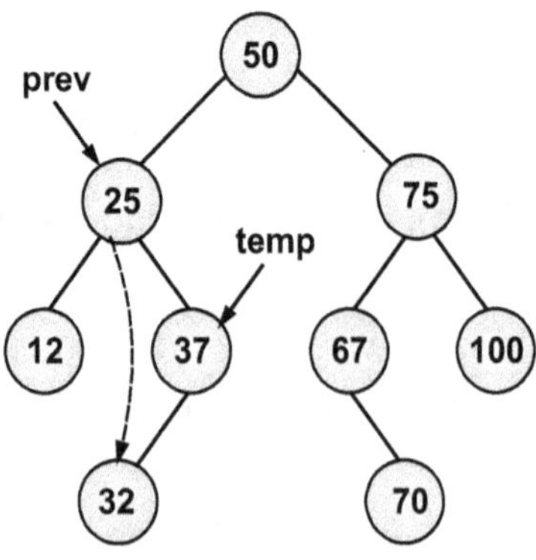

Fig. 5.30 (c): Delete operation node with *lchild*

If the node to be deleted has left child as shown in figure 5.30(c). If 37 is deleted, its successor should be made right child of 25. We can have the node to be deleted as right or left child of its parent node. Hence, we will have two options.'

```
if (temp->rchild==NULL &&temp->lchild!=NULL)
{
    if (prev->lchild==temp)
        prev->lchild=temp->lchild;
    else
        prev->rchild=temp->lchild;
}
```

Case 4: The node to be deleted has both children as shown in Fig. 5.30(d).

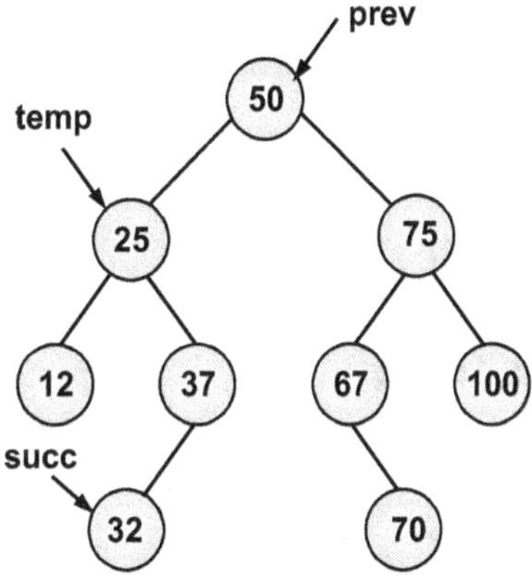

Fig. 5.30 (d): Delete operation node with *l*child and rchild

Let us say we want to delete 25. The inorder successor of 25 is 32. We can copy 32 in place of 25 and delete 32. Hence, the process is to find inorder successor of the node. Copy the successor in its place and delete the inorder successor node.

```
if (temp->lchild!=NULL, &&temp->rchild!=NULL)
{
    succ= temp;
    x=temp->rchild;
    while(x!=NULL)
    {
        prev=succ;
        succ=x;
        x=x->lchild;
    }
    temp->data=succ->data;
    temp=succ;
}
```

This will copy the value of inorder, successor into the node to be deleted. Now, that we have a pointer temp to the inorder successor node and prev to its parent node, this node will fall into one of the 3 cases considered earlier. If we write the cases after this case, automatically one of them will get executed and the-node will be deleted.

5.5.5 Insert Operation

If new data is to be inserted in already existing BST, the position for this new data has to be located. It will be inserted as a leaf node in the BST. The algorithm will be as follows:

1. Read x (Data to be added)
2. Create a new node ptr and store the data in it
3. temp=root
4. while(temp!=NULL)
       {   prev=temp;
            if(temp->data>x)
                 temp=temp->lchild; flag=1;
            else
                 temp=temp->rchild; flag=0;
       }
5. if (flag==1)
            prev->lchild=ptr;
       else
            prev->rchild=ptr;

Explanation:

1. The new data to be inserted is accepted and stored into a new node ptr.
2. Start from root node till you go bottom of tree. Compare at each node and move to left or right. Before we move to left or right keep a pointer prev to previous node so that if you fall into null, we have a pointer to the node on whose left or right side new node is to be attached. The decision of whether the new node will be attached to right or left will be made from the value of flag.

     Now let us write a menu driven program to implement all these operations.

     The functions that we are going to write are

     (i)   Create   : Creates a binary search tree and returns address of root node,
     (ii) Search   : Searches an element in BST.
     (iii) Inorder   : Display inorder traversal.

(iv) Preorder   : Display preorder traversal.

(v)   Postorder   : Display postorder traversal.

(vi) Delete   : Deletes a node.

(vii) insert   : Inserts a new node.

Program 5.1: To create and implement binary search tree

```c
#include <stdio.h>
#include <conio.h>
typedef struct node
{
    int data;
    struct node *lchild,*rchild;
}NODE;
NODE*create( );
int search (NODE*, int);
void inorder (NODE*);
void preorder (NODE*)
void postorder (NODE*);
NODE*del(NODE*);
NODE* insert (NODE*);
void main( )
{
    int ch, s;
    NODE*root=NULL;
    do
    {
        clrscr( );
        printf("1.Create \n 2.Search \n 3.Inorder \n 4.Preorder \n 5.Postorder \n
        6.Delete \n 7.Insert \n8.Exit \n");
        printf("Enter your choice \n");
        scanf("%d", &ch);
        switch(ch)
        {
            case 1 :   root=create( );
                       break;
            case 2 :   printf("Enter number to be searched \n");
```

```c
                        scanf("%d", &s);
                        search(root, s)
                        break;
            case 3 :    inorder(root);
                        break;
            case 4 :    preorder(root);
                        break;
            case 5 :    postorder(root);
                        break;
            case 6 :    root=del(root)
                        break;
            case 7 :    root=insert(root);
                        break;
        }
        getch();
    }while(ch!=8);
}
NODE *create( )
{
    int x, i, n, flag;
    NODE *root, *ptr, *temp, *prev;
    root=NULL;
    printf("How many elements? \n");
    scanf("%d", &n);
    for(i=1;i<=n;i++)
    {
        printf("Enter the number");
        scanf("%d", &x);
        ptr=(NODE*)malloc(sizeof(NODE));
        ptr->data=x;
        ptr->rchild=ptr->lchild=NULL;
        if (root==NULL)
            root=ptr;
        else
        {
            temp=root;
```

```c
                while (temp!=NULL)
                {
                        prev=temp;
                        if (temp->data>x)
                        {
                                temp=temp->lchild;
                                flag=1;
                        }
                        else
                        {
                                temp=temp->rchild;
                                flag=0;
                        }
                }
                if (flag==1)
                        prev->lchild=ptr;
                else
                        prev->rchild=ptr;
        }
}
return (root);
}
int search (NODE *root, int x)
{
    NODE *temp;
    temp=root;
    while (temp!=NULL && temp->data!=x)
    {
        if(temp->data>x)
            temp=temp->lchild;
        else
            temp=temp->rchild;
    }
    if (temp!= NULL)
        return (1);
    else
```

```c
            return (0);
}
void inorder (NODE *temp)
{
    if (temp!= NULL)
    {
        inorder (temp->lchild);
        printf("%d \n", temp->data);
        inorder(temp->rchild);
    }
}
void preorder (NODE *temp)
{
    if (temp!=NULL)
    {
        printf("%d \n", temp->data);
        preorder(temp->lchild);
        preorder(temp->rchild);
    }
}
void postorder (NODE *temp)
{
    if (temp!=NULL)
    {
        postorder(temp->lchild);
        postorder(temp->rchild);
        printf("%d \n", temp->data);
    }
}
NODE *del(NODE*root)
{
    NODE *temp, *prev, *x, *succ;
    int s;
    printf("Enter data to be deleted \n");
    scanf("%d", &s);
    temp=root;
```

```c
        prev=temp;
        while(temp!=NULL)
        {
            if (temp->data==s)
                break;
            prev=temp;
            if(temp->data>s)
                temp=temp->lchild;
            else
                temp=temp->rchild;
        }
        if(temp==NULL)
        {
            printf("Not in the BST \n");
            exit(0);
        }
        if(temp->lchild!=NULL &&temp->rchild!=NULL)
        {
            succ=temp;
            x=temp->rchild;
            while(x!=NULL)
            {
                prev=succ;
                succ=x;
                x=x-Achild;
            }
            temp->data=succ->data;
            temp=succ;
        }
        if(temp->rchild== NULL & temp->lchild!=NULL)
        {
            if(prev->lchild == temp)
                prev->rchild=temp->lchild;
            else
                prev->rchild=temp->lchild;
        }
```

```c
        if(temp->rchild!=NULL &&temp->lchild==NULL)
        {
            if(prev->lchild==temp)
                prev->lchild=temp->rchild;
            else
                prev->rchild=temp->rchild;
        }
        if(temp->lchild == NULL &&temp->rchild == NULL)
        {
            if(prev->lchild==temp)
                prev->lchild=NULL;
            else
                prev->rchild=NULL;
        }
        free(temp);
        return(root);
}
NODE *insert(NODE *root)
{
    NODE *temp, *prev, *ptr;
    int x, flag;
    printf("Enter data to be inserted \n");
    scanf("%d", &x);
    ptr =(NODE*)malloc(sizeof(NODE));
    ptr->data=x;
    ptr->lchild=ptr->rchild=NULL;
    temp=root;
    while (temp!=NULL)
    {
        prev=temp;
        if(temp->data>x)
        {
            temp=temp->child;
            flag=1;
        }
        else
```

```
            {
                temp=temp->rchild;
                flag=0;
            }
        }
        if(root==NULL)
            root=ptr;
        else
        {
        if(flag==1)
            prev->lchild=ptr;
        else
            prev->rchild=ptr;
        }
        return (root);
    }
```

5.6 Operations on Binary Tree

We have seen Binary search tree and operations on it. The BST was relatively easy to implement along with the operations such as create, insert, delete traversals, etc. It was because of the relation that exists among the elements in BST. Now, if you are given a binary tree and asked. to create it as it is, we will have to ask the user to manually enter the data and their positions in the tree. The operators that we can have on this tree are insert, traversals (all three). The algorithms of these operations are as follows.

5.6.1 Creating a binary tree

1. Read n
2. root=Null
3. for (i=1;i<=n;i++)
   {
4.   Read x
       Create a new node ptr
       store x in ptr->data
5.   if(root==NULL)
           root=ptr
       else

```
                {
6.              temp=root;
7.              while(temp!=NULL)
                {
                        prev=temp;
                        read side
                        if(side=='l')
                                temp=temp->lchild
                        else
                                temp=temp->rchild;
                }
8.              if(side=='l')
                        prev->child=ptr
                else
                        prev->rchild=ptr
        }
    }
9.  Stop
```

Explanation:

1. Read number of nodes (n) in the tree.

2   root=NULL.

3. Repeat for each element the following process

4. Read data and store it in a node ptr.

5. If it is first node let it be pointed by root.

6, 7. If it is not first node, start from root node and traverse in the tree every time asking the user about which side of current node the new node is to be added.

8. When temp becomes NULL, prev will be at a node in the tree on whose left or right side new node is to be inserted. Insert the node accordingly.

5.6.2 Traversal Operation

The inorder, preorder and postorder traversals can be implemented in the same way as discussed in BST.

5.6.3 Insert Operation

It will be similar to create operation except that the process is to be carried out only once.

Program 5.2: To implement a binary tree

```c
typedef struct node
{
    int data;
    struct node *lchild, *rchild;
} NODE;
NODE *create( );
void    inorder(NODE*);
void    preorder (NODE*);
void    postorder(NODE*);
NODE *insert(NODE*);
void main( )
{
    int ch;
    NODE *root;
    root=NULL;
    do
    {
        printf("1.Create \n2. Inorder W. preorder \n4. Postorder \n5. Insert \n6. Exit \n");
        printf("Enter your choice \n");
        scanf("%d", &ch);
        switch(ch)
        {
            case 1 :  root=create( );
                      break;
            case 2 :  inorder(root);
                      break
            case 3 :  preorder(root);
                      break;
            case 4 :  postorder(root);
                      break;
```

```c
                    case 5 :  root=insert(root);
            }
        getch( );
    } while(ch!=6);
}
NODE *create( )
{
    NODE *ptr, *temp, *prev;
    int x; n, i;
    char ch;
    printf("Enter number of nodes \n");
    scanf("%d",&n);
    root=NULL;
    for(i=1;i<=n;i++)
    {
        printf("Enter data \n");
        scanf("%d", &x);
        ptr=(NODE*) malloc(sizeof (NODE));
        ptr->lchild=ptr->rchild=NULL;
        if(root == NULL)
            root=ptr;
        else
        {
            temp=root;
            while(temp!=NULL)
            {   prev=temp;
                printf("which side of %d? (l/r) \n", temp->data);
                ch=getch( );
                if(ch=='l' || ch=='L')
                    temp=temp->lchild;
                else
                    temp=temp->rchild;
            }
            if(ch=='l' || ch=='L')
                prev->child=ptr;
            else
```

```c
                    prev->rchild=ptr;
            }
    }
    return (root);
}
void inorder(NODE*root)
{   NODE *temp;
    temp=root;
    if (temp!=NULL)
    {
        inorder(temp->lchild);
        printf("%d \n", temp->data);
        inorder(temp->rchild);
    }
}
void preorder(NODE*root)
{   NODE *temp;
    temp=root;
    if (temp!=NULL)
    {
        printf("%d \n", temp->data);
        preorder(temp->lchild);
        preorder(temp->rchild);
    }
}
void postorder(NODE*root)
{
    NODE*temp;
    temp=root;
        if(temp!=NULL)
        {
            postorder(temp->lchild);
            postorder(temp->rchild);
            printf("%d \n", temp->data);
        }
}
```

```
NODE *insert(NODE*root)
{
    NODE *temp,*ptr, *prev;
    int x;
    char ch;
    printf("Enter data \n");
    scanf("%d", &x);
    ptr=(NODE*)malloc(sizeof(NODE));
    ptr->data=x;
    ptr->child=ptr->rchild=NULL;
    if (root==NULL)
        root=ptr;
    else
    {
        temp=root;
        while(temp!=NULL)
        {
            printf("which side of %d (l/r) \n", temp->data);
            ch=getch( );
            if(ch=='l' || ch=='L')
                temp=temp->lchild;
            else
                temp=temp->rchild;
        }
        if(ch=='l' || ch=='L')
            prev->lchild=ptr;
        else
            prev->rchild=ptr;
    }
    return(root);
}
```

5.6.4 Non-Recursive Traversal

The recursive inorder, preorder and postorder traversals use the program's recursion stack.
The recursion can be removed by implementing user defined stack. Let us see, how we can
write inorder and preorder traversals using stack.

1. Inorder traversal

Algorithm: Inorder traversal

1. temp=root
2. do

```
    {
        while(temp!=NULL)
        {
            push(temp);
            temp=temp->lchild;
        }
            temp=pop( );
            print temp->data
            temp=temp->rchild;
    }while(stack is not empty OR temp!=NULL);
```

3. Stop.

Explanation:

1. Start with root node.
2. Traverse on left side while storing the address of each node on stack.
3. Pop the address of a node from stack (it will be left most node). Display the data.
4. Move to right side.
5. Repeat above till all nodes are traversed.
6. The stack will be stack of pointers as it has to store addresses of nodes.

Consider a binary tree as:

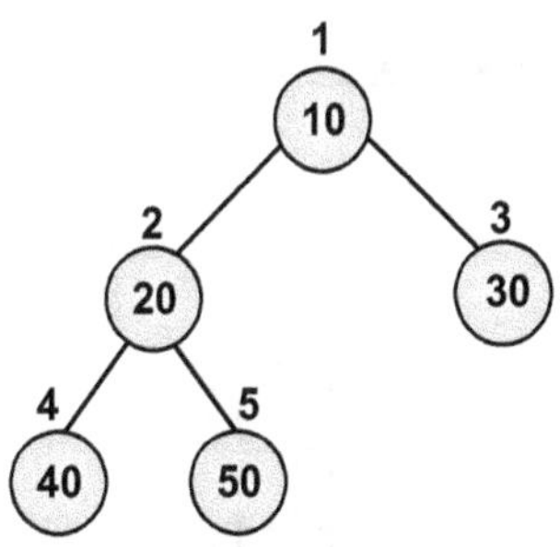

Fig. 5.31(a): Binary tree

Let 1, 2, 3, 4, 5, be the addresses of the nodes.

1. We start with root node and move to left pushing every time address of node on the stack. At the end of inner while, the stack will be

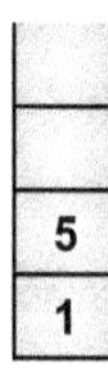

Fig. 5.31(b): Stack contents for non-recursive inorder traversal

2. temp=pop( ) will pop node 4.

    data at node 4 i.e. 40 will be displayed.

3. temp will be Null as rchild of 4 is Null.

    Since temp is NULL, 2 is poped.

    Data at 2 i.e. 20 is displayed.

    temp will move to rchild of 2.

    Hence, 5 will be pushed and stack will be

Fig. 5.31(c): Stack contents for non-recursive inorder traversal

4. 5 is popped and data at 5 is displayed i.e. 50.

    Since temp is NULL

    1 is popped and data 1 is displayed i.e. 11.

    temp will move to rchild 3.

    3 is pushed and stock will be'

Fig. 5.31(d): Stack contents for non-recursive inorder traversal

3 is popped data at 3. i.e. 30 displayed.

stack becomes empty and temp is null hence the function gets over.

2. Preorder traversal: For preorder traversal (VLR) we used to make only one change the print statement will be written before left move as follows:

1. temp=root
2. do
   {   while(temp!=NULL)
       {

           print temp->data

           push(temp);

           temp=temp->lchild;

       }
       temp=pop( );
       temp=temp->rchild;

   }   while (stack is not empty OR temp!=NULL)
3. Stop

5.7 Applications of Trees

In computer science, trees have number of applications because they are most efficient for searching the data. Hence, they are used to store large databases. Some of the applications are as below.

1. Expression Tree

The compilers and interpreters evaluate the expression based on the precedence of operators. Any arithmetic expression can be represented using binary tree. The evaluation of the expression becomes convenient with such representation. For example, the expression a + b * c/d can be represented as below:

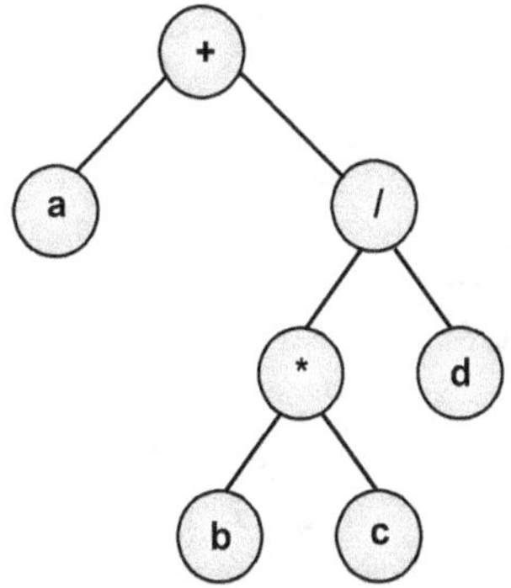

Fig. 5.32: Expression tree for a + b * c/d

The expression 3 * 4 + (8 + 7) can be represented as

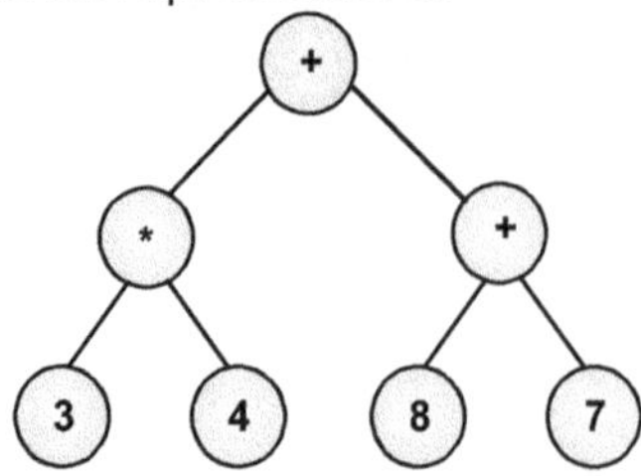

Fig. 5.33: Expression for tree 3*4+(8+7)

Inorder traversal of tree will result into evaluation of the expression. Some more examples are as below.

d=a * b/d − 4.

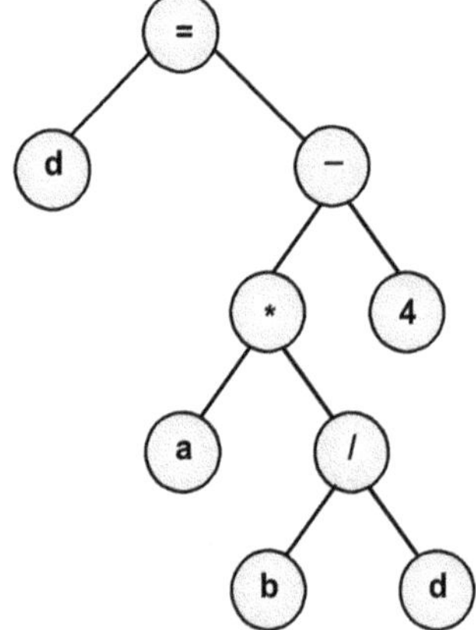

Fig. 5.34: Expression tree for d = a*b/d−4

x=4 * 5 + 6 * 7 − 3/2

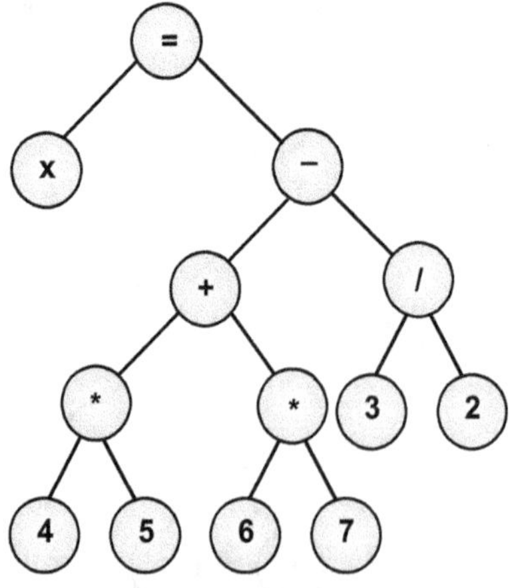

Fig. 5.35: Expression tree for x = 4*5+6*7−3/2

2. Game Trees

The trees can be used in many gaming applications. The different moves in the game can be represented using trees. From a given board position, we can represent all possible moves so that we can select best possible move.

Consider the problem of implementing a computer program to play a game. To simplify things a bit, we will only consider games with the following two properties:

(i)   Two player - we do not deal with coalitions etc.

(ii) Zero sum - one player's win is the other's loss; there are no co-operative victories

Examples of these kinds of games include many classic board games, such as tic-tac-toe, chess, checkers, and go. For these types of games, we can model the game using what is called a *game tree*.

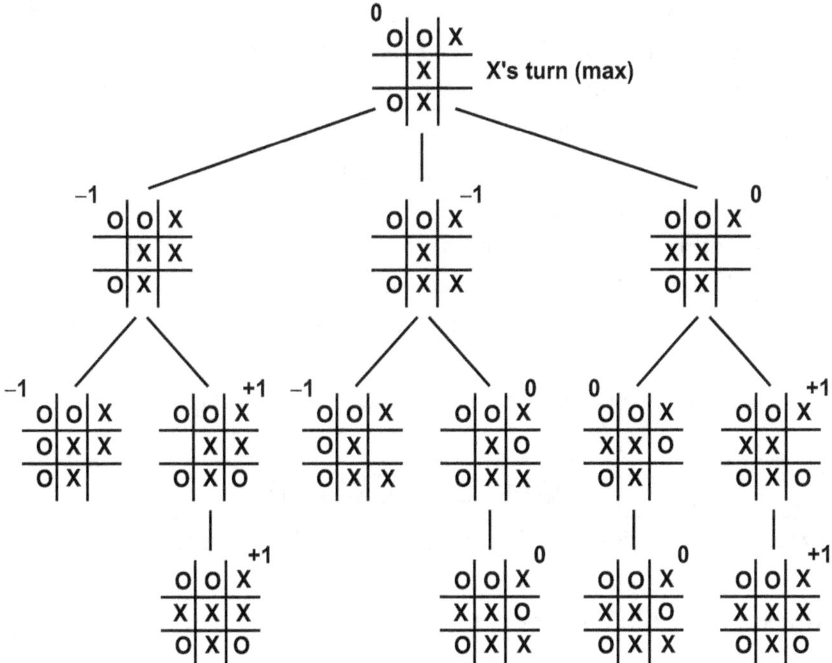

Fig. 5.36: Game tree

Fig. 5.36 shows a section of a game tree for tic-tac-toe. Each node represents a board position, and the children of each node are the legal moves from that position. To score each position, we will give each position which is favorable for player 1 a positive number (the more positive, the more favorable). Similarly, we will give each position which is favorable for player 2 a negative number (the more negative, the more favorable). In our tic tac toe example, player 1 is 'X', player 2 is 'O', and the only three scores we will have are +1 for a win by 'X', −1 for a win by 'O', and 0 for a draw. Note that scores of current positions can only be calculated. To calculate the scores for the other positions, we must look ahead a few moves, by using tree traversal algorithms.

SUMMARY

- Tree is a nonlinear data structure used for efficient access or retrieval of elements.
- A tree (T) is a set of nodes. The set can be empty. If it is non-empty set, it consists of a specially designated node called root node and zero or more sub-trees (T_1, T_2, ..., T_n) each whose roots are connected by a directed edge from the root of T.
- Binary tree is a tree in which no node has more than two sub-trees.
- A binary tree can be represented using array or linked representation.
- A binary tree can be traversed in three different ways inorder (LVR), preorder (VLR) and postorder (LRV).
- A Binary Search Tree (BST) is used to store data for searching applications. A binary search tree is a binary tree in which for each node, the left sub-tree elements are less than the node elements and right sub-tree elements are greater than the node element.
- If binary search tree is height balanced, the time complexity of search is $0(\log_2 n)$.
- The traversals of binary tree can be implemented using recursive or non-recursive ways.
- A threaded binary tree makes use of NULL fields in the nodes of binary tree for spreading up the operations on binary tree.
- A height balanced or AVL tree is a binary tree with T_l and T_r as left and right sub-trees having heights h_l and h_r such that $|h_l - h_r| \leq 1$.
- In order to make a binary tree height balanced, we can use one of the four rotations LL, RR, LR or RL.
- Trees can be used for expression storage and evaluation and gaming applications.

SOLVED PROBLEMS

1. Write a recursive function to print leaf nodes of binary tree.

Solution:

```c
void leaf node_check(NODE *temp)
{
    printf("The leaf nodes are \n");
    if (temp!=NULL)
    {
        leaf-node-check (temp->lchild);
        if(temp->lchild==NULL && temp->rchild=NULL)
        {
            printf("%d \n", temp->data);
        }
        leaf_node_check(temp->rchild);
    }
}
```

2. Write Inorder, Preoder and Postorder traversals for following tree.

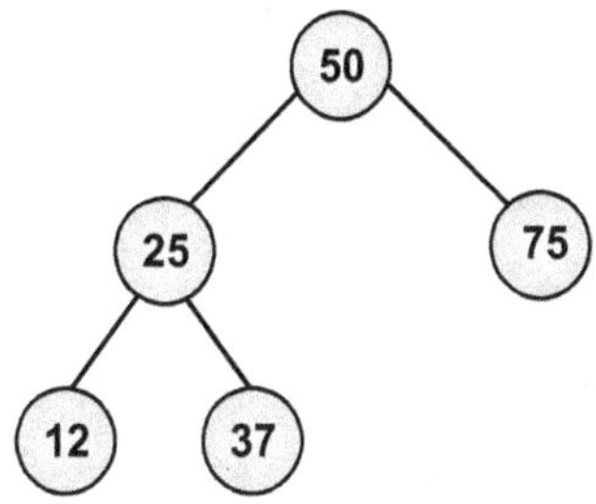

Fig. 5.37: Binary Tree

Solution:

Inorder	12 25 37 50 75
Preoder	50 25 12 37 75
Postorder	12 37 25 75 50

3. For the following data draw a binary search tree. Show all steps.

50 80 30 20 100 75 25 15 68

Solution: A binary search tree is shown in figure 5.38.

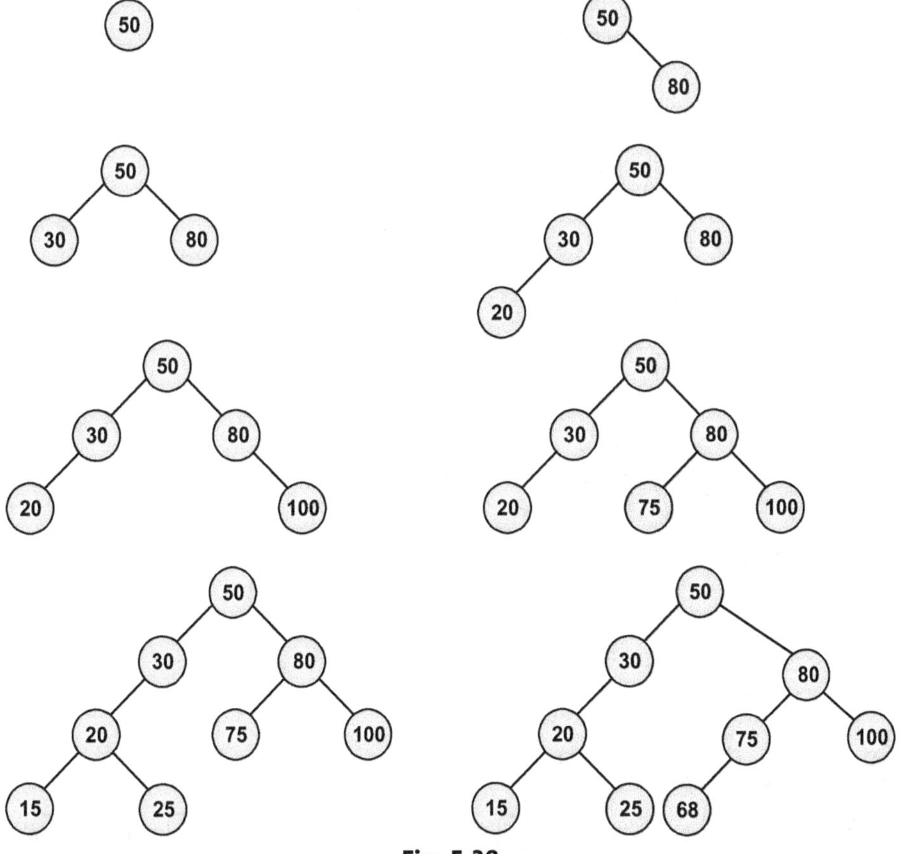

Fig. 5.38

4. Write Inorder, Preoder and Postorder traversals for the following.
Solution:

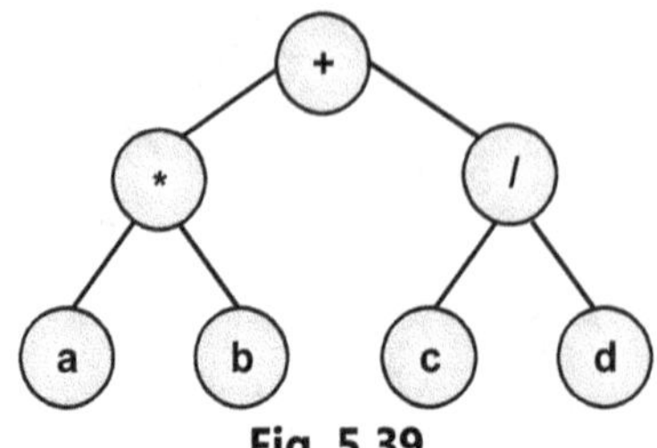

Fig. 5.39

Solution:

Inorder	:	+ *ab/cd
Preoder	:	a * b + c/d
Postorder	:	ab * cd \+

5. From gives traversal, construct the binary tree.

Inorder	:	DBFEAGCLJHK
Preorder	:	DFEBGLJKHCA

Solution:

Step I: From postorder we can see last element is root.

Hence, the left sub-tree and right sub-tree from inorder traversal is

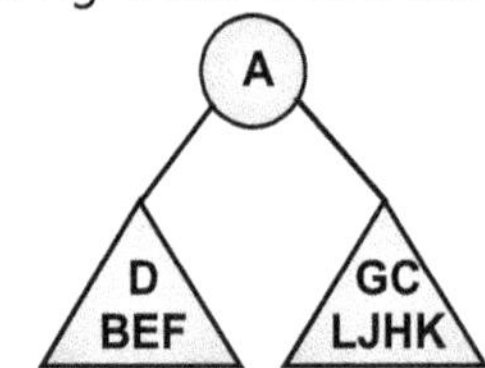

Step II:

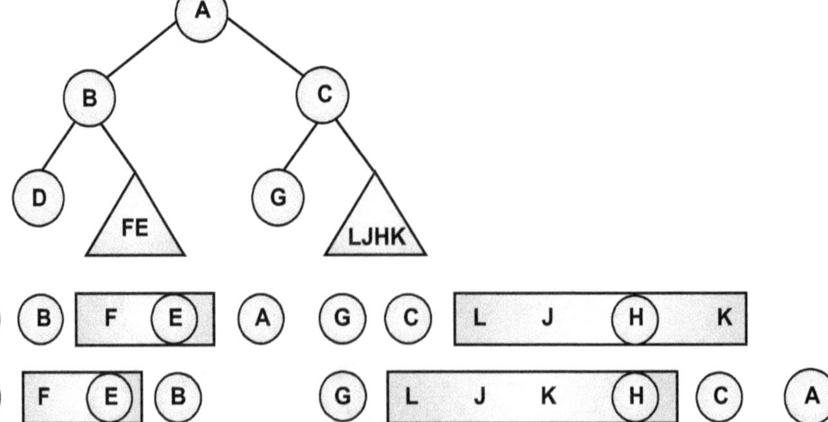

Step IV:

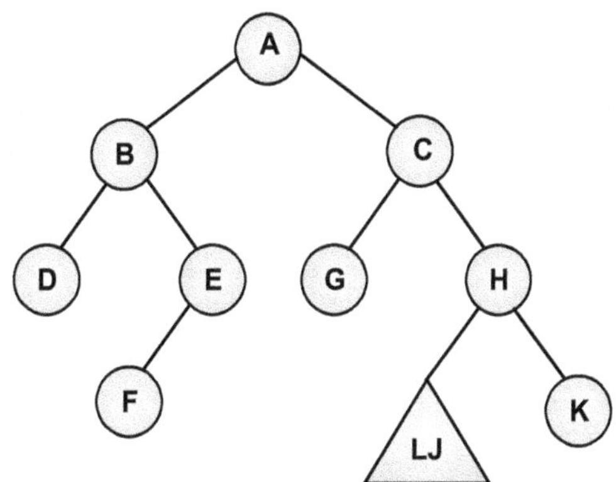

Step V:

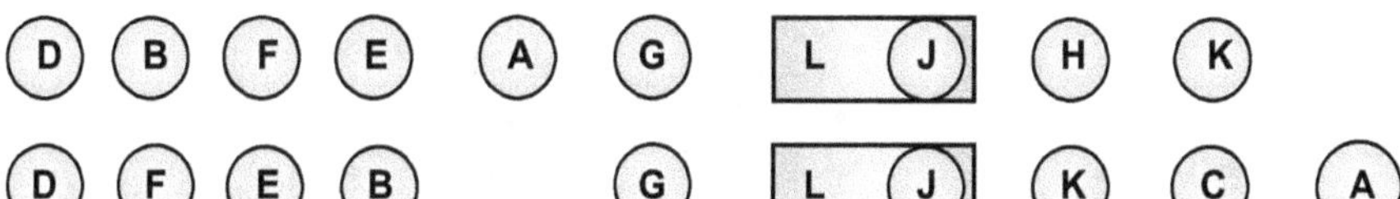

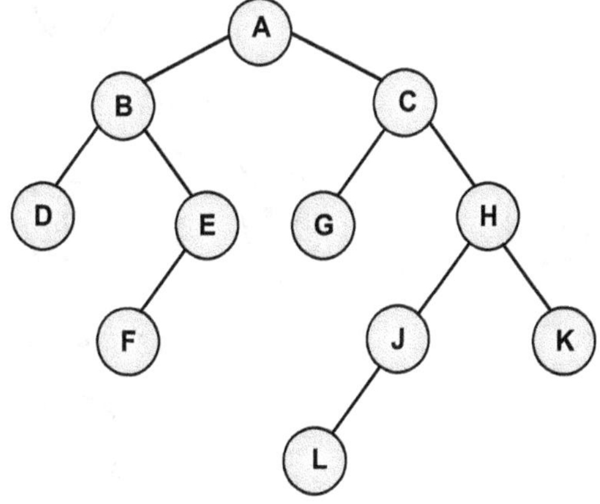

Fig. 5.40

6. **Define binary search tree. Construct binary search tree from following set of strings. Show all steps. Also write height of final tree.**

   JAN FEB MAR APR MAY JUN JUL AUG SEP OCT NOV DEC

   Solution: (Refer section 5.4 for definition)

Steps for creation of BST.

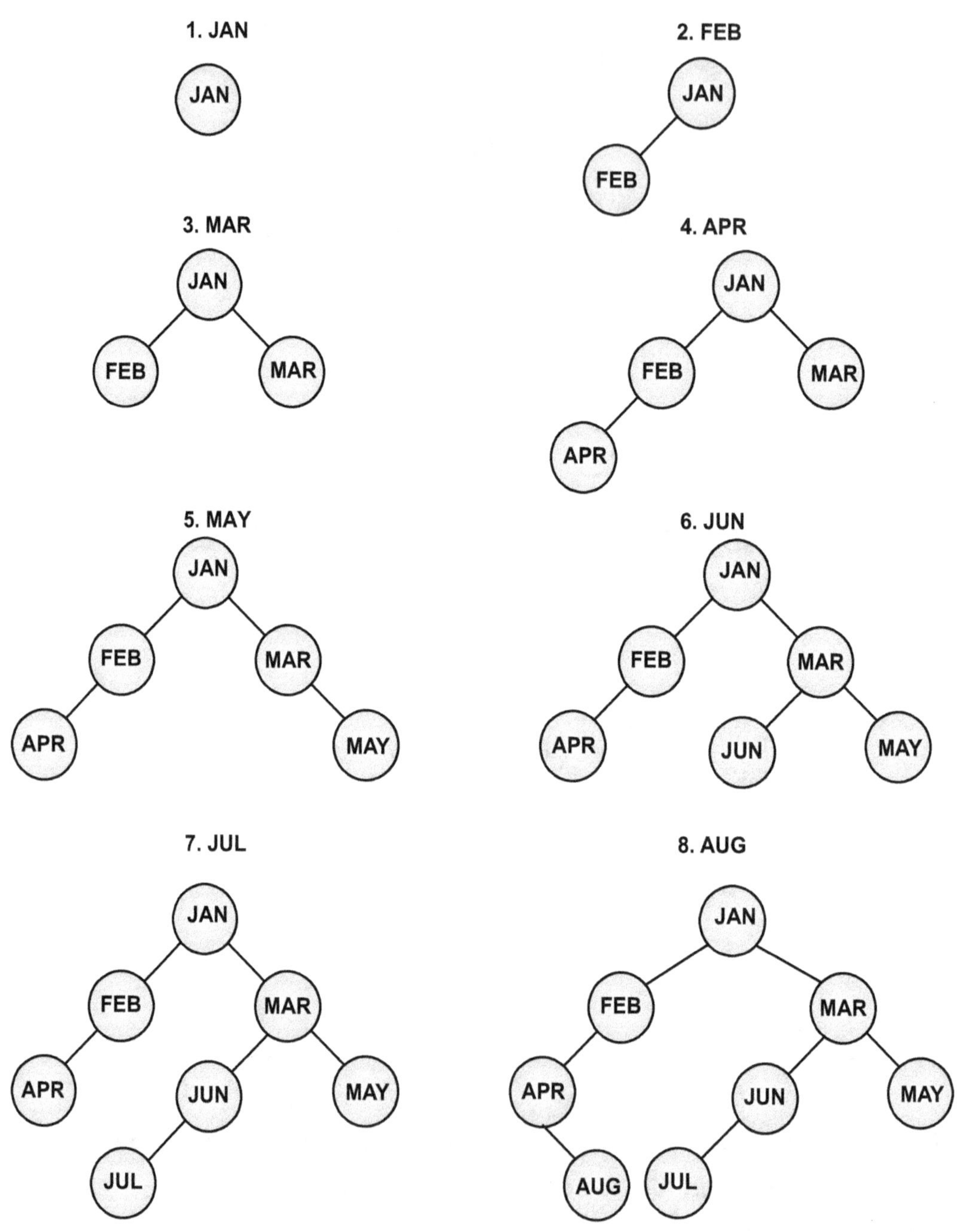

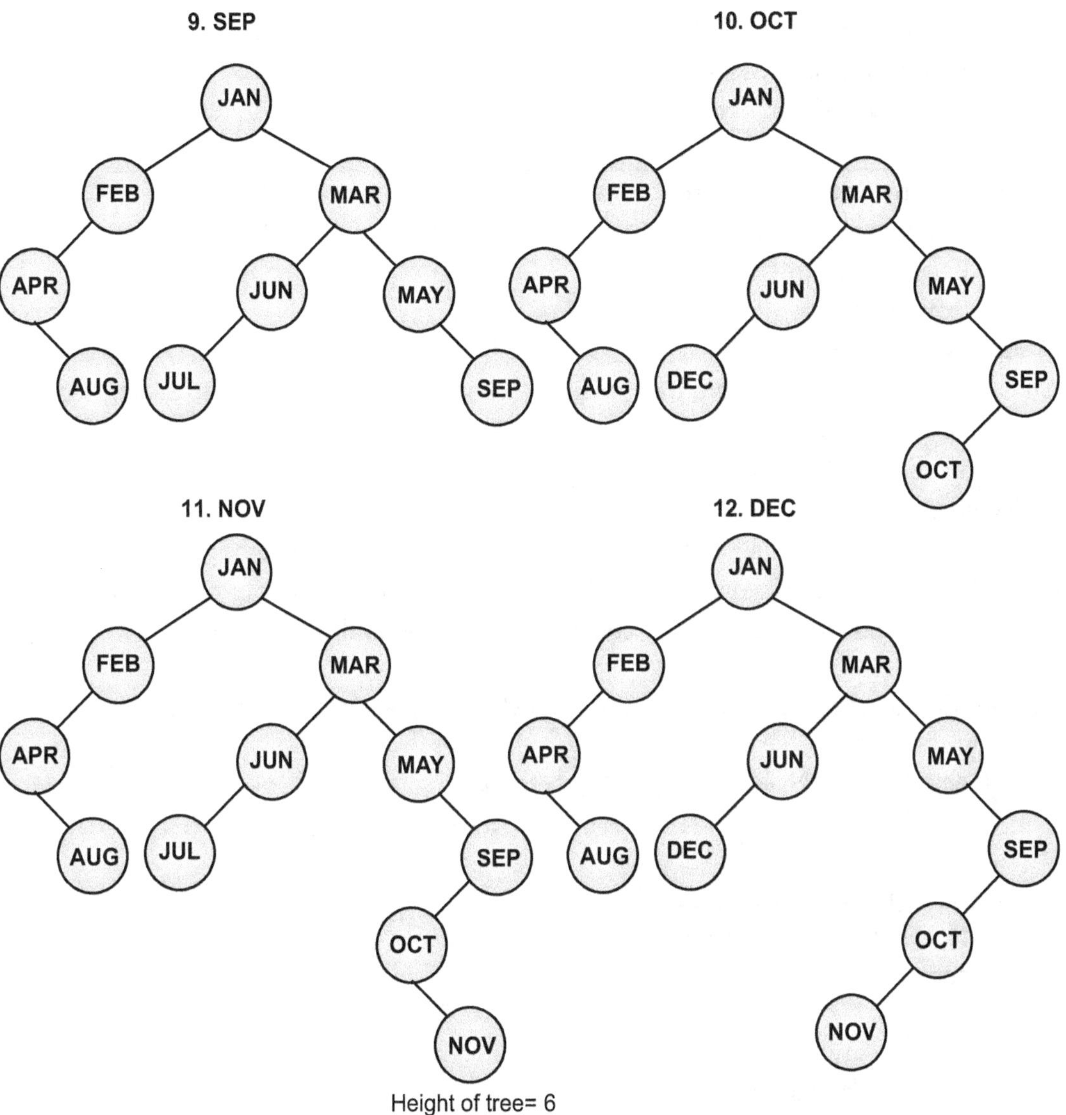

Fig. 5.41

7. **Write a recursive function to find.**

    (i) **Height of a binary tree.**

    (ii) **To count and print leaf nodes of binary tree.**

Solution: Refer Solved Problem 3.

8. **Give pseudo code to print the leaves of tree using any traversal.**

Solution:

```
void print_leaves(NODE *root)
{
    if (root!=NULL)
        print_leaves(root->lchild);
```

```
        if (root->lchild == NULL & root->rchild == NULL)
        printf("%d \n", root->data);
        print_leaves(root->rchild);
    }
```

9. Explain any one application of binary tree with suitable example.

Solution: There are two applications of binary tree that we can list out.

- (i)   Binary search tree.
- (ii) Expression tree.

(i) Binary search tree:

We can use binary tree to store data in such a way that it will be easier to search required data. We can store the binary search tree such that at each node on the left side we will have smaller numbers and on right side we will have larger numbers than the data at node.

(ii) Expression tree:

Another application can be expression tree. We can store an infix expression into the binary tree so that we can have its prefix or postfix conversion using preorder or postorder traversal.

12. Write a non-recursive function to count number of leaf nodes in a binary tree.

Solution:

We can use non-recursive inorder traversal function. In place of print statement, we can use following statement.

```
    if (temp->lchild==NULL&&temp->rchild==NULL)
        count=count + 1;


    int count_leaves(NODE *root)
    {   NODE *temp;   int count;
        temp=root;
        do
        {
            while(temp!=NULL)
            {
                push(temp);
                temp temp->lchild;
            }
            temp=pop( );
            if(temp-lchild==NULL && temp->rchild==NULL)
                count=count + 1;
            temp=temp->rchild;
        } while(!stack empty( ) || temp!=NULL);
        return(count);
    }
```

EXERCISE

1. Define the following related to tree:

    1. Complete binary tree,

    2. Siblings,

    3. Non-terminals, (All non-leaf nodes are known as non-terminals)

    4. Forest,

    5. Height or Depth,

    6. Ancestors. (All nodes on the path joining the current node and the root node are ancestors of the current node.)

2. Define following terms with example.

    (i) Complete binary tree.   (ii) Siblings.

    (iii) Height.   (iv) Binary search tree.

    (v) Forest.

3. Define the following terms.

    1. Binary tree,   2. Complete Binary tree,

    3. Threaded Binary Tree.   4. What is binary tree?

5. Define the following:

    (a) Binary tree,   (b) Complete binary tree,

    (c) Full binary, tree,   (d) Sibling.

6. Define the following terms with respect to tree.

    (i) Complete binary tree.   (ii) Forest.

    (iii) Height of binary tree.   (iv) Skewed binary tree.

    (v) Full binary tree.

7. Explain the sequential representation of binary tree with example.

8. Define the term binary search tree. Give a 'C' declaration to define a node structure for the same. Write a function in 'C' to insert a node in a binary search tree.

9. What do you mean by binary search tree? Write a C function to search an element from a given binary search tree.

10. What is binary search tree? Explain its application.

11. What is binary search tree? Explain its application.

12. What is Binary search tree? Explain the application of BST.

13. Define binary search tree. Write a function to delete a node from a BST. Consider all possible cases.

14. Write necessary 'C' functions to search given data in BST.

15. Write a function to search an element in BST.

16. Traverse the tree built in Q. 47 in inorder, postorder and preorder and display the sequence of numbers.

17. Write a 'C' function (non-recursive) for deleting a node from binary search tree.

18. Write a C function to delete a node from binary search tree. Consider all cases.

19. Write necessary 'C' functions to delete a node in BST.

20. Write a non-recursive function to delete a node from BST. Explain all cases with suitable example.

21. Define binary search tree. Write a function to delete a node from BST.

22. Write a C function to insert a node in binary search tree.

23. Write a function to insert an element in BST.

24. Write necessary 'C' functions to implement inorder traversal in a binary tree non-recursively.

25. Write a non-recursive C function to traverse a binary tree in in-order traversal.

26. Write a non-recursive function in 'C' to perform a pre-order traversal on a binary tree.

27. Write necessary 'C' functions to implement preorder traversal in a binary tree non-recursively.

28. Write a pseudo code to traverse a given binary tree in preorder without recursion.

29. Write a non-recursive 'C' function to traverse binary tree in preorder. Explain with suitable example.

30. Explain non-recursive inorder traversal of binary tree.

31. Write an algorithm to implement non-recursive inorder traversal of binary tree.

32. Comment on "Threaded binary tree can be traversed without using stack".

33. What is threaded binary tree? State its advantage and disadvantages.

34. What is threaded binary tree? State its advantages and disadvantages.

35. State and explain the advantages of threaded binary tree.

36. Explain the term threaded binary tree. Give a 'C declaration to define the node structure of a threaded binary tree. What are the advantages of threaded binary trees over normal binary trees?

37. What do you mean by threaded binary tree? Also write pseudo code to perform non-recursive preorder traversal of TBT without using stack.

38. What is threaded binary tree? Explain its application.

39. What is threaded binary tree? Explain the application of threaded binary tree.

40. (i)   Give declaration in 'C' for TBT.

    (ii) Write a function in 'C' to perform traversal of threaded binary tree.

    (iii) Compare traversal of TBT with binary tree.

41. List the advantages of using a threaded binary tree. Give node structure for defining a threaded binary tree. Write a function in 'C' to find the pre-order successor of any node pointed by P in a threaded binary tree.

42. List advantages of threaded binary tree. Give its node structure. Write a function in 'C' to find preorder successor of any node pointed by 7 in TBT.

43. What is threaded binary tree? Explain its advantages/applications.

44. Comment on "Threaded binary tree can be traversed without stack".

45. Write a non-recursive algorithm for pre-order traversal of a binary tree.

46. What is AVL tree? Explain RR and LL rotations with example.

47. Build a binary search tree from the following set of elements:

    100, 50, 200, 300, 20, 150, 70, 180, 120, 30

48. Construct binary search tree from the following set of strings:

    JAN, FEB, MAR, APR, MAY, JUN, JUL, AUG, SEP, OCT, NOV and DEC.

49. Construct Binary tree if following traversals are give.

    Inorder   :   D, F, E, G, A, H, I, C

    Postorder   :   D, F, G, E, B, I, H, C, A

50. Construct BST from following elements:

    (i)   MAT, TAN, BAN, BAT, SUN, CAT, RAT Show all steps.

    (ii) 100, 50, 200, 300, 20, 150, 70, 180, 120, 30

51. Construct binary search tree from the following set of strings:

    MAR, MAY, NOV, AUG, APR, JAN, DEC, JUL, FEB, JUN, OCT and SEP. Show all steps.

52. Create Binary Search Tree for the following data and print the tree using all tree traversals.

    MAR, OCT, JAN, APR, NOV, FEB, MAY, DEC, JUN, AUG, JUL, SEP.

53. Write a recursive function to count and print leaf nodes of binary tree.

54. Write a recursive function to find height of binary tree.

55. Write recursive functions to obtain:

    (i)   Height of a binary tree,

    (ii) To count and print the leaf nodes of a binary tree.

56. Explain any one application of binary tree with suitable example.

57. Construct a threaded binary search tree for the following set of elements:

                100, 50, 200, 300, 20, 150, 150, 70, 180, 120, 30 show all steps

Unit VI

SORTING AND SEARCHING

6.1 Sorting Methods

Sorting is one of the most common data processing applications. Sorting is a process of arranging data according to their values. The data that we get after sorting is called ordered data. Ordered data will be useful in searching a particular data item.

Just like searching, sorting is classified as internal and external sort.

Internal sort is a sort in which all of the data is held in primary memory.

External sort uses primary memory for data being sorted currently and secondary storage for data that cannot fit into primary memory.

There are number of sorting techniques such as selection, bubble, insertion, quick sort, merge sort, heap sort, shell sort etc.

A sorting technique is said to be stable, if elements with equal keys/values maintain their relative input order in the sorted list also.

Data may be sorted in ascending or descending order. It is called sort order. If the order is not specified it is by default ascending.

Since, there are number of methods of sorting, efficiency of these methods should be known to the programmer. The efficiency considerations are nothing but Time and Space complexity also the implementation complexity. The time complexity of sorting algorithm is specified in terms of comparisons and exchanges required.

When elements in the list are sorted, we have to traverse the list. When we traverse the list once, it is called as one pass of the sort.

6.2 Selection Sort

In selection sort, successive elements are selected in order and placed into their proper sorted position.

One way of implementing this is, if you are given an array a[ ], find maximum of the elements in the list and interchange it with the last element. It means we are selecting largest element in the list and placing it in its position. Then reduce the size of list by 1 and repeat the process. This will be continued till the list size is reduced to 1.

Another way of implementing it is, find minimum of the elements in the list and interchange it with first element. Both versions are implemented below. Let us first write an algorithm for the first case.

Algorithm 6.1: Selection Sort

```
1.  Read n
2.  for(i=0; i<n−1;i++)
    Read a[i]
3.  for (i=n-1;i>0;i−−)
    {
        max = a[0];
        index = 0
        for(j=1;j<=i;j++)
        {
            if(a[j]>max)
            {
                max = a[j];
                index = j;
            }
        }
        a [index] = a [i]
        a[i] = max;
    }
4.  for(i=0;i<k;i++)
        print a[i]
5.  stop
```

Explanation:
1. Read number of element to be sorted.
2. Read the numbers and store them in an array a.
3. Repeat the process of selecting maximum element and placing it at the end, n − 1 times (corresponds to n − 1 passes).
4. Find maximum of the elements from j = 0 to i = 1 (meaning current list size i). The variable index stores the location of the element and max stores the maximum element.
5, Put i^{th} number (i.e., last number in current list of size i) in the location given by index and the maximum number in i^{th} location, i.e., at the end of current list.
6. Display the sorted list.

Example 6.1: Let us take, following 7 numbers to be sorted. Here, n = 7.

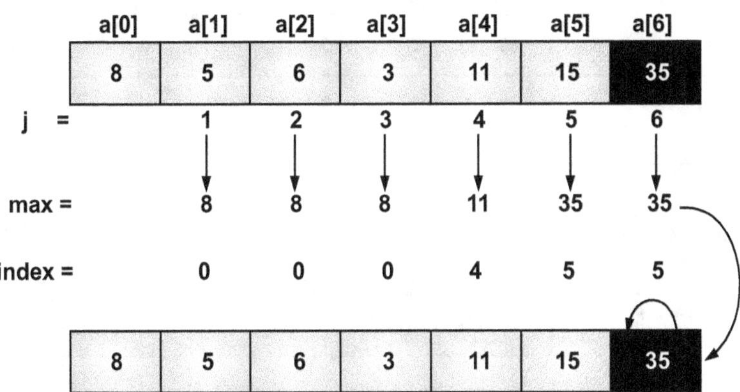

Pass 1: i = n − 1 = 6; max = a[0] = 8

Pass 2: i = 5, max = a[0] = 8

Pass 3: i = 4; max = a[0] = 8

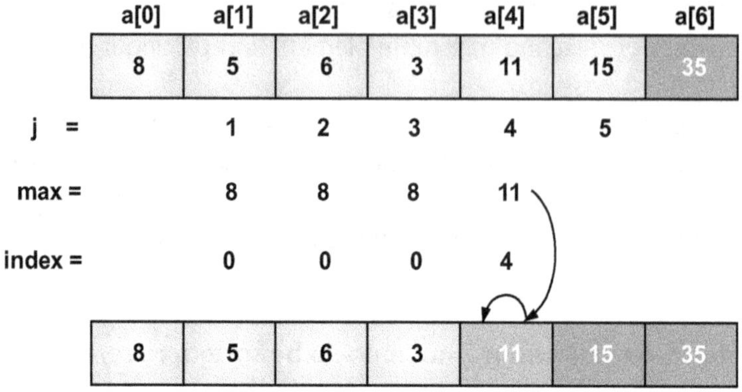

	a[0]	a[1]	a[2]	a[3]	a[4]	a[5]	a[6]
	8	5	6	3	11	15	35

j =		1	2	3	4	5
max =		8	8	8	11	
index =		0	0	0	4	

8	5	6	3	11	15	35

Pass 4: i = 3; max = a[0] = 8

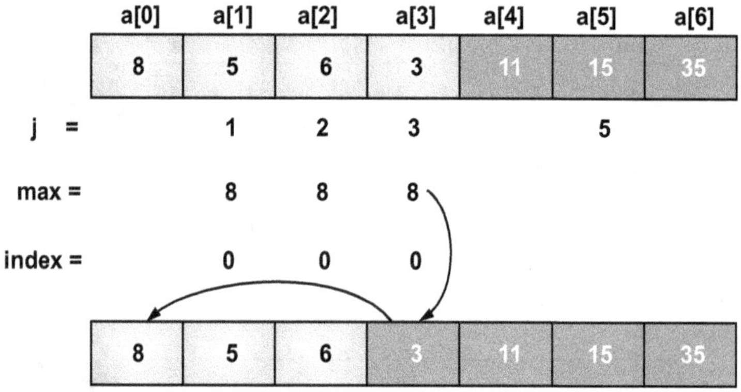

	a[0]	a[1]	a[2]	a[3]	a[4]	a[5]	a[6]
	8	5	6	3	11	15	35

j =		1	2	3		5
max =		8	8	8		
index =		0	0	0		

8	5	6	3	11	15	35

Pass 5: i = 2; max = a[0] = 3

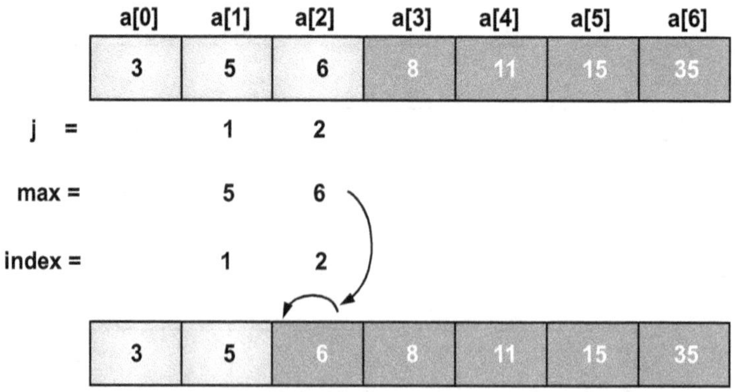

	a[0]	a[1]	a[2]	a[3]	a[4]	a[5]	a[6]
	3	5	6	8	11	15	35

j =		1	2
max =		5	6
index =		1	2

3	5	6	8	11	15	35

Pass 6: i = 1; max = a[0] = 3

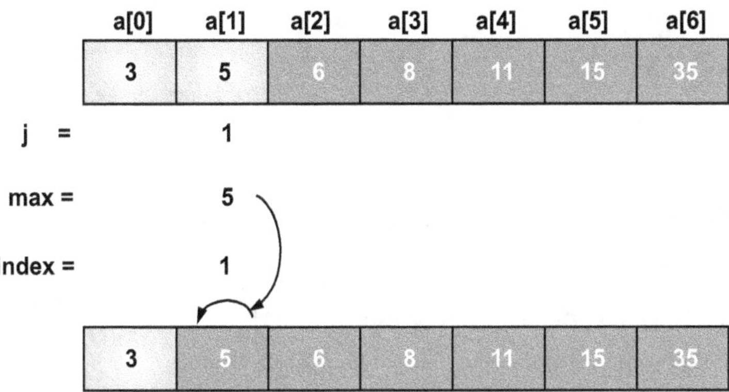

Analysis:

1. In the first pass, number of comparisons (a[j] > max) will be n − 1. In each successive pass, the number of comparisons reduces by 1. In the last pass, there will be only one comparison. Hence, the total number of comparisons will be,

   (n − 1) + (n − 2) + (n − 3) + ... + 3 + 2 + 1

   $$= \frac{n(n - 1)}{2} = O(n^2)$$

   Hence, time complexity of the algorithm will be $O(n^2)$.

2. The number of interchanges will be (n − 1). Note that there are some interchanges with the elements itself.

3. There is no additional memory requirement except to hold the element temporarily like max, index, etc.

4. The number of comparisons and swaps required for this algorithm are as below:

(i) Number of comparisons

Best case $\dfrac{n(n - 1)}{2}$ i.e. $O(n^2)$

Worst case $\dfrac{n(n - 1)}{2}$ i.e. $O(n^2)$

(ii) Number of swaps

Best case n − 1 i.e. O(n)

Worst case n − 1 i.e. O(n)

Program 6.1: Selection Sort

```c
#include <stdio.h>
#include <conio.h>
#define MAX 100
void main( )
{
    int a[MAX], i, j, n, index, max;
    clrscr( );
    printf ("Enter number of elements in the list \n");
    scanf ("%d", &n);
    printf ("Enter the number \n")
    for(i=0;i<n;i++)
        scanf("%d" , &a[i]);
    for(i=n-1;i>0;i--)
    {
        max = a[0];
        index = 0;
        for(j=1;j<=i;j++)
        {
            if (a[j]>max)
            {
                max = a[j];
                index = j;
            }
        }
        a[index] = a[i];
        a[i] = max;
    }
    printf ("Sorted list is \n");
    for(i=0;i<n;i++)
        printf("%d \n", a[i]);
}
```

Algorithm 6.2: Selection sort (version 2)

Another approach to selection sort can be find minimum number in the list and interchange the first location in the list with this number. Hence, step number 3 and 4 in above algorithm will be changed as follows:

```
3.  for(i=0;i<n−1;i++)
    {
        min = a[i];
        index = i;
4.          for(j=i+1;j<n;j++)
        {
            if(a[j]<min)
            {
                min = a[j];
                index = j;
            }
        }
        a[index] = a[i];
        a[i] = min;
    }
```

There is one more way in which selection sort is implemented. We can start with, first number in the array. Compare it with all the elements one by one. If we find the number to be smaller than this number, we interchange them. In the next pass, we start the process from second number and so on. In this case, the number of swaps is more compared to the methods discussed earlier.

The algorithm is as follows:

Algorithm 6.3: Selection sort (version 3)

```
1.  Read n
2.  for(i=0;i<n;i++)
    Read a[i]
```

```
3.  for(i=0;i<n-1;i++)
    {
        for(j=i+1;j<n;j++)
        {
            if (a[i] > a[i])
            {
                temp = a[i];
                a[i] = a[j];
                a[j] = temp;
            }
        }
    }
3.  for (i=0; i<n; i++)
        print a[i]
4.  Stop
```

6.3 Bubble Sort

This technique is relatively easy to implement and understand. In bubble sort, we compare each element with its successor. If we find that the successor is smaller, then it is interchanged with its predecessor. By doing so, we will be shifting the smaller numbers one position up in every pass. The largest number will move to last location at the end of 1st pass. Then we again start from first location and repeat the process in 2nd pass. The second largest number will move to second last position. We continue this till n – 1 passes. The algorithm for bubble sort is as follows:

Algorithm 6.4: Bubble sort

```
1.  Read n
2.  for(i=0; i<n; i++)
    Read a[i]
```

```
3.  for (i=0; i<n−1; i++)

    {

4.          for j=0; j<n−1−i; j++)

            {

                if (a[j] > a[j + 1]

                {

                        temp = a[j];

                        a[j] = a[j + 1];

                        a[j + 1] = temp;

                }

            }

    }

5.  for (i = 0; i<n; i++)

            print a[i]
```

Explanation:

1. Read number of element in the list (n).

2. Read the number and store them in the array a.

3. Repeat for n − 1 times i.e., i taking values from 0 to n − 2 (n − 1 passes).

4. In each pass, start with the first element in the array and go on comparing the adjacent elements a[j] and a[j + 1]. Interchange them if a[j] > a[j + 1], otherwise do not interchange. During pass 1, i = 0 and j starts with 0 and goes upto location (n − 1). Note that the inner for loop starts with j = 0 and goes upto n − 1 − i means, when i = 0 (1st pass) we go upto location n − 2 i.e., when i = 0 (1st pass) we go upto second last location. When i = 1, we go upto third location from last. When i = 2, we go upto 4th location from last and so on. Thus in every pass, largest number will go to down the list in its position.

5. The sorted numbers are displayed.

Example 6.2: Let the numbers to be sorted be 25 38 33 11 73 29. Here, n = 6.

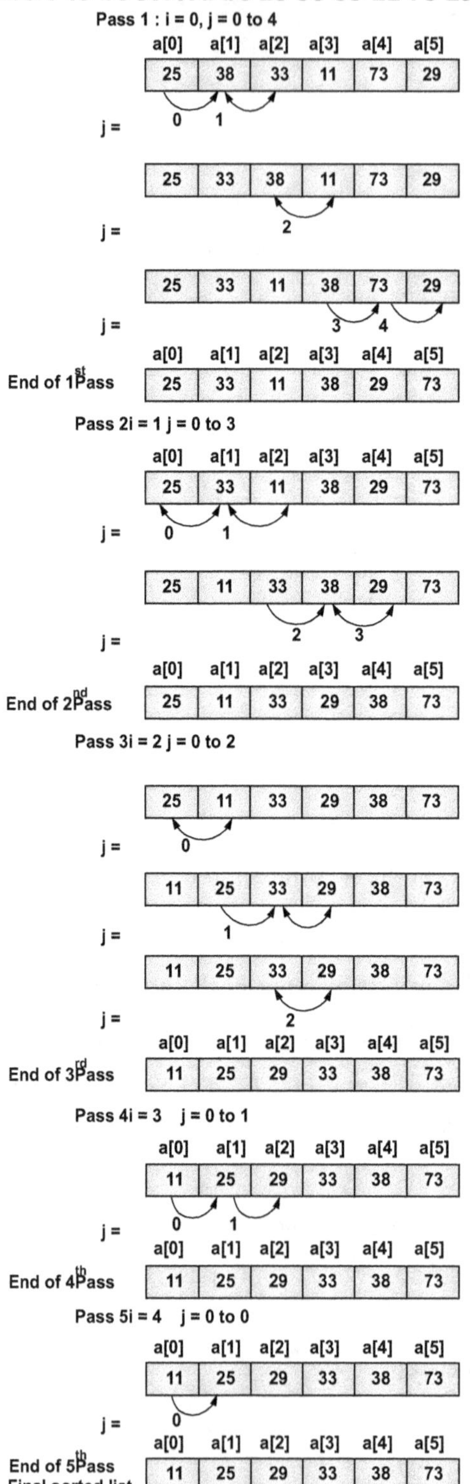

Analysis:

1. As indicated in the above example, the first pass will require n – 1 comparison and interchanges. The second pass will have n – 2, third pass n – 3 and so on. Hence, the total number of comparisons and interchanges will be,

   (n – 1) + (n – 2) + (n – 3) + ... + 3 + 2 + 1

   $$= \frac{n(n-1)}{2} = O(n^2)$$

   Hence, the time complexity of bubble sort will be $O(n^2)$.

2. This time complexity will be same, whatever may be the order of numbers i.e., even if the list is already sorted it will be $O(n^2)$.

3. There is no additional space required except the temp variable required for interchanging.

4. Thus, bubble sort algorithm will require number of comparisons and swaps as below.

   (i)   Number of comparisons

   Best case: $\dfrac{n(n-1)}{2}$ i.e. $O(n^2)$

   Worst case: $\dfrac{n(n-1)}{2}$ i.e. $O(n^2)$

   (ii)   Number of swaps

   Best case: n – 1 i.e. $O(n)$

   Worst case: $\dfrac{n(n-1)}{2}$ i.e. $O(n^2)$

Program 6.2: Bubble sort.

```c
#include <stdio.h>
#include <conio.h>
#define MAX 100
void main( )
{
    int a[MAX], i, j, n, temp;
    clrscr( );
    printf("Enter number of elements in the list \n");
    scanf("%d", &n);
    printf("Enter the number \n")
    for(i=0;i<n;i++)
```

```
            scanf("%d" , &a[i]);
        for(i=0;i<n-1;i--)
        {
                for(j=0;j<n-1-i;j++)
                {
                        if(a[j]>a[j+1])
                        {
                                temp = a[j];
                                a[j] = a[j + 1];
                                a[j + 1] = temp;
                        }
                }
        }
        printf("Sorted list is \n");
        for(i=0;i<n;i++)
                printf("%d \n", a[i]);
}
```

6.4 Merge Sort

Combing the two lists is called as merging. For example A is a sorted list with r elements and B is a sorted list with s elements. The operation that combines the elements of A and B into a single sorted list C with n = r + s elements is called merging. After combing the two lists the elements are sorted by using the following merging algorithm.

Suppose one is given two sorted decks of cards. The decks are merged as in Fig. 2.1. That is, at each step, the two front cards are compared and the smaller one is placed in the combined deck. When one of the decks is empty, all of the remaining cards in the other deck are put at the end of the combined deck. Similarly, suppose we have two lines of students sorted by increasing heights, and suppose we want to merge them into a single sorted line. The new line is formed by choosing, at each step, the shorter of the two students who are at the head of their respective lines. When one of the lines has no more students, the remaining students line up at the end of the combined line.

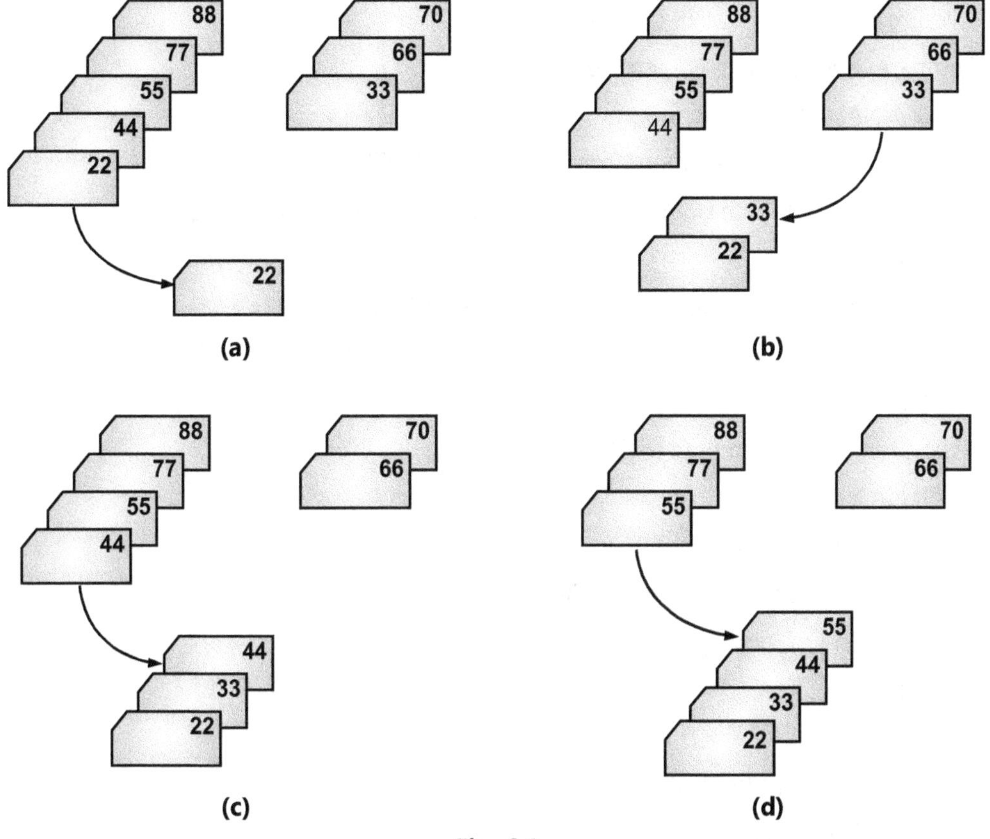

Fig. 6.1

The above discussion will now be translated into a formal algorithm which merges a sorted r-element array A and a sorted s-element array B into a sorted array C, with n = r + s elements. First of all, we must always keep track of the locations of the smallest element of A and the smallest element of B which have not yet been placed in C. Let NA and NB denote these locations, respectively. Also, let PTR denote the location in C to be filled. Thus, initially, we set NA : = 1, NB : = 1 and PTR : = 1. At each step of the algorithm, we compare A[NA] and B[NB] and assign the smaller element to C[PTR]. Then we increment PTR by setting PTR:= PTR + 1, and we either increment NA by setting NA: = NA + 1 or increment NB by setting NB: = NB + 1, according to whether the new element in C has come from A or from B. Furthermore, if NA> r, then the remaining elements of B are assigned to C; or if NB > s, then the remaining elements of A are assigned to C.

Algorithm 6.5

MERGING (A, R, B, S, C)

Let A and B be sorted arrays with R and S elements. This algorithm merges A and B into an array C with N = R + S elements.

1. [Initialize] Set NA : = 1 , NB := 1 AND PTR : = 1

2. [Compare] Repeat while NA <= R and NB <= S

      If A[NA] < B[NB], then

          (a) [Assign element from A to C] set C[PTR] := A[NA]

          (b) [Update pointers] Set PTR := PTR +1 and NA := NA +1

      Else

          (a) [Assign element from B to C] Set C[PTR] := B[NB]

          (b) [Update Pointers] Set PTR := PTR +1 and NB := NB +1

      [End of loop]

3. [Assign remaining elements to C]

      If NA > R, then

          Repeat for K = 0 ,1,2,.........,S- NB

             Set C[PTR+K] := B[NB+K]

          [End of loop

      Else

          Repeat for K = 0,1,2,.......,R-NA

             Set C[PTR+K] := A[NA+K]

          [End of loop]

4. Exit

The total computing time = $O(n \log_2 n)$.

The disadvantages of using mergesort is that it requires two arrays of the same size and type for the merge phase

6.5 Radix Sort

Radix sort is the method that many people intuitively use or begin to use when alphabetizing a large list of names. Specifically, the list of names is first sorted according to the first letter of each name. That is, the names are arranged in 26 classes, where the first class consists of those names that begin with "A," the second class consists of those names that begin with "B," and so on. During the second pass, each class is alphabetized according to the second letter of the name. And so on. If no name contains, for example, more than 12 letters, the names are alphabetized with at most 12 passes.

The radix sort is the method used by a card sorter. A card sorter contains 13 receiving pockets labeled as follows:

9, 8, 7, 6, 5, 4, 3, 2, 1, 0, 11, 12, R (reject)

Each pocket other than R corresponds to a row on a card in which a hole can be punched. Decimal numbers, where the radix is 10, are punched in the obvious way and hence use only the first 10 pockets of the sorter. The sorter uses a radix reverse-digit sort on numbers. That is, suppose a card sorter is given a collection of cards where each card contains a 3-digit number punched in columns 1 to 3. The cards are first sorted according to the units digit. On the second pass, the cards are sorted according to the tens digit. On the third and last pass, the cards are sorted according to the hundreds digit. We illustrate with an example.

Example 6.3:

Suppose 9 cards are punched as follows:

348, 143, 361, 423, 538, 128, 321, 543, 366

Given to a card sorter, the numbers would be sorted in three phases, as pictured in Fig. 6.

(a) In the first pass, the units digits are sorted into pockets. (The pockets are pictured upside down, so 348 is at the bottom of pocket 8.) The cards are collected pocket by pocket, from pocket 9 to pocket 0. (Note that 361 will now be at the bottom of the pile and 128 at the top of the pile.) The cards are now reinput to the sorter.

(b) In the second pass, the tens digits are sorted into pockets. Again the cards are collected pocket by pocket and reinput to the sorter.

(c) In the third and final pass, the hundreds digits are sorted into pockets.

Input	0	1	2	3	4	5	6	7	8	9
348									348	
143				143						
361		361								
423				423						
538									538	
128									128	
321		321								
543				543						
366										

(a) First pass

Input	0	1	2	3	4	5	6	7	8	9
361							361			
321			321							
143					143					
423			423							
543					543					
366					543					
366							366			
348					348					
538				538						
128			128							

(b) Second pass

Input	0	1	2	3	4	5	6	7	8	9
321				321					348	
423					423					
128		128								
538										
143		143							538	
543									128	
348				348						
361				361						
366				366						

When the cards are collected after the third pass, the numbers are in the following order:

128, 143, 321, 348, 361, 366, 423, 538, 543

Thus the cards are now sorted.

The number C of comparisons needed to sort nine such 3-digit numbers is bounded as follows:

$$C \leq 9 * 3 * 10$$

The 9 comes from the nine cards, the 3 comes from the three digits in each number, and the 10 comes from radix d = 10 digits.

Complexity of Radix Sort

Suppose a list A of n items $A_1, A_2, \ldots, A_n$ is given. Let d denote the radix (e.g., d = 10 for decimal digits, d = 26 for letters and d = 2 for bits), and suppose each item Ai is represented by means of s of the digits:

$$A_i = d_{i1} \, d_{i2} \ldots d_{is}$$

The radix sort algorithm will require 5 passes, the number of digits in each item. Pass K will compare each d_{ik} with each of the d digits. Hence the number C(n) of comparisons for the algorithm is bounded as follows:

$$C(n) \leq d * s * n$$

Although d is independent of n, the number s does depend on n. In the worst case, s = n, so $C(n) = O(n^2)$. In the best case, s = logd n, so C(n) = O(n log n). In other words, radix sort performs well only when the number s of digits in the representation of the A_i's is small.

Another drawback of radix sort is that one may need d*n memory locations. This comes from the fact that all the items may be "sent to the same pocket" during a given pass. This drawback may be minimized by using linked lists rather than arrays to store the items during a given pass. However, one will still require 2*n memory locations.

6.6 Quick Sort

As the name suggest is the fastest one. The quick sort is an in-place, divide-and-conquer, massively recursive sort. The algorithm is simple in theory, but very difficult to put into code. The purpose of the quick sort is to move a data item in the correct direction just enough for it to reach its final place in the array. The method, therefore, reduces unnecessary swaps, and moves an item a great distance in one move. A pivotal item near the middle of the array is chosen, and then items on either side are moved so that the data items on one side of the pivot are smaller than the pivot, whereas those on the other side are larger. The middle (pivot) item is now in its correct position. The procedure is then applied recursively to the two parts of the array, on either side of the pivot, until the whole of numbers.

The recursive algorithm consists of four steps :
1. If there is one or less element in the array to be sorted, return immediately.
2. Pick an element in the array to serve as a "pivot" point. (Usually the left-most element in the array is used.)
3. Split the array into two parts - one with elements smaller than the pivot and the other with elements larger than the pivot.
4. Recursively repeat the algorithm for both halves of the original array.

Quick Sort in details :
In this method an array a[1] ------- a[n] is sorted by picking some value in the array as a key element. We then swap the first element of the list with the key element so that the key will come in the first position. We then find out the proper place of key in the list.

The proper place is that position in the list where, if a key is placed, then all elements to the left of it are smaller than the key, and all the elements to the right of it a greater than the key.

To obtain the proper position of the key we traverse the list in both the directions using the indices i and j, respectively. We initialize i to that index which is one more than index of the key element, i.e. if the list to be sorted has the indices running from m to n, then the key element is the at index m, hence we initialize i to (m+l).

The index i is incremented till we get an element at the ith position greater than key value. Similarly, we initialize j to n and go on decrementing j till we get an element having the value less than the key value.

We then check whether i and j have crossed each other. If not then we interchange elements at the ith and j^{th} position, and continue the process of incrementing i and decrementing j till i and j cross each other. When i and j cross each other, we interchange the elements at the key position (i.e. at m^{th} position) and the elements at the jth position.

This brings the key element to the jth position, and we find that the elements to its left are less than it, and the elements to its right are greater than it. Therefore we can split the given list into two sub-lists. The first one made of elements from m^{th} position to the $(j-1)^{th}$ position, and the second one made of elements from the $(j+1)^{th}$ position to n^{th}, position, and repeat the same procedure with each of the sub-lists separately.

Choice of the key
We can choose any entry in the list as the key. The choice of the first entry is often a poor choice for key, since if the list is already sorted, then there will be no element less than the first element selected as key, and so one of the sub-lists will be, empty.

Hence we choose a key near the center of the list, in the hope that our choice will position the list in such a manner that about half come one each side of the key.

The choice of the key near the center is also arbitrary, and hence it is not necessary that it will always divide the list nicely in half. It may also happen that one sub-list is much larger than other. Hence some other method of selecting a key should be used. A good way to choose a key is to use a random number generator to choose the position of next key in each activation of quicksort.

Program 6.3: Quick Sort

```c
#define MAX 10
void swap(int *x, int *y)
{
    int temp;
    temp = *x;
    *x = *y;
    *y = temp;
}
void qsort(int list[ ],int m,int n)
{
    int key,i,j,k;
    if(m<n)
    {
        k = (m+n)/2;
        swap(&list[m],&list[k]);
        key = list[m];
        i=m+1;
        j=n;
        while(i<=j)
        {
            while((i<=n)&&(list[i] <= key))
                i++;
            while((j>=m)&&(list[j]>key))
                j--;
            if (i<j)
                swap(&list[i],&list[j]);
        }
        swap(&list[m],&list[j]);
        qsort(list,m,j-1) ;
        qsort (list,j+1,n);
    }
}
```

Consider the following list:

0	1	2	3	4	5	6
10	5	23	67	20	30	60

1. When qsort is called first time, key = 67, and i = 1, and j = 6, i is incremented till it becomes 7, because there is no element greater than key, j is not decremented, because at position 6, the value that we have is less than the key. Since i > j, we interchange the key element that is the element at position 0, with the element at position 6, and call qsort recursively with the left sub-list made of elements from position 0 to 5, and right sub-list which is empty is shown below :

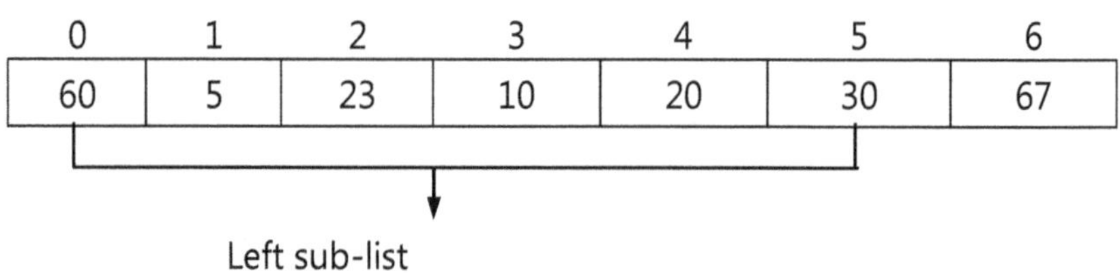

Left sub-list

Fig. 6.3

2. When qsort is called second time with left sub-list as shown above, key = 23, and i = 1, and j = 5. i is incremented till it becomes 2. Because the element at position 2 is greater than key, j is decremented to 4 because the value at position 4 is less than the key. Since I < j, the element at position 2 and 4 are swapped, i is then incremeneted to 4 and j is decremented to 3. Since i > j, we interchange the key element that is the element at position 0, with the element at position 3, and call qsort recursively with the left sub-list made of elements from position 0 to 2, and right sub-list made of elements from position 4 to 5 as shown below.

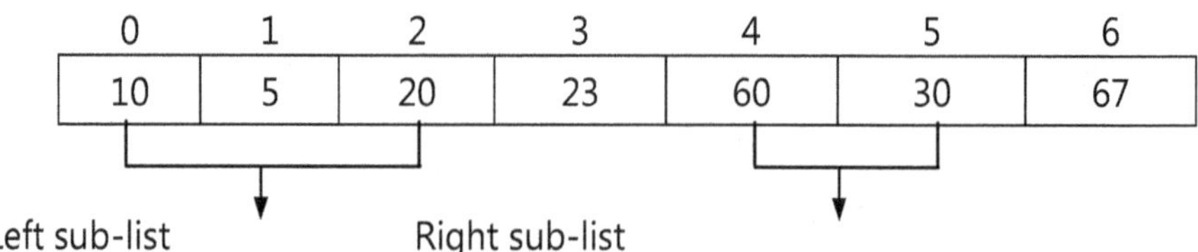

Left sub-list   Right sub-list

Fig. 6.4

3. By continuing in this fashion, finally we get the sorted list.

    Let us see details of all passes through following example.

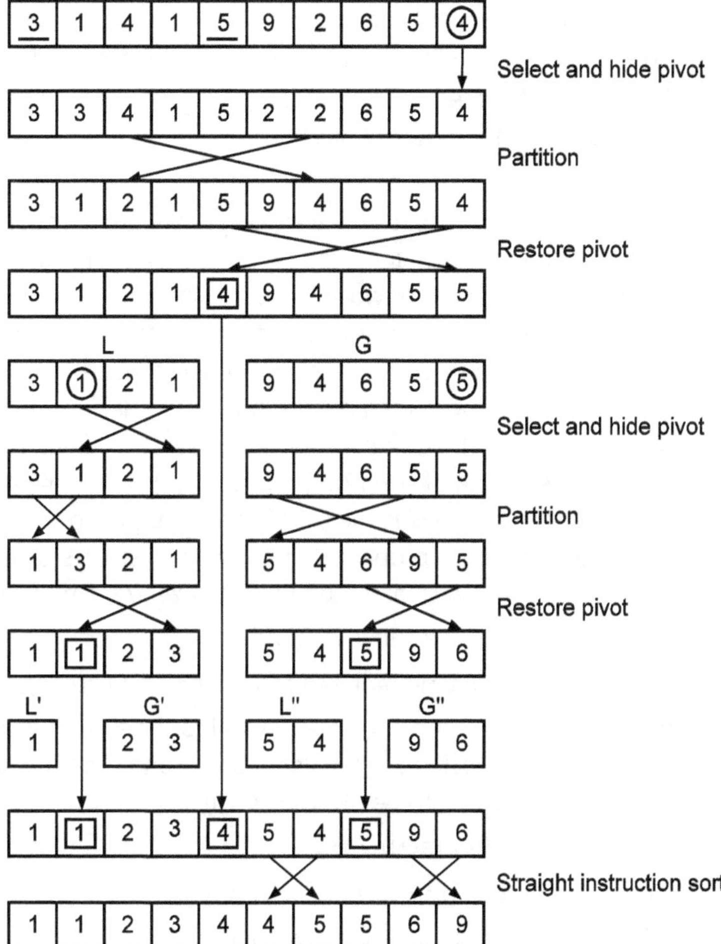

Fig. 6.5: Quick Sorting

The purpose of the quick sort is to move a data item in the correct direction just enough for it to reach its final place in the array. The method, therefore, reduces unnecessary swaps, and moves an item a great distance in one move.

Now, let us see the efficiency of quick sort. On the first pass, every element in the array is compared to the pivot, so there are n comparisons. The array is then divided into two parts each of size (n/2) approximately. (We assume that the array is divided into approximately one half each time). For each of these sub arrays, (n/2) comparisons are made and four sub arrays of size (n/4) are formed. So at each level, the number of sub arrays doubles. It will take up $\log_2 n$ divisions if we are dividing the array approximately one half each time. Therefore, quick sort is **O ($n\log_2 n$)** on the average.

If the original array is sorted and array[left] is chosen as a pivot, the quick sort turns out to be $O(n_2)$. Therefore, when we choose array[left] as pivot, quick sort works best for files that are completely unsorted and worst for files which are completely sorted. In the case of nearly sorted arrays choose a random element as a pivot value.

We assume that every time the list gets splitted into two approximately equal sized sub-lists. If the size of a given list is n, then it gets split into two sub-lists of size approximately n/2. Each of these sub-lists further gets split into two sub-lists of size n/4, and this is continued till the size becomes equal to 1. When the quick sort works with a list of size n, it places the key element (which we take the first element of the list under consideration) at its proper position in the list. This requires no more than n iterations. After placing the key element at its proper position in the list of size n, quick sort activates itself two times to work with left and right sub-lists, each assumed to be of size n/2. Therefore T(n) is the time required to' sort a list of size n. Since the time required to sort the list of size n is equal to the sum of the time required to put the key element at its proper position in the list of size n and the time required to the left and right sub-lists each assumed to be of size n/2, T(n) turns out to be :

$$T(n) = c*n + 2*T(n/2)$$

where, c is a constant and T(n/2) is the time required to sort the list of size n/2.

Similarly the time required to sort the list of size n/2 is equal to the sum of 1 time required to place the key element at its proper position in the list of size 2 and the time required to sort the left and right sub-lists each assumed to be of size n/4 T(n/2) turns out to be :

$$T(n/2)=c*n/2+-2*T(n/4)$$

where, T(n/4) is the time required to sort the list of size n/4.

∴   T(n/4) = c*n/4 + 2*T(n/8), and so on and finally we get T(1) = 1.

∴   T(n) = c*n + 2(c*n(n/2) + 2T(n/4)) '

∴   T(n) = c*n + c*n + 4T(n/4)) = 2*c*n +4T(n/4) = 2*c*n + 4(c*(n/4) + 2T(n/8))

∴   T(n) = 2*c*n + c*n + 8T(n/8) = 3*c*n + 8T(n/8).

∴   T(n) = (log n)*c*n + nT(n/n)= (log n)*c*n + nT(1) = n + n*(log n) *c

∴   T(n) = nlog(n)

Therefore we conclude that the average complexity of the quick sort algorithm is O(nlog n). But the worst-case time complexity is of the $O(n^2)$. The reason for this is in the worst case one of the two subsists wild always be empty, and the other will be of size (n-1), where n is the size of the original list. Therefore in the worst case, T(n) turns out to be

T(n) = c*n + T(n-1)

= c*n + c*(n-1) + T(n-2)

= 2*c*n - c + T(n-2)

$$= 2*c*n - c + c*(n-2) + T(n-3)$$
$$= 3*c*n - 3*c + T(n-3)$$
$$\cdots$$
$$\cdots$$
$$= n*c*n - n*c + T(1)$$
$$= n^2c - nc + l$$

Therefore the order is $O(n^2)$.

Space Complexity:

The average-case space complexity is $\log_2 t$, because the space complexity depends on the maximum number of activations that can exist. We find that if we assume that every time the list gets split into approximately two equal-sized lists, the maximum number of activations that will exists simultaneously will be $\log_2 n$.

In the worst case, there exist n activations because the depth of the recursion is n. Hence the worst case space complexity is $O(n)$.

Pros and Cons of Quick Sort :

- Extremely fast.
- This quick sort can be implemented efficiently by using recursion; but
- Very complex algorithm, massively recursive.
- Gives good results when an array is in random order.
- Quick sort is O (nlog2n) on the average.

6.7 Heap Sort

Heapsort is a sorting technique that sorts a list of length n with $O(n \log_2(n))$ comparisons and movement of entries, even in the worst case.

Hence it achieves the worst-case bounds better than those of quicksort; and for the list it is better than mergesort, since it needs only a small and constant amount of space apart from the list being sorted.

Heapsort works in two steps. First all the entries in the list are arranged to satisfy heap property, and then the top of the heap is removed and another entry is promoted to take its place repeatedly. Therefore we need a function that builds an initial heap to arrange all the entries in the list to satisfy heap property. The function that builds an initial heap uses a function that adjusts its entry in the list whose entries at 2i and 2i + 1 positions already satisfy heap property in such a manner that the entry at i^{th} position in the list will also satisfy heap property.

In brief,

Algorithm

(I)   Build a heap tree with a gives set of data.

(II)   (a) Delete root node from heap

       (b) Rebuild the heap after deletion

       (c) Place the deleted node in the output

(III) Continue with step (II) until the heap tree is empty.

Program 6.4: Heap Sort

```
#define MAX 10
   void swap(int *x,int *y)
   {
       int temp;
       temp = *x;
       *x = *y;
       *y = temp;
   }
   void Adjust( int list[ ],int i, int n)
   {
       int j,k,flag;
       k=list[i];
       flag=1;
       j = 2 * i;
       while(j<=n&&flag)
       {
           if(j<=n&&listlj]<list[j+1])
           j++;
           if(k>=list[j])
               flag = 0;
           else
           {
               list[j/2]=list[i];
```

```
            }
        }
    }
    list [j/2] = k;
}
void Build-Heap(int list[], int n)
{
    int i;
    for(i=(n/2);i>=0;i-)
        Adjust(list,i,n-1);
}
void HeapSort(int list[ ],int n)
{
    int i;
    Build_Heap(list,n);
    for(i=(n-2);i>=0;i-),
    {
        swap(&list[0], &list[i+1]);
        Adjust(list,i,n-i);
    }
}
void main( )
    {
    int list [MAX], n;

    .

    .

    .

    HeapSort (list,n);

    .

    .

    .
}
```

Let the elements of the list are:

1   11   12   21 34 42 56 66 87 90.

In each pass of while loop in function Adjust (x, i, n), the position i is double hence the number of passes cannot exceed log(n/i). Therefore the computation time adjust is O(logn/i).

The function Build-Heap calls the Adjust procedure n/2 for values ranging from nl/2 to 0. Hence the total number of iterations will be:

$$= \log(n) + \log(n/2) + \ldots + \log(n/n/2)$$

$$= \sum_{i=1}^{n/2} \log(n/i)$$

$$= n/2 \, \log(n) - \log(in/2)$$

This turns out to be some constant times n. Hence the computation time of build_initial_heap is O(n). The heapsort function calls the adjust (x, 1, –i) (nod) times. Hence the total number of iterations made in the heapsort will be

$$\log(i/1)$$

$$= \sum_{i=1}^{n-1} \log(i)$$

$$= \log(1) + \log(2) + \ldots + \log(n-1)$$

which turns out to be approximately nlogn. Hence the computing time of heap sort it is O(n log(n)) + O(n). The only additional space needed by heapsort is the space for one record to carry out swap.

6.8 Shell Sort

The technique used by Shellsort (named for its inventor Donald Shell) is interesting, and the algorithm is easy to program and runs fairly quickly. Its analysis, however, is very difficult.

Algorithm 6.6: Shell Sort

1.   Input an unsorted array A of size N
2.   Initialize step size, Let h =N/2
3.   While(h > 0) do
Begin
    J=h
    While(J<N) do
    Begin
        J=J+1
        K=J+1
        While (K>0) do
        Begin
            If(A[K]>A[K+1]) then
            Begin
                Temp=A[K]
                A[K]=A[K+1]

```
                A[k+1]=Temp
                 K=K-J
          End
          Else
            K=0;
        End
    End
 h=h/2
End
```
4.   Stop

Program 6.5: Shell Sort

```c
void shellSort(int numbers[], int array_size)
{
  int i, j, increment, temp;

  increment = 3;
  while (increment > 0)
  {
    for (i=0; i < array_size; i++)
    {
      j = i;
      temp = numbers[i];
      while ((j>=increment)&&(numbers[j-increment]>temp))
      {
        numbers[j] = numbers[j - increment];
        j=j - increment;
      }
      numbers[j] = temp;
    }
    if (increment/2!=0)
      increment = increment/2;
    else if (increment==1)
      increment = 0;
    else
      increment = 1;
  }
}
```

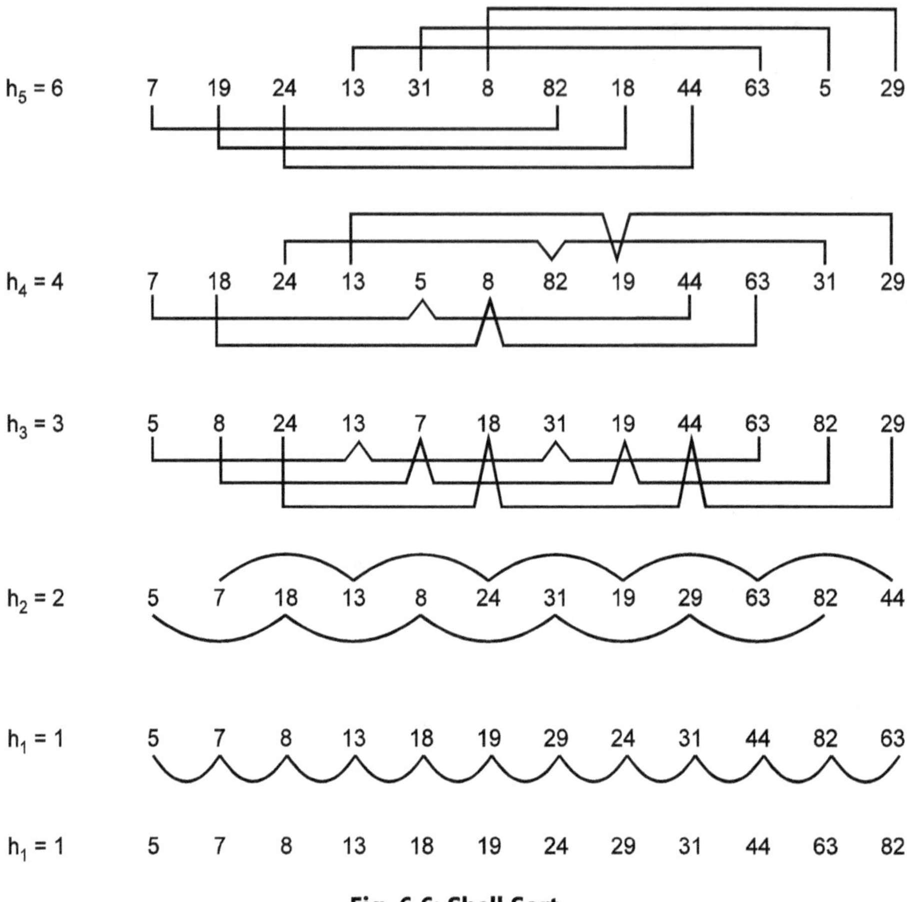

Fig. 6.6: Shell Sort

As we see, the subsequences skip through the array at intervals of 6, in this example, and at intervals of h.

After these subsequences are sorted, the next increment h_{t-1} is used to separate the array again into subsequences, this time with entries h_{t-1} elements apart, and again subsequences are sorted. The process is repeated for each increment. The final increment, h_1, is always 1, so at the end, the entire array will be sorted.

Considering that the last increment is 1 and the entire array is sorted in the last pass. Is Shellsort any more efficient than the algorithm used to sort the subsequences? Can the algorithm be written to minimize all the bookkeeping that seems to be needed to control the sorting of all the subsequences? What increments should be used?

As the example in Figure above shows, when the last few passes are made using small increments, few elements will be out of order because of all the work that was done in earlier passes. So Shellsort may be efficient if, and indeed would be efficient only if, the method used to sort subsequences is one that does very little work if the array is already sorted or nearly sorted. Insertion Sort has this property. It does only n–1 comparisons if the array is completely sorted, it is simple to program, and it has very little overhead.

Pros and Cons:

The number of comparisons done by Shellsort is a function of the sequence of increments used. A complete analysis is extremely difficult and requires answers to some mathematical problems that have not yet been solved. Therefore the best possible sequence of increments has not been determined, but some specific cases have been thoroughly studied. One of these is the case where t = 2, that is, where exactly two increments, h and 1, are used. It has been shown that the best choice for h is approximately $1.72 \sqrt[3]{n}$ and with this choice the average running time is proportional to n5/3. This may seem surprising since using the increment 1 is the same as doing Insertion Sort, which has $\Theta(n^2)$ average behavior; just doing one preliminary pass through the array with increment h lowers the asymptotic order of the running time. By using more than two increments, the running time can be improved even more.

It is known that if the increments are $h_k = 2^k - 1$ for $1 \le k \le [\lg n]$, the number of comparisons done in the worst case is in $O(n^{3/2})$. Empirical studies (with values of n as high as 250,000) have shown that another set of increments gives rise to very fast-running programs. These are defined by $h_i = (3^i - 1)/2$ for $1 \le i \le t$, where t is chosen as the smallest integer such that $h_{t+2} \le n$. These increments are easy to compute iteratively. We can find ht at the beginning of the sort by using the relation $h_{s+1} = 3h_s + 1$ and comparing the results to n. Instead of storing all the increments, we can recompute them in reverse order during the sort using the formula $h_s = (h_{s+1} - 1)/3$.

It has been proven that, if the increments consist of all integers of the form $2^i 3^j$ that are less than n (used in decreasing order), then the number of comparisons done is in $O(n(\log n)^2)$. The worst-case running times for the other sets of increments are known or expected to be of higher asymptotic order. However, because of the large number of integers of the form $2^i 3^j$, there will be more passes through the array, hence more overhead, with these increments than with others. Therefore they are not particularly useful unless n is fairly large.

Shellsort is clearly an in-place sort. Although the analysis of the algorithm is far from complete, and it is not known which increments are best, its speed and simplicity make it a good choice in practice.

6.9 Comparison of Sorting Methods

	Bubble sort	**Selection sort**
Number of comparisons		
Best case	$\dfrac{n(n-1)}{2}$	$\dfrac{n(n-1)}{2}$
Worst case	$\dfrac{n(n-1)}{2}$	$\dfrac{n(n-1)}{2}$
Number of swaps/shifts		
Best case	$n-1$	$n-1$
Worst case	$\dfrac{n(n-1)}{2}$	$n-1$
Overall time complexity		
Best case	$O(n^2)$	$O(n^2)$
Worst case	$O(n^2)$	$O(n^2)$
Average	$O(n^2)$	$O(n^2)$
Additional memory	Not required In place algorithm	Not required In place algorithm
Implementation	Simple	Complex
Stability of algorithm	Stable	Stable

6.10 Searching and Sorting

Searching and sorting are the most common operations required to be performed in programs. Almost 90% of times in the programs these operations are used. Hence, it is important to study these techniques and their efficiency, their advantages, disadvantages etc. Though we will be concentrating on only single dimensional arrays of integer and real numbers, we can extend these techniques to strings, records, linked list as well.

6.11 Searching Techniques

Searching is a process of finding the location of required data in the given list of objects. The algorithm used for searching depends on how data is organized in the list. But we will be studying only search operations with arrays. The two important techniques used for searching in an array are linear of sequential search and binary search. Apart from these two searching techniques indexed sequential search technique. Before we look into these techniques, let us define some terms.

1. **List:** It is an ordered set of data contained in main memory.
2. **Record:** It is collection of related fields.
3. **Table or file:** It is collection of ordered set of records.
4. **Key:** It is a field in the record used to differentiate each record.
5. **Search Algorithm:** It is an algorithm that accepts an argument (say s) and tries to find a record whose key is s.
6. **Retrieval:** Successful search is called retrieval.
7. **Internal Search:** The search operation in which entire table is constantly stored in main memory is called internal search.
8. **External Search:** The search operation in which part of the table is in secondary memory is called external search.

6.12 Sequential Search

It is also called linear search. It is simplest searching technique and can be applied to a table organized as an array or linked list. Sequential search can be used when the list is not ordered or ordered.

In sequential search, we start searching from first element in the list and continue until we find the element. If we don't find the element, we reach the end of list and stop.

Example 6.4: Suppose we have 6 elements stored in an array as shown and we want to search element 5 in the list (i.e. array).

The steps are shown in Fig. 6.7.

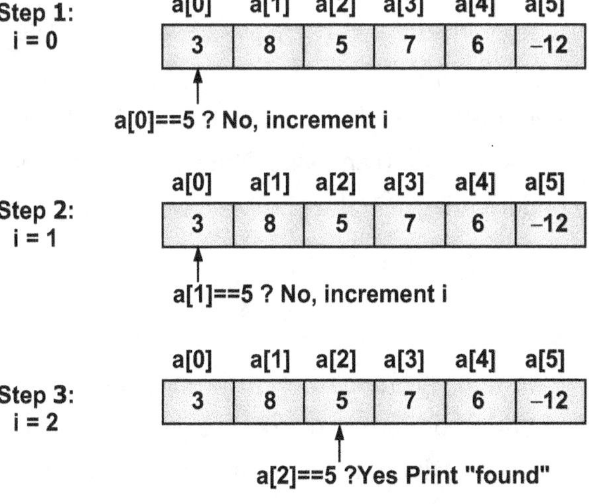

Fig. 6.7: Process of linear search

The algorithm for sequential search is as follows:

Algorithm 6.7: Sequential search or linear search.

Step 1:　Read n {Number of elements in list}

Step 2:　i=0

Step 3:　while i<n repeat step 4 and 5

Step 4:　Read a[i]

Step 5:　i=i+1

Step 6:　Read s {Number to be searched}

Step 7:　i=0; flag=1

Step 8:　While i<n repeat step 9 to 13

Step 9:　if a[i]==s execute step 10 to 12

Step 10: print "found" i+1

Step 11: flag=0;

Step 12: go to step 14

Step 13: i=i+1

Step 14: if flag==1 print "Not found"

Step 15: Stop

Explanation:

1. First we read number of element stored in the list (n).
2. We read the element in the list and store it in the array a.
3. Read the number to be searched (s).
4. Set initial value of i = 0 and flag = 1. Flag is used to indicate or sense whether the number is present in the list or not.
5, We repeatedly compare number in the ith location with s. If the number is found, we print the location number, make flag = 0 and exit. Otherwise we continue searching.
6. When we exit loop and find flag = 1, the number s will not be there in the list.
7. Stop.

Analysis:

1. While comparing, if we find the number s in the first location i.e., when i = 0 we exit. Hence, the minimum time required to search is 1. i.e., we require only one comparison. Hence, best case time complexity of the algorithm is 1. i.e., O(1).
2. If the element to be searched is at the end of the list or not there at all, we require to do n comparisons i.e., the loop, runs for n times. Hence, worst case time complexity is O(n).

3. On an average to find the element in the list, we will require (n+1)/2 comparisons. Hence, average case time complexity will be O(n), since (n+1)/2 = O(n).

It can be found as below.

If these are n numbers in the list, the number to be searched can be at any position from 1 to n.

The probability of finding the number at a location will be 1/n. Hence average number of comparisons will be,

$$T(n) = 1 \times \frac{1}{n} + 2 \times \frac{1}{n} + 3 \times \frac{1}{n} + \ldots\ldots + n \times \frac{1}{n}$$

$$= \frac{1}{n}(1 + 2 + 3 + \ldots\ldots + n)$$

$$= \frac{1}{n}\frac{n(n + 1)}{2}$$

$$= \frac{n + 1}{2}$$

4. For large number of elements (n), this algorithm will be slow.

Program 6.6: To search a number in a list using sequential search.

```c
#include <stdio.h>
#include <conio.h>
# define MAX 100
void main( )
{
    int a[MAX], i, s, n, flag;
    printf ("Enter number of elements in the list \n");
    scanf("%d", &n);
    printf ("Enter the elements in the list \n");
    for (i=0;i<n;i++)
        scanf ("%d", &a[i]);
    printf("Enter the number to be searched \n");
    scanf ("%d", &s);
    flag = 1
    i = 0;
    while (i<n)
    {
        if (a[i]==s)
        {
            printf("Found at location %d", i+1);
            flag = 0;
```

```
                break;
        }
    }
    if (flag==1)
        printf ("Not found");
    getch( );
}
```

6.13 Binary Search

Sequential search is very slow for large n. We can make the searching process faster provided, we have the elements in the list in sorted order.

The binary search starts with the middle element of the list instead of first element. If the element to be searched is at the middle, we exit; otherwise we check whether the element in the middle location is smaller or greater than element to be searched. If it is greater, the number will be above this middle location and the second half need not be checked. If it is smaller, the number will be below the middle location and first half need not be checked. Hence, in the first comparison we eliminate half the numbers in the list. We repeat the same process for remaining half in which the number may be present. We continue this process till we find the target or determine that the number is not there in the list.

Example 6.5: Suppose we have 10 elements as shown and we want to search s = 70.

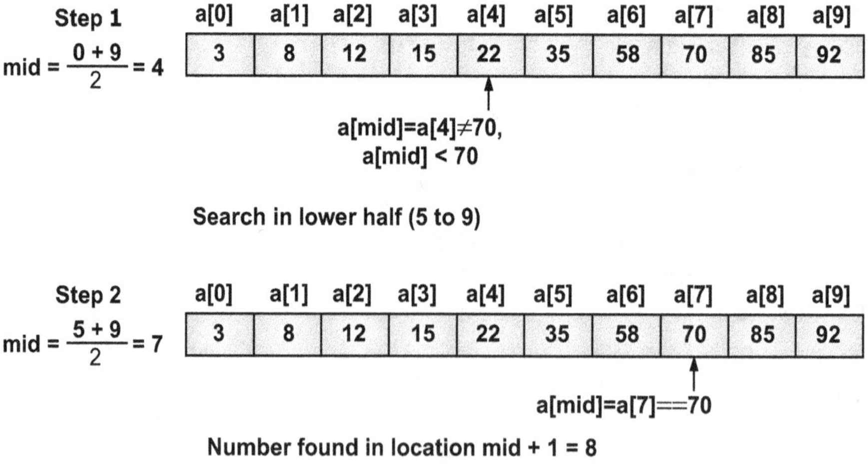

Step 1

$$mid = \frac{0+9}{2} = 4$$

a[0]	a[1]	a[2]	a[3]	a[4]	a[5]	a[6]	a[7]	a[8]	a[9]
3	8	12	15	22	35	58	70	85	92

a[mid]=a[4]≠70,
a[mid] < 70

Search in lower half (5 to 9)

Step 2

$$mid = \frac{5+9}{2} = 7$$

a[0]	a[1]	a[2]	a[3]	a[4]	a[5]	a[6]	a[7]	a[8]	a[9]
3	8	12	15	22	35	58	70	85	92

a[mid]=a[7]==70

Number found in location mid + 1 = 8

Fig. 6.8: Binary search process

As it can be seen above, number 70 is present at location 7. It is found in the second comparison only.

Algorithm 6.8: Binary Search

Step 1: Read n {Number of elements}

Step 2: i=0

Step 3: while i<n repeat step 4 and 5

Step 4: Read a[i]

Step 5: i=i+1

Step 6: Read s {Number to be searched}

Step 7: l=0, u=n−1; flag=1

Step 8: While (l<=u) Repeat step 9 to 15

Step 9: mid=(l+u)/2

Step 10: if a[mid]==s execute step 11 to 13

Step 11: printf "found at" mid+1

Step 12: flag=0

Step 13: go to step 17

Step 14: if a[mid] > s   u=mid−1

Step 15: if a[mid] < s l=mid+1

Step 17: if flag==1 print "Not found"

Step 18: Stop

Explanation:

1. First we read number the number of elements stored in the list (n).

2. We read the element in the list and store it in the array a.

3. Read the number to be searched.

4. Set l = 0 (location of first element in the list) u = n − 1 (location of last element in the list) and flag=1 to determine whether the number is present in the list or not.

5. While (l ≤ u) means the list to be checked has more than 1 element. We go to the middle location in the list and check whether number is present. If yes, we print the location and exit after setting flag = 0. If the number is greater than number to be searched, we have to check upper half. Hence, make u = mid − 1 and keeping and same for the new list. If the number is less than number to be searched, we have to check lower half. Hence, make l = mid + 1 keeping u same for new list.

    We repeat the process till the list to be checked has more than or equal to 1 element.

6. If we exit above loop with flag = 1, it means we did not find the number.

Analysis:

1. When we enter the loop (statement 5) and find the number is in the mid-locations, then we exit. Only 1 comparison will be required. Hence, the minimum time required to search is 1. Hence, best case time complexity is $O(1)$.

2. If the element to be searched is not there in the table, we will keep on dividing the list into two parts and search in one half. The process is continued till there is single element left out finally. Suppose we have 32 element in the list i.e., $n = 32$, first comparison will reduce the list to 16 element, second comparison to 8, third to 4, fourth to 2 and fifth comparison will reduce to 1 element. Hence, the maximum number of comparison will be 5, which is $\log_2 32$. In general, sappose we have n elements, after first comparison the number elements will reduce to $n/2$. The second comparison will leave $n/4$ elements. Comparison number x will leave $n/2^x$ elements. Hence, maximum number of comparisons $\times$ x = $\log_2 n$. Hence, worst case time complexity of the algorithm is $O(\log_2 n)$.

3. On an average, the number of comparisons to find and element of the algorithm is $O(\log_2 n)$.

4. Compared to linear search, this algorithm is faster for example, sequential search has time complexity 1000 whereas, binary search $\log_2 n = \log_2 1000 = 10$

Program 6.7: Binary Search */

```c
#include <stdio.h>
#include <conio.h>
#define MAX 100
void main
{
    int a[MAX], i, n, s, mid, l, u, flag,
    clrscr( );
    printf ("Enter number of element in the list \n")
    printf ("%d", &n);
    printf ("Enter the element in the list \n")
    for (i=0;i<n;i++)
        scanf ("%d", &a[i]);
    printf ("Enter number to be searched \n")
    scanf ("%d", &s);
    flag = 1; l=0; u = n – 1;
```

```c
while (l<=u)
{
        mid=(l + u)/2;
        if (a[mid]==s)
        {
                printf("Number found at location %d", mid + 1);
                flag = 0;
                break;
        }
        if (a[mid]>s)
                u = mid - 1;
        if (a[mid]<s)
                l = mid + 1;
}
if (flag==1)
        printf ("Not found");
}
```

6.14 Comparison of Searching Methods

No.	Parameter	Sequential search	Binary Search
1.	Time complexity	Best case: O(1) Worst case: O(n)	Best case: O(1) Worst case: $O(\log_2 n)$
2.	Prerequisite	No prerequisite of elements to be in sorted order	Element are to be in sorted ordered
3.	Performance	Works better for small n and slow for large n	Works better for large n
4.	Application	Can be used when the list is dynamic (i.e. changing)	Can be used when the list is not changing (i.e. fixed).

6.15 B-Trees and B⁺ Trees

Dictionaries for very large files typically reside on secondary storage, such as a disk. The dictionary is implemented as an index to the actual file and contains the key and record address of data. To implement a dictionary we could use red-black trees, replacing pointers with offsets from the beginning of the index file, and use random access to reference nodes of the tree. However, every transition on a link would imply a disk access, and would be prohibitively expensive. Recall that low-level disk I/O accesses disk by sectors (typically 256 bytes). We could equate node size to sector size, and group several keys together in each node to minimize the number of I/O operations. This is the principle behind B-trees.

Theory

Figure 6.9 illustrates a B-tree with 3 keys/node. Keys in internal nodes are surrounded by pointers, or record offsets, to keys that are less than or greater than, the key value. For example, all keys less than 22 are to the left and all keys greater than 22 are to the right. For simplicity, I have not shown the record address associated with each key.

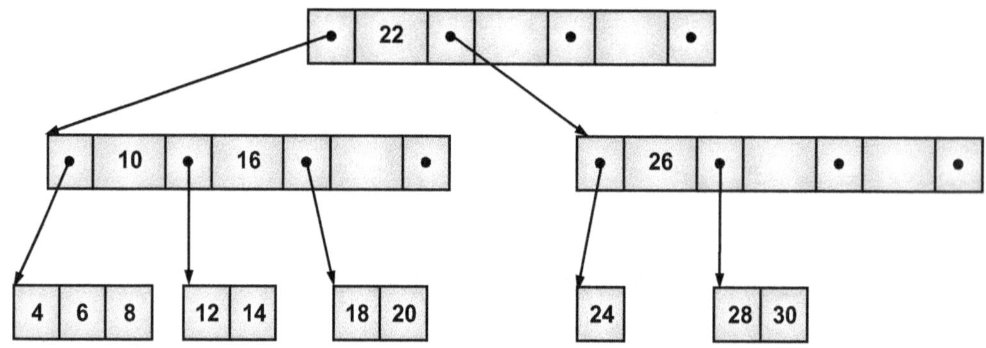

Fig. 6.9: B-Tree

We can locate any key in this 2-level tree with three disk accesses. If we were to group 100 keys/node, we could search over 1,000,000 keys in only three reads. To ensure this property holds, we must maintain a balanced tree during insertion and deletion. During insertion, we examine the child node to verify that it is able to hold an additional node. If not, then a new sibling node is added to the tree, and the child's keys are redistributed to make room for the new node. When descending for insertion and the root is full, then the root is spilled to new children, and the level of the tree increases. A similar action is taken on deletion, where child nodes may be absorbed by the root. This technique for altering the height of the tree maintains a balanced tree.

Table 6.1: Tree Implementations

	B-Tree	**B*-Tree**	**B$^+$-Tree**	**B^{++}-Tree**
data stored in	any node	any node	leaf only	Leaf only
on insert, split	$1 \times 1 \to 2 \times 1/2$	$2 \times 1 \to 3 \times 2/3$	$1 \times 1 \to 2 \times 1/2$	$3 \times 1 \to 4 \times 3/4$
on delete, join	$2 \times 1/2 \to 1 \times 1$	$3 \times 2/3 \to 2 \times 1$	$2 \times 1/2 \to 1 \times 1$	$3 \times 1/2 \to 2 \times 3/4$

Several variants of the B-tree are listed in Table 6.1. The standard B-tree stores keys and data in both internal and leaf nodes. When descending the tree during insertion, a full child node is first redistributed to adjacent nodes. If the adjacent nodes are also full, then a new node is created, and ½ the keys in the child are moved to the newly created node. During deletion, children that are ½ full first attempt to obtain keys from adjacent nodes. If the adjacent nodes are also ½ full, then two nodes are joined to form one full node. B*-trees are similar, only the nodes are kept 2/3 full. This results in better utilization of space in the tree, and slightly better performance.

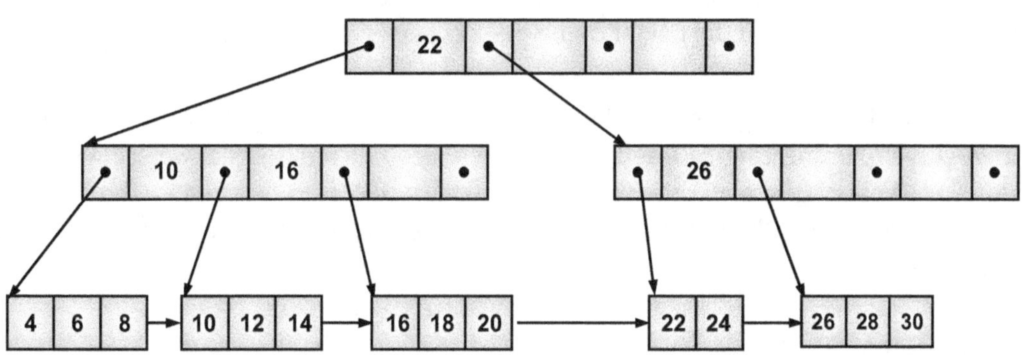

Fig. 6.10: B-$^+$Tree

Figure 6.10 illustrates a B+-tree. All keys are stored at the leaf level, with their associated data values. Duplicates of the keys appear in internal parent nodes to guide the search. Pointers have a slightly different meaning than in conventional B-trees. The left pointer designates all keys less than the value, while the right pointer designates all keys greater than or equal to (GE) the value. For example, all keys less than 22 are on the left pointer, and all keys greater than or equal to 22 are on the right. Notice that key 22 is duplicated in the leaf, where the associated data may be found. During insertion and deletion, care must be taken to properly update parent nodes. When modifying the first key in a leaf, the last GE pointer found while descending the tree will require modification to reflect the new key value. Since all keys are in leaf nodes, we may link them for sequential access.

The last method, B^{++}-trees, is something of my own invention. The organization is similar to B$^+$-trees, except for the split/join strategy. Assume each node can hold k keys, and the root node holds 3k keys. Before we descend to a child node during insertion, we check to see if it is full. If it is, the keys in the child node and two nodes adjacent to the child are all merged and redistributed. If the two adjacent nodes are also full, then another node is added, resulting in four nodes, each ¾ full. Before we descend to a child node during deletion, we check to see if it is ½ full. If it is, the keys in the child node and two nodes adjacent to the child are all merged and redistributed. If the two adjacent nodes are also ½ full, then they are merged into two nodes, each ¾ full. Note that in each case, the resulting nodes are ¾ full. This is halfway between ½ full and completely full, allowing for an equal number of insertions or deletions in the future.

Recall that the root node holds 3k keys. If the root is full during insertion, we distribute the keys to four new nodes, each ¾ full. This increases the height of the tree. During deletion, we inspect the child nodes. If there are only three child nodes, and they are all ½ full, they are gathered into the root, and the height of the tree decreases.

Another way of expressing the operation is to say we are gathering three nodes, and then *scattering* them. In the case of insertion, where we need an extra node, we scatter to four nodes. For deletion, where a node must be deleted, we scatter to two nodes. The symmetry of the operation allows the gather/scatter routines to be shared by insertion and deletion in the implementation.

Implementation

Source for the B^{++}-tree algorithm may be found in file **btr.c**. In the implementation-dependent section, you'll need to define **bAdrType** and **eAdrType**, the types associated with B-tree file offsets and data file offsets, respectively. You'll also need to provide a callback function that is used by the B^{++}-tree algorithm to compare keys. Functions are provided to insert/delete keys, find keys, and access keys sequentially. Function main, at the bottom of the file, provides a simple illustration for insertion.

The code provided allows for multiple indices to the same data. This was implemented by returning a handle when the index is opened. Subsequent accesses are done using the supplied handle. Duplicate keys are allowed. Within one index, all keys must be the same length. A binary search was implemented to search each node. A flexible buffering scheme allows nodes to be retained in memory until the space is needed. If you expect access to be somewhat ordered, increasing the **bufCt** will reduce paging.

SUMMARY

- Efficient and reliable data processing depends upon sorted data.
- The internal and external sorting methods each have their relative efficiencies in different applications.
- It should be clear that no single sort is best for all applications. Certain properties such as the number, size, distribution and order of keys of a given key set plays an important role in determination of sorting technique which should be used for that particular application.
- If the number of entries in the array is small, the simpler bubble sort or selection sort as well and sometimes better and they require relatively little programming effort to write and maintain. If n is larger and the keys are short, the radix sort can perform well. For large n with long keys, we can use quick sort, heap sort or a merge sort.
- The order of the original data is an important consideration in choosing a sort algorithm. If the data are already sorted, quick sort should be avoided. If keys are uniformly distributed, address-calculation sort is the best choice.
- It appears that the quick sort is faster, and handle arrays of heterogeneous data fairly efficiently. The shell short is more efficient than the bubble sort, selection sort, and insertion sort.
- Sorting of larger files that cannot fit in main memory is best accomplished by external sorting techniques such as the merge sort.

SOLVED PROBLEMS

1. Sort Following numbers using bubble, Selection and Insertion. Show all steps. How many swaps and comparisons are required for each method?

10 30 20 40 60 50

Solution:

i)   Bubble Sort...

List after Pass 1...

10 20 30 40 50 60

List after Pass 2...

10 20 30 40 50 60

List after Pass 3...

10 20 30 40 50 60

List after Pass 4...

10 20 30 40 50 60

List after Pass 5...

10 20 30 40 50 60

Sorted list is...

10 20 30 40 50 60

Number of comparisons = 15
Number of swaps = 2

ii) Selection Sort...

List after Pass 1

10 30 20 40 50 60

List after Pass 2

10 30 20 40 50 60

List after Pass 3

10 30 20 40 50 60

List after Pass 4

10 20 30 40 50 60

List after Pass 5

10 20 30 40 50 60

Sorted list is...

10 20 30 40 50 60

Number of comparisons = 15

Number of swaps = 5

2. Sort Following numbers uning bubble, Selection. Show all steps. How many swaps and comparisons are required for each method?

50 40 30 20 10

Solution:

i) Bubble Sort...

List after Pass 1...

40 30 20 10 50

List after Pass 2...

30 20 10 40 50

List after Pass 3...

20 10 30 40 50

List after Pass 4...

10 20 30 40 50

Sorted list is...

10 20 30 40 50

Number of comparisons = 10

Number of swaps = 10

ii) Selection Sort...

List after Pass 5

10 40 30 20 50

List after Pass 4

10 20 30 40 50

List after Pass 3

10 20 30 40 50

List after Pass 2

10 20 30 40 50

Sorted list is...

10 20 30 40 50

Number of comparisons = 10

Number of swaps = 4

3. Sort Following numbers uning bubble, Selection. Show all steps. How many swaps and comparisons are required for each method?

10 20 30 40 50

Solution:

(i) Bubble Sort...

List after Pass 1...

10 20 30 40 50

List after Pass 2...

10 20 30 40 50

List after Pass 3...

10 20 30 40 50

List after Pass 4...

10 20 30 40 50

Sorted list is...

10 20 30 40 50

Number of comparisons = 10

Number of swaps = 0

(ii) Selection Sort...

List after Pass 5
10 20 30 40 50
List after Pass 4
10 20 30 40 50
List after Pass 3
10 20 30 40 50
List after Pass 2
10 20 30 40 50
Sorted list is...
10 20 30 40 50
Number of comparisons = 10
Number of swaps = 4

4. Sort Following numbers uning bubble, Selection. Show all steps. How many swaps and comparisons are required for each method?
15 3 18 7 21 10

Solution:

(i) Bubble Sort...

List after Pass 1...
3   15 7   18 10 21
List after Pass 2...
3   7   15 10 18 21
List after Pass 3...
3   7   10 15 18 21
List after Pass 4...
3   7   10 15 18 21
List after Pass 5...
3   7   10 15 18 21
Sorted list is...
3   7   10 15 18 21
Number of comparisons = 15
Number of swaps = 6

(ii) Selection Sort...

List after Pass 6
15 3   18 7   10 21
List after Pass 5
15 3   10 7   18 21

List after Pass 4
7　3　10　15　18　21
List after Pass 3
7　3　10　15　18　21
List after Pass 2
3　7　10　15　18　21
Sorted list is...
3　7　10　15　18　21
Number of comparisons = 15
Number of swaps = 5

5. Sort Following numbers using bubble, Selection. Show all steps. How many swaps and comparisons are required for each method?
100 50 70 40 30

Solution:

(i)　Bubble Sort...
List after Pass 1...
50　70　40　30　100
List after Pass 2...
50　40　30　70　100
List after Pass 3...
40　30　50　70　100
List after Pass 4...
30　40　50　70　100
Sorted list is...
30　40　50　70　100
Number of comparisons = 10
Number of swaps = 9

(ii)　Selection Sort...
List after Pass 5
30　50　70　40　100
List after Pass 4
30　50　40　70　100
List after Pass 3
30　40　50　70　100
List after Pass 2
30　40　50　70　100

Sorted list is...

30 40 50   70   100

Number of comparisons = 10

Number of swaps = 4

EXERCISE

1. Write algorithms for
    (i)   Bubble sort
    (ii)   Insertion sort
    (iii) Selection sort
2. Compare the sorting methods.
    Bubble sort, Selection sort.
3. Modify the programs for sorting to display output after each pass.
4. What are the different searching techniques? Compare them on the basis of time complexity?
5. Give the algorithm for searching any elements using binary search method. Comment on complexity.

✳✳✳